Facebook **facebook.com/idwpublishing**
Twitter **@idwpublishing**
YouTube **youtube.com/idwpublishing**
Tumblr **tumblr.idwpublishing.com**
Instagram **instagram.com/idwpublishing**

COVER ARTIST
ANGEL HERNANDEZ

COVER COLORIST
J.D. METTLER

SERIES EDITORIAL ASSISTANT
ANNI PERHEENTUPA

SERIES EDITOR
CHASE MAROTZ

SERIES GROUP EDITOR
DENTON J. TIPTON

COLLECTION EDITORS
ALONZO SIMON
AND ZAC BOONE

COLLECTION DESIGNER
CLAUDIA CHONG

ISBN: 978-1-68405-650-7   23 22 21 20   1 2 3 4

Originally published as STAR TREK: DISCOVERY – AFTERMATH issues #1–3 and STAR TREK: DISCOVERY: CAPTAIN SARU.

Chris Ryall, President & Publisher/CCO

Cara Morrison, Chief Financial Officer

Matthew Ruzicka, Chief Accounting Officer

David Hedgecock, Associate Publisher

John Barber, Editor-in-Chief

Justin Eisinger, Editorial Director, Graphic Novels and Collections

Jerry Bennington, VP of New Product Development

Lorelei Bunjes, VP of Technology & Information Services

Jud Meyers, Sales Director

Anna Morrow, Marketing Director

Tara McCrillis, Director of Design & Production

Mike Ford, Director of Operations

Rebekah Cahalin, General Manager

Special thanks to Risa Kessler, Marian Cordry, Dayton Ward, and John Van Citters of CBS Consumer Products for their invaluable assistance.

STAR TREK® DISCOVERY: AFTERMATH

WRITTEN BY **KIRSTEN BEYER** & **MIKE JOHNSON**

AFTERMATH

ART BY **TONY SHASTEEN**

COLORS BY **J.D. METTLER**

LETTERS BY **NEIL UYETAKE**

CAPTAIN SARU

ART BY **ANGEL HERNANDEZ**

COLORS BY **J.L. RIO** & **VALENTINA PINTO**

LETTERS BY **CHRISTA MIESNER**

STAR TREK CREATED BY GENE RODDENBERRY

ART BY **ANGEL HERNANDEZ** | COLORS BY **J.D. METTLER**

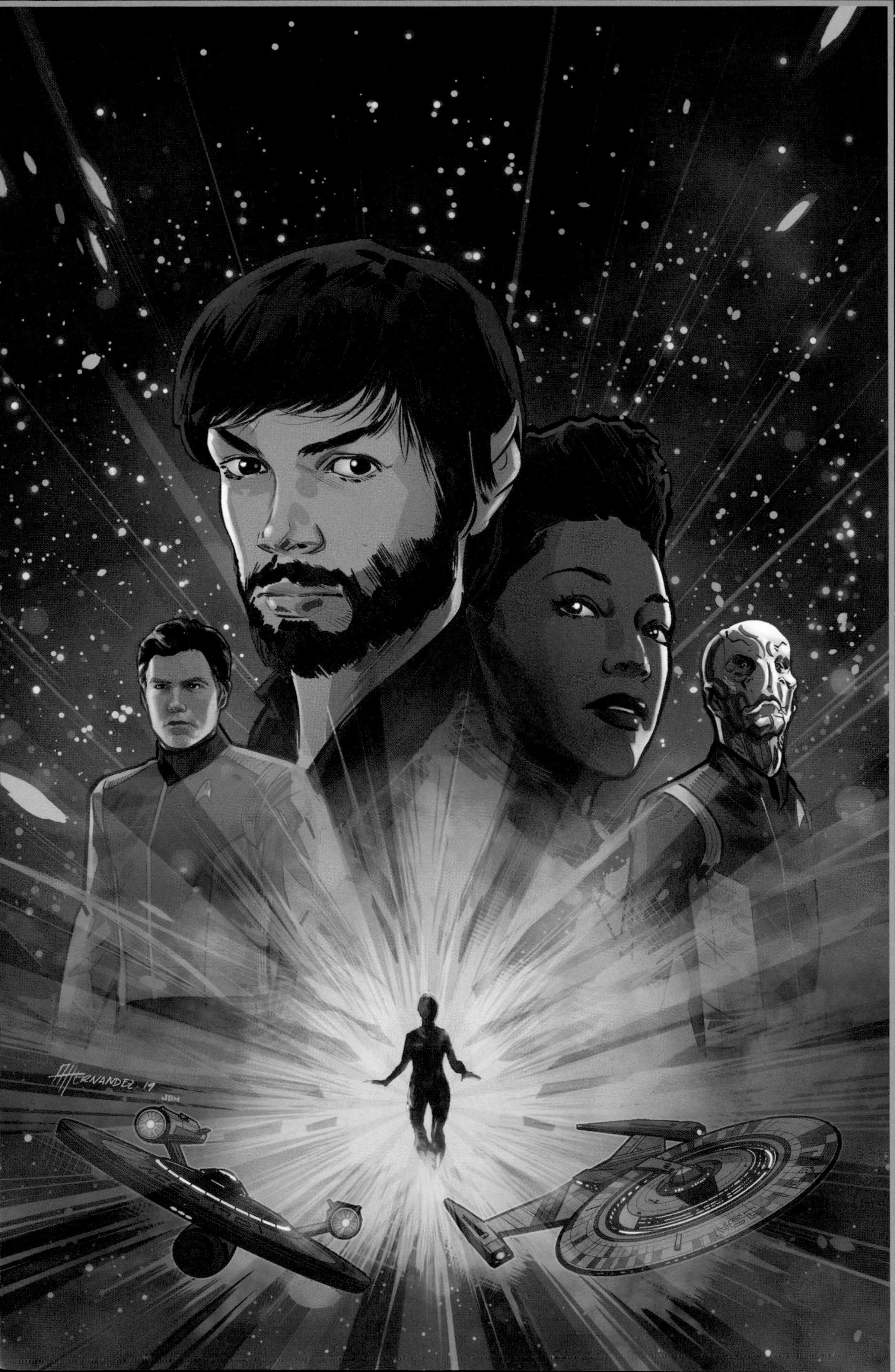
AHERNANDEZ '19
JDM

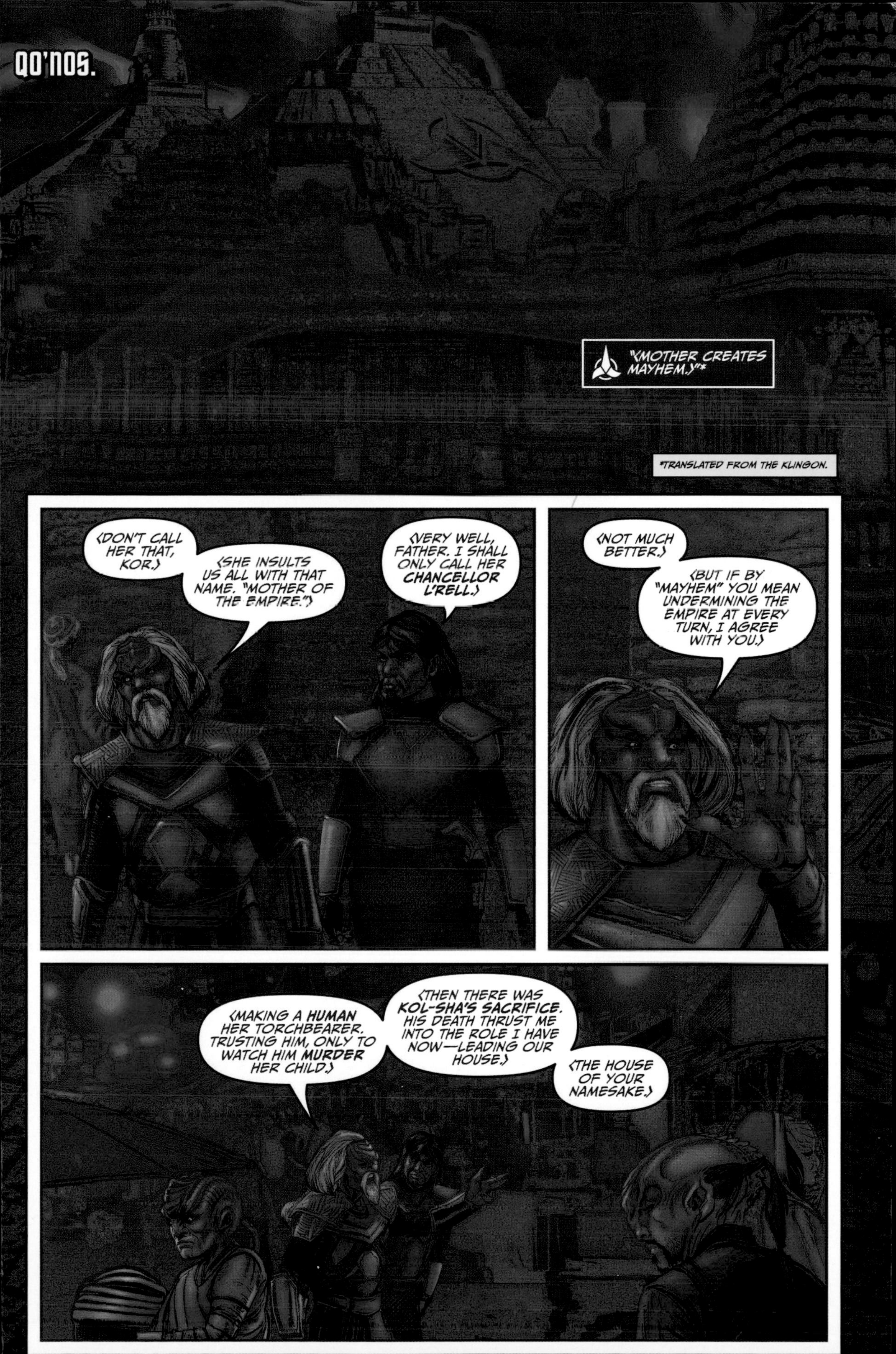
QO'NOS.
"<MOTHER CREATES MAYHEM.>"*
*TRANSLATED FROM THE KLINGON.
<DON'T CALL HER THAT, KOR.>
<SHE INSULTS US ALL WITH THAT NAME. "MOTHER OF THE EMPIRE.">
<VERY WELL, FATHER. I SHALL ONLY CALL HER CHANCELLOR L'RELL.>
<NOT MUCH BETTER.>
<BUT IF BY "MAYHEM" YOU MEAN UNDERMINING THE EMPIRE AT EVERY TURN, I AGREE WITH YOU.>
<MAKING A HUMAN HER TORCHBEARER. TRUSTING HIM, ONLY TO WATCH HIM MURDER HER CHILD.>
<THEN THERE WAS KOL-SHA'S SACRIFICE. HIS DEATH THRUST ME INTO THE ROLE I HAVE NOW—LEADING OUR HOUSE.>
<THE HOUSE OF YOUR NAMESAKE.>

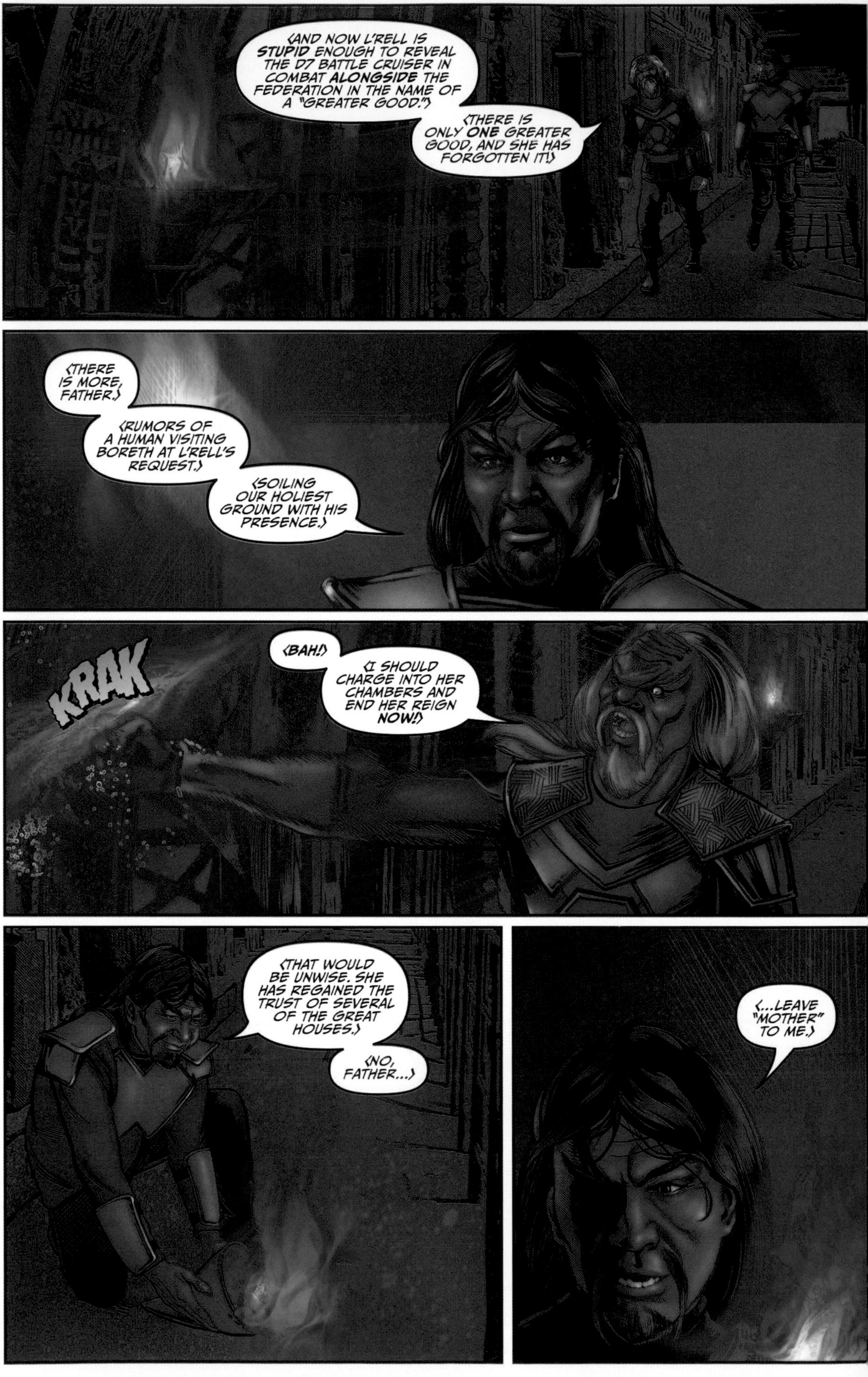

‹AND NOW L'RELL IS STUPID ENOUGH TO REVEAL THE D7 BATTLE CRUISER IN COMBAT ALONGSIDE THE FEDERATION IN THE NAME OF A "GREATER GOOD."›
‹THERE IS ONLY ONE GREATER GOOD, AND SHE HAS FORGOTTEN IT!›
‹THERE IS MORE, FATHER.›
‹RUMORS OF A HUMAN VISITING BORETH AT L'RELL'S REQUEST.›
‹SOILING OUR HOLIEST GROUND WITH HIS PRESENCE.›
KRAK
‹BAH!›
‹I SHOULD CHARGE INTO HER CHAMBERS AND END HER REIGN NOW!›
‹THAT WOULD BE UNWISE. SHE HAS REGAINED THE TRUST OF SEVERAL OF THE GREAT HOUSES.›
‹NO, FATHER...›
‹...LEAVE "MOTHER" TO ME.›

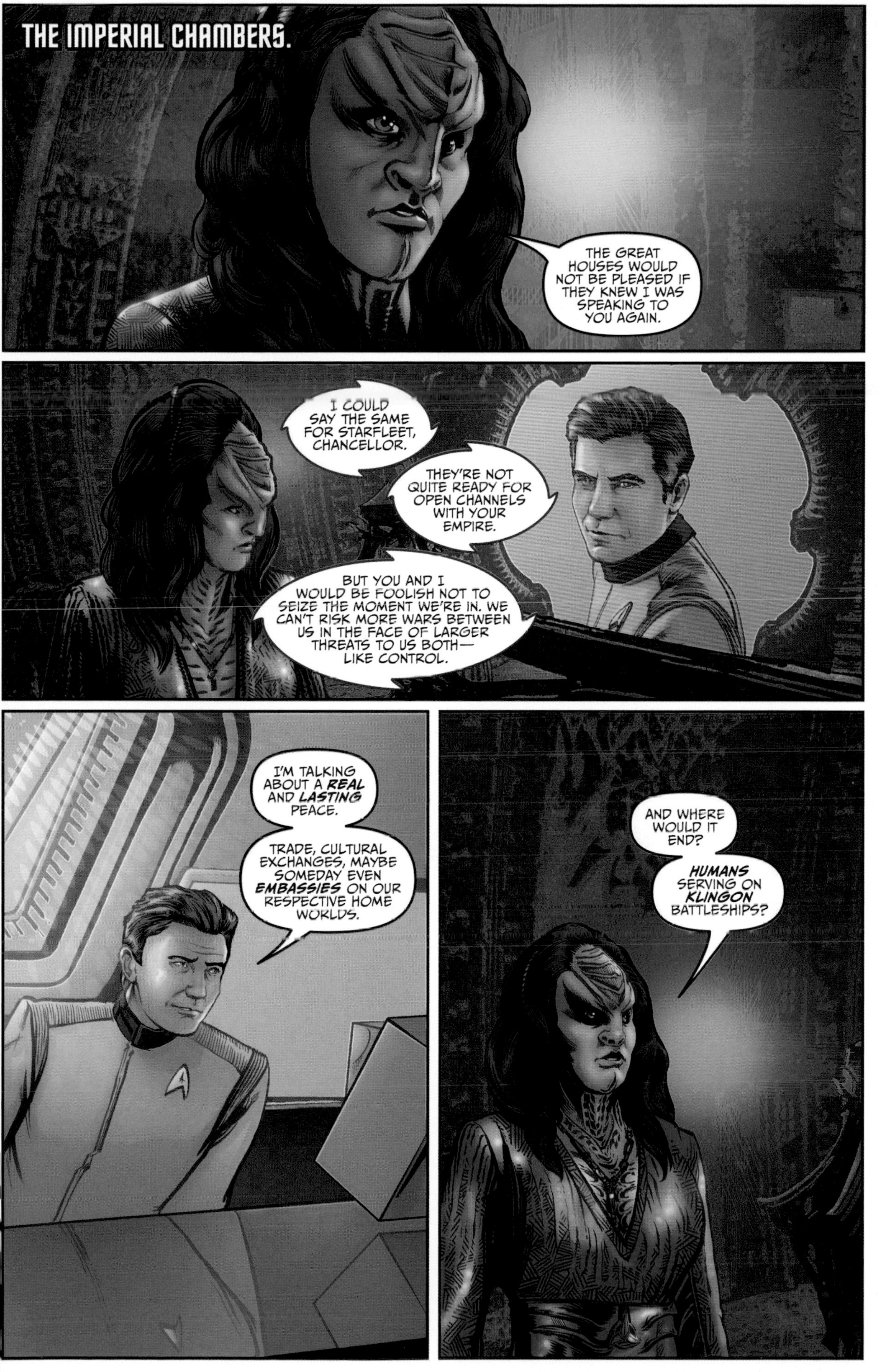
THE IMPERIAL CHAMBERS.
THE GREAT HOUSES WOULD NOT BE PLEASED IF THEY KNEW I WAS SPEAKING TO YOU AGAIN.
I COULD SAY THE SAME FOR STARFLEET, CHANCELLOR.
THEY'RE NOT QUITE READY FOR OPEN CHANNELS WITH YOUR EMPIRE.
BUT YOU AND I WOULD BE FOOLISH NOT TO SEIZE THE MOMENT WE'RE IN. WE CAN'T RISK MORE WARS BETWEEN US IN THE FACE OF LARGER THREATS TO US BOTH—LIKE CONTROL.
I'M TALKING ABOUT A REAL AND LASTING PEACE.
TRADE, CULTURAL EXCHANGES, MAYBE SOMEDAY EVEN EMBASSIES ON OUR RESPECTIVE HOME WORLDS.
AND WHERE WOULD IT END?
HUMANS SERVING ON KLINGON BATTLESHIPS?

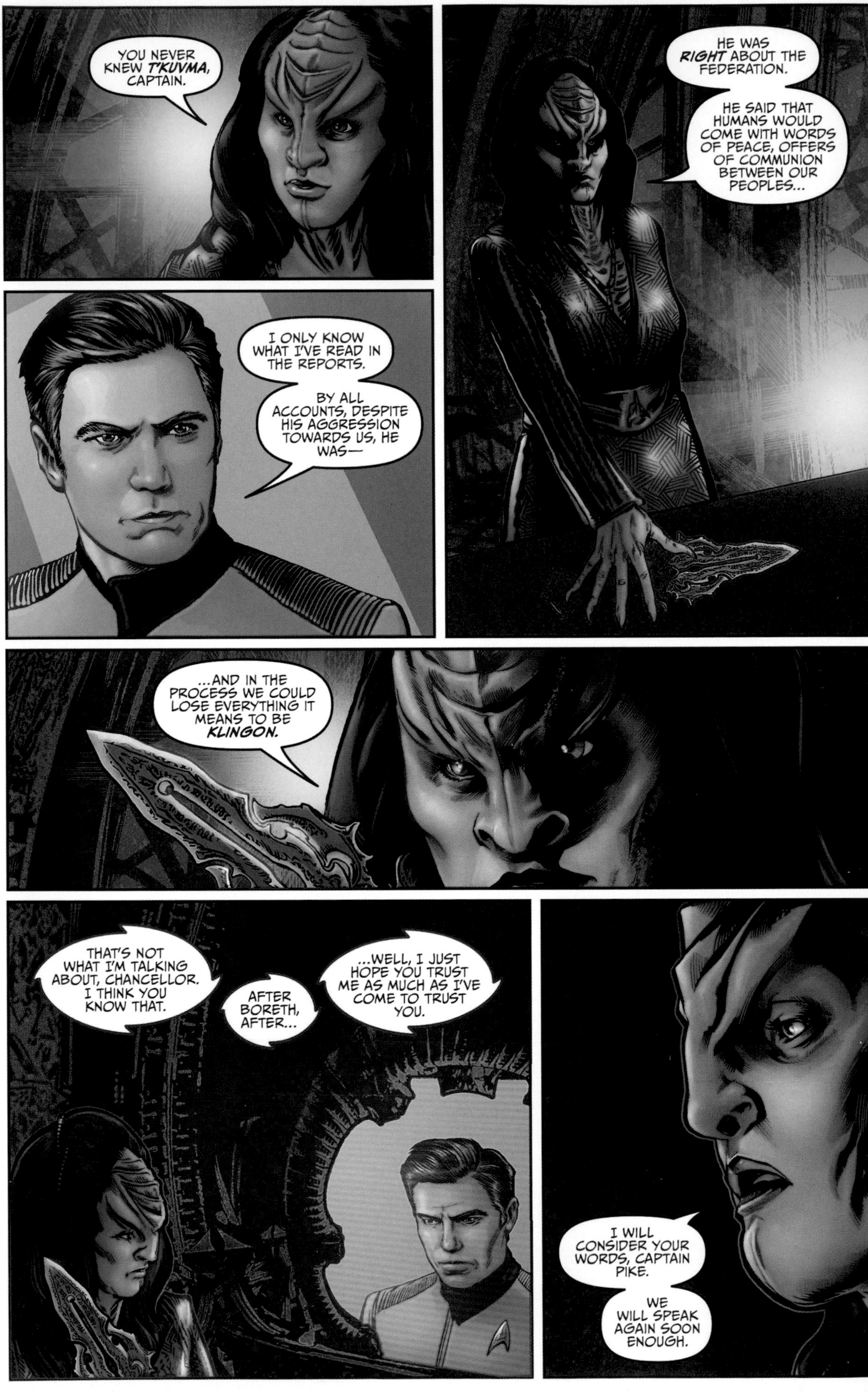
YOU NEVER KNEW *T'KUVMA*, CAPTAIN.
HE WAS ***RIGHT*** ABOUT THE FEDERATION.
HE SAID THAT HUMANS WOULD COME WITH WORDS OF PEACE, OFFERS OF COMMUNION BETWEEN OUR PEOPLES...
I ONLY KNOW WHAT I'VE READ IN THE REPORTS.
BY ALL ACCOUNTS, DESPITE HIS AGGRESSION TOWARDS US, HE WAS—
...AND IN THE PROCESS WE COULD LOSE EVERYTHING IT MEANS TO BE ***KLINGON.***
THAT'S NOT WHAT I'M TALKING ABOUT, CHANCELLOR. I THINK YOU KNOW THAT.
AFTER BORETH, AFTER...
...WELL, I JUST HOPE YOU TRUST ME AS MUCH AS I'VE COME TO TRUST YOU.
I WILL CONSIDER YOUR WORDS, CAPTAIN PIKE.
WE WILL SPEAK AGAIN SOON ENOUGH.

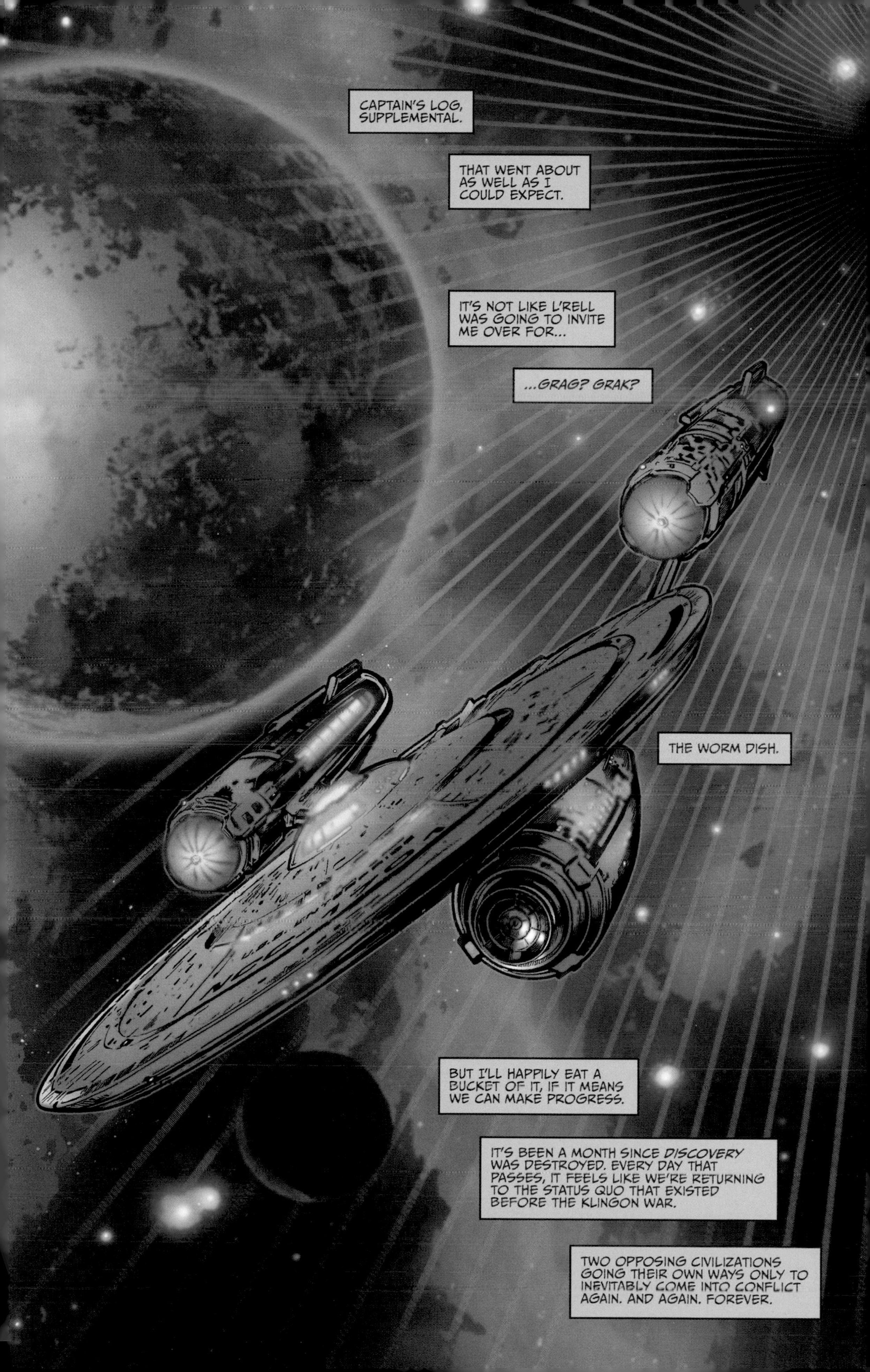
CAPTAIN'S LOG, SUPPLEMENTAL.
THAT WENT ABOUT AS WELL AS I COULD EXPECT.
IT'S NOT LIKE L'RELL WAS GOING TO INVITE ME OVER FOR...
...GRAG? GRAK?
THE WORM DISH.
BUT I'LL HAPPILY EAT A BUCKET OF IT, IF IT MEANS WE CAN MAKE PROGRESS.
IT'S BEEN A MONTH SINCE DISCOVERY WAS DESTROYED. EVERY DAY THAT PASSES, IT FEELS LIKE WE'RE RETURNING TO THE STATUS QUO THAT EXISTED BEFORE THE KLINGON WAR.
TWO OPPOSING CIVILIZATIONS GOING THEIR OWN WAYS ONLY TO INEVITABLY COME INTO CONFLICT AGAIN. AND AGAIN. FOREVER.

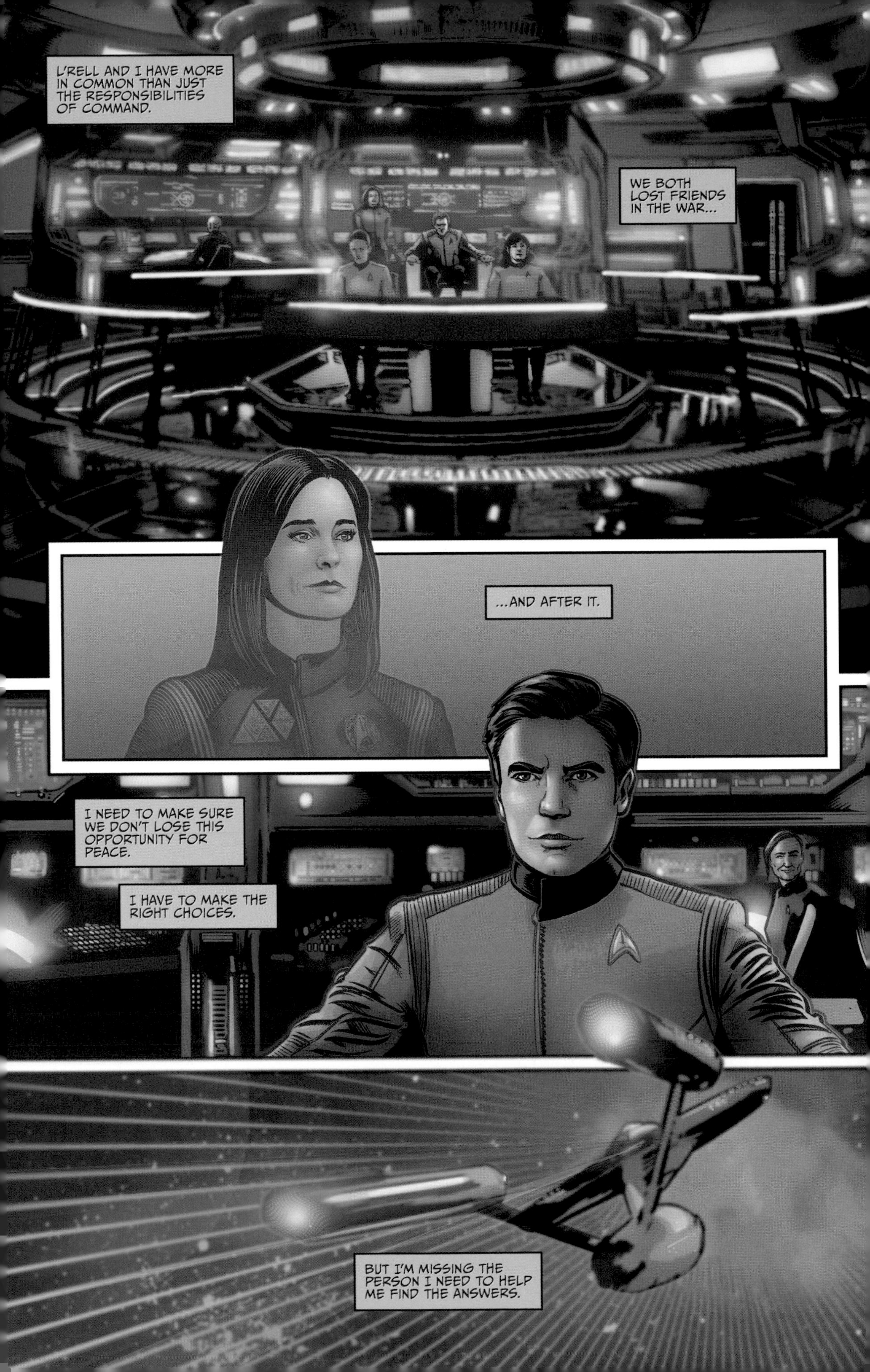
L'RELL AND I HAVE MORE IN COMMON THAN JUST THE RESPONSIBILITIES OF COMMAND.
WE BOTH LOST FRIENDS IN THE WAR...
...AND AFTER IT.
I NEED TO MAKE SURE WE DON'T LOSE THIS OPPORTUNITY FOR PEACE.
I HAVE TO MAKE THE RIGHT CHOICES.
BUT I'M MISSING THE PERSON I NEED TO HELP ME FIND THE ANSWERS.

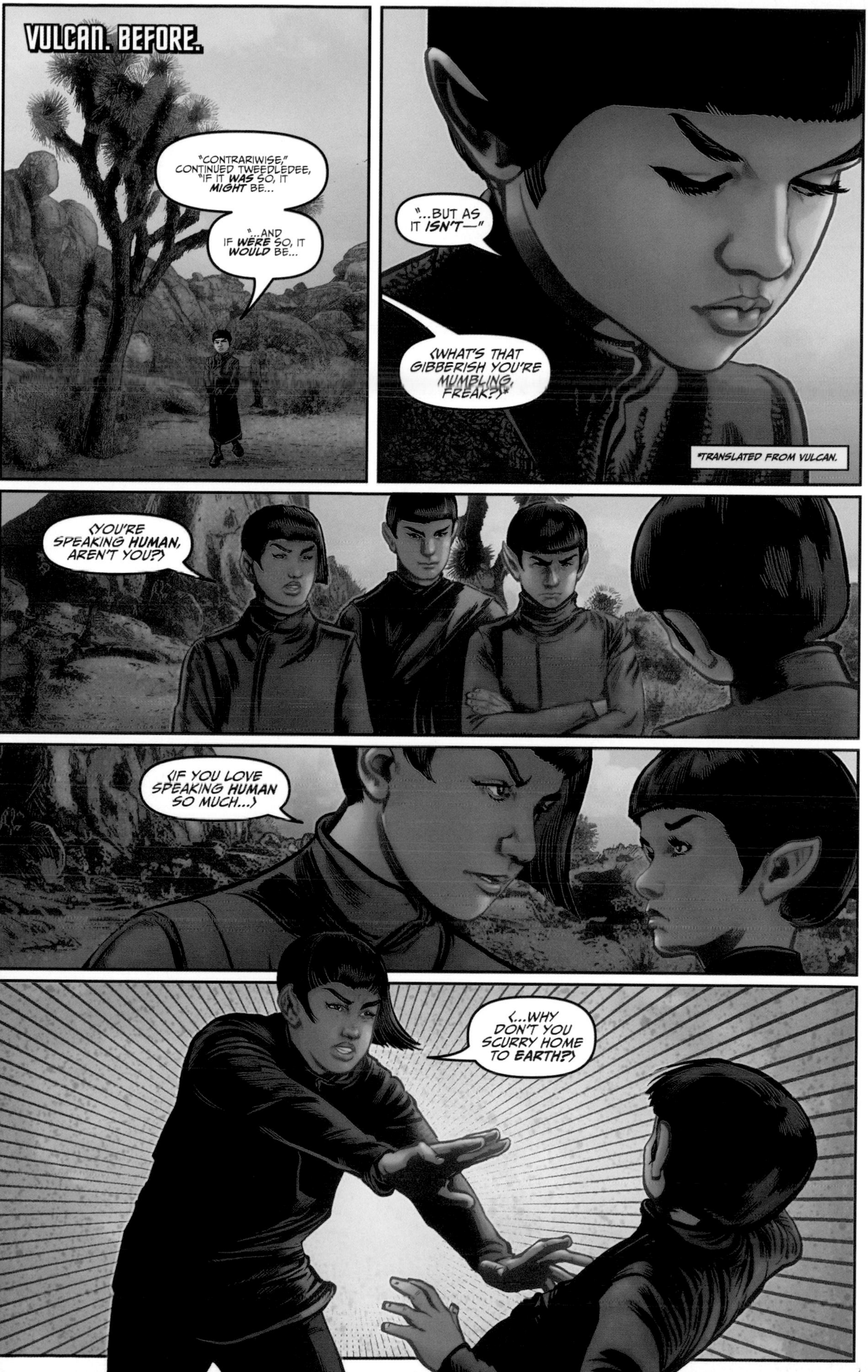

VULCAN. BEFORE.
"CONTRARIWISE," CONTINUED TWEEDLEDEE, "IF IT WAS SO, IT MIGHT BE...
"...AND IF WERE SO, IT WOULD BE...
"...BUT AS IT ISN'T—"
‹WHAT'S THAT GIBBERISH YOU'RE MUMBLING, FREAK?›*
*TRANSLATED FROM VULCAN.
‹YOU'RE SPEAKING HUMAN, AREN'T YOU?›
‹IF YOU LOVE SPEAKING HUMAN SO MUCH...›
‹...WHY DON'T YOU SCURRY HOME TO EARTH?›

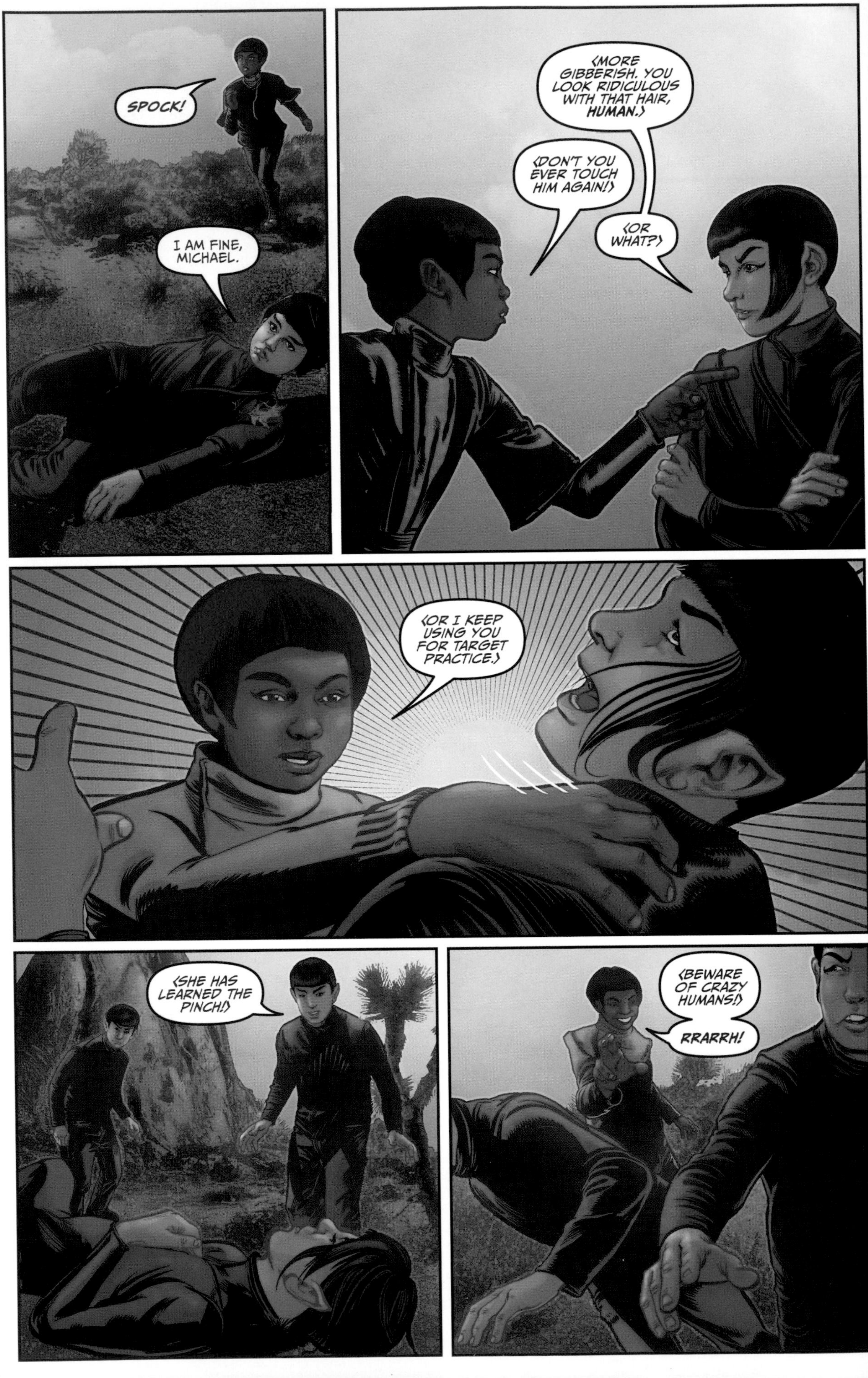
SPOCK!
I AM FINE, MICHAEL.
⟨MORE GIBBERISH. YOU LOOK RIDICULOUS WITH THAT HAIR, HUMAN.⟩
⟨DON'T YOU EVER TOUCH HIM AGAIN!⟩
⟨OR WHAT?⟩
⟨OR I KEEP USING YOU FOR TARGET PRACTICE.⟩
⟨SHE HAS LEARNED THE PINCH!⟩
⟨BEWARE OF CRAZY HUMANS!⟩
RRARRH!

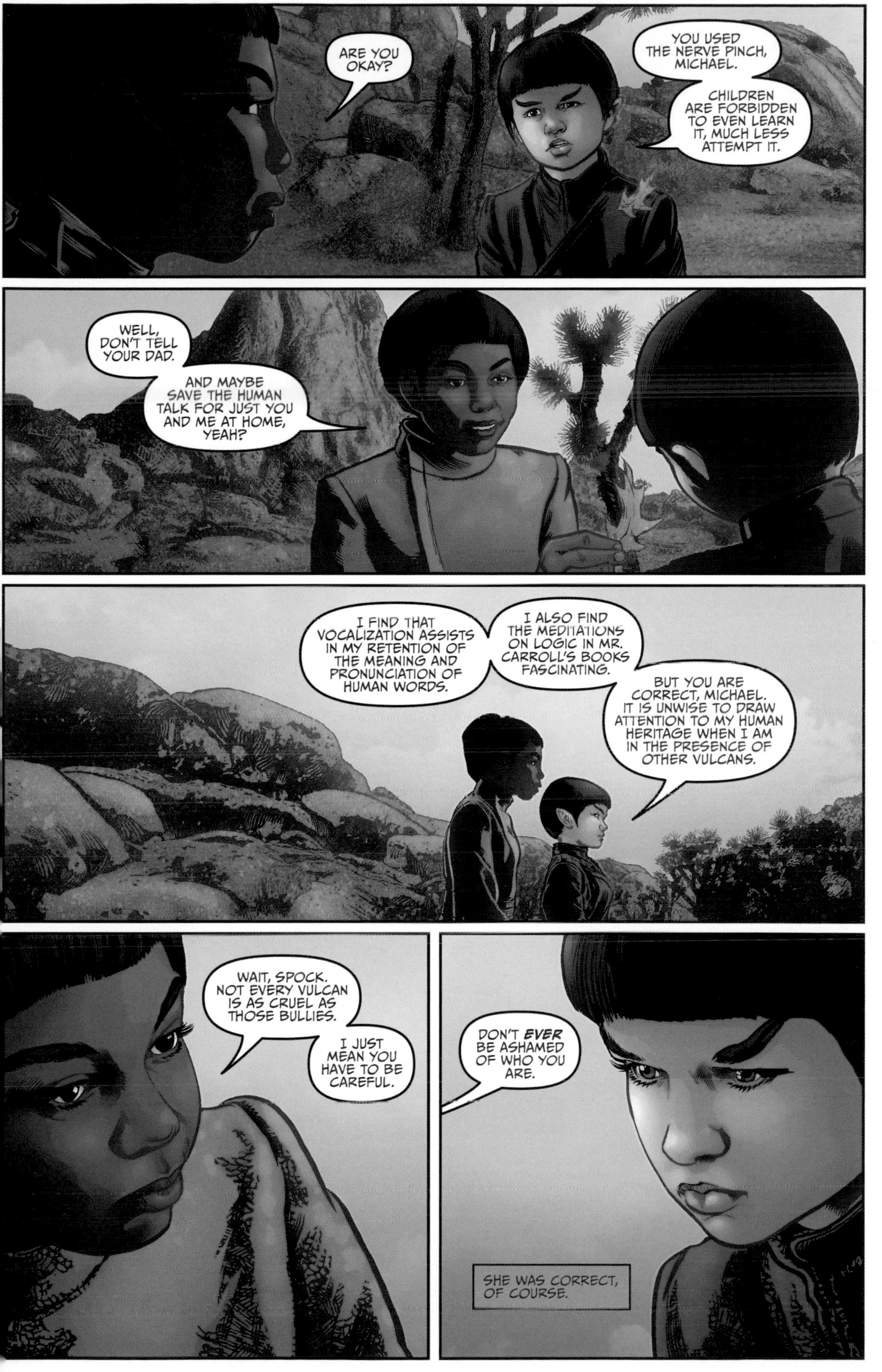
ARE YOU OKAY?
YOU USED THE NERVE PINCH, MICHAEL.
CHILDREN ARE FORBIDDEN TO EVEN LEARN IT, MUCH LESS ATTEMPT IT.
WELL, DON'T TELL YOUR DAD.
AND MAYBE SAVE THE HUMAN TALK FOR JUST YOU AND ME AT HOME, YEAH?
I FIND THAT VOCALIZATION ASSISTS IN MY RETENTION OF THE MEANING AND PRONUNCIATION OF HUMAN WORDS.
I ALSO FIND THE MEDITATIONS ON LOGIC IN MR. CARROLL'S BOOKS FASCINATING.
BUT YOU ARE CORRECT, MICHAEL. IT IS UNWISE TO DRAW ATTENTION TO MY HUMAN HERITAGE WHEN I AM IN THE PRESENCE OF OTHER VULCANS.
WAIT, SPOCK. NOT EVERY VULCAN IS AS CRUEL AS THOSE BULLIES.
I JUST MEAN YOU HAVE TO BE CAREFUL.
DON'T ***EVER*** BE ASHAMED OF WHO YOU ARE.
SHE WAS CORRECT, OF COURSE.

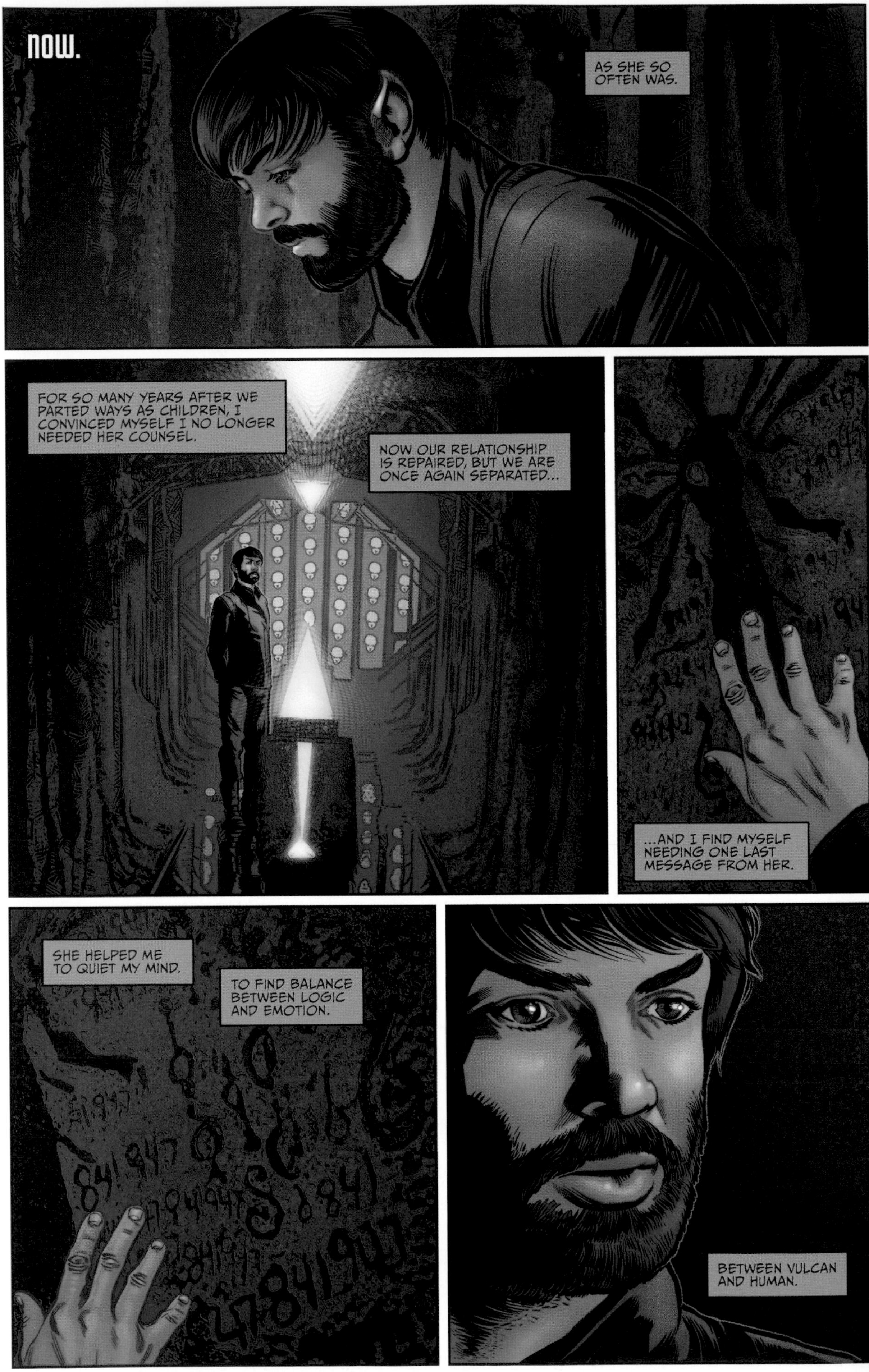
NOW.
AS SHE SO OFTEN WAS.
FOR SO MANY YEARS AFTER WE PARTED WAYS AS CHILDREN, I CONVINCED MYSELF I NO LONGER NEEDED HER COUNSEL.
NOW OUR RELATIONSHIP IS REPAIRED, BUT WE ARE ONCE AGAIN SEPARATED...
...AND I FIND MYSELF NEEDING ONE LAST MESSAGE FROM HER.
SHE HELPED ME TO QUIET MY MIND.
TO FIND BALANCE BETWEEN LOGIC AND EMOTION.
BETWEEN VULCAN AND HUMAN.

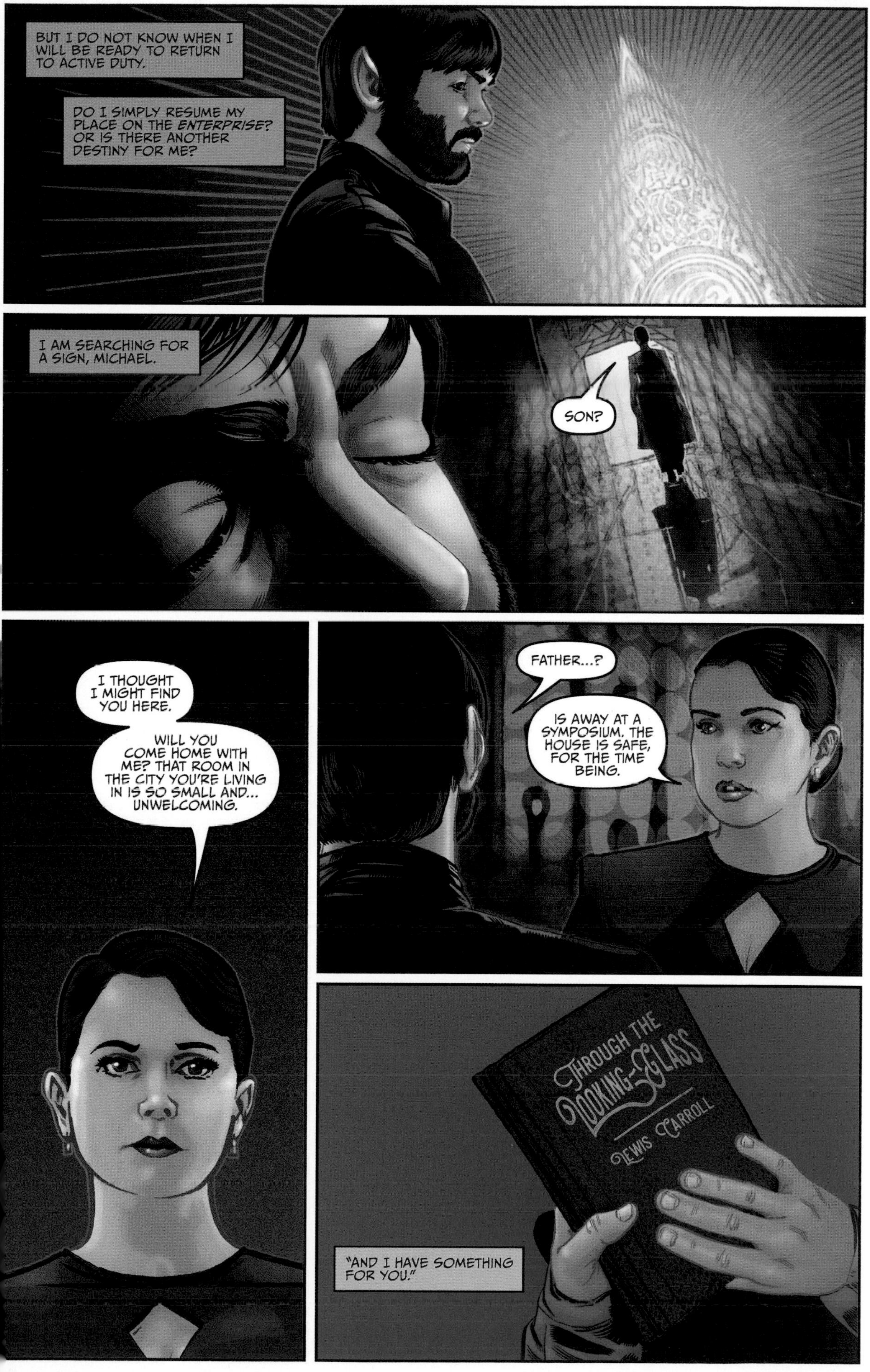
BUT I DO NOT KNOW WHEN I WILL BE READY TO RETURN TO ACTIVE DUTY.
DO I SIMPLY RESUME MY PLACE ON THE *ENTERPRISE*? OR IS THERE ANOTHER DESTINY FOR ME?
I AM SEARCHING FOR A SIGN, MICHAEL.
SON?
I THOUGHT I MIGHT FIND YOU HERE.
WILL YOU COME HOME WITH ME? THAT ROOM IN THE CITY YOU'RE LIVING IN IS SO SMALL AND... UNWELCOMING.
FATHER...?
IS AWAY AT A SYMPOSIUM. THE HOUSE IS SAFE, FOR THE TIME BEING.
THROUGH THE LOOKING-GLASS
LEWIS CARROLL
"AND I HAVE SOMETHING FOR YOU."

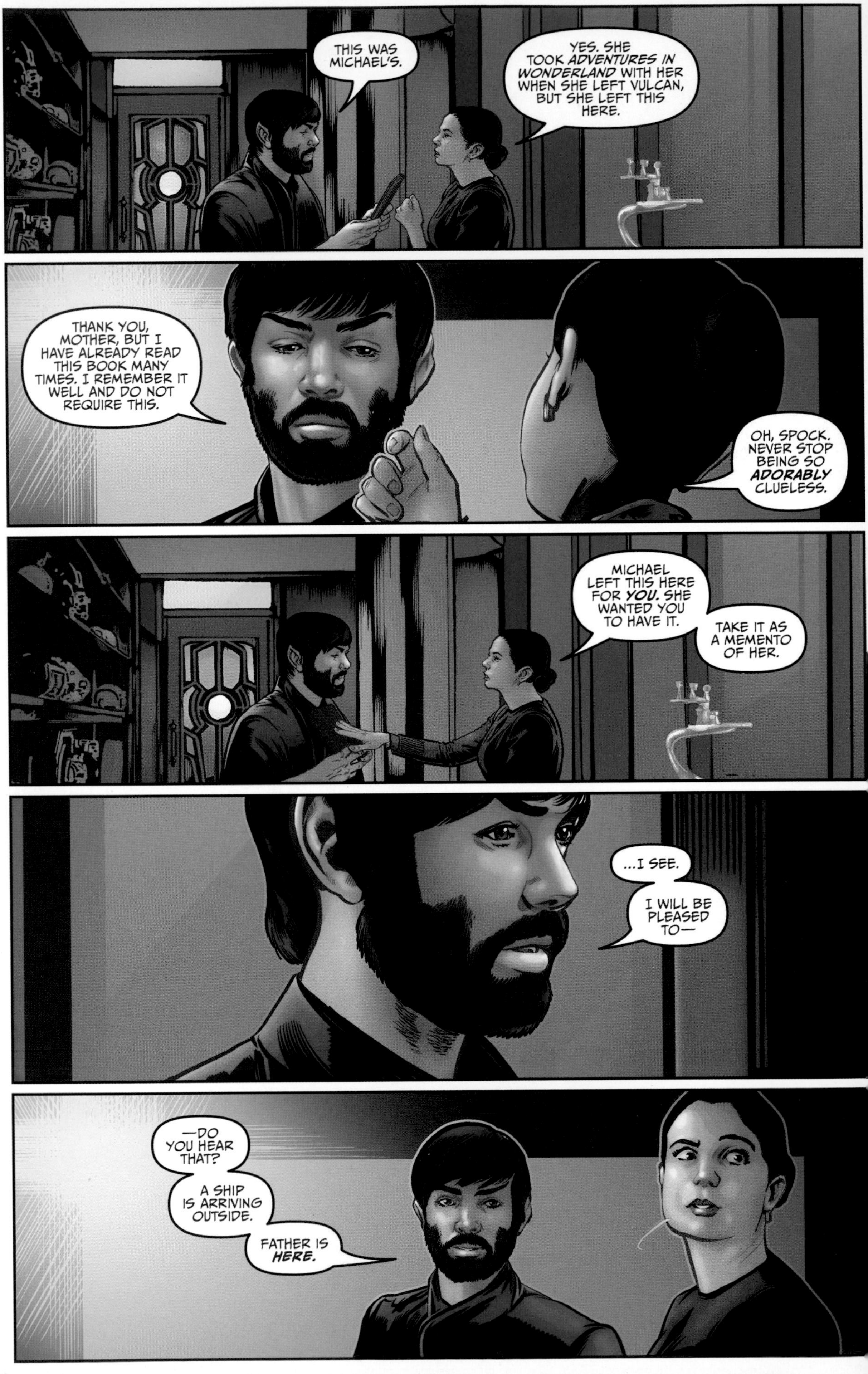
THIS WAS MICHAEL'S.
YES. SHE TOOK *ADVENTURES IN WONDERLAND* WITH HER WHEN SHE LEFT VULCAN, BUT SHE LEFT THIS HERE.
THANK YOU, MOTHER, BUT I HAVE ALREADY READ THIS BOOK MANY TIMES. I REMEMBER IT WELL AND DO NOT REQUIRE THIS.
OH, SPOCK. NEVER STOP BEING SO ***ADORABLY*** CLUELESS.
MICHAEL LEFT THIS HERE FOR ***YOU.*** SHE WANTED YOU TO HAVE IT.
TAKE IT AS A MEMENTO OF HER.
...I SEE.
I WILL BE PLEASED TO—
—DO YOU HEAR THAT?
A SHIP IS ARRIVING OUTSIDE.
FATHER IS ***HERE.***

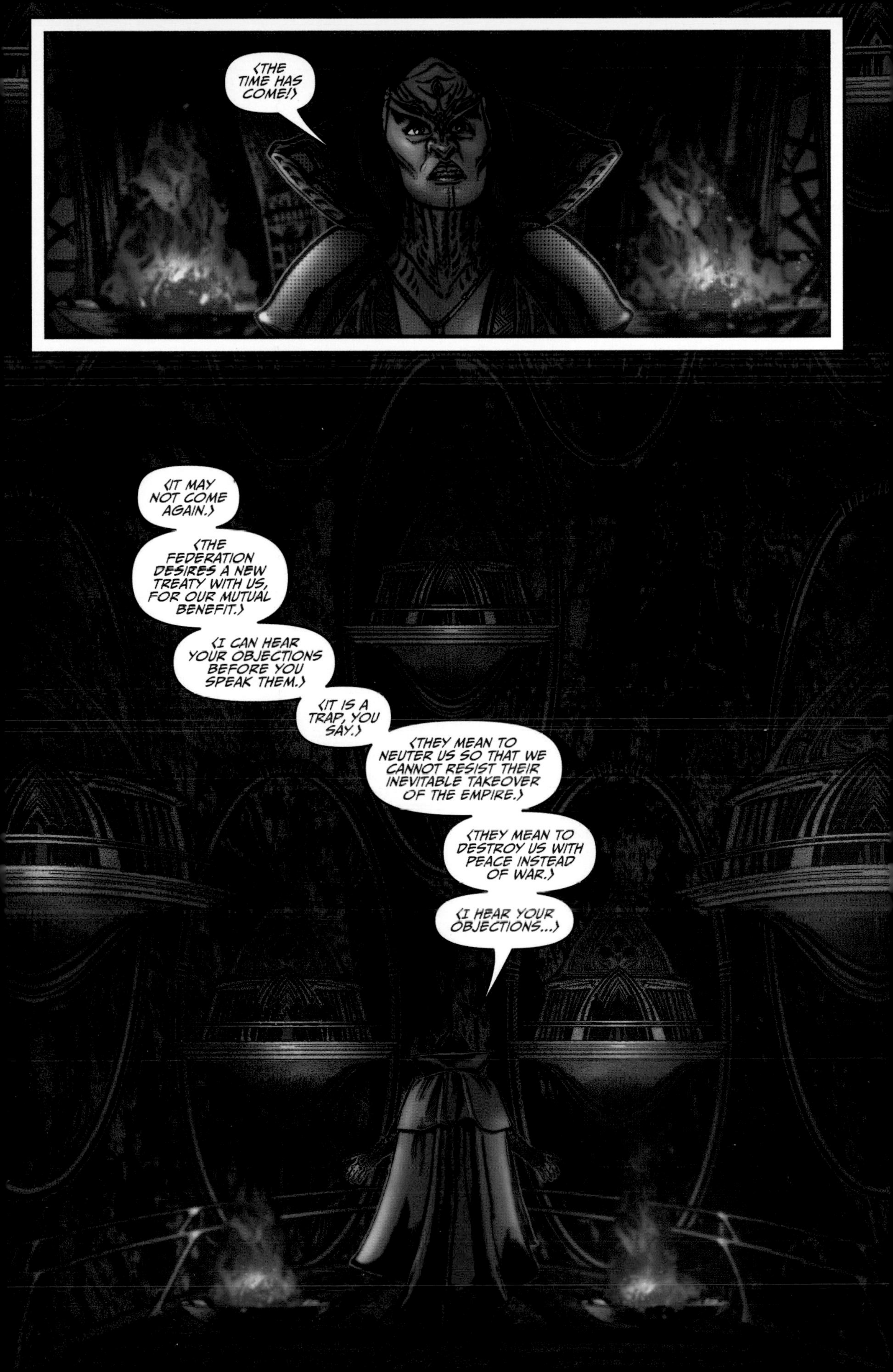

<THE TIME HAS COME!>
<IT MAY NOT COME AGAIN.>
<THE FEDERATION DESIRES A NEW TREATY WITH US, FOR OUR MUTUAL BENEFIT.>
<I CAN HEAR YOUR OBJECTIONS BEFORE YOU SPEAK THEM.>
<IT IS A TRAP, YOU SAY.>
<THEY MEAN TO NEUTER US SO THAT WE CANNOT RESIST THEIR INEVITABLE TAKEOVER OF THE EMPIRE.>
<THEY MEAN TO DESTROY US WITH PEACE INSTEAD OF WAR.>
<I HEAR YOUR OBJECTIONS...>

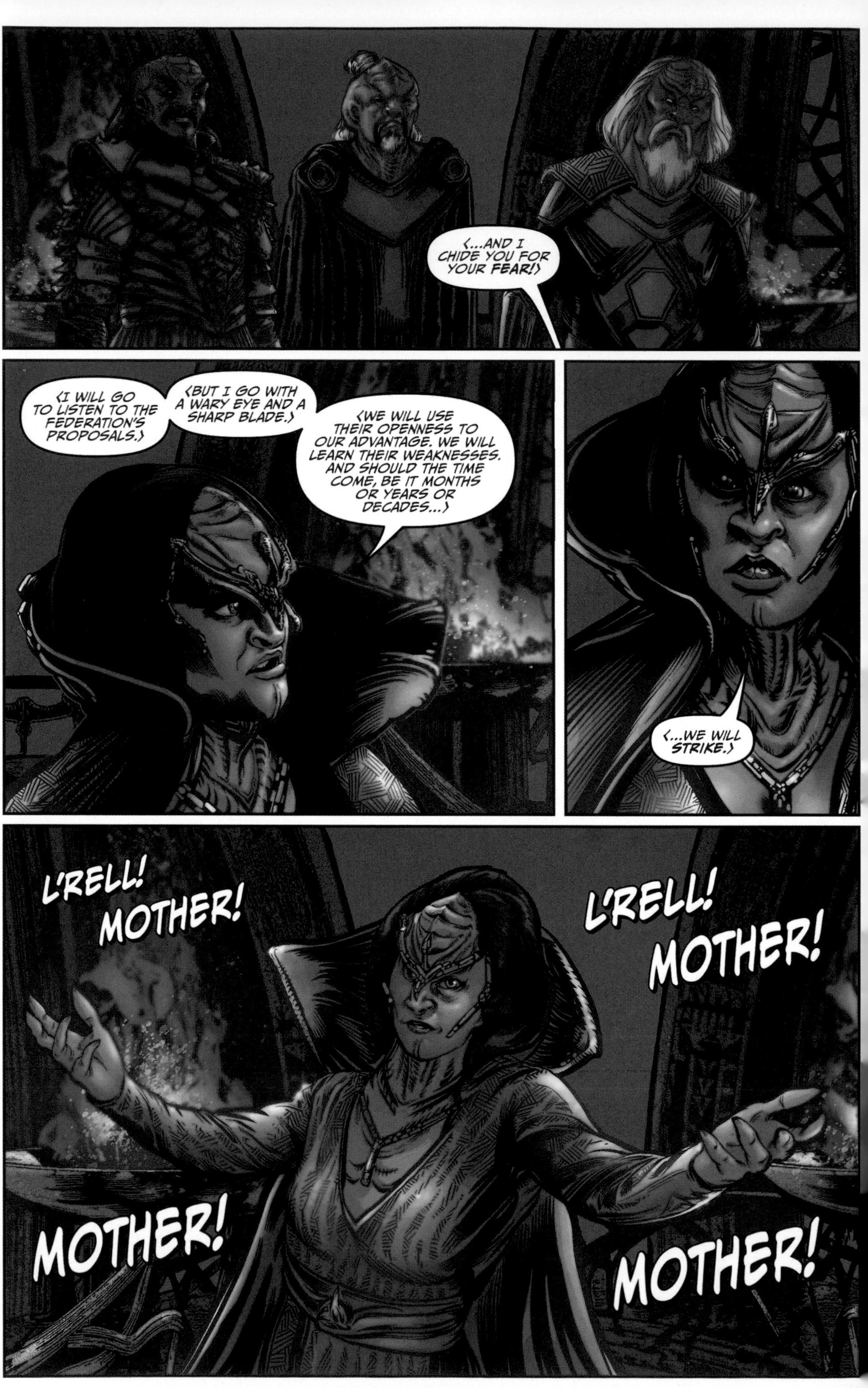
⟨...AND I CHIDE YOU FOR YOUR FEAR!⟩
⟨I WILL GO TO LISTEN TO THE FEDERATION'S PROPOSALS.⟩
⟨BUT I GO WITH A WARY EYE AND A SHARP BLADE.⟩
⟨WE WILL USE THEIR OPENNESS TO OUR ADVANTAGE. WE WILL LEARN THEIR WEAKNESSES. AND SHOULD THE TIME COME, BE IT MONTHS OR YEARS OR DECADES...⟩
⟨...WE WILL STRIKE.⟩
L'RELL! MOTHER!
L'RELL! MOTHER!
MOTHER!
MOTHER!

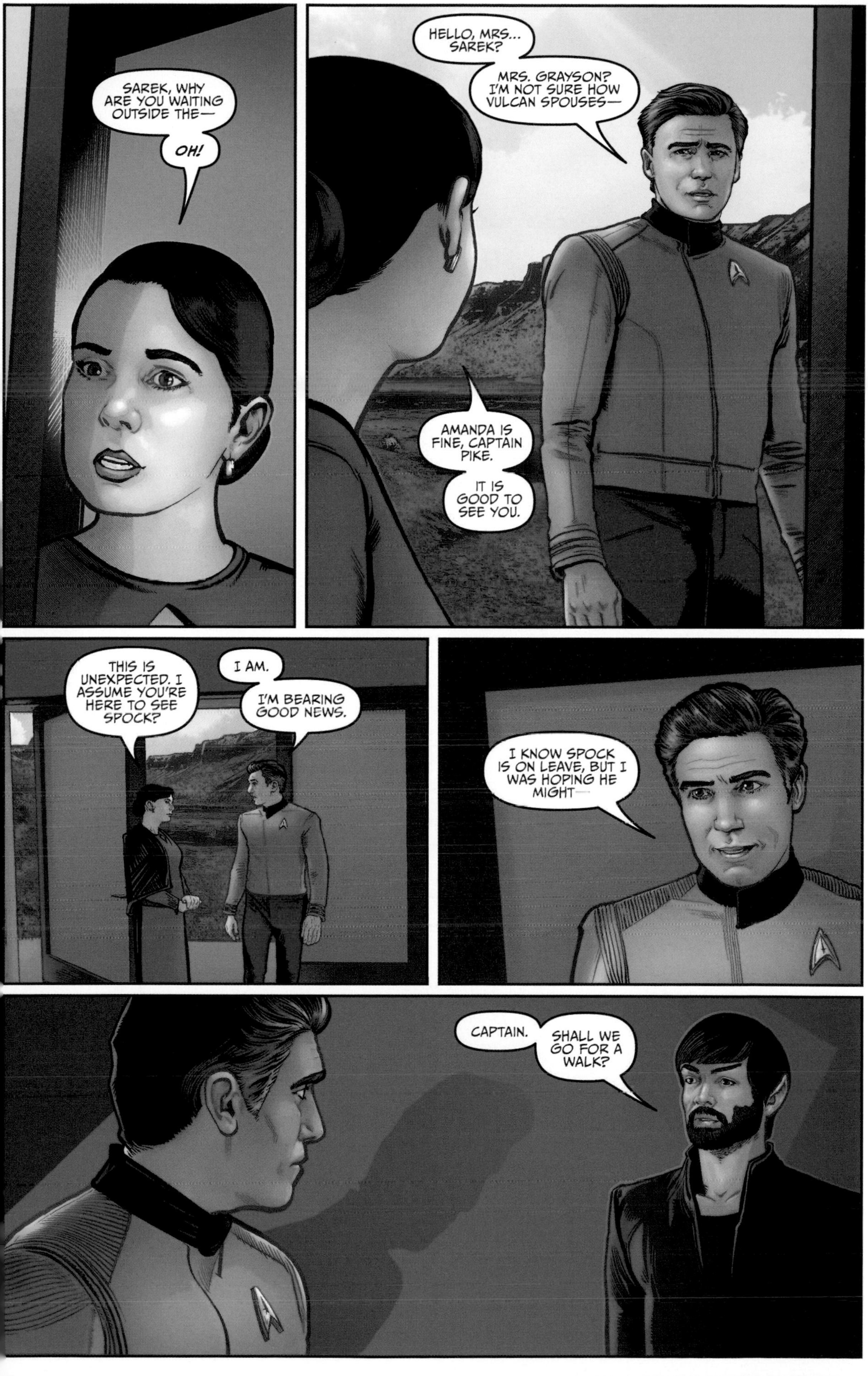
SAREK, WHY ARE YOU WAITING OUTSIDE THE—
OH!
HELLO, MRS... SAREK?
MRS. GRAYSON? I'M NOT SURE HOW VULCAN SPOUSES—
AMANDA IS FINE, CAPTAIN PIKE.
IT IS GOOD TO SEE YOU.
THIS IS UNEXPECTED. I ASSUME YOU'RE HERE TO SEE SPOCK?
I AM.
I'M BEARING GOOD NEWS.
I KNOW SPOCK IS ON LEAVE, BUT I WAS HOPING HE MIGHT—
CAPTAIN.
SHALL WE GO FOR A WALK?

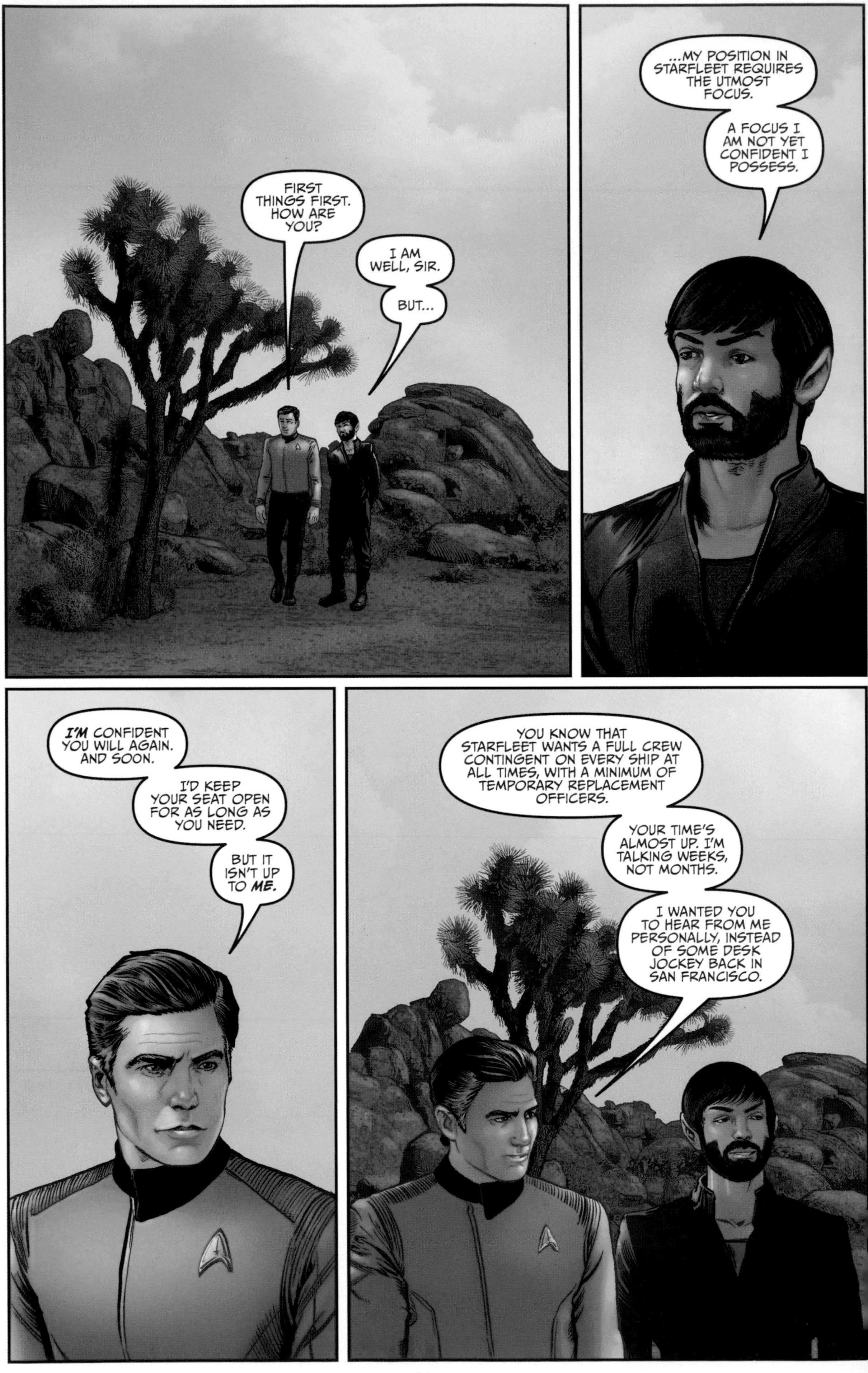
FIRST THINGS FIRST. HOW ARE YOU?
I AM WELL, SIR.
BUT...
...MY POSITION IN STARFLEET REQUIRES THE UTMOST FOCUS.
A FOCUS I AM NOT YET CONFIDENT I POSSESS.
I'M CONFIDENT YOU WILL AGAIN. AND SOON.
I'D KEEP YOUR SEAT OPEN FOR AS LONG AS YOU NEED.
BUT IT ISN'T UP TO ME.
YOU KNOW THAT STARFLEET WANTS A FULL CREW CONTINGENT ON EVERY SHIP AT ALL TIMES, WITH A MINIMUM OF TEMPORARY REPLACEMENT OFFICERS.
YOUR TIME'S ALMOST UP. I'M TALKING WEEKS, NOT MONTHS.
I WANTED YOU TO HEAR FROM ME PERSONALLY, INSTEAD OF SOME DESK JOCKEY BACK IN SAN FRANCISCO.

BUT THAT'S NOT THE ONLY REASON I'M HERE. I NEED YOU BACK NOW, EVEN IF IT'S NOT OFFICIAL REINSTATEMENT.

I WANT YOU BY MY SIDE WHEN I MEET WITH THE KLINGONS AT THE SUMMIT ON VASET.

I DO NOT UNDERSTAND WHAT USE I WOULD BE TO YOU THERE. EVEN AS A SCIENCE OFFICER.

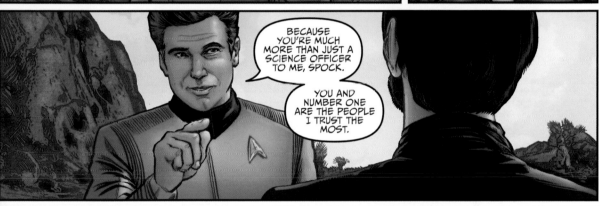

BECAUSE YOU'RE MUCH MORE THAN JUST A SCIENCE OFFICER TO ME, SPOCK.

YOU AND NUMBER ONE ARE THE PEOPLE I TRUST THE MOST.

BESIDES, IT MIGHT BE GOOD FOR YOU TO GET BACK ON THE *ENTERPRISE*, EVEN UNOFFICIALLY.

YOU MIGHT FIND SOME OF THAT FOCUS YOU'RE LOOKING FOR.

PERHAPS YOU ARE RIGHT, CAPTAIN.

I DID LEAVE SEVERAL ONGOING EXPERIMENTS ABOARD THAT MIGHT BENEFIT FROM MY ATTENTION.

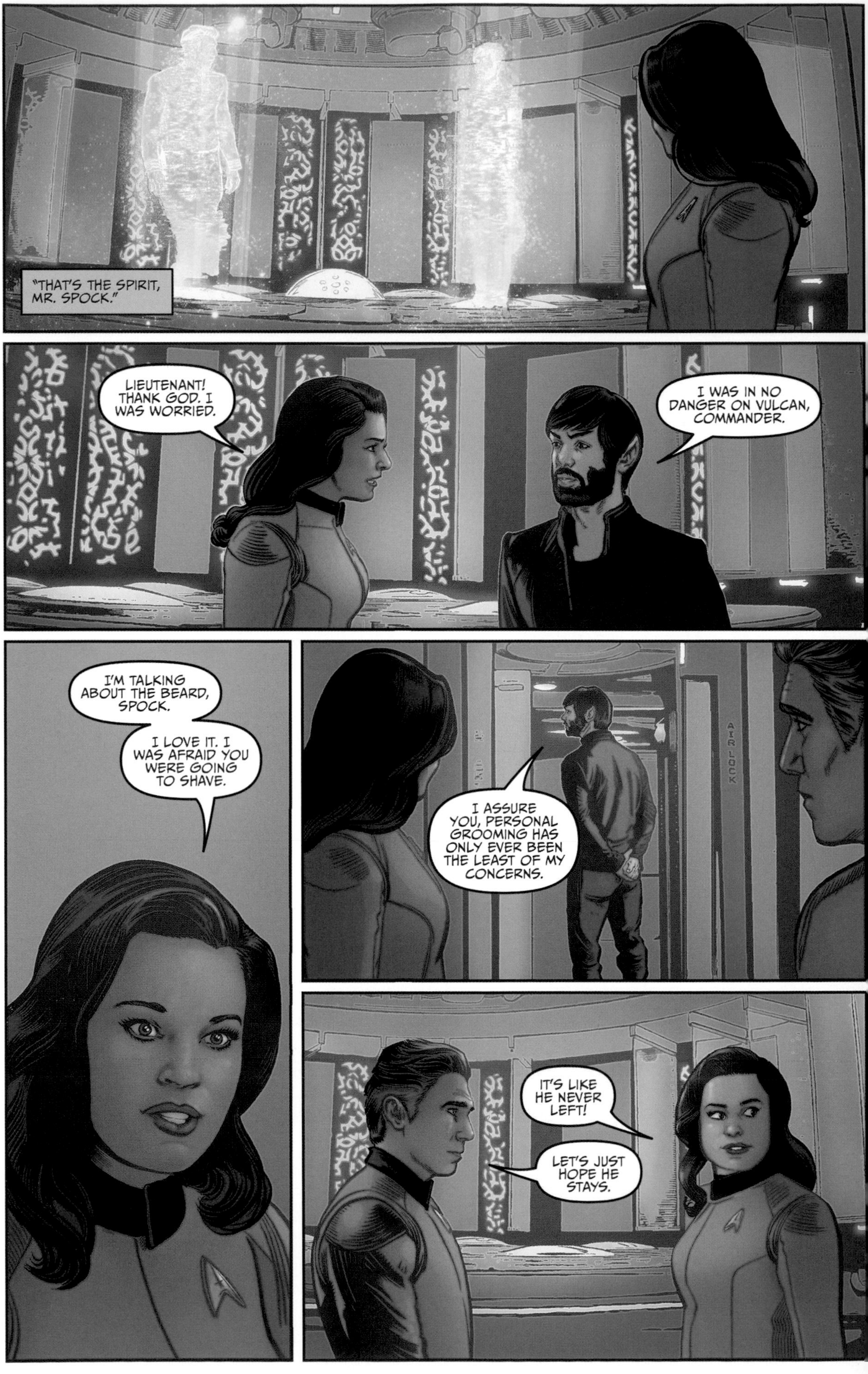
"THAT'S THE SPIRIT, MR. SPOCK."
LIEUTENANT! THANK GOD. I WAS WORRIED.
I WAS IN NO DANGER ON VULCAN, COMMANDER.
I'M TALKING ABOUT THE BEARD, SPOCK.
I LOVE IT. I WAS AFRAID YOU WERE GOING TO SHAVE.
I ASSURE YOU, PERSONAL GROOMING HAS ONLY EVER BEEN THE LEAST OF MY CONCERNS.
AIR LOCK
IT'S LIKE HE NEVER LEFT!
LET'S JUST HOPE HE STAYS.

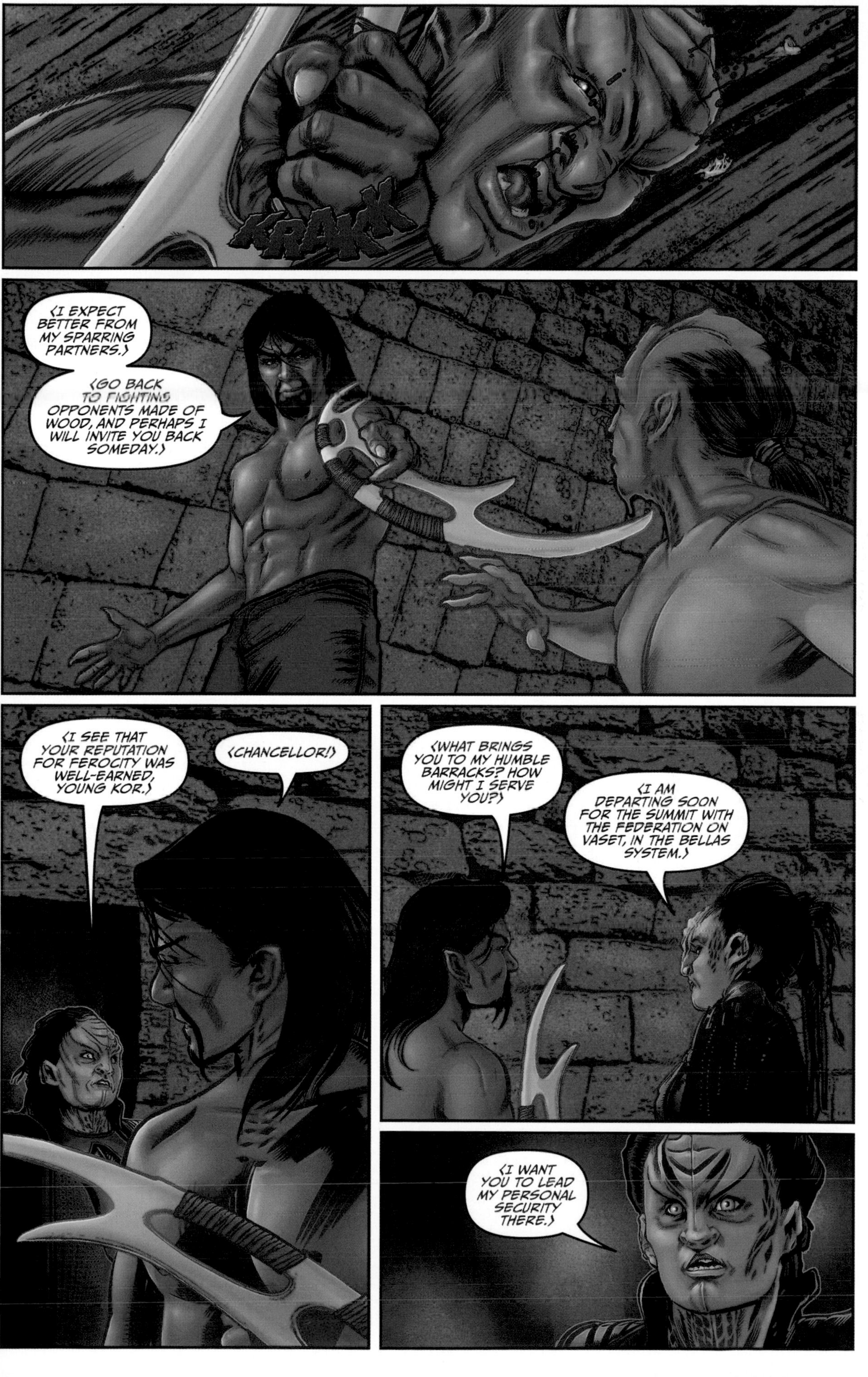
KRAKK
‹I EXPECT BETTER FROM MY SPARRING PARTNERS.›
‹GO BACK TO FIGHTING OPPONENTS MADE OF WOOD, AND PERHAPS I WILL INVITE YOU BACK SOMEDAY.›
‹I SEE THAT YOUR REPUTATION FOR FEROCITY WAS WELL-EARNED, YOUNG KOR.›
‹CHANCELLOR!›
‹WHAT BRINGS YOU TO MY HUMBLE BARRACKS? HOW MIGHT I SERVE YOU?›
‹I AM DEPARTING SOON FOR THE SUMMIT WITH THE FEDERATION ON VASET, IN THE BELLAS SYSTEM.›
‹I WANT YOU TO LEAD MY PERSONAL SECURITY THERE.›

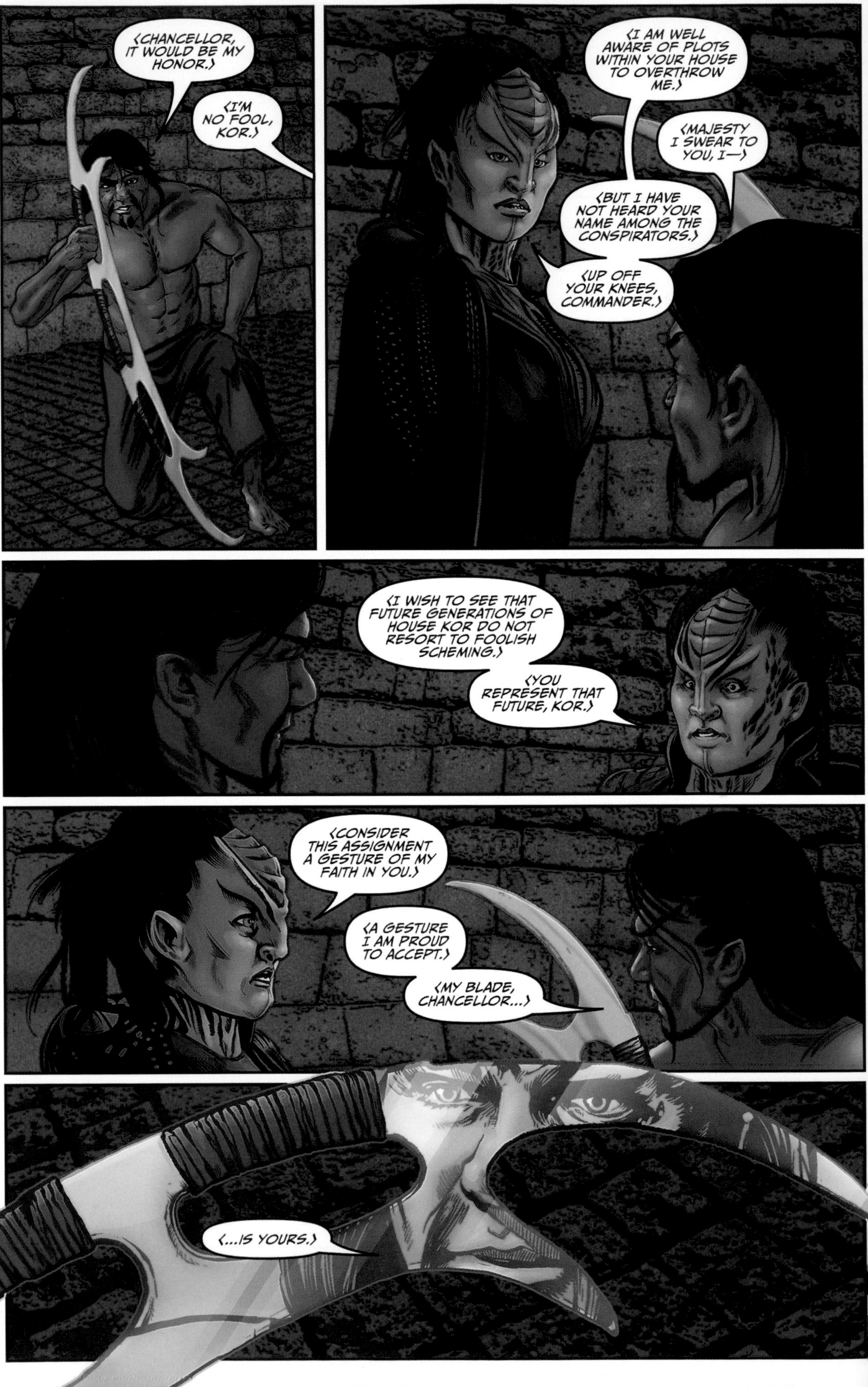
‹CHANCELLOR, IT WOULD BE MY HONOR.›
‹I'M NO FOOL, KOR.›
‹I AM WELL AWARE OF PLOTS WITHIN YOUR HOUSE TO OVERTHROW ME.›
‹MAJESTY I SWEAR TO YOU, I—›
‹BUT I HAVE NOT HEARD YOUR NAME AMONG THE CONSPIRATORS.›
‹UP OFF YOUR KNEES, COMMANDER.›
‹I WISH TO SEE THAT FUTURE GENERATIONS OF HOUSE KOR DO NOT RESORT TO FOOLISH SCHEMING.›
‹YOU REPRESENT THAT FUTURE, KOR.›
‹CONSIDER THIS ASSIGNMENT A GESTURE OF MY FAITH IN YOU.›
‹A GESTURE I AM PROUD TO ACCEPT.›
‹MY BLADE, CHANCELLOR...›
‹...IS YOURS.›

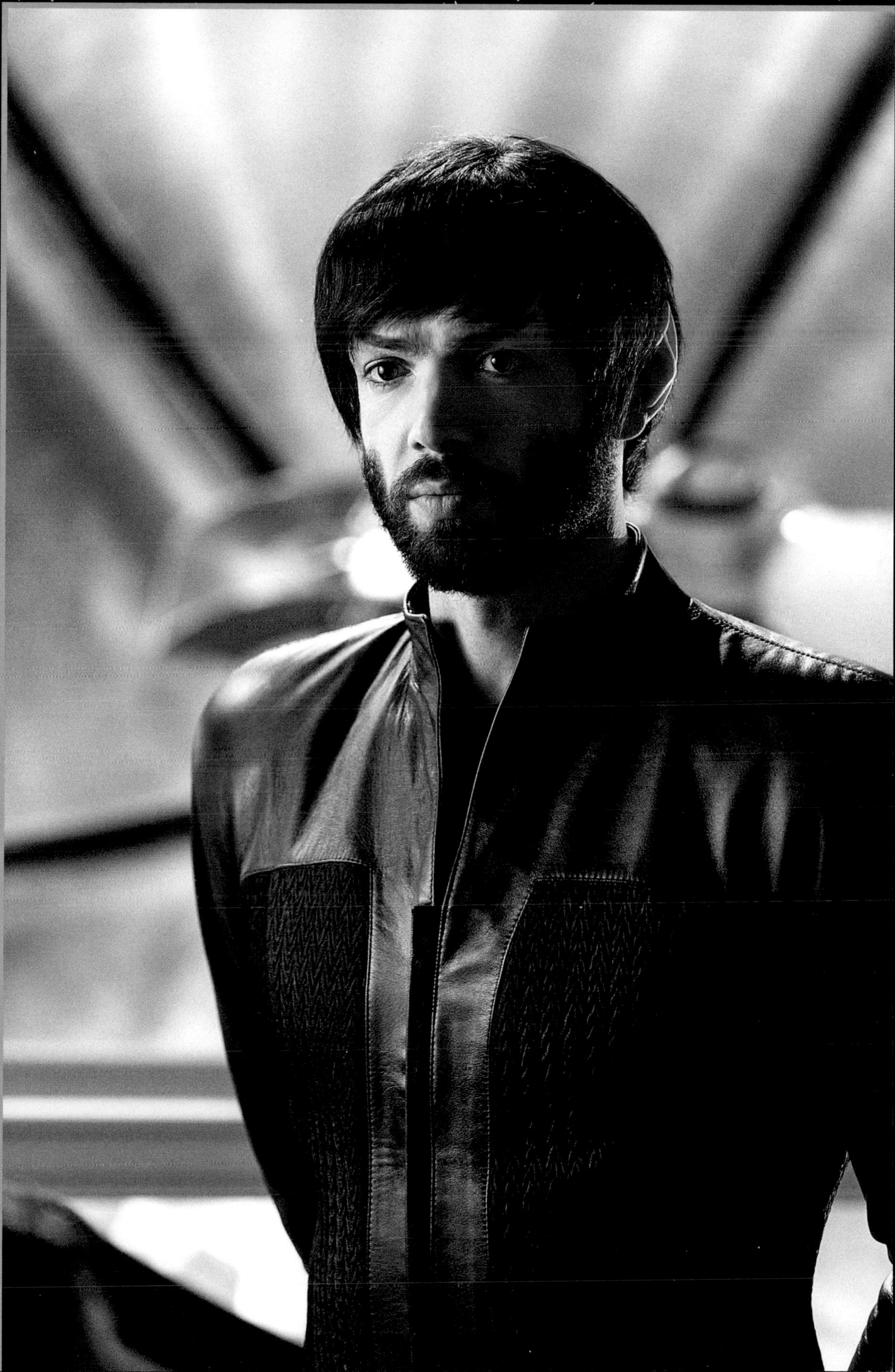

ART BY **ANGEL HERNANDEZ** | COLORS BY **J.D. METTLER**

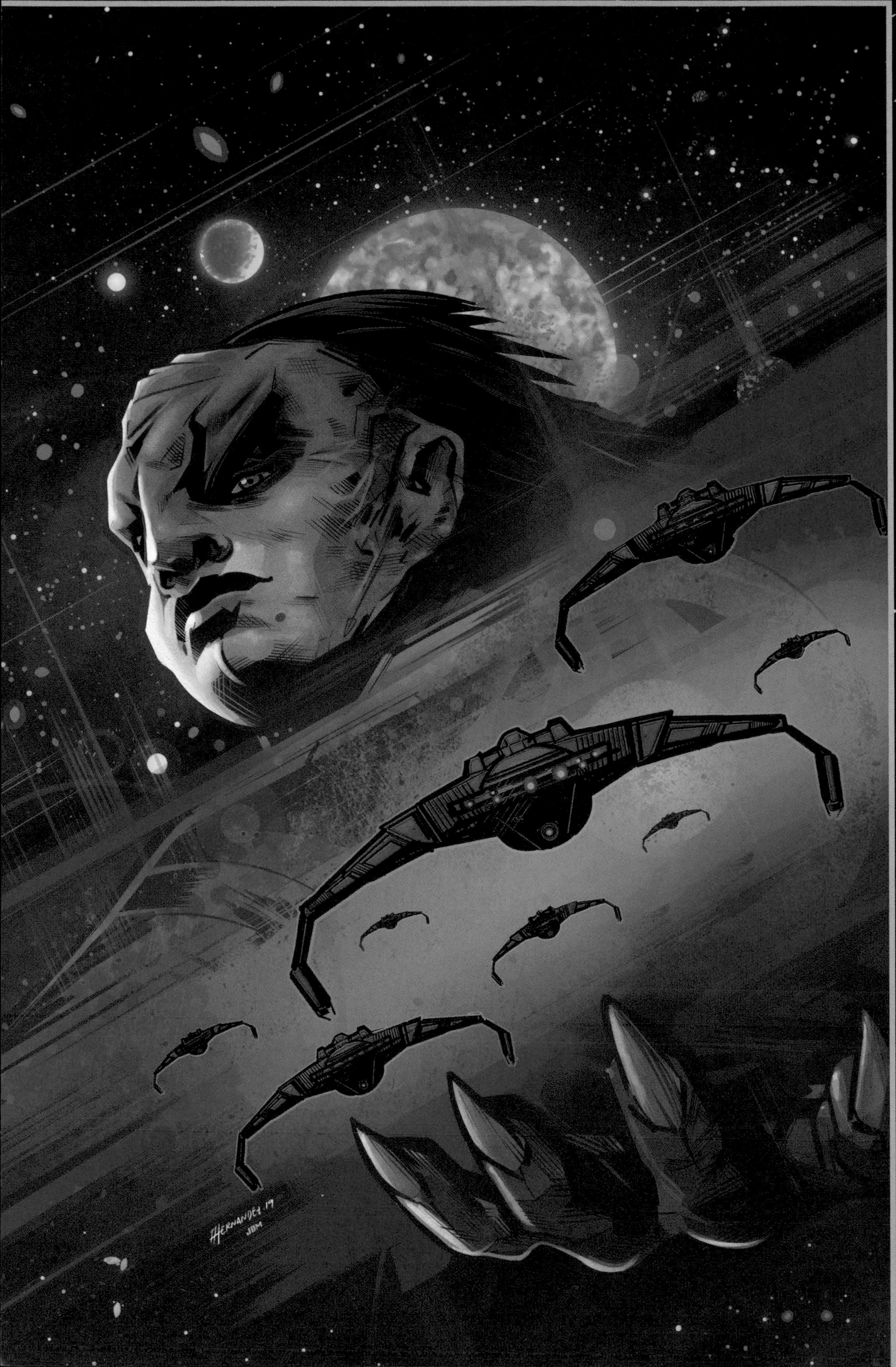
HERNANDEZ 17
JDM

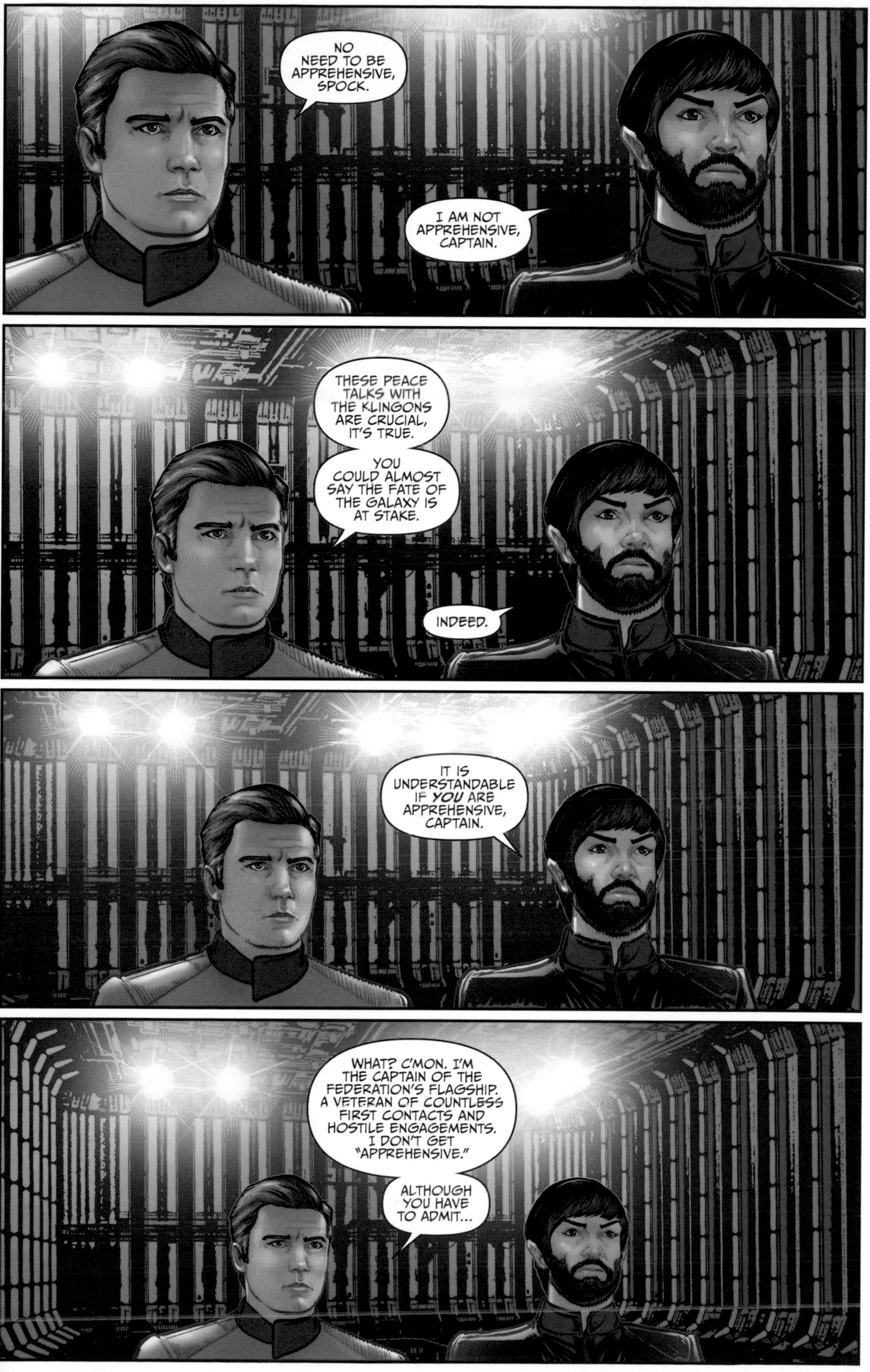
NO NEED TO BE APPREHENSIVE, SPOCK.
I AM NOT APPREHENSIVE, CAPTAIN.
THESE PEACE TALKS WITH THE KLINGONS ARE CRUCIAL, IT'S TRUE.
YOU COULD ALMOST SAY THE FATE OF THE GALAXY IS AT STAKE.
INDEED.
IT IS UNDERSTANDABLE IF *YOU* ARE APPREHENSIVE, CAPTAIN.
WHAT? C'MON. I'M THE CAPTAIN OF THE FEDERATION'S FLAGSHIP. A VETERAN OF COUNTLESS FIRST CONTACTS AND HOSTILE ENGAGEMENTS. I DON'T GET "APPREHENSIVE."
ALTHOUGH YOU HAVE TO ADMIT...

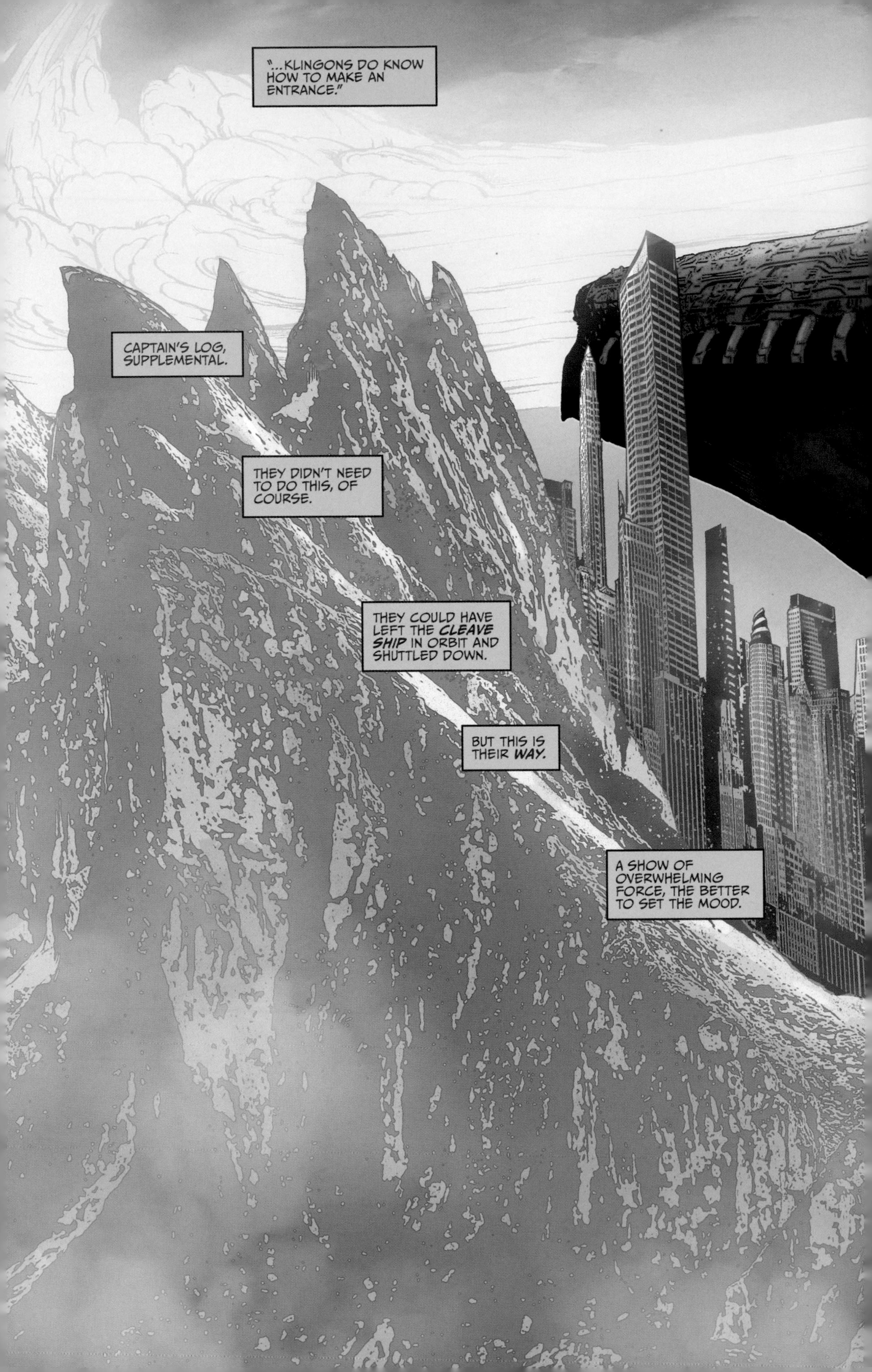
"...KLINGONS DO KNOW HOW TO MAKE AN ENTRANCE."
CAPTAIN'S LOG, SUPPLEMENTAL.
THEY DIDN'T NEED TO DO THIS, OF COURSE.
THEY COULD HAVE LEFT THE **CLEAVE SHIP** IN ORBIT AND SHUTTLED DOWN.
BUT THIS IS THEIR **WAY**.
A SHOW OF OVERWHELMING FORCE, THE BETTER TO SET THE MOOD.

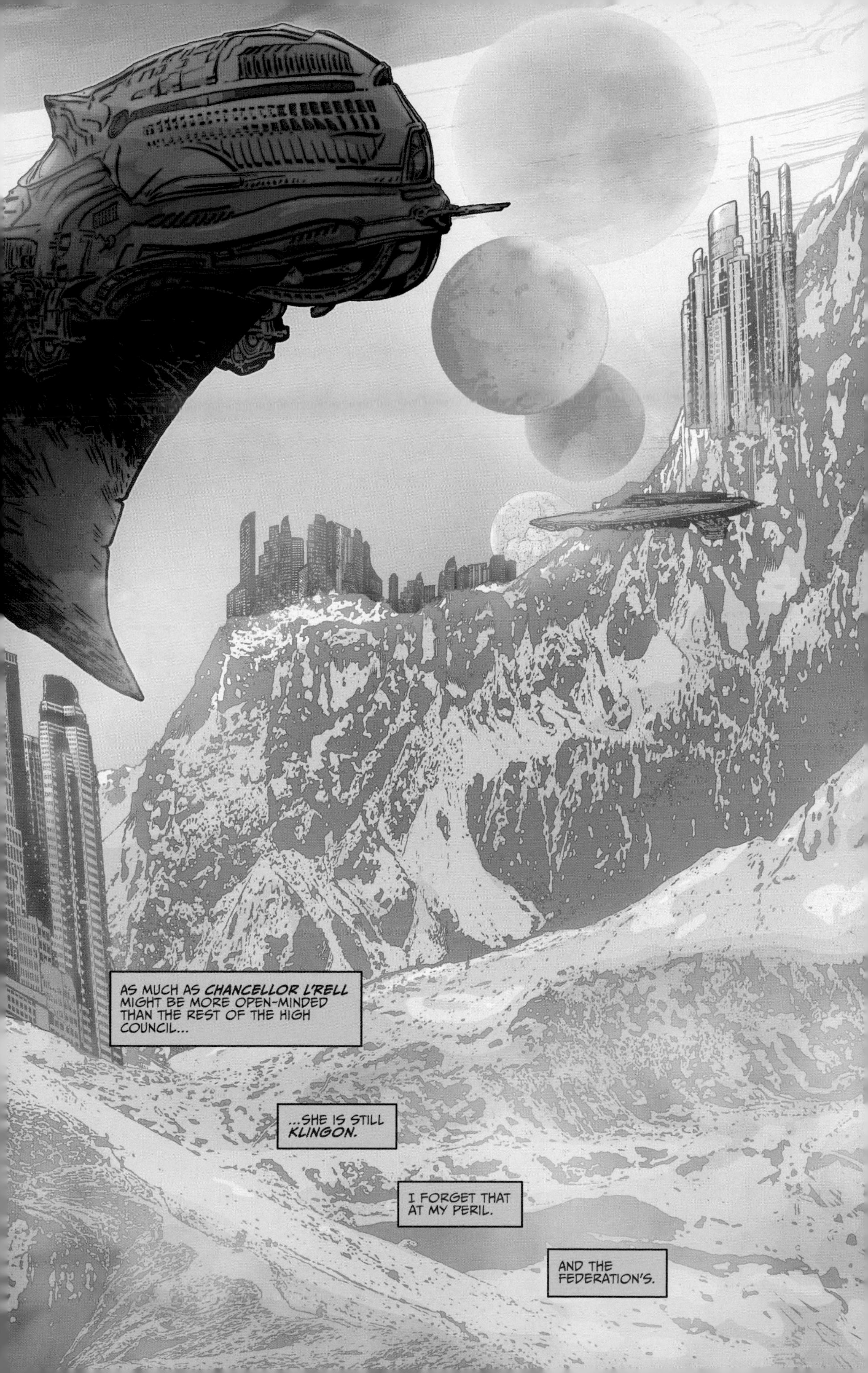
AS MUCH AS **CHANCELLOR L'RELL** MIGHT BE MORE OPEN-MINDED THAN THE REST OF THE HIGH COUNCIL...
...SHE IS STILL **KLINGON.**
I FORGET THAT AT MY PERIL.
AND THE FEDERATION'S.

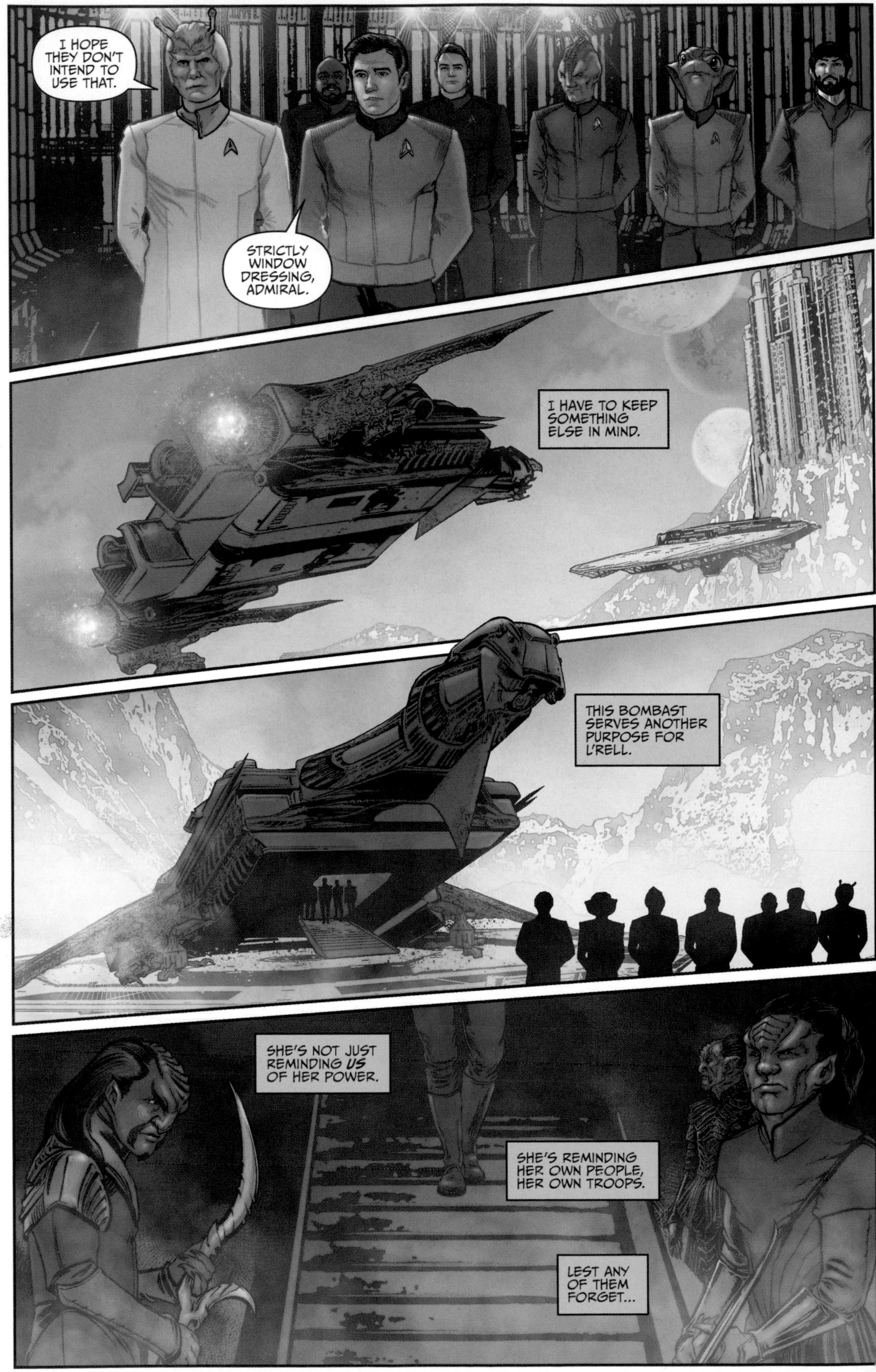
I HOPE THEY DON'T INTEND TO USE THAT.
STRICTLY WINDOW DRESSING, ADMIRAL.
I HAVE TO KEEP SOMETHING ELSE IN MIND.
THIS BOMBAST SERVES ANOTHER PURPOSE FOR L'RELL.
SHE'S NOT JUST REMINDING *US* OF HER POWER.
SHE'S REMINDING HER OWN PEOPLE, HER OWN TROOPS.
LEST ANY OF THEM FORGET...

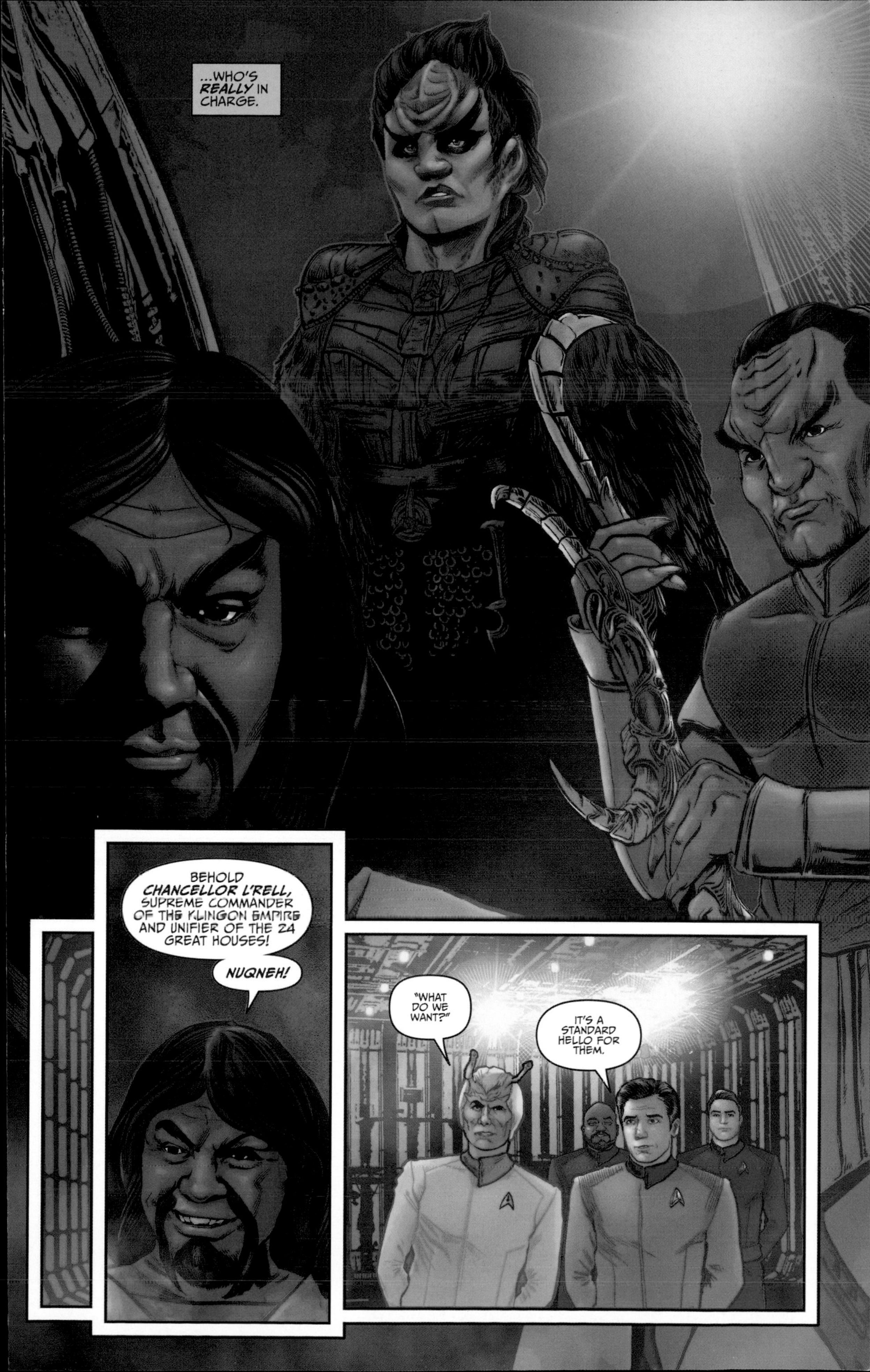
...WHO'S *REALLY* IN CHARGE.
BEHOLD *CHANCELLOR L'RELL,* SUPREME COMMANDER OF THE KLINGON EMPIRE AND UNIFIER OF THE 24 GREAT HOUSES!
NUQNEH!
"WHAT DO WE WANT?"
IT'S A STANDARD HELLO FOR THEM.

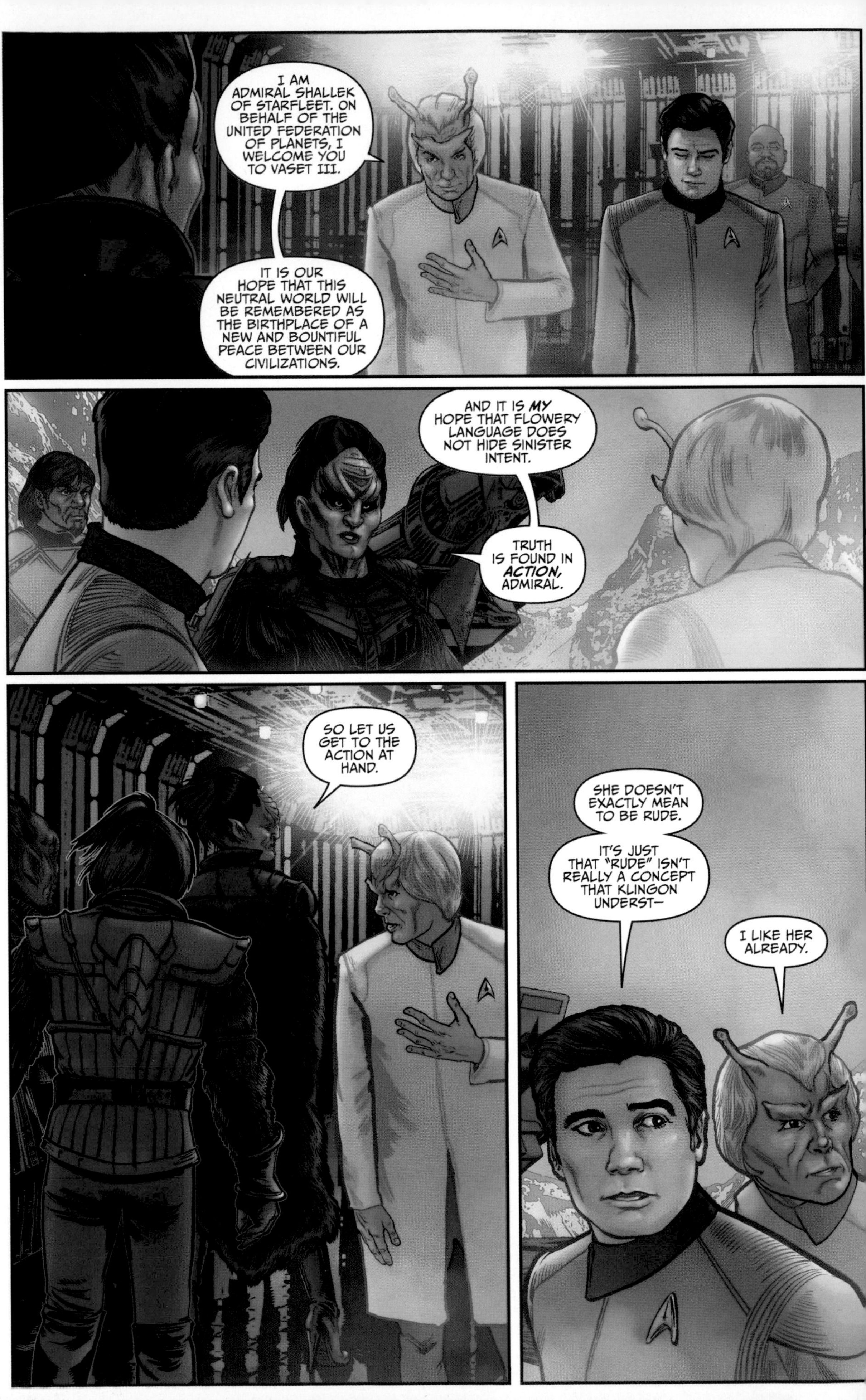
I AM ADMIRAL SHALLEK OF STARFLEET. ON BEHALF OF THE UNITED FEDERATION OF PLANETS, I WELCOME YOU TO VASET III.
IT IS OUR HOPE THAT THIS NEUTRAL WORLD WILL BE REMEMBERED AS THE BIRTHPLACE OF A NEW AND BOUNTIFUL PEACE BETWEEN OUR CIVILIZATIONS.
AND IT IS *MY* HOPE THAT FLOWERY LANGUAGE DOES NOT HIDE SINISTER INTENT.
TRUTH IS FOUND IN *ACTION,* ADMIRAL.
SO LET US GET TO THE ACTION AT HAND.
SHE DOESN'T EXACTLY MEAN TO BE RUDE.
IT'S JUST THAT "RUDE" ISN'T REALLY A CONCEPT THAT KLINGON UNDERST—
I LIKE HER ALREADY.

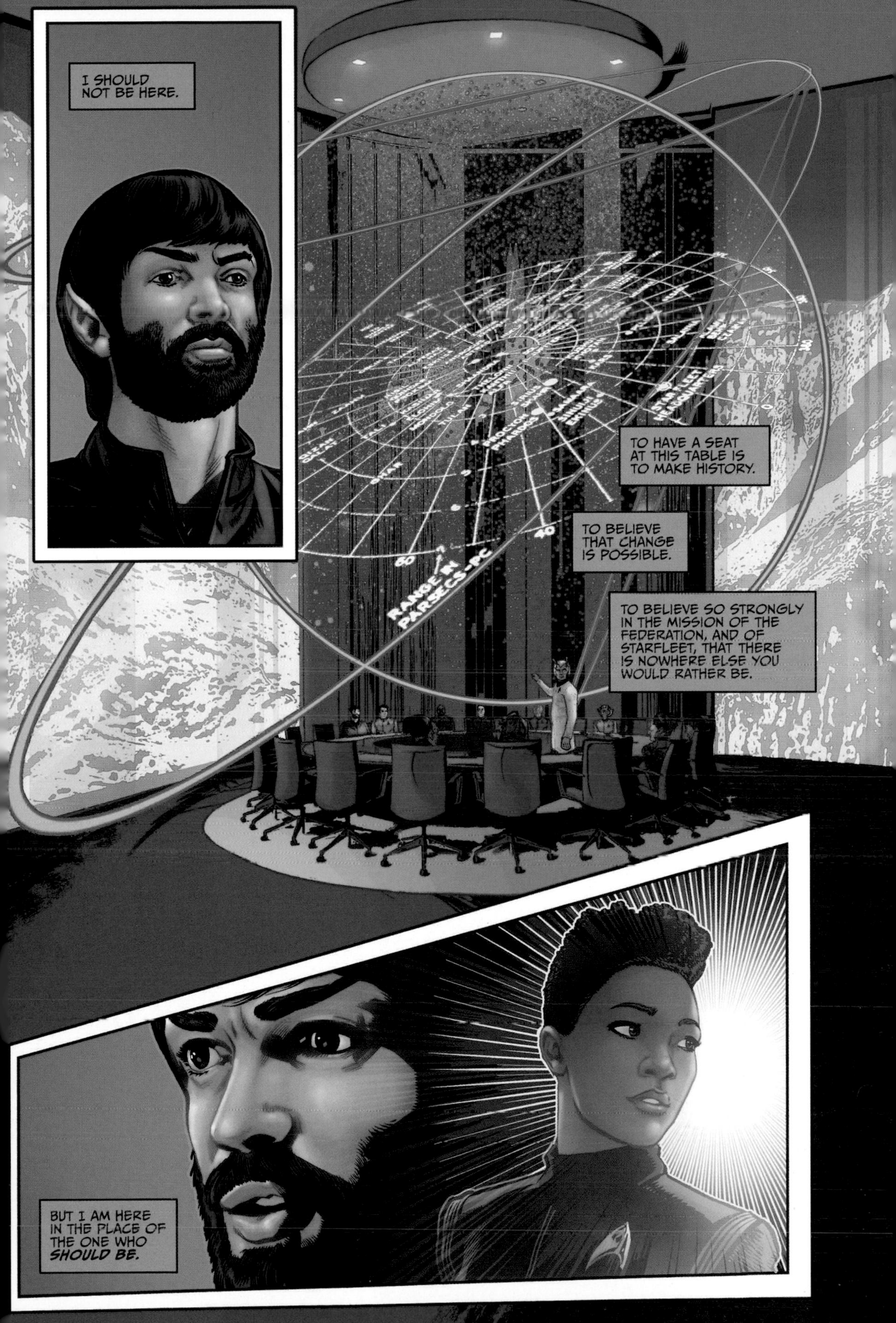
I SHOULD NOT BE HERE.
TO HAVE A SEAT AT THIS TABLE IS TO MAKE HISTORY.
TO BELIEVE THAT CHANGE IS POSSIBLE.
TO BELIEVE SO STRONGLY IN THE MISSION OF THE FEDERATION, AND OF STARFLEET, THAT THERE IS NOWHERE ELSE YOU WOULD RATHER BE.
BUT I AM HERE IN THE PLACE OF THE ONE WHO *SHOULD BE.*

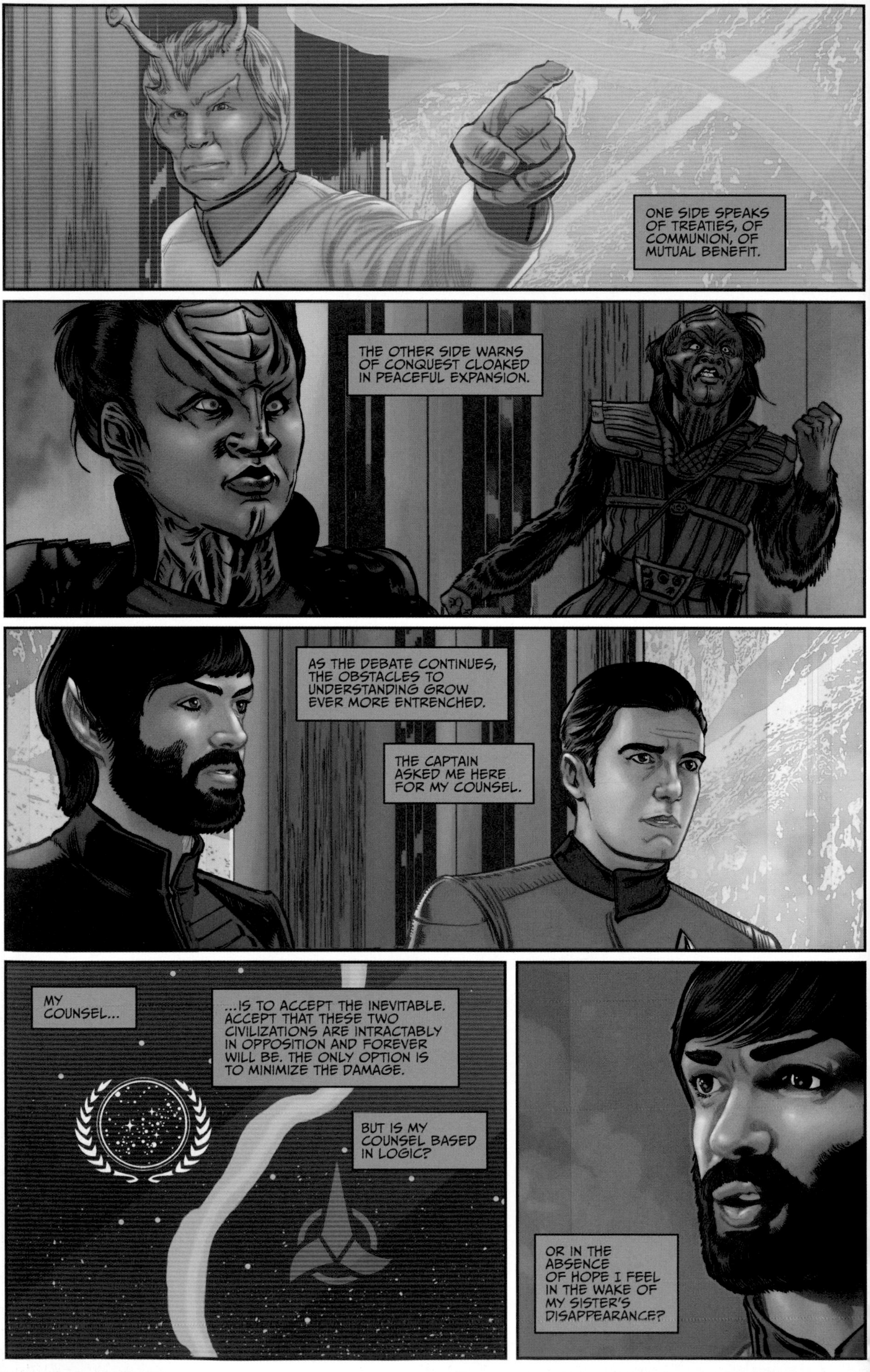
ONE SIDE SPEAKS OF TREATIES, OF COMMUNION, OF MUTUAL BENEFIT.
THE OTHER SIDE WARNS OF CONQUEST CLOAKED IN PEACEFUL EXPANSION.
AS THE DEBATE CONTINUES, THE OBSTACLES TO UNDERSTANDING GROW EVER MORE ENTRENCHED.
THE CAPTAIN ASKED ME HERE FOR MY COUNSEL.
MY COUNSEL...
...IS TO ACCEPT THE INEVITABLE. ACCEPT THAT THESE TWO CIVILIZATIONS ARE INTRACTABLY IN OPPOSITION AND FOREVER WILL BE. THE ONLY OPTION IS TO MINIMIZE THE DAMAGE.
BUT IS MY COUNSEL BASED IN LOGIC?
OR IN THE ABSENCE OF HOPE I FEEL IN THE WAKE OF MY SISTER'S DISAPPEARANCE?

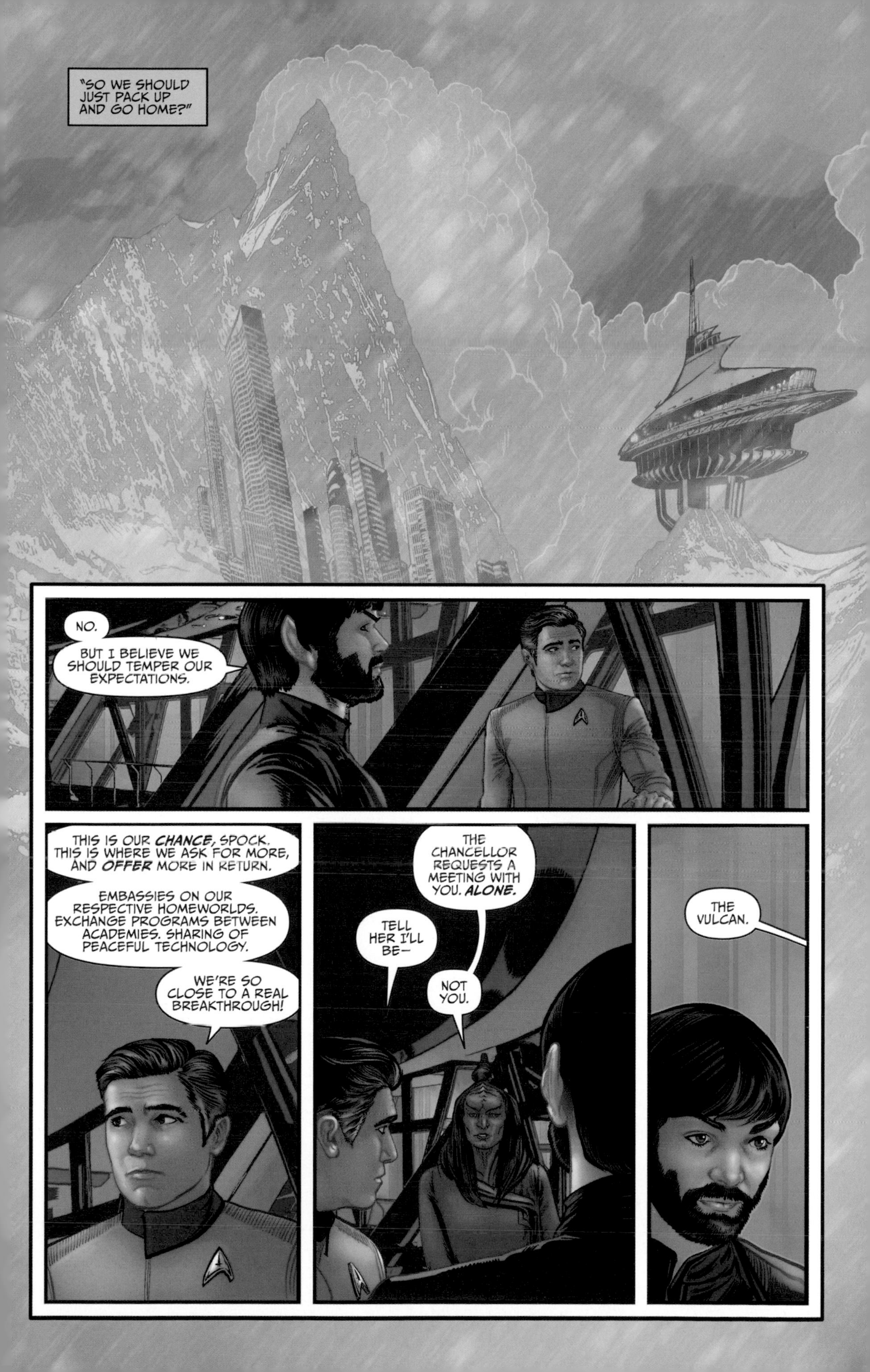
"SO WE SHOULD JUST PACK UP AND GO HOME?"
NO.
BUT I BELIEVE WE SHOULD TEMPER OUR EXPECTATIONS.
THIS IS OUR CHANCE, SPOCK. THIS IS WHERE WE ASK FOR MORE, AND OFFER MORE IN RETURN.
EMBASSIES ON OUR RESPECTIVE HOMEWORLDS. EXCHANGE PROGRAMS BETWEEN ACADEMIES. SHARING OF PEACEFUL TECHNOLOGY.
WE'RE SO CLOSE TO A REAL BREAKTHROUGH!
THE CHANCELLOR REQUESTS A MEETING WITH YOU. ALONE.
TELL HER I'LL BE—
NOT YOU.
THE VULCAN.

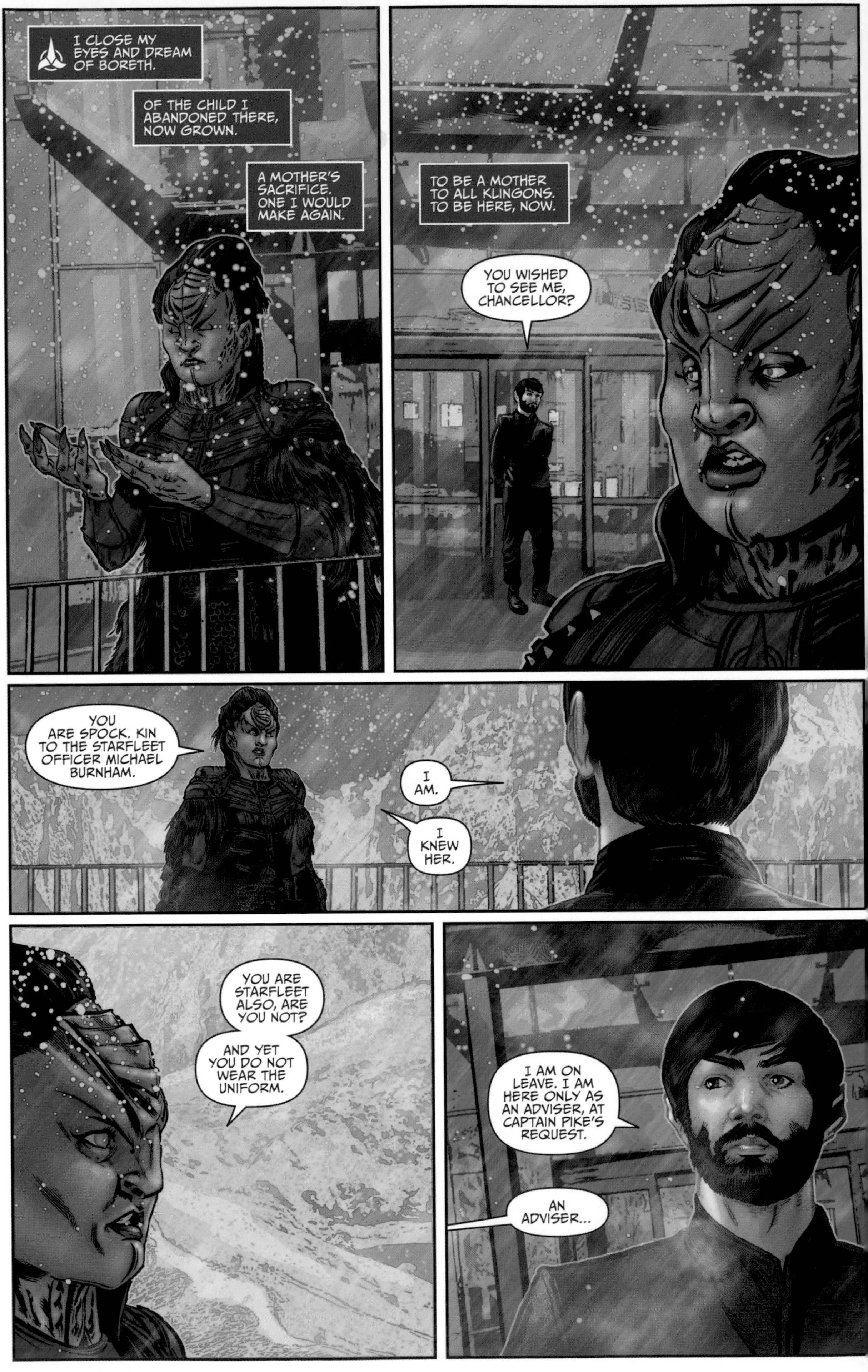
I CLOSE MY EYES AND DREAM OF BORETH.
OF THE CHILD I ABANDONED THERE, NOW GROWN.
A MOTHER'S SACRIFICE. ONE I WOULD MAKE AGAIN.
TO BE A MOTHER TO ALL KLINGONS. TO BE HERE, NOW.
YOU WISHED TO SEE ME, CHANCELLOR?
YOU ARE SPOCK. KIN TO THE STARFLEET OFFICER MICHAEL BURNHAM.
I AM.
I KNEW HER.
YOU ARE STARFLEET ALSO, ARE YOU NOT?
AND YET YOU DO NOT WEAR THE UNIFORM.
I AM ON LEAVE. I AM HERE ONLY AS AN ADVISER, AT CAPTAIN PIKE'S REQUEST.
AN ADVISER...

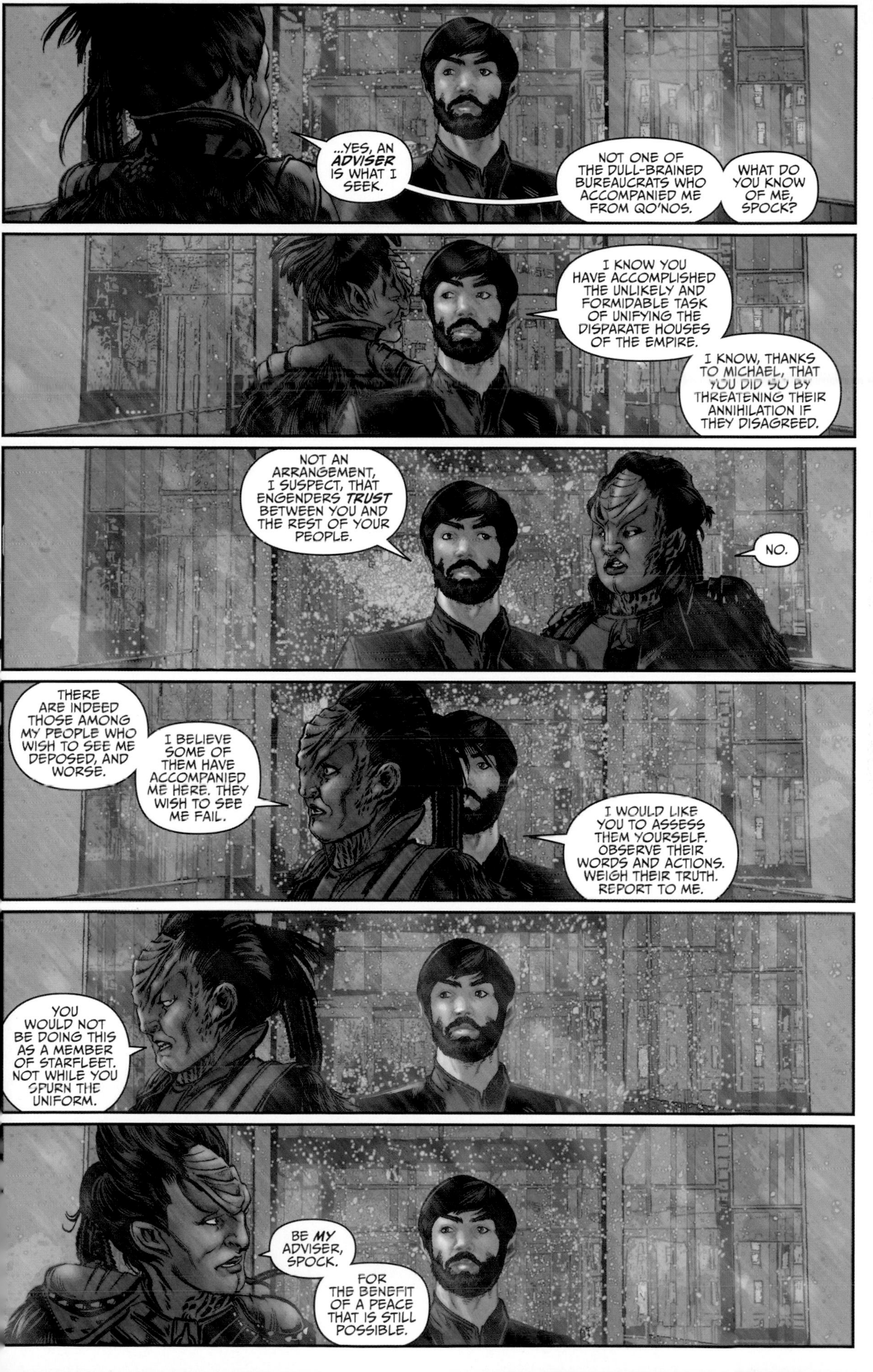
...YES, AN ADVISER IS WHAT I SEEK.
NOT ONE OF THE DULL-BRAINED BUREAUCRATS WHO ACCOMPANIED ME FROM QO'NOS.
WHAT DO YOU KNOW OF ME, SPOCK?
I KNOW YOU HAVE ACCOMPLISHED THE UNLIKELY AND FORMIDABLE TASK OF UNIFYING THE DISPARATE HOUSES OF THE EMPIRE.
I KNOW, THANKS TO MICHAEL, THAT YOU DID SO BY THREATENING THEIR ANNIHILATION IF THEY DISAGREED.
NOT AN ARRANGEMENT, I SUSPECT, THAT ENGENDERS TRUST BETWEEN YOU AND THE REST OF YOUR PEOPLE.
NO.
THERE ARE INDEED THOSE AMONG MY PEOPLE WHO WISH TO SEE ME DEPOSED, AND WORSE.
I BELIEVE SOME OF THEM HAVE ACCOMPANIED ME HERE. THEY WISH TO SEE ME FAIL.
I WOULD LIKE YOU TO ASSESS THEM YOURSELF. OBSERVE THEIR WORDS AND ACTIONS. WEIGH THEIR TRUTH. REPORT TO ME.
YOU WOULD NOT BE DOING THIS AS A MEMBER OF STARFLEET. NOT WHILE YOU SPURN THE UNIFORM.
BE MY ADVISER, SPOCK.
FOR THE BENEFIT OF A PEACE THAT IS STILL POSSIBLE.

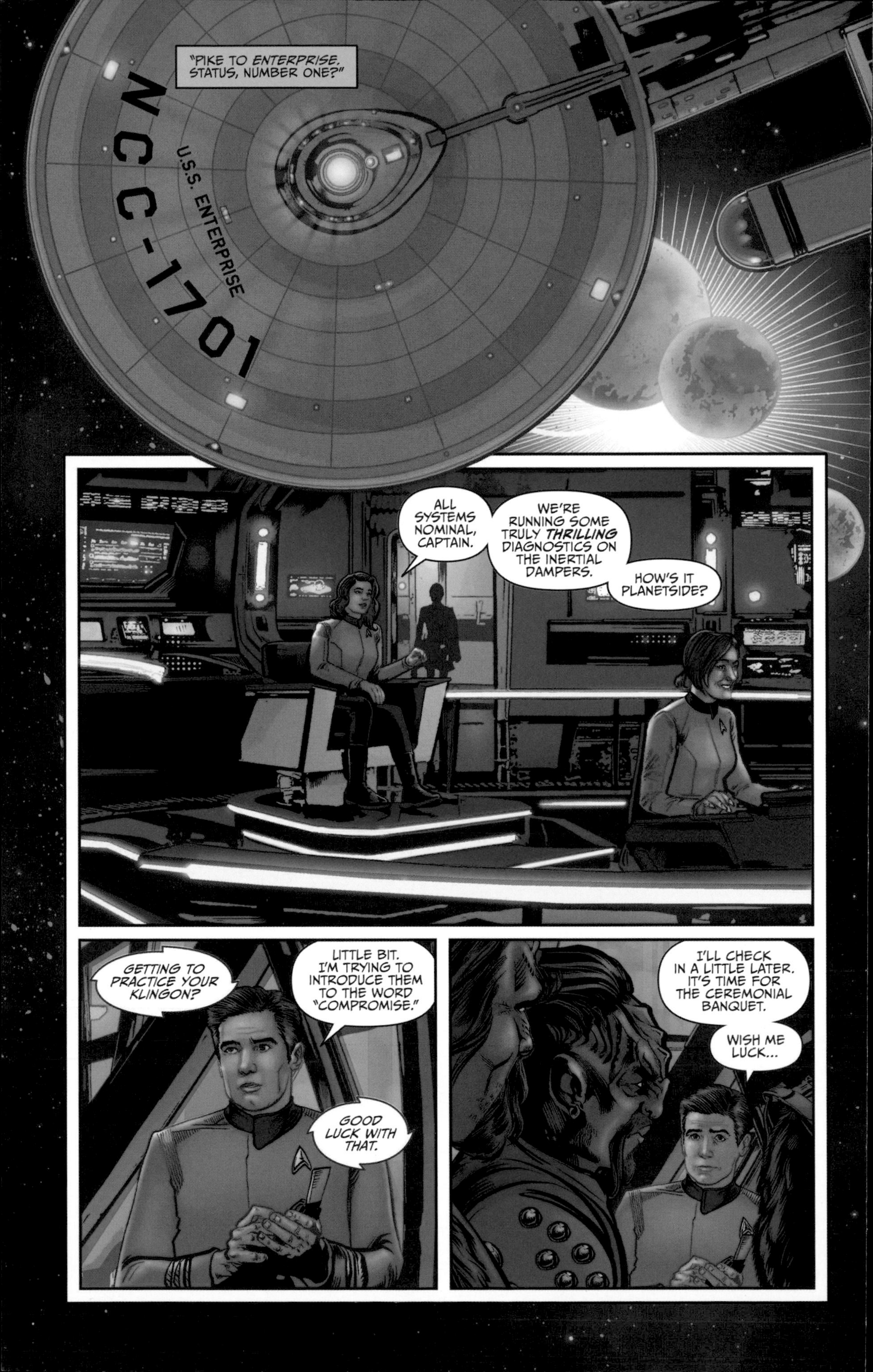
"PIKE TO ENTERPRISE. STATUS, NUMBER ONE?"
NCC-1701
U.S.S. ENTERPRISE
ALL SYSTEMS NOMINAL, CAPTAIN.
WE'RE RUNNING SOME TRULY THRILLING DIAGNOSTICS ON THE INERTIAL DAMPERS.
HOW'S IT PLANETSIDE?
GETTING TO PRACTICE YOUR KLINGON?
LITTLE BIT. I'M TRYING TO INTRODUCE THEM TO THE WORD "COMPROMISE."
GOOD LUCK WITH THAT.
I'LL CHECK IN A LITTLE LATER. IT'S TIME FOR THE CEREMONIAL BANQUET.
WISH ME LUCK...

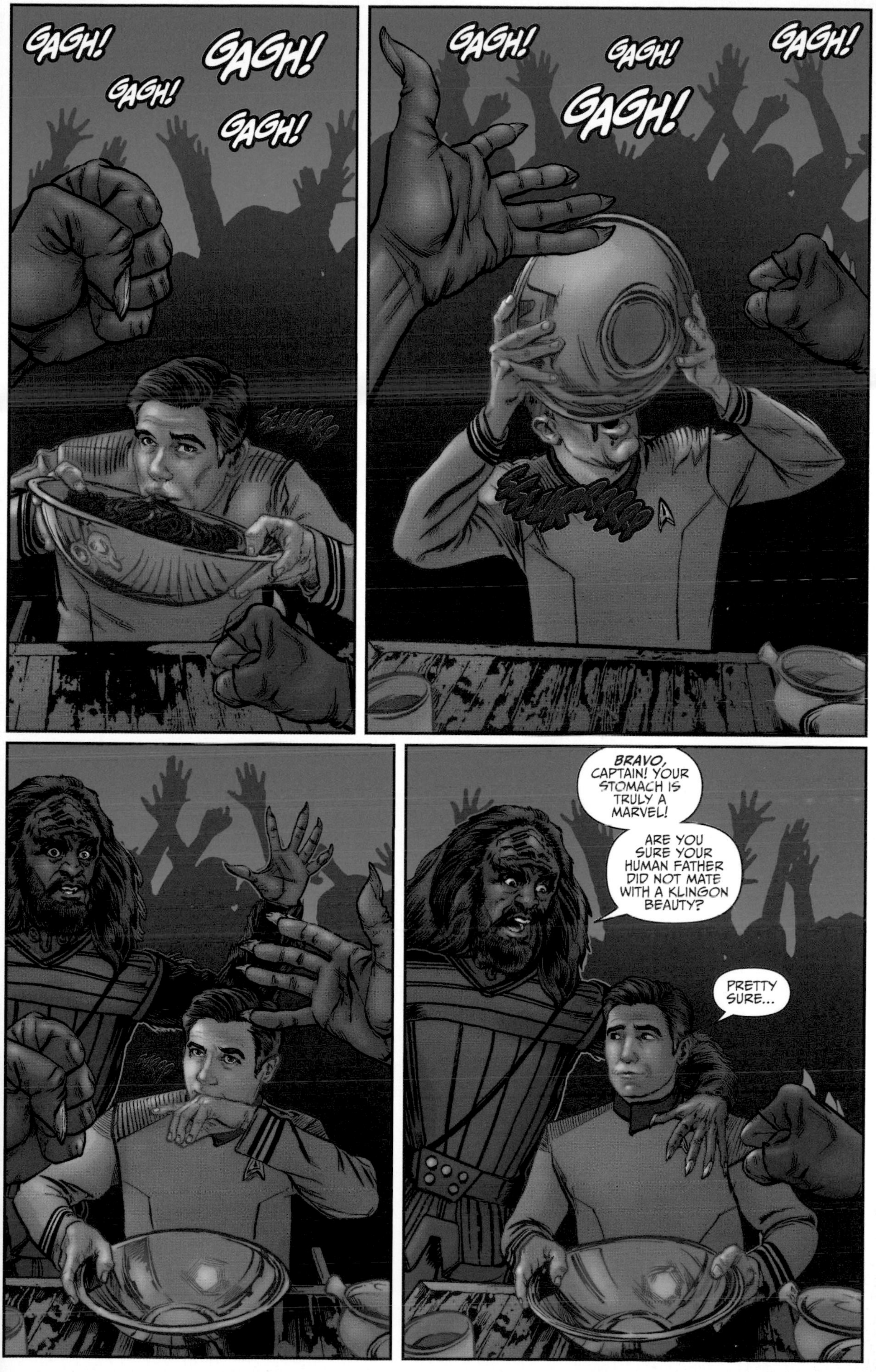
GAGH!
GAGH!
GAGH!
GAGH!
GAGH!
GAGH!
GAGH!
GAGH!
BRAVO, CAPTAIN! YOUR STOMACH IS TRULY A MARVEL!
ARE YOU SURE YOUR HUMAN FATHER DID NOT MATE WITH A KLINGON BEAUTY?
PRETTY SURE...

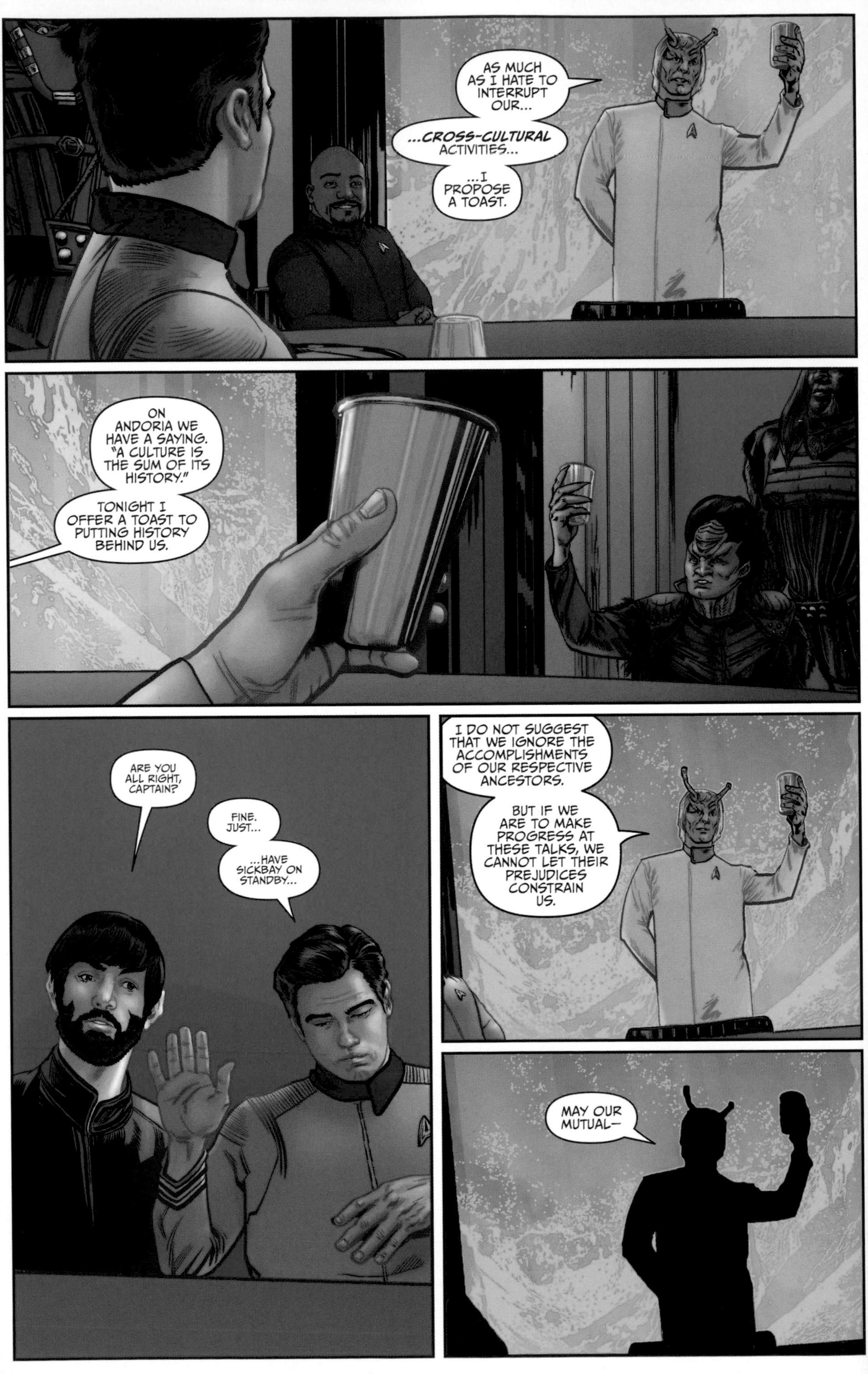
AS MUCH AS I HATE TO INTERRUPT OUR...
...CROSS-CULTURAL ACTIVITIES...
...I PROPOSE A TOAST.
ON ANDORIA WE HAVE A SAYING. "A CULTURE IS THE SUM OF ITS HISTORY."
TONIGHT I OFFER A TOAST TO PUTTING HISTORY BEHIND US.
ARE YOU ALL RIGHT, CAPTAIN?
FINE. JUST...
...HAVE SICKBAY ON STANDBY...
I DO NOT SUGGEST THAT WE IGNORE THE ACCOMPLISHMENTS OF OUR RESPECTIVE ANCESTORS.
BUT IF WE ARE TO MAKE PROGRESS AT THESE TALKS, WE CANNOT LET THEIR PREJUDICES CONSTRAIN US.
MAY OUR MUTUAL—

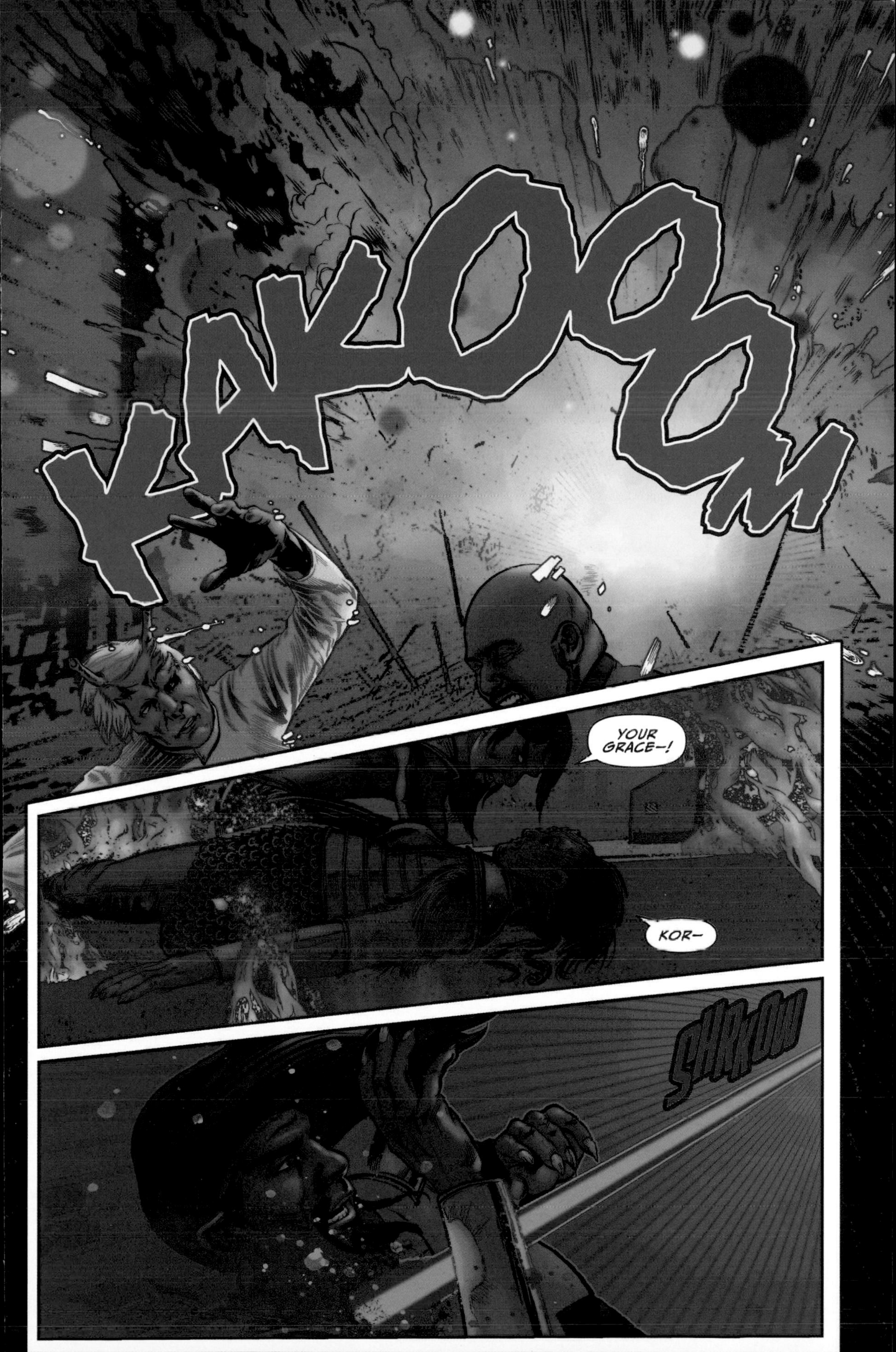
KAKOOOM
YOUR GRACE—!
KOR—
SHRKOW

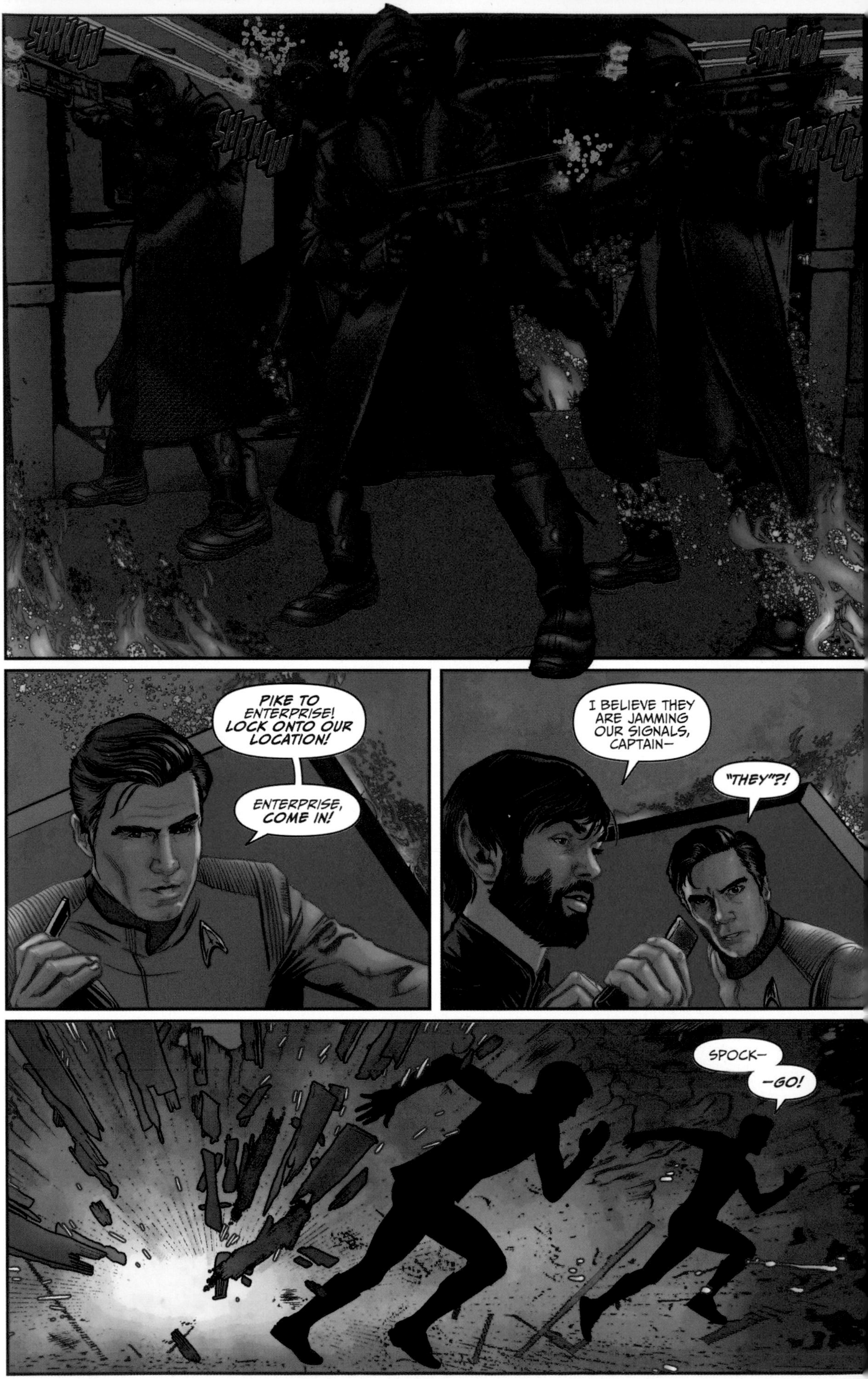
SHKKOW
SHKKOW
SHKKOW
SHKKOW
PIKE TO ENTERPRISE! LOCK ONTO OUR LOCATION!
ENTERPRISE, COME IN!
I BELIEVE THEY ARE JAMMING OUR SIGNALS, CAPTAIN—
"THEY"?!
SPOCK—
—GO!

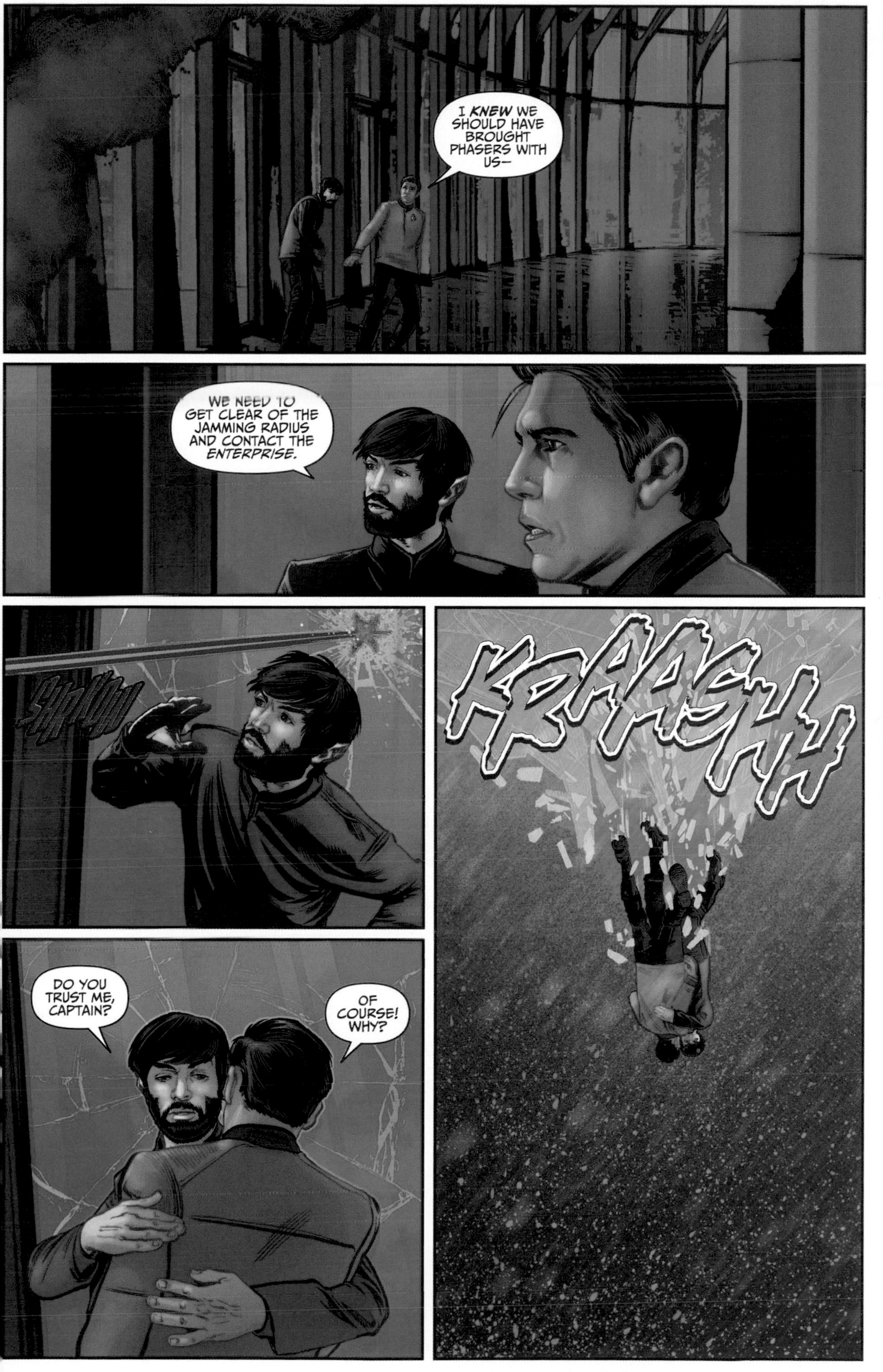
I *KNEW* WE SHOULD HAVE BROUGHT PHASERS WITH US—
WE NEED TO GET CLEAR OF THE JAMMING RADIUS AND CONTACT THE *ENTERPRISE.*
KRAASHH
DO YOU TRUST ME, CAPTAIN?
OF COURSE! WHY?

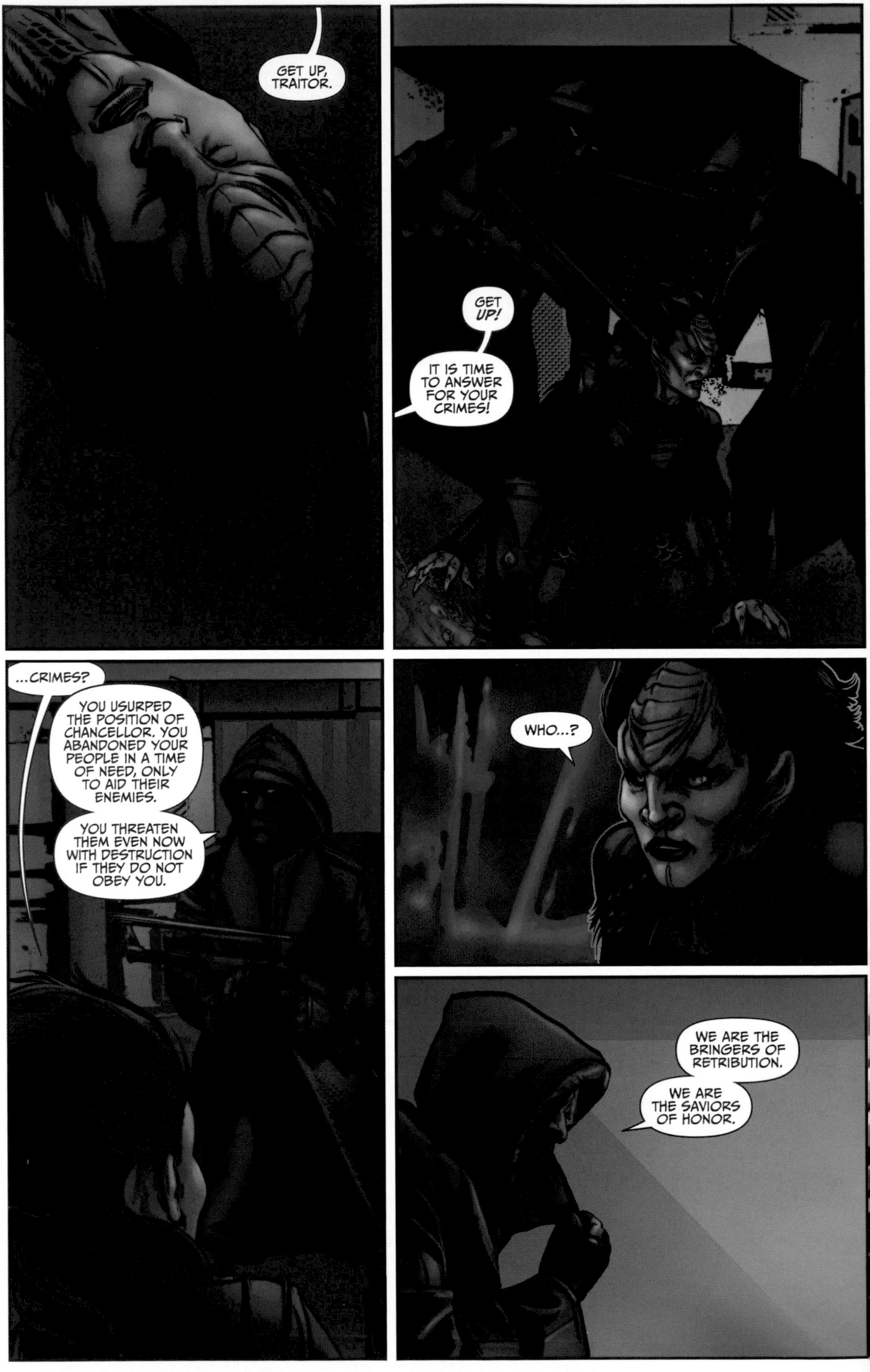
GET UP, TRAITOR.
GET UP!
IT IS TIME TO ANSWER FOR YOUR CRIMES!
...CRIMES?
YOU USURPED THE POSITION OF CHANCELLOR. YOU ABANDONED YOUR PEOPLE IN A TIME OF NEED, ONLY TO AID THEIR ENEMIES.
YOU THREATEN THEM EVEN NOW WITH DESTRUCTION IF THEY DO NOT OBEY YOU.
WHO...?
WE ARE THE BRINGERS OF RETRIBUTION.
WE ARE THE SAVIORS OF HONOR.

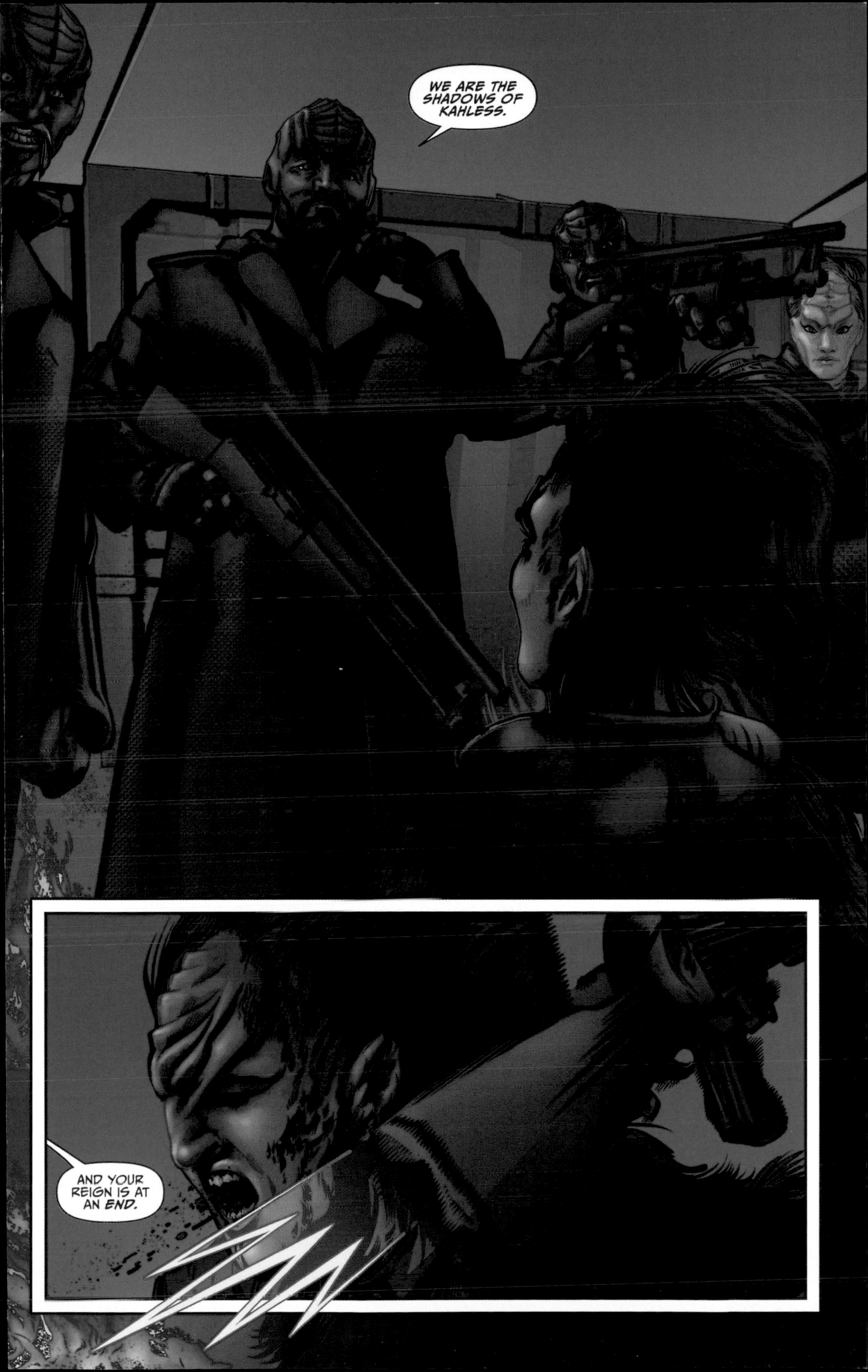
WE ARE THE SHADOWS OF KAHLESS.
AND YOUR REIGN IS AT AN *END*.

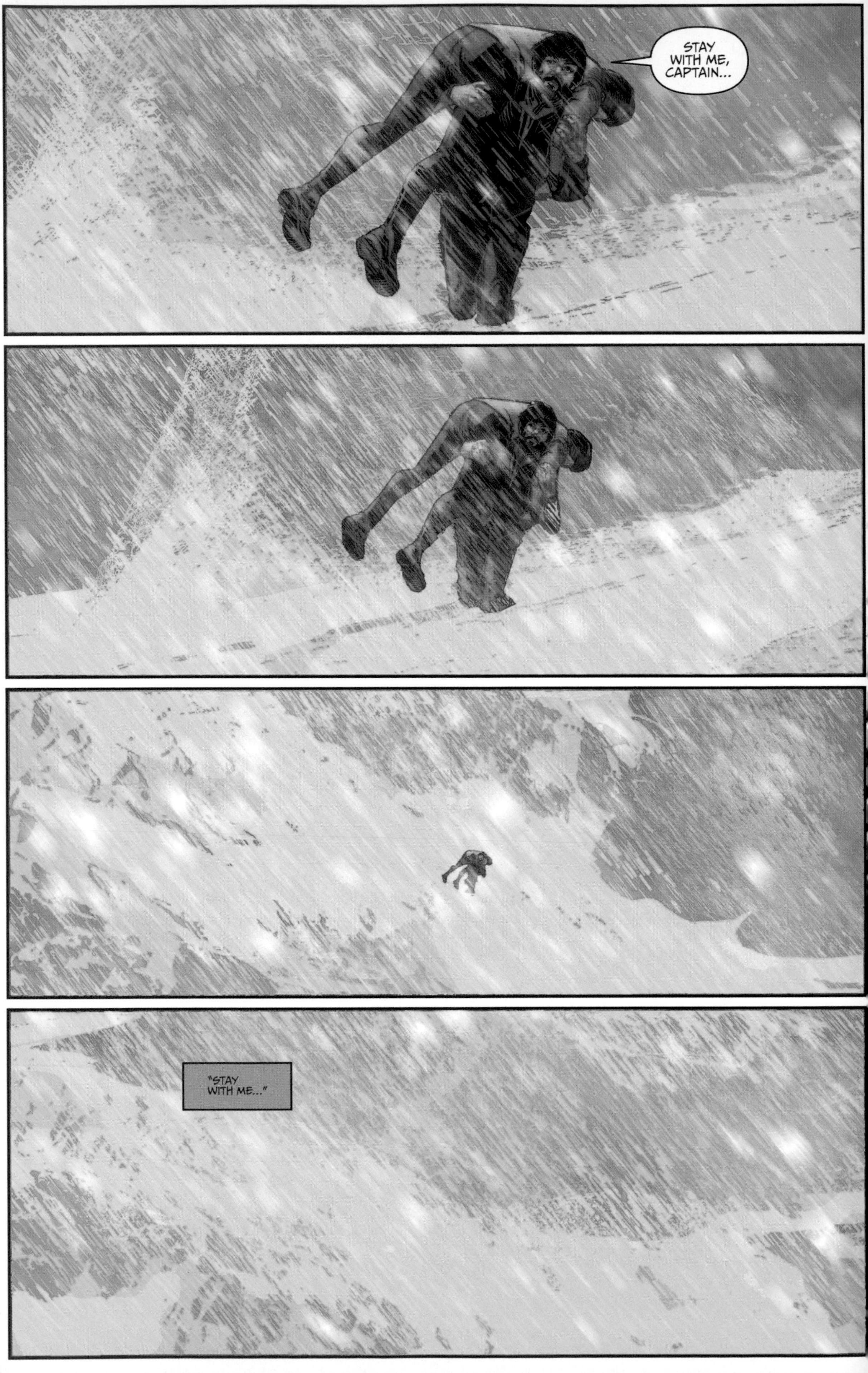
STAY WITH ME, CAPTAIN...
"STAY WITH ME..."

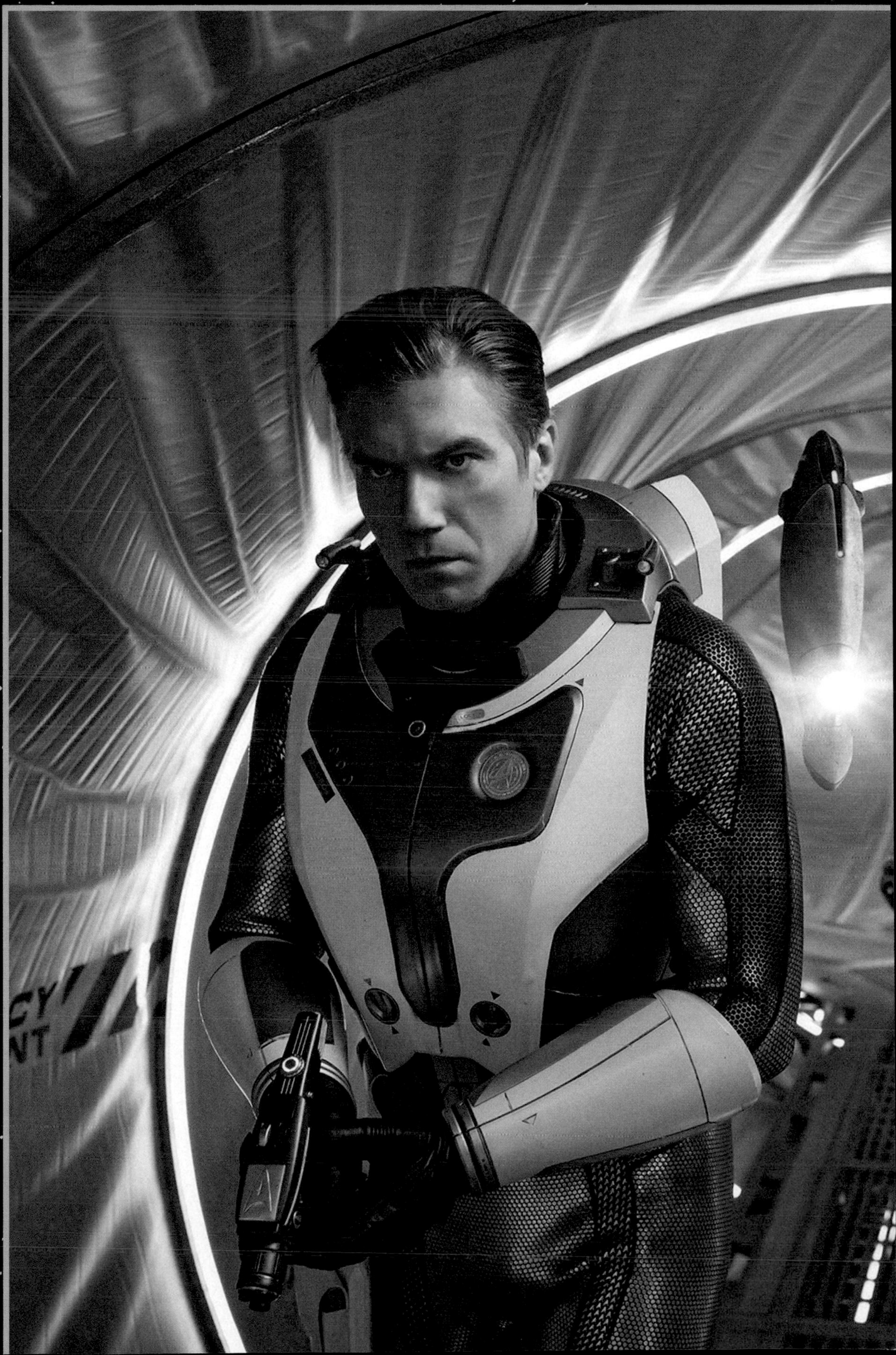

ART BY **ANGEL HERNANDEZ** | COLORS BY **J.D. METTLER**

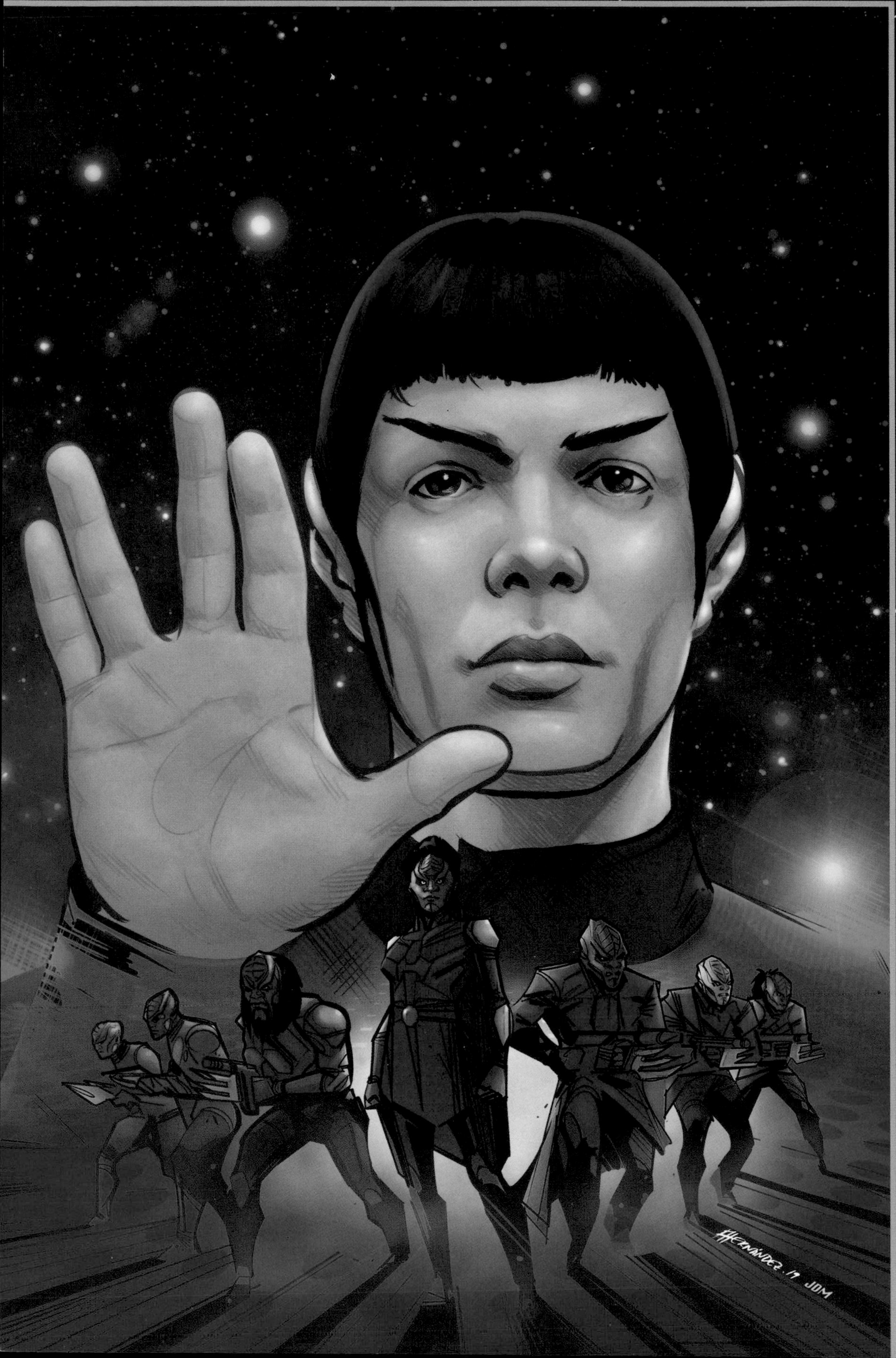
HERNÁNDEZ.17 JDM

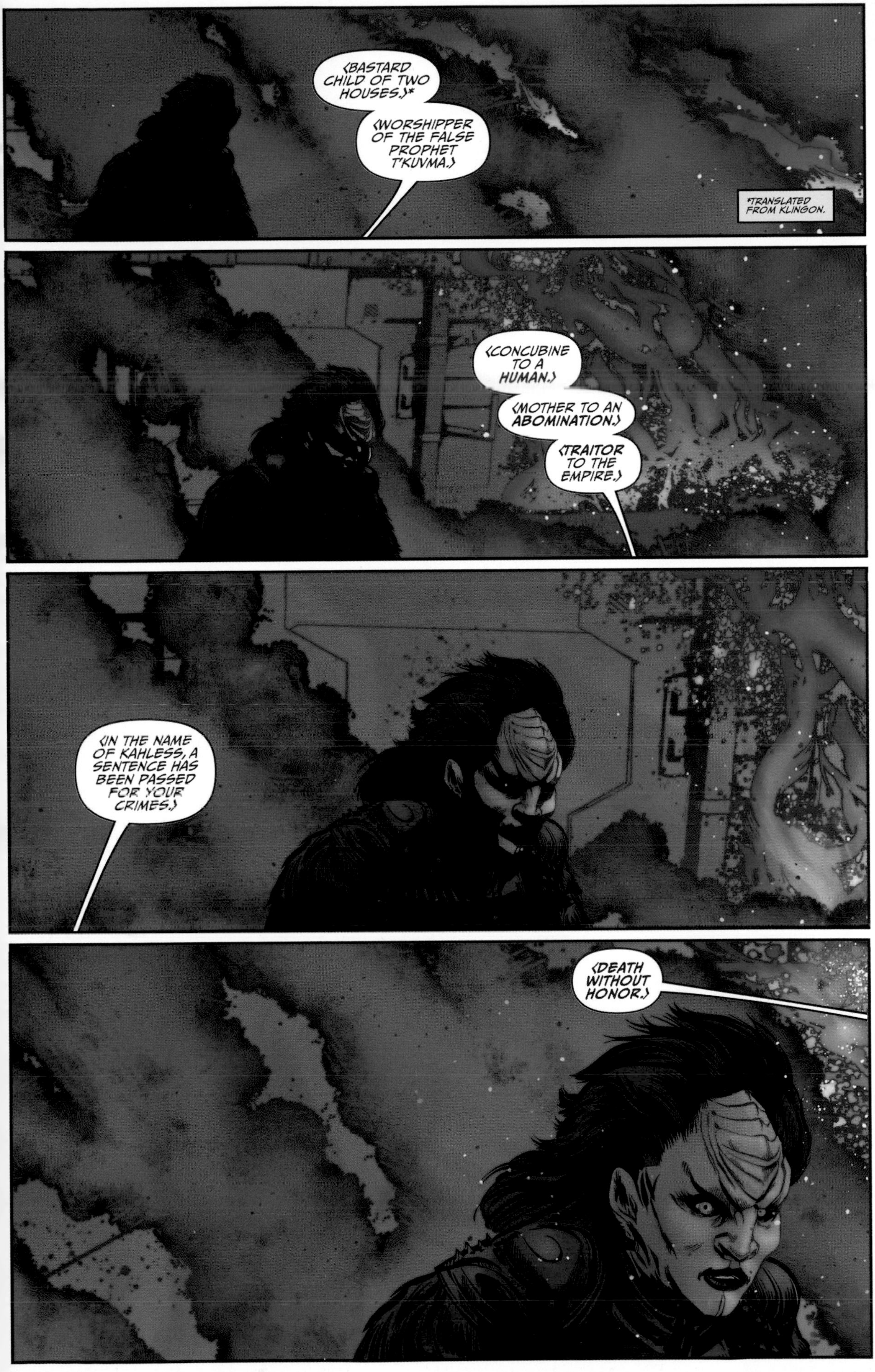
<BASTARD CHILD OF TWO HOUSES.>*
<WORSHIPPER OF THE FALSE PROPHET T'KUVMA.>
*TRANSLATED FROM KLINGON.
<CONCUBINE TO A HUMAN.>
<MOTHER TO AN ABOMINATION.>
<TRAITOR TO THE EMPIRE.>
<IN THE NAME OF KAHLESS, A SENTENCE HAS BEEN PASSED FOR YOUR CRIMES.>
<DEATH WITHOUT HONOR.>

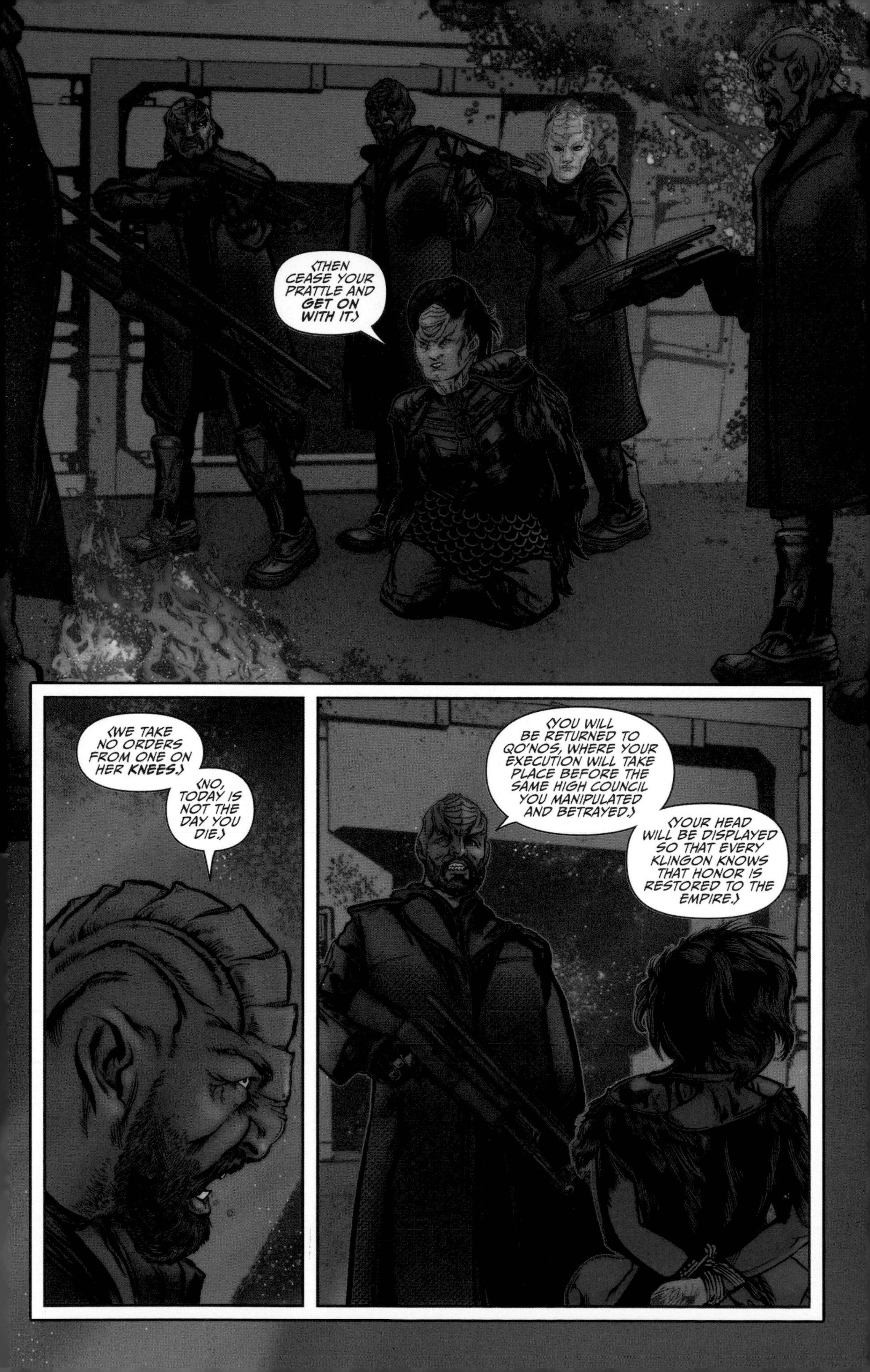

<THEN CEASE YOUR PRATTLE AND GET ON WITH IT.>
<WE TAKE NO ORDERS FROM ONE ON HER KNEES.>
<NO, TODAY IS NOT THE DAY YOU DIE.>
<YOU WILL BE RETURNED TO QO'NOS, WHERE YOUR EXECUTION WILL TAKE PLACE BEFORE THE SAME HIGH COUNCIL YOU MANIPULATED AND BETRAYED.>
<YOUR HEAD WILL BE DISPLAYED SO THAT EVERY KLINGON KNOWS THAT HONOR IS RESTORED TO THE EMPIRE.>

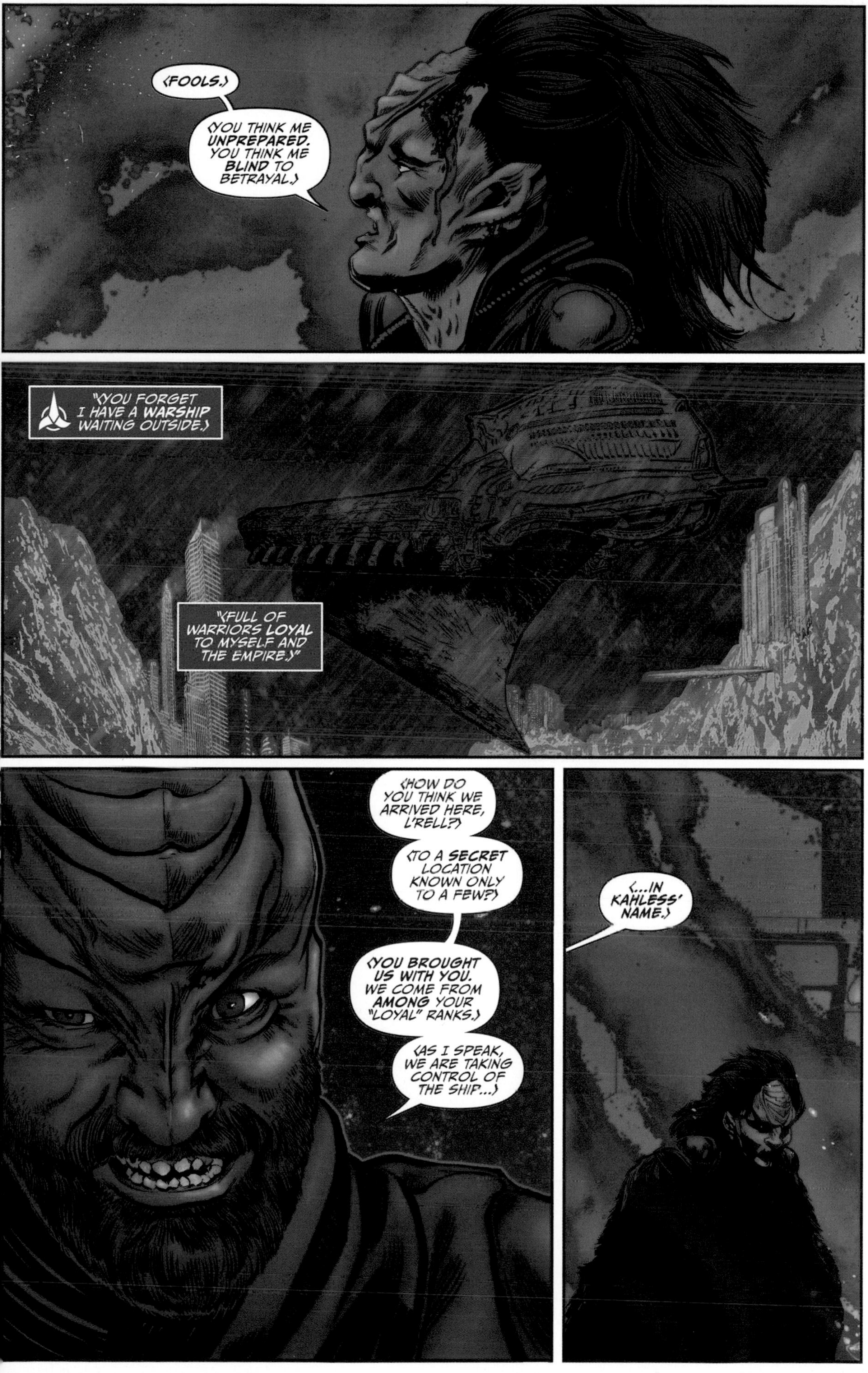

‹FOOLS.›
‹YOU THINK ME UNPREPARED. YOU THINK ME BLIND TO BETRAYAL.›
"‹YOU FORGET I HAVE A WARSHIP WAITING OUTSIDE.›
"‹FULL OF WARRIORS LOYAL TO MYSELF AND THE EMPIRE.›"
‹HOW DO YOU THINK WE ARRIVED HERE, L'RELL?›
‹TO A SECRET LOCATION KNOWN ONLY TO A FEW?›
‹YOU BROUGHT US WITH YOU. WE COME FROM AMONG YOUR "LOYAL" RANKS.›
‹AS I SPEAK, WE ARE TAKING CONTROL OF THE SHIP...›
‹...IN KAHLESS' NAME.›

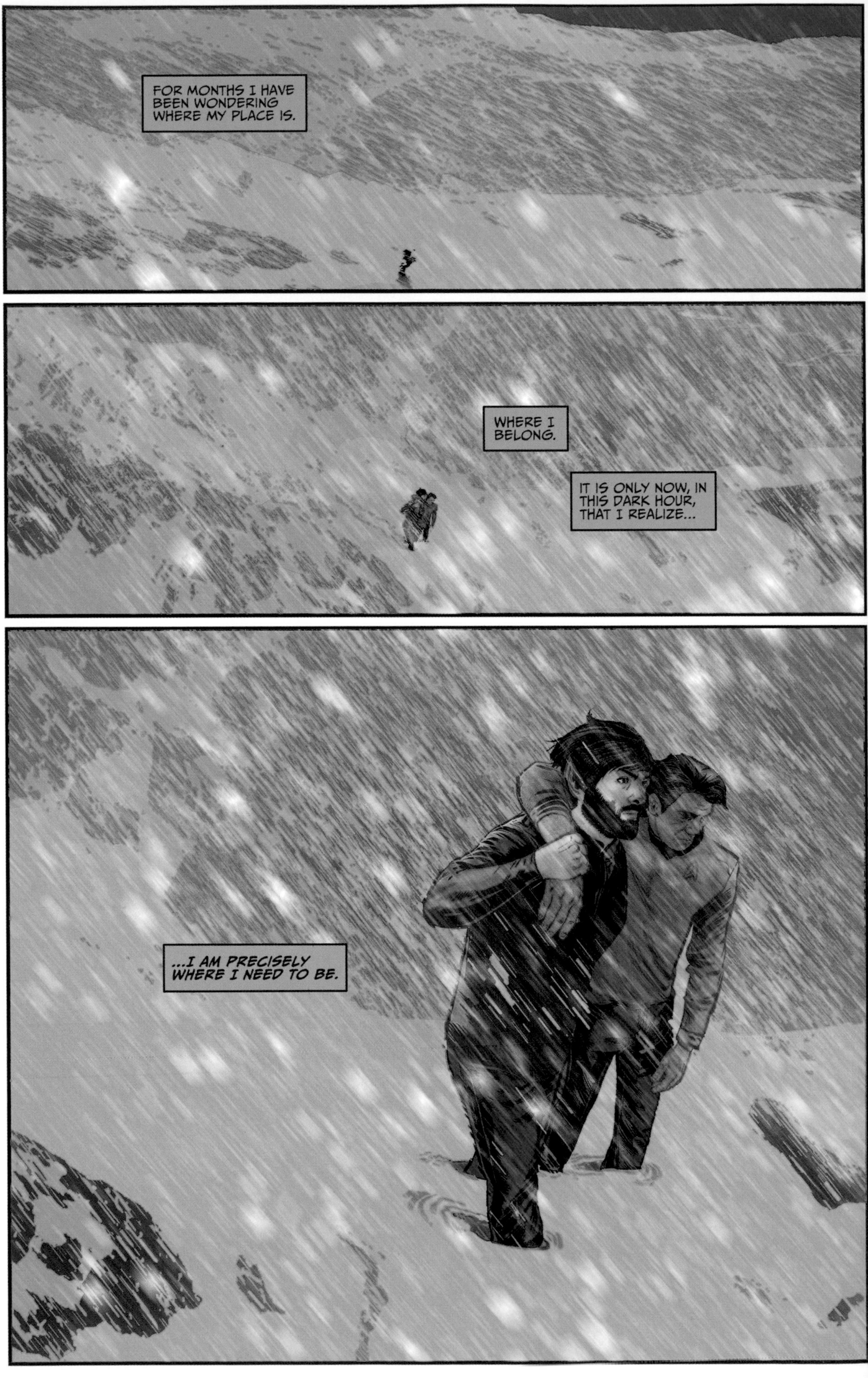
FOR MONTHS I HAVE BEEN WONDERING WHERE MY PLACE IS.
WHERE I BELONG.
IT IS ONLY NOW, IN THIS DARK HOUR, THAT I REALIZE...
...I AM PRECISELY WHERE I NEED TO BE.

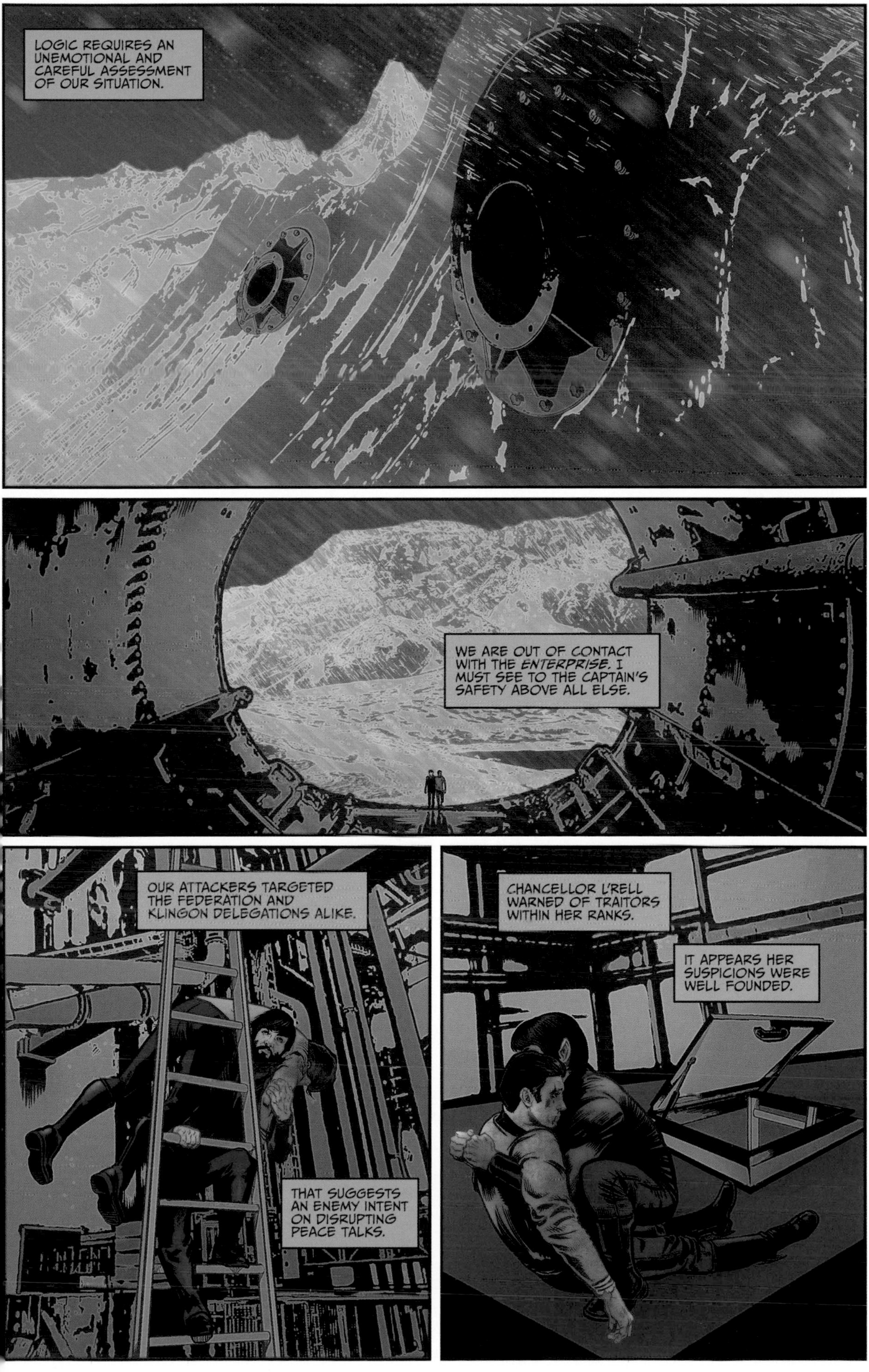
LOGIC REQUIRES AN UNEMOTIONAL AND CAREFUL ASSESSMENT OF OUR SITUATION.
WE ARE OUT OF CONTACT WITH THE *ENTERPRISE*. I MUST SEE TO THE CAPTAIN'S SAFETY ABOVE ALL ELSE.
OUR ATTACKERS TARGETED THE FEDERATION AND KLINGON DELEGATIONS ALIKE.
THAT SUGGESTS AN ENEMY INTENT ON DISRUPTING PEACE TALKS.
CHANCELLOR L'RELL WARNED OF TRAITORS WITHIN HER RANKS.
IT APPEARS HER SUSPICIONS WERE WELL FOUNDED.

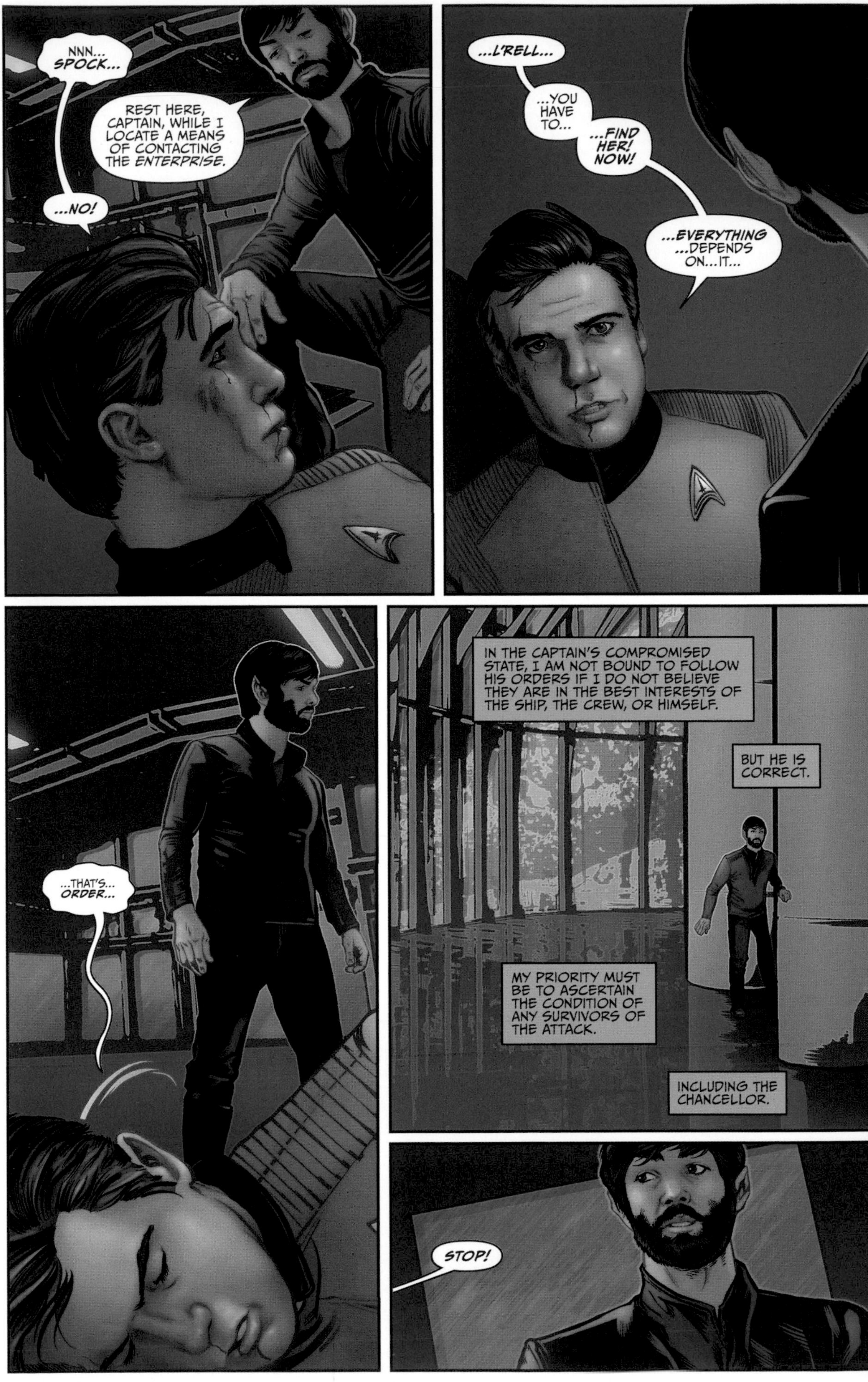
NNN... SPOCK...
REST HERE, CAPTAIN, WHILE I LOCATE A MEANS OF CONTACTING THE ENTERPRISE.
...NO!
...L'RELL...
...YOU HAVE TO...
...FIND HER! NOW!
...EVERYTHING ...DEPENDS ON...IT...
...THAT'S... ORDER...
IN THE CAPTAIN'S COMPROMISED STATE, I AM NOT BOUND TO FOLLOW HIS ORDERS IF I DO NOT BELIEVE THEY ARE IN THE BEST INTERESTS OF THE SHIP, THE CREW, OR HIMSELF.
BUT HE IS CORRECT.
MY PRIORITY MUST BE TO ASCERTAIN THE CONDITION OF ANY SURVIVORS OF THE ATTACK.
INCLUDING THE CHANCELLOR.
STOP!

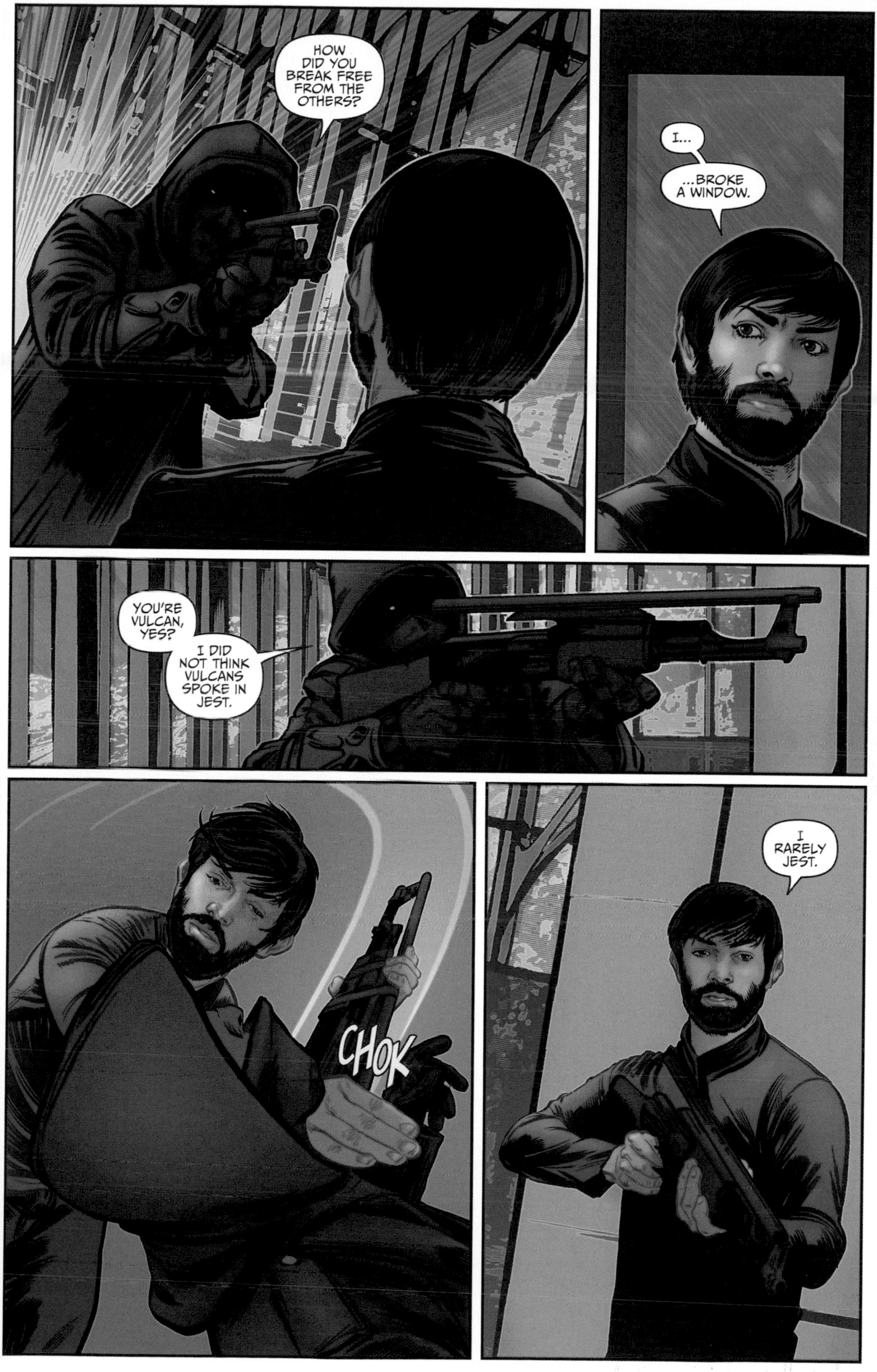
HOW DID YOU BREAK FREE FROM THE OTHERS?
I...
...BROKE A WINDOW.
YOU'RE VULCAN, YES?
I DID NOT THINK VULCANS SPOKE IN JEST.
CHOK
I RARELY JEST.

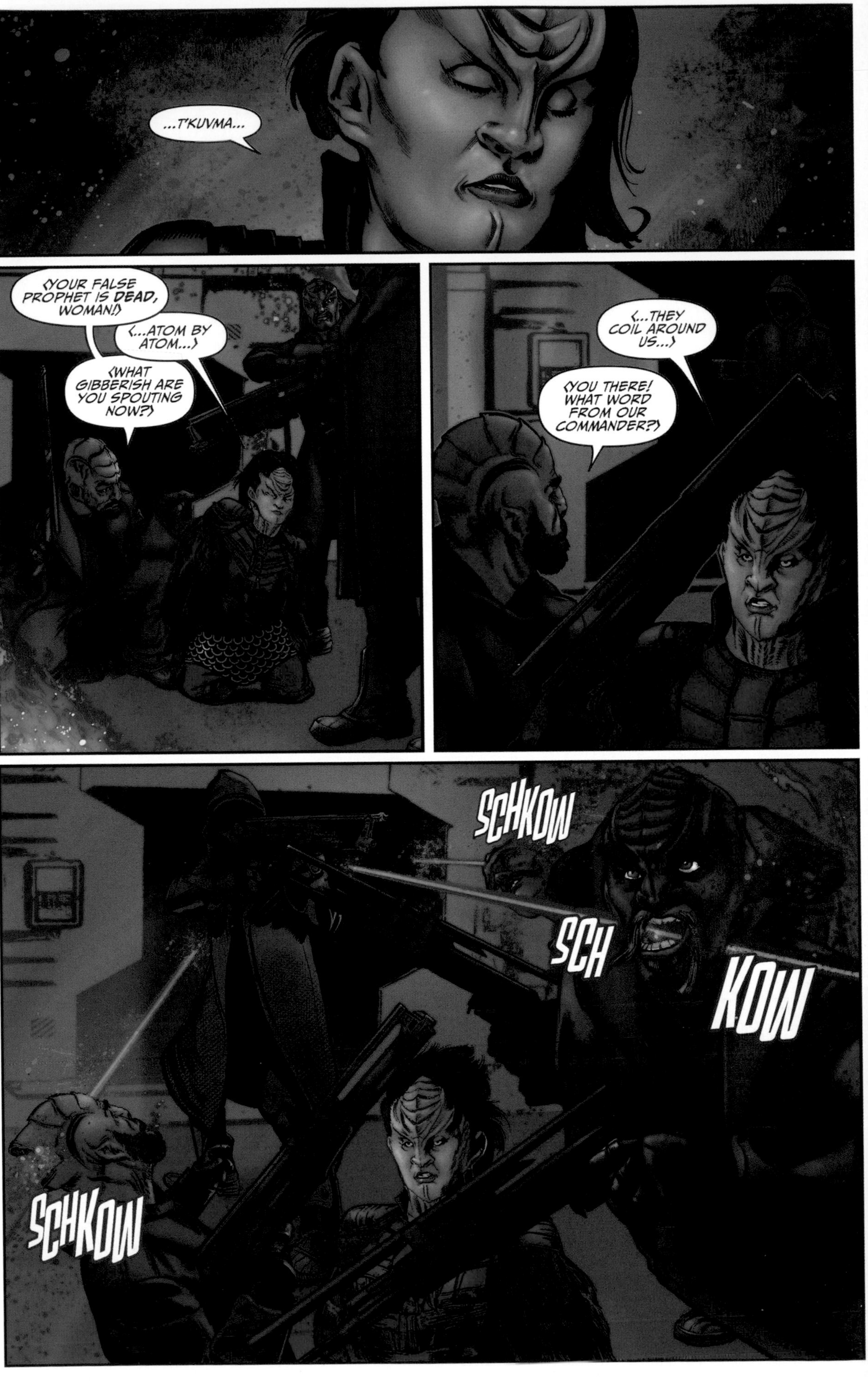
...T'KUVMA...
‹YOUR FALSE PROPHET IS DEAD, WOMAN!›
‹...ATOM BY ATOM...›
‹WHAT GIBBERISH ARE YOU SPOUTING NOW?›
‹...THEY COIL AROUND US...›
‹YOU THERE! WHAT WORD FROM OUR COMMANDER?›
SCHKOW
SCH
KOW
SCHKOW

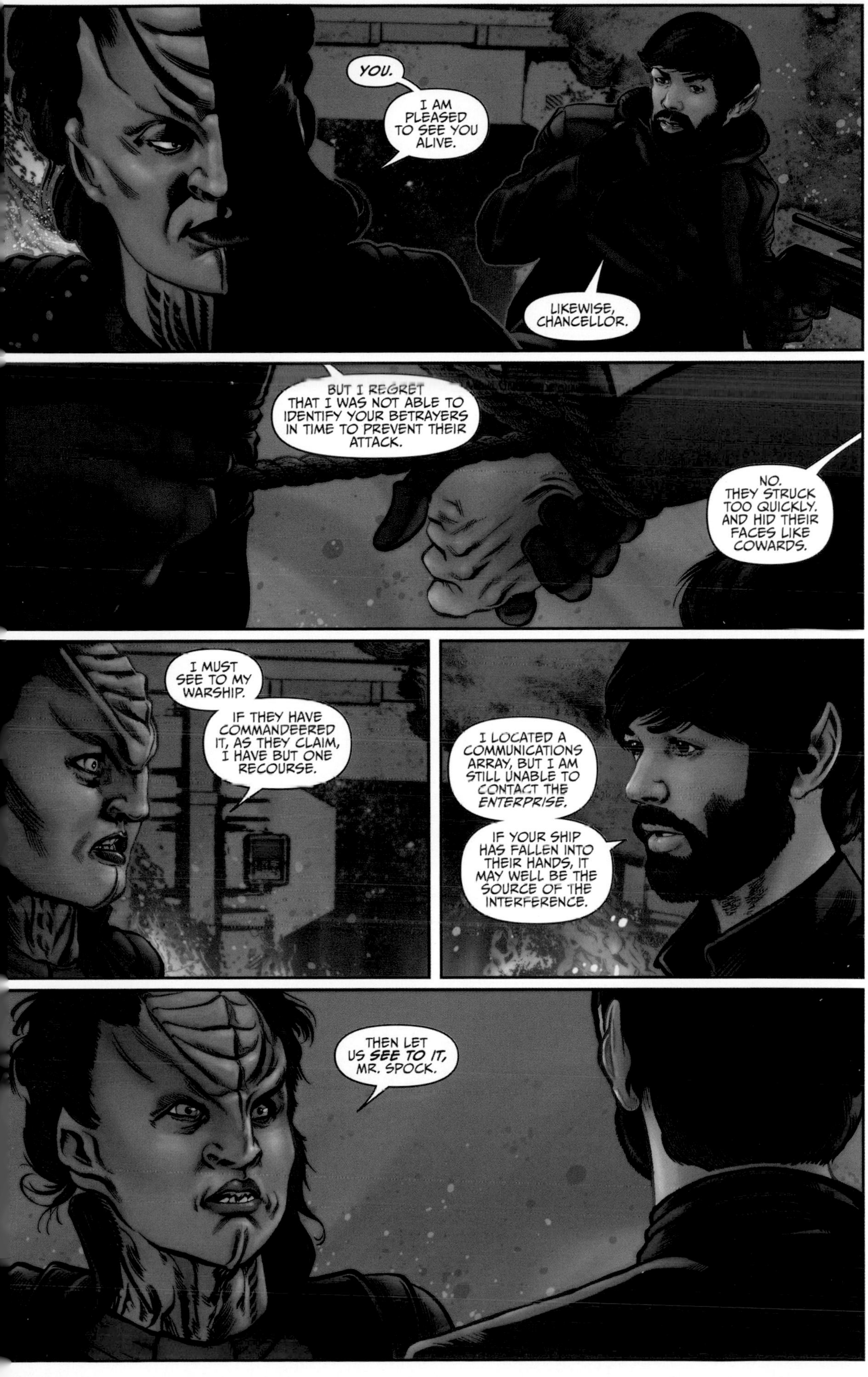
YOU.
I AM PLEASED TO SEE YOU ALIVE.
LIKEWISE, CHANCELLOR.
BUT I REGRET THAT I WAS NOT ABLE TO IDENTIFY YOUR BETRAYERS IN TIME TO PREVENT THEIR ATTACK.
NO. THEY STRUCK TOO QUICKLY. AND HID THEIR FACES LIKE COWARDS.
I MUST SEE TO MY WARSHIP.
IF THEY HAVE COMMANDEERED IT, AS THEY CLAIM, I HAVE BUT ONE RECOURSE.
I LOCATED A COMMUNICATIONS ARRAY, BUT I AM STILL UNABLE TO CONTACT THE *ENTERPRISE*.
IF YOUR SHIP HAS FALLEN INTO THEIR HANDS, IT MAY WELL BE THE SOURCE OF THE INTERFERENCE.
THEN LET US ***SEE TO IT***, MR. SPOCK.

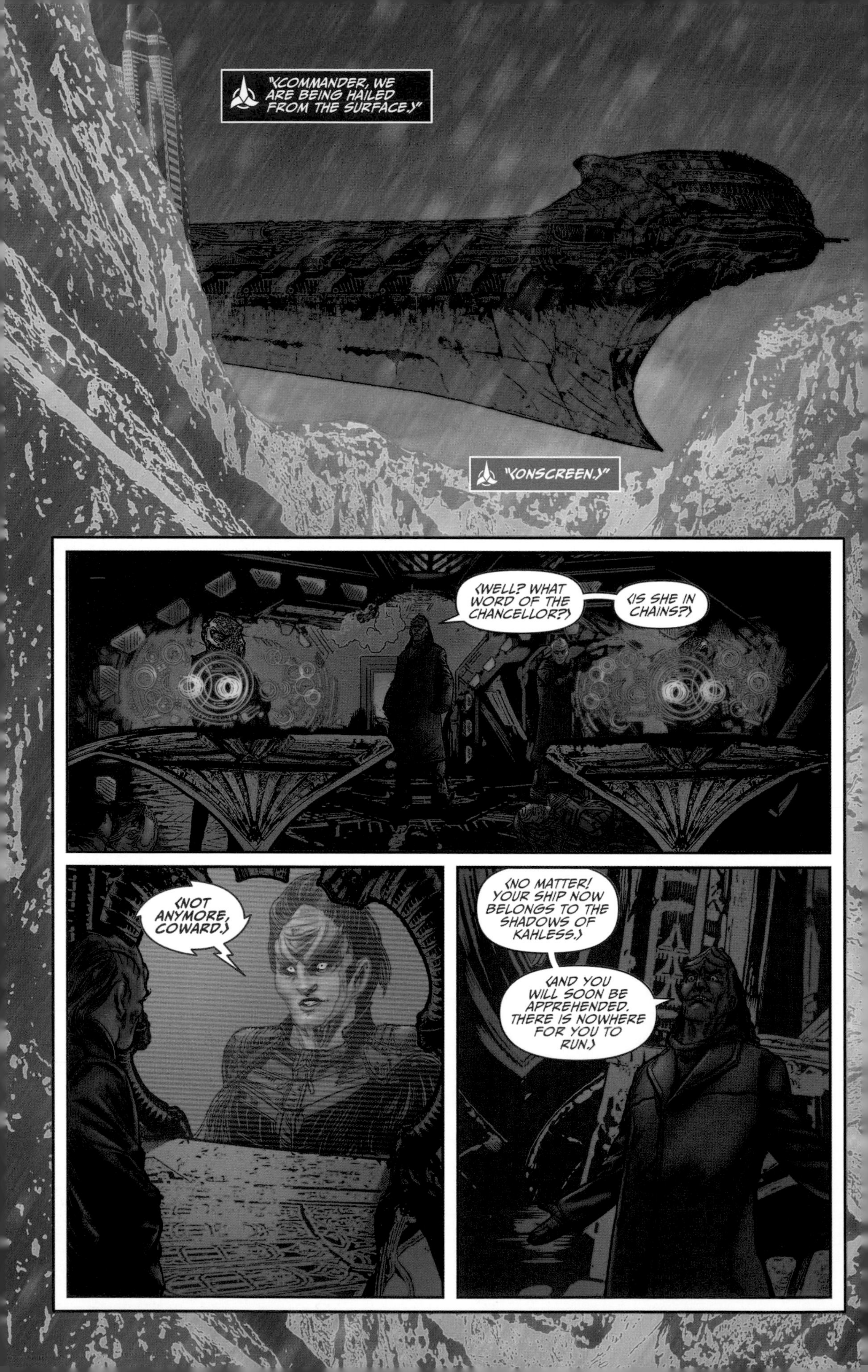
"‹COMMANDER, WE ARE BEING HAILED FROM THE SURFACE.›"
"‹ONSCREEN.›"
‹WELL? WHAT WORD OF THE CHANCELLOR?›
‹IS SHE IN CHAINS?›
‹NOT ANYMORE, COWARD.›
‹NO MATTER! YOUR SHIP NOW BELONGS TO THE SHADOWS OF KAHLESS.›
‹AND YOU WILL SOON BE APPREHENDED. THERE IS NOWHERE FOR YOU TO RUN.›

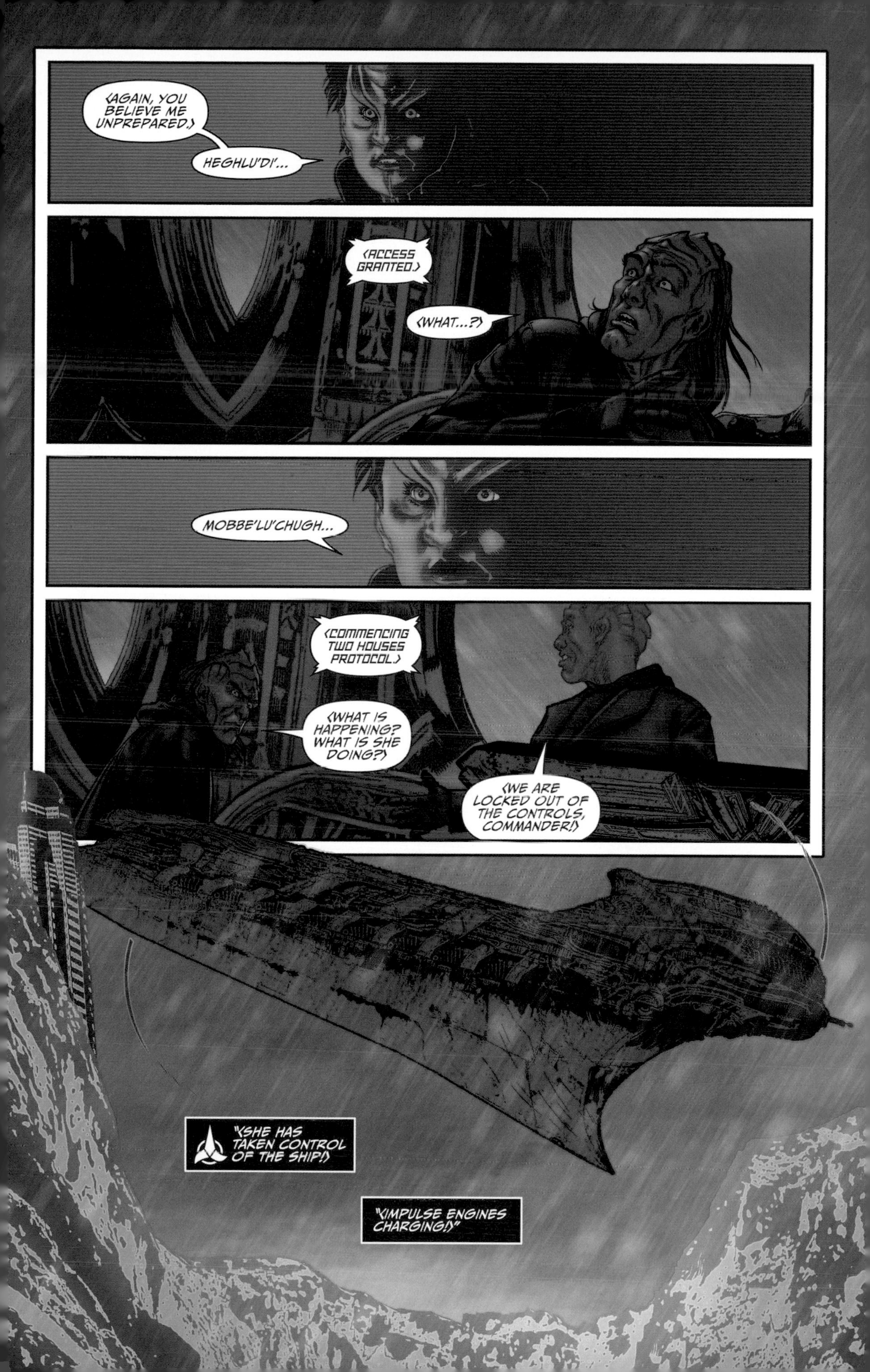

‹AGAIN, YOU BELIEVE ME UNPREPARED.›
HEGHLU'DI'...
‹ACCESS GRANTED.›
‹WHAT...?›
MOBBE'LU'CHUGH...
‹COMMENCING TWO HOUSES PROTOCOL.›
‹WHAT IS HAPPENING? WHAT IS SHE DOING?›
‹WE ARE LOCKED OUT OF THE CONTROLS, COMMANDER!›
"‹SHE HAS TAKEN CONTROL OF THE SHIP!›
"‹IMPULSE ENGINES CHARGING!›"

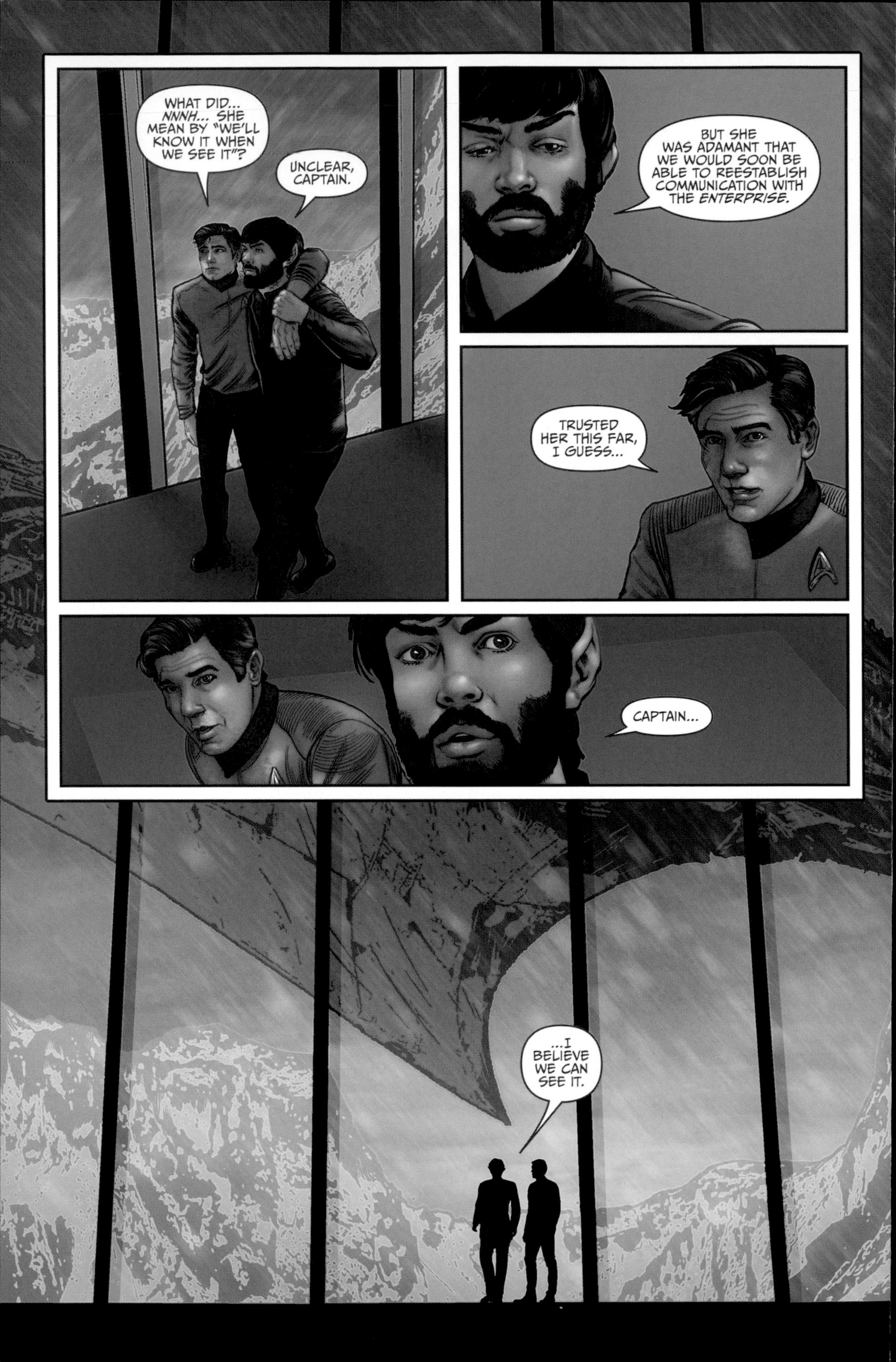
WHAT DID... NNNH... SHE MEAN BY "WE'LL KNOW IT WHEN WE SEE IT"?
UNCLEAR, CAPTAIN.
BUT SHE WAS ADAMANT THAT WE WOULD SOON BE ABLE TO REESTABLISH COMMUNICATION WITH THE ENTERPRISE.
TRUSTED HER THIS FAR, I GUESS...
CAPTAIN...
...I BELIEVE WE CAN SEE IT.

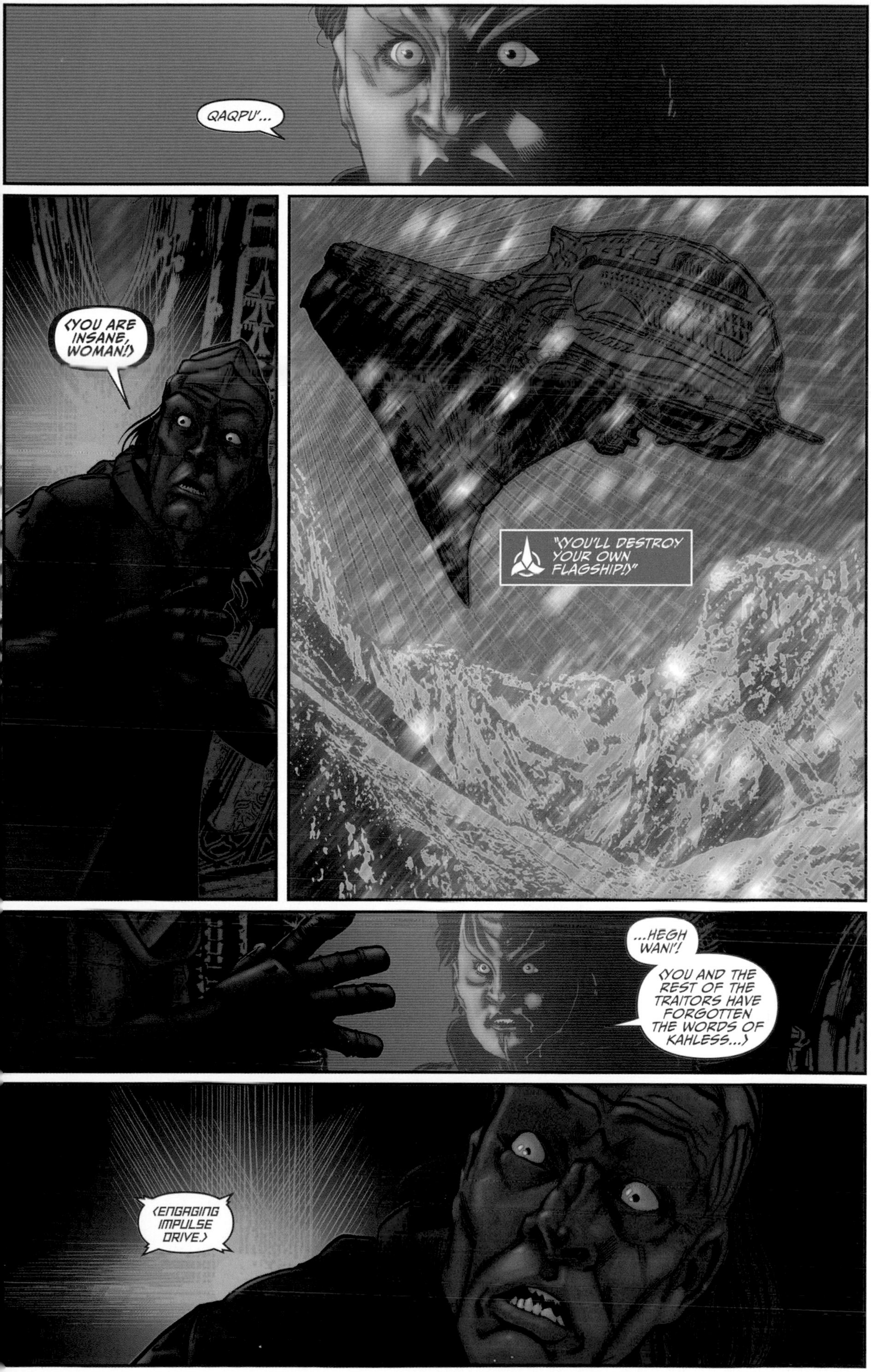
QAQPU'...
<YOU ARE INSANE, WOMAN!>
"<YOU'LL DESTROY YOUR OWN FLAGSHIP!>"
...HEGH WANI'!
<YOU AND THE REST OF THE TRAITORS HAVE FORGOTTEN THE WORDS OF KAHLESS...>
<ENGAGING IMPULSE DRIVE.>

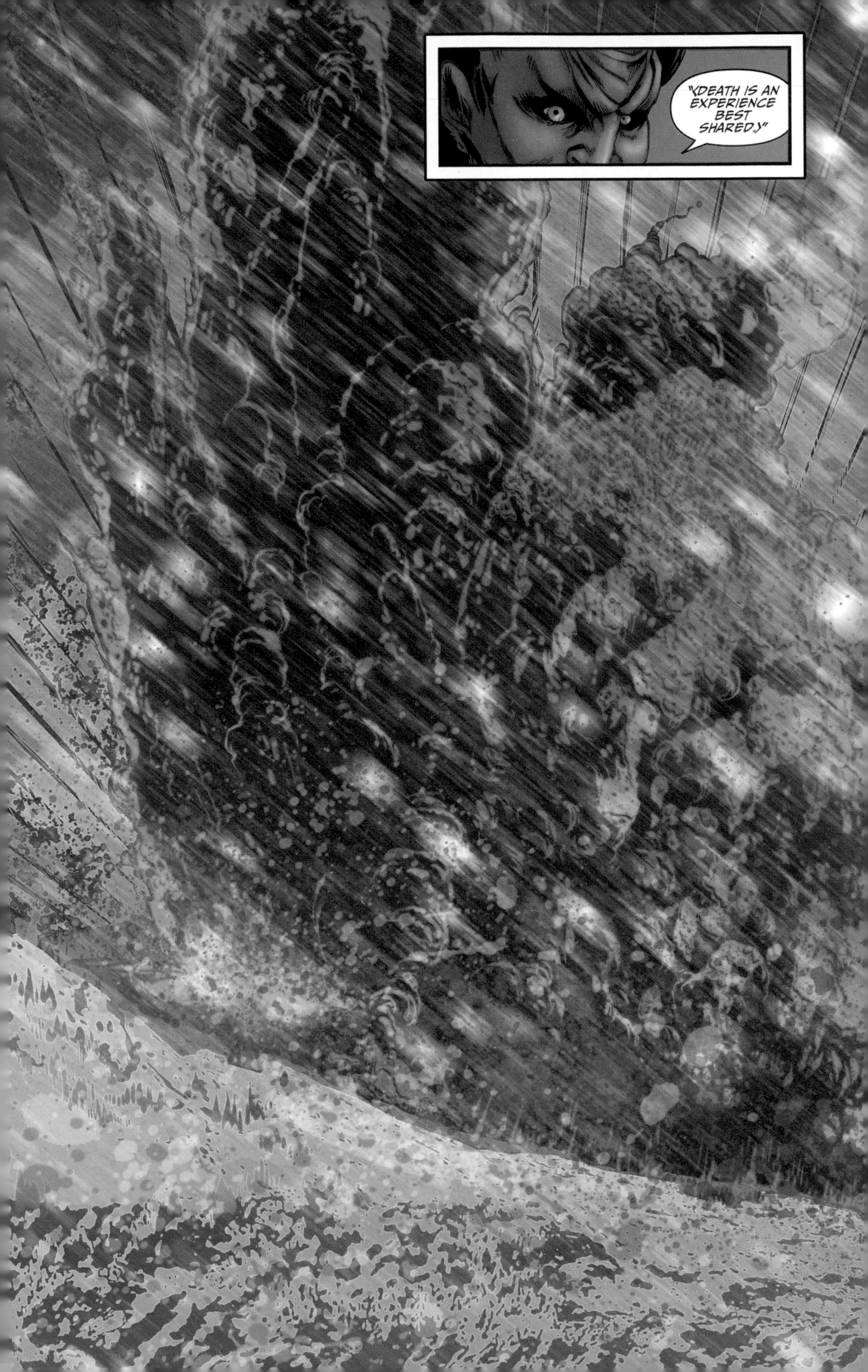
"‹DEATH IS AN EXPERIENCE BEST SHARED.›"

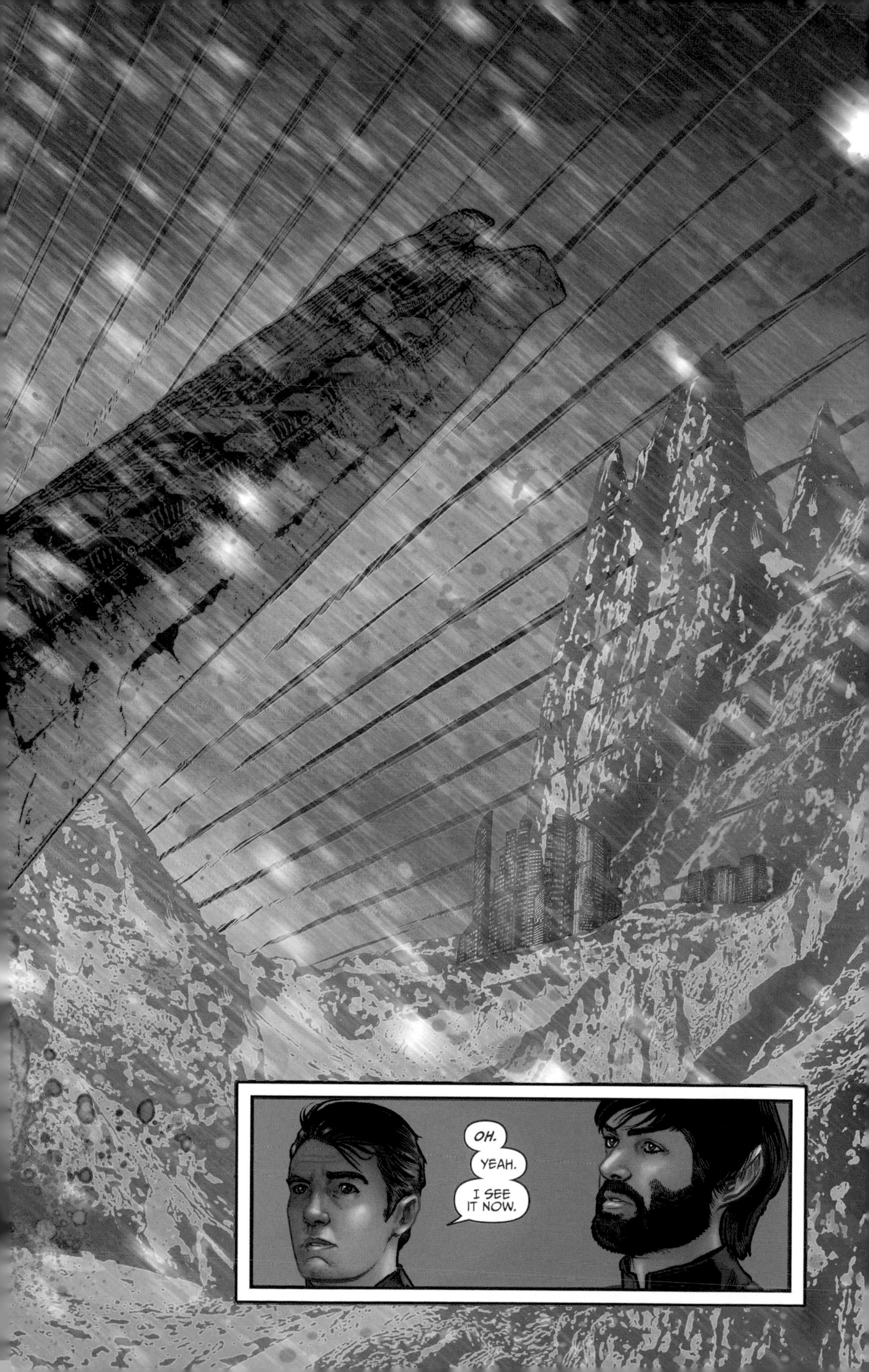
OH.
YEAH.
I SEE IT NOW.

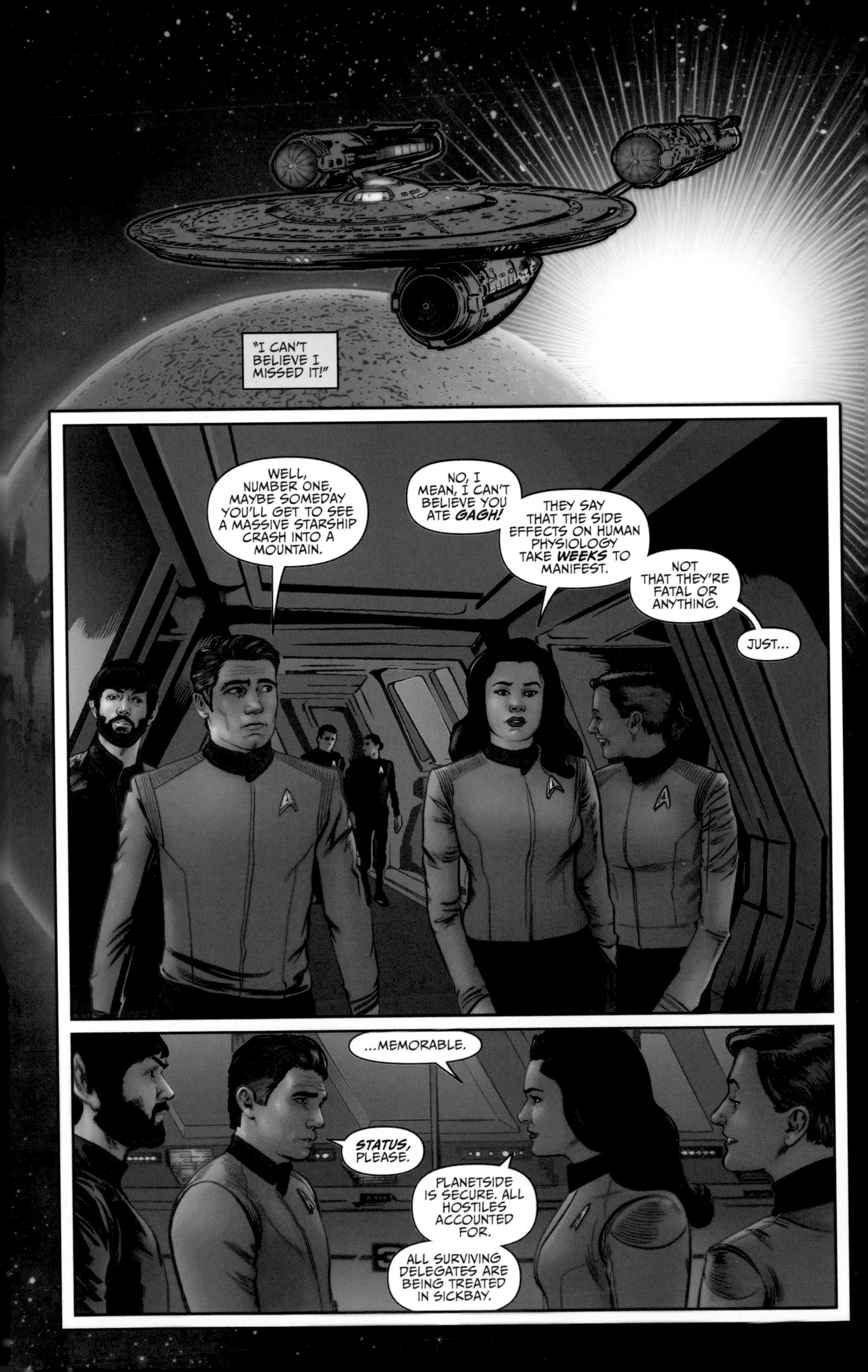
"I CAN'T BELIEVE I MISSED IT!"
WELL, NUMBER ONE, MAYBE SOMEDAY YOU'LL GET TO SEE A MASSIVE STARSHIP CRASH INTO A MOUNTAIN.
NO, I MEAN, I CAN'T BELIEVE YOU ATE *GAGH!*
THEY SAY THAT THE SIDE EFFECTS ON HUMAN PHYSIOLOGY TAKE *WEEKS* TO MANIFEST.
NOT THAT THEY'RE FATAL OR ANYTHING.
JUST...
...MEMORABLE.
STATUS, PLEASE.
PLANETSIDE IS SECURE. ALL HOSTILES ACCOUNTED FOR.
ALL SURVIVING DELEGATES ARE BEING TREATED IN SICKBAY.

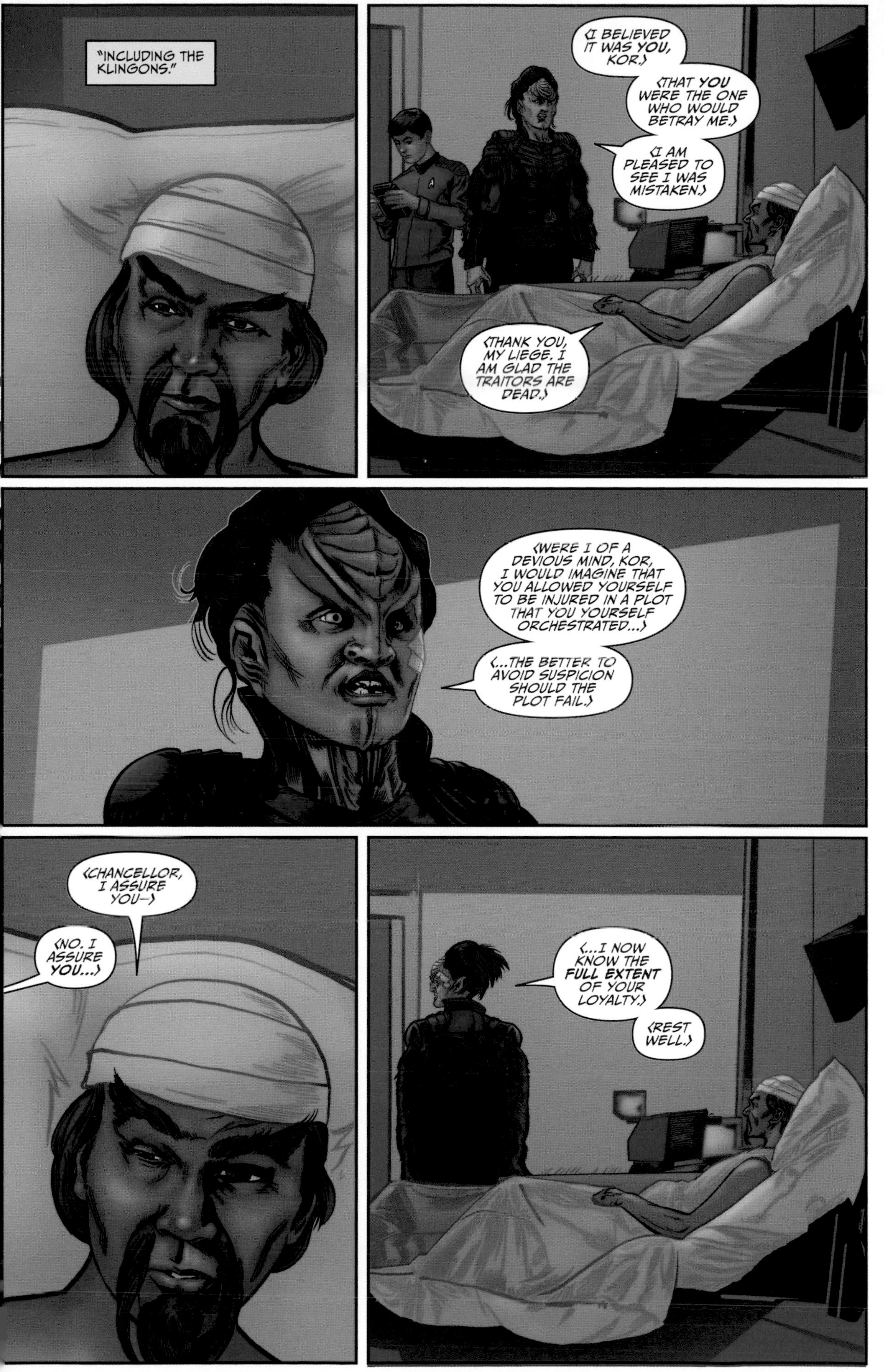
"INCLUDING THE KLINGONS."
‹I BELIEVED IT WAS YOU, KOR.›
‹THAT YOU WERE THE ONE WHO WOULD BETRAY ME.›
‹I AM PLEASED TO SEE I WAS MISTAKEN.›
‹THANK YOU, MY LIEGE. I AM GLAD THE TRAITORS ARE DEAD.›
‹WERE I OF A DEVIOUS MIND, KOR, I WOULD IMAGINE THAT YOU ALLOWED YOURSELF TO BE INJURED IN A PLOT THAT YOU YOURSELF ORCHESTRATED...›
‹...THE BETTER TO AVOID SUSPICION SHOULD THE PLOT FAIL.›
‹CHANCELLOR, I ASSURE YOU--›
‹NO. I ASSURE YOU...›
‹...I NOW KNOW THE FULL EXTENT OF YOUR LOYALTY.›
‹REST WELL.›

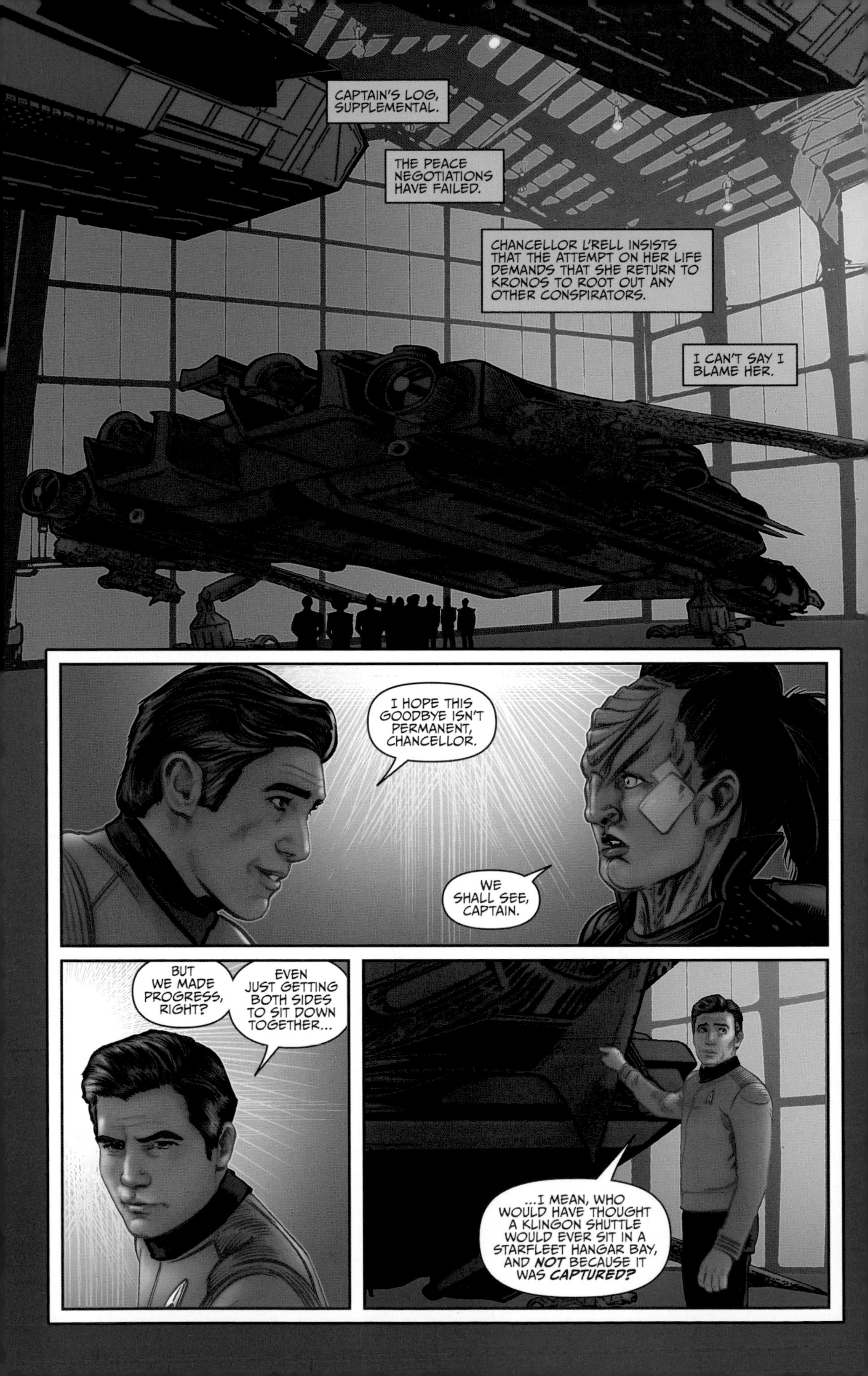
CAPTAIN'S LOG, SUPPLEMENTAL.
THE PEACE NEGOTIATIONS HAVE FAILED.
CHANCELLOR L'RELL INSISTS THAT THE ATTEMPT ON HER LIFE DEMANDS THAT SHE RETURN TO KRONOS TO ROOT OUT ANY OTHER CONSPIRATORS.
I CAN'T SAY I BLAME HER.
I HOPE THIS GOODBYE ISN'T PERMANENT, CHANCELLOR.
WE SHALL SEE, CAPTAIN.
BUT WE MADE PROGRESS, RIGHT?
EVEN JUST GETTING BOTH SIDES TO SIT DOWN TOGETHER...
...I MEAN, WHO WOULD HAVE THOUGHT A KLINGON SHUTTLE WOULD EVER SIT IN A STARFLEET HANGAR BAY, AND NOT BECAUSE IT WAS CAPTURED?

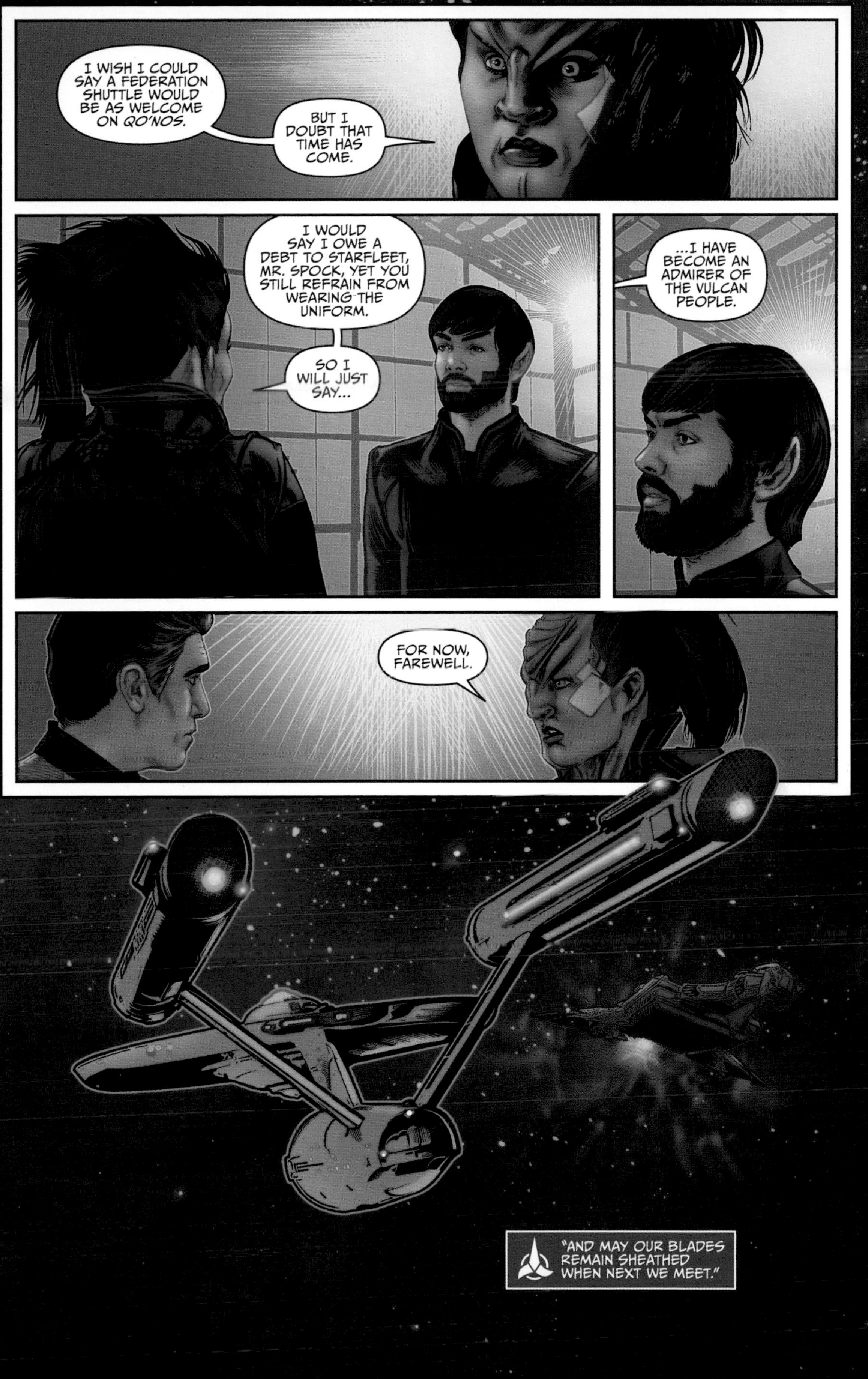
I WISH I COULD SAY A FEDERATION SHUTTLE WOULD BE AS WELCOME ON QO'NOS.
BUT I DOUBT THAT TIME HAS COME.
I WOULD SAY I OWE A DEBT TO STARFLEET, MR. SPOCK, YET YOU STILL REFRAIN FROM WEARING THE UNIFORM.
SO I WILL JUST SAY...
...I HAVE BECOME AN ADMIRER OF THE VULCAN PEOPLE.
FOR NOW, FAREWELL.
"AND MAY OUR BLADES REMAIN SHEATHED WHEN NEXT WE MEET."

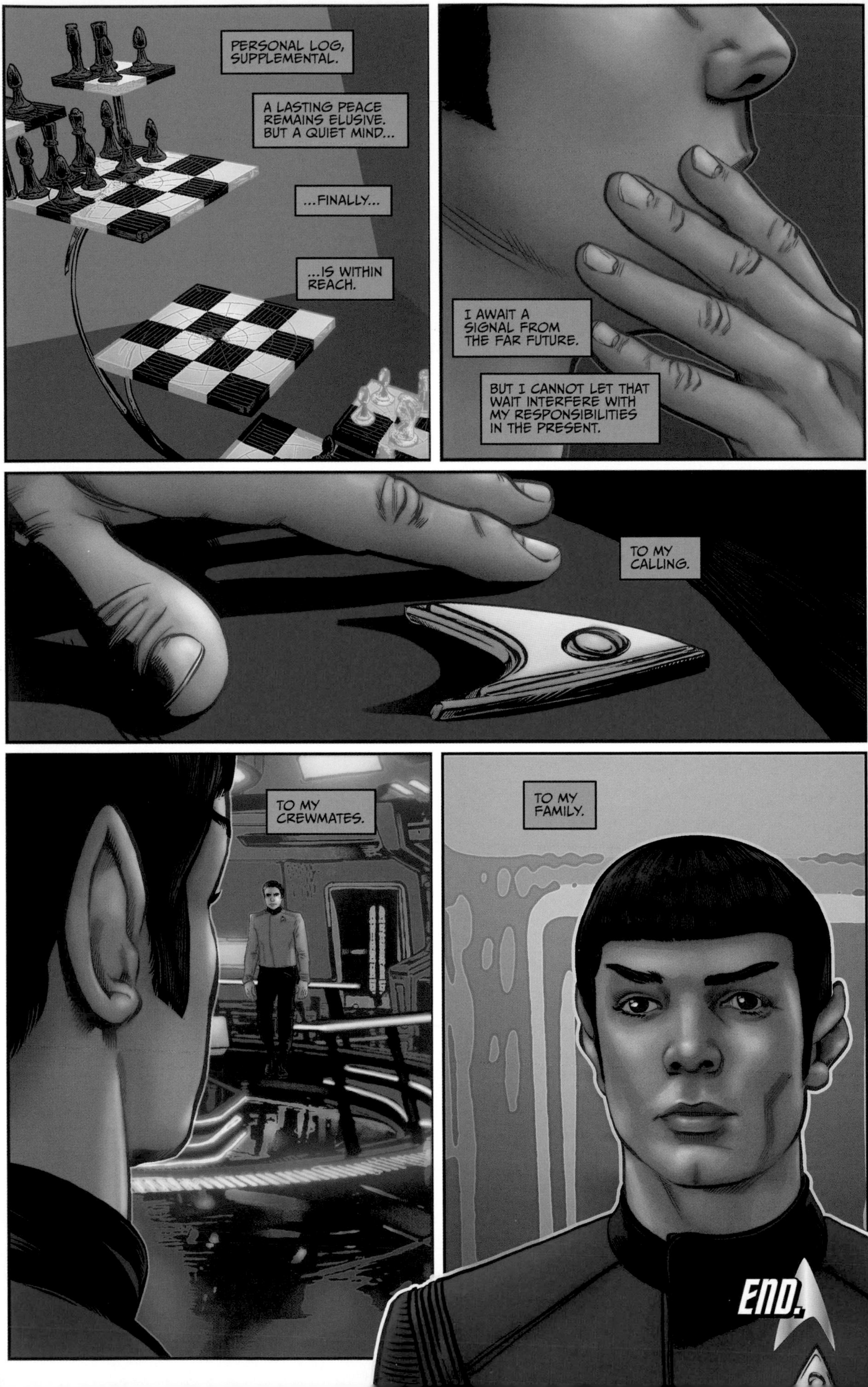
PERSONAL LOG, SUPPLEMENTAL.
A LASTING PEACE REMAINS ELUSIVE. BUT A QUIET MIND...
...FINALLY...
...IS WITHIN REACH.
I AWAIT A SIGNAL FROM THE FAR FUTURE.
BUT I CANNOT LET THAT WAIT INTERFERE WITH MY RESPONSIBILITIES IN THE PRESENT.
TO MY CALLING.
TO MY CREWMATES.
TO MY FAMILY.
END.

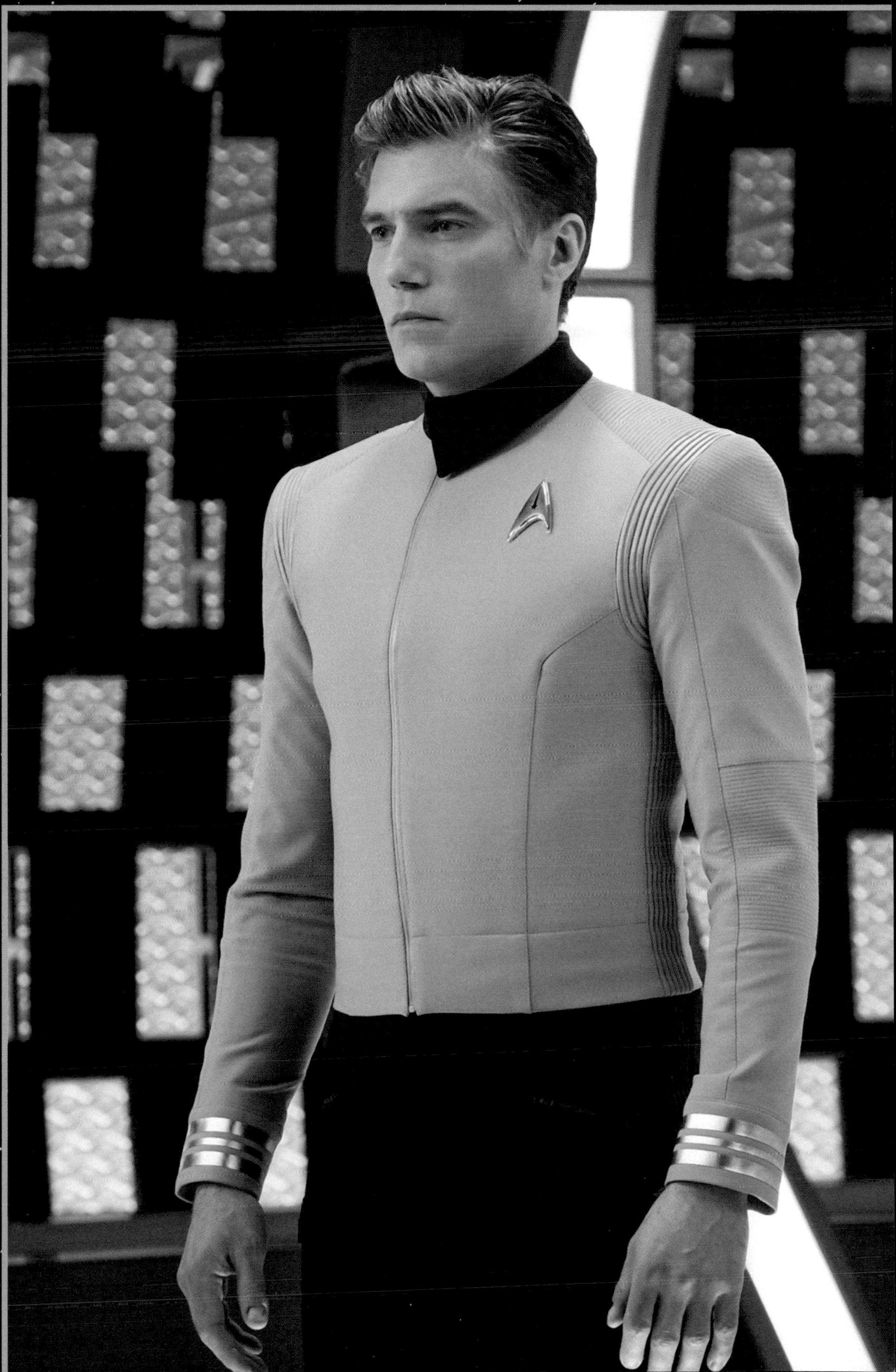

ART BY **PAUL SHIPPER**

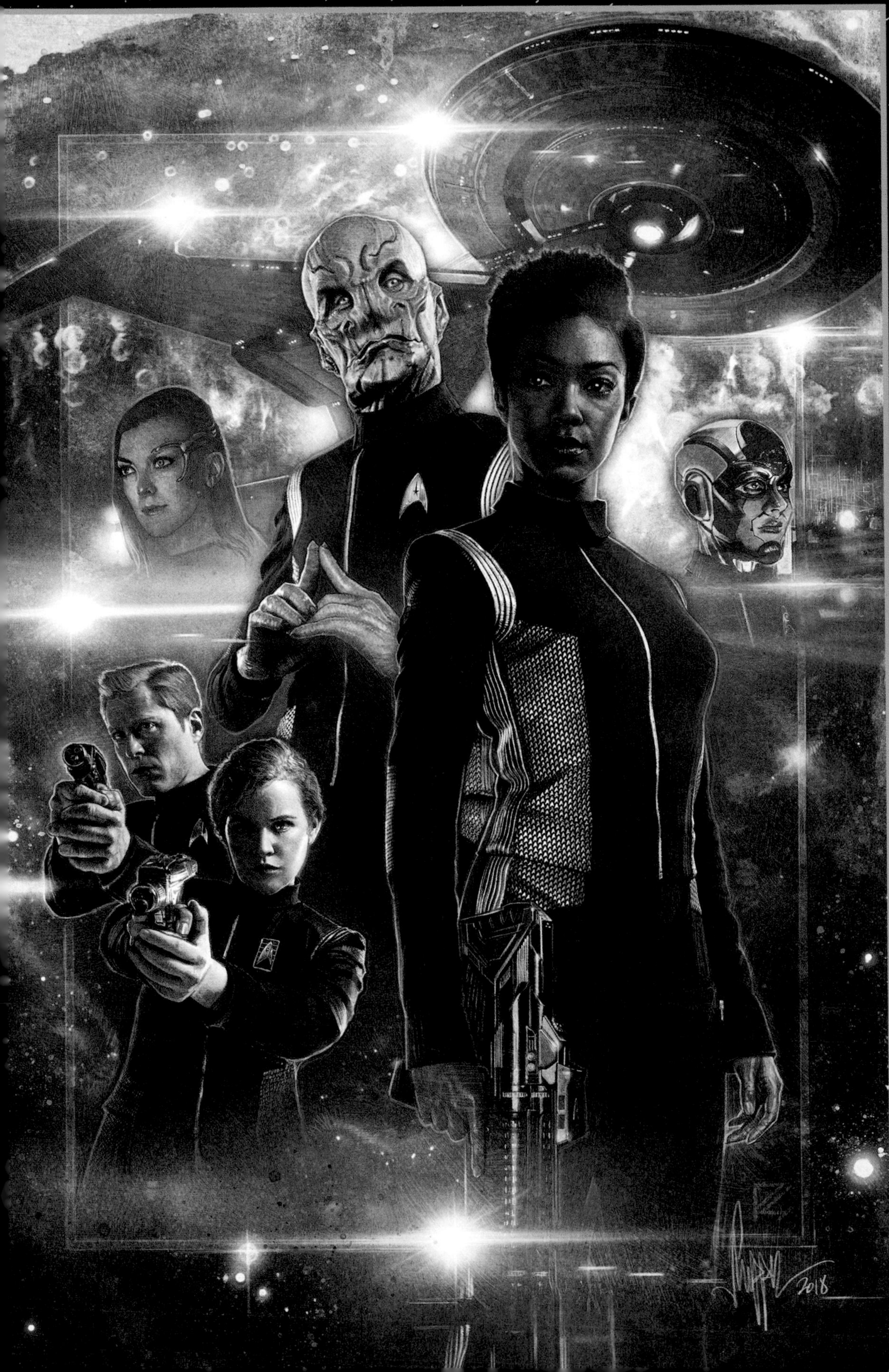

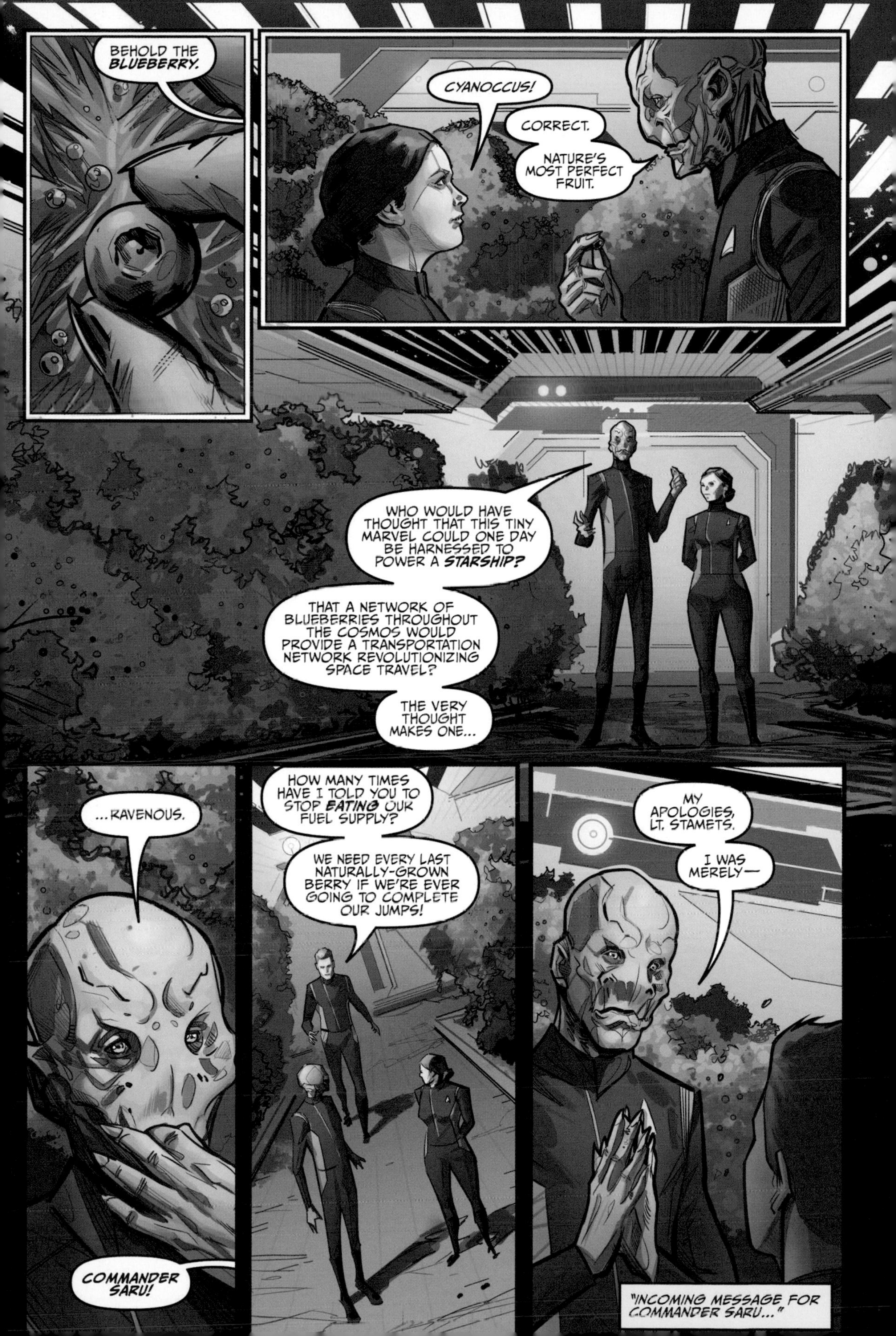
BEHOLD THE BLUEBERRY.
CYANOCCUS!
CORRECT.
NATURE'S MOST PERFECT FRUIT.
WHO WOULD HAVE THOUGHT THAT THIS TINY MARVEL COULD ONE DAY BE HARNESSED TO POWER A STARSHIP?
THAT A NETWORK OF BLUEBERRIES THROUGHOUT THE COSMOS WOULD PROVIDE A TRANSPORTATION NETWORK REVOLUTIONIZING SPACE TRAVEL?
THE VERY THOUGHT MAKES ONE...
...RAVENOUS.
COMMANDER SARU!
HOW MANY TIMES HAVE I TOLD YOU TO STOP EATING OUR FUEL SUPPLY?
WE NEED EVERY LAST NATURALLY-GROWN BERRY IF WE'RE EVER GOING TO COMPLETE OUR JUMPS!
MY APOLOGIES, LT. STAMETS.
I WAS MERELY—
"INCOMING MESSAGE FOR COMMANDER SARU..."

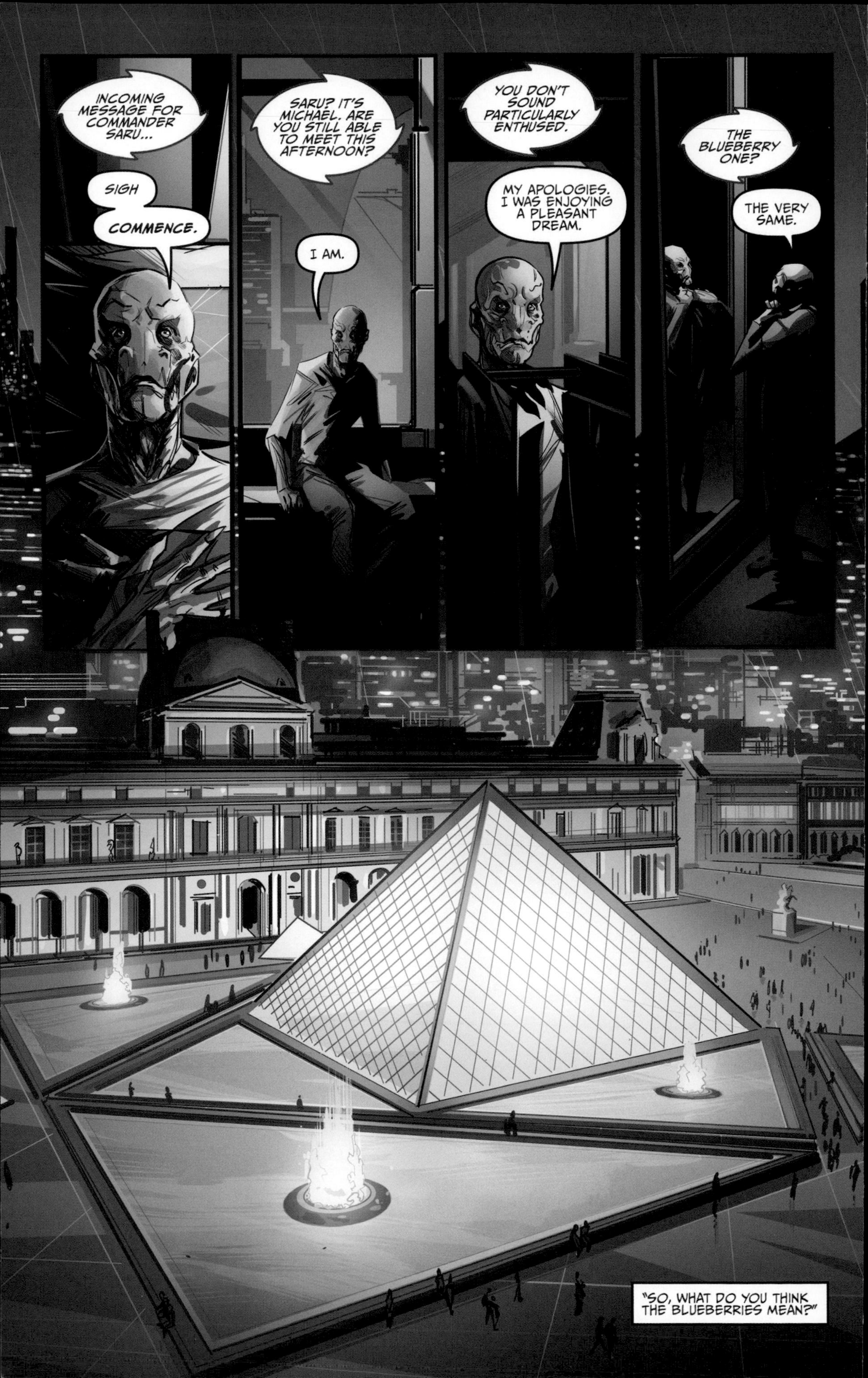
INCOMING MESSAGE FOR COMMANDER SARU...
SIGH
COMMENCE.
SARU? IT'S MICHAEL. ARE YOU STILL ABLE TO MEET THIS AFTERNOON?
I AM.
YOU DON'T SOUND PARTICULARLY ENTHUSED.
MY APOLOGIES. I WAS ENJOYING A PLEASANT DREAM.
THE BLUEBERRY ONE?
THE VERY SAME.
"SO, WHAT DO YOU THINK THE BLUEBERRIES MEAN?"

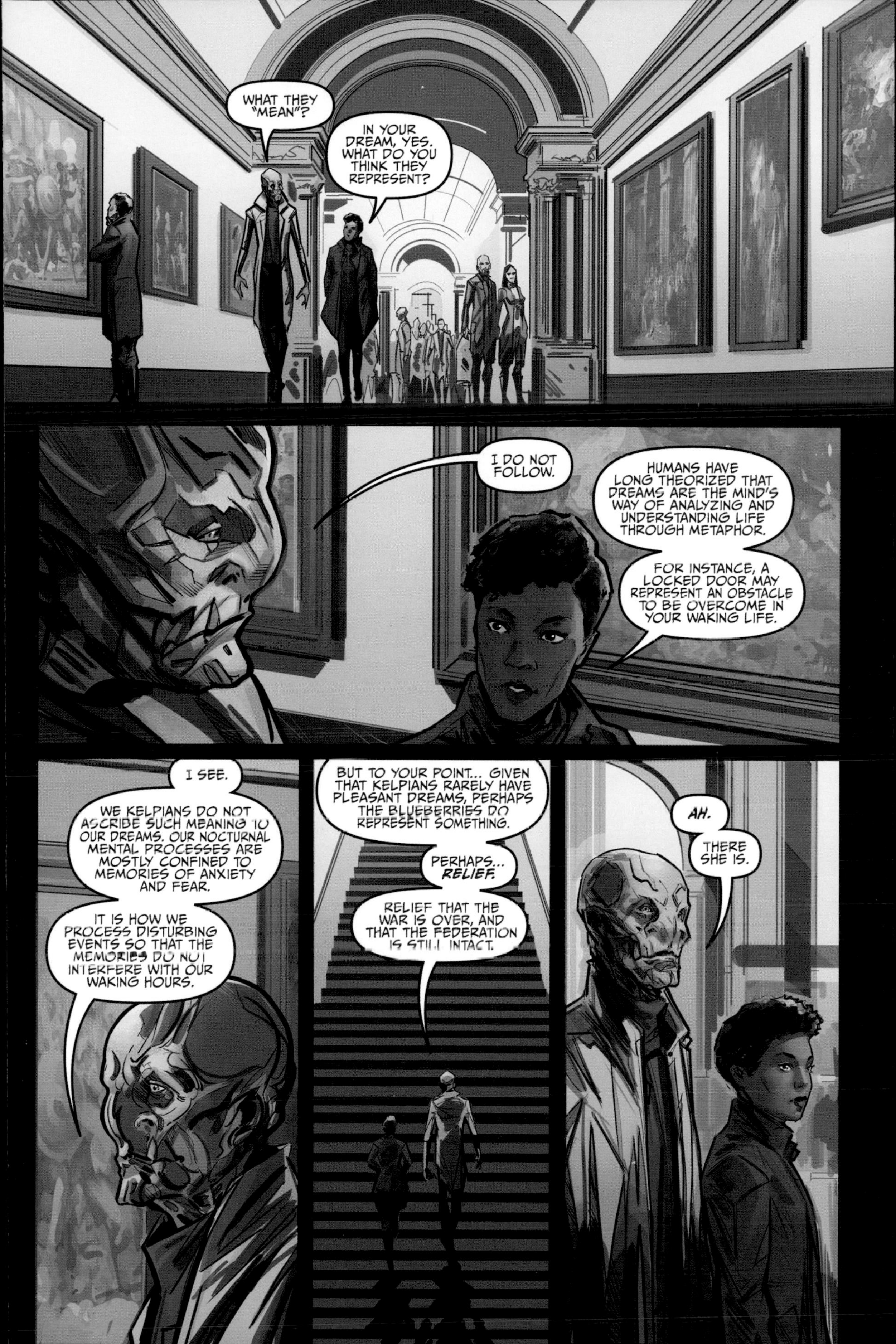
WHAT THEY "MEAN"?
IN YOUR DREAM, YES. WHAT DO YOU THINK THEY REPRESENT?
I DO NOT FOLLOW.
HUMANS HAVE LONG THEORIZED THAT DREAMS ARE THE MIND'S WAY OF ANALYZING AND UNDERSTANDING LIFE THROUGH METAPHOR.
FOR INSTANCE, A LOCKED DOOR MAY REPRESENT AN OBSTACLE TO BE OVERCOME IN YOUR WAKING LIFE.
I SEE.
WE KELPIANS DO NOT ASCRIBE SUCH MEANING TO OUR DREAMS. OUR NOCTURNAL MENTAL PROCESSES ARE MOSTLY CONFINED TO MEMORIES OF ANXIETY AND FEAR.
IT IS HOW WE PROCESS DISTURBING EVENTS SO THAT THE MEMORIES DO NOT INTERFERE WITH OUR WAKING HOURS.
BUT TO YOUR POINT... GIVEN THAT KELPIANS RARELY HAVE PLEASANT DREAMS, PERHAPS THE BLUEBERRIES DO REPRESENT SOMETHING.
PERHAPS... *RELIEF.*
RELIEF THAT THE WAR IS OVER, AND THAT THE FEDERATION IS STILL INTACT.
AH.
THERE SHE IS.

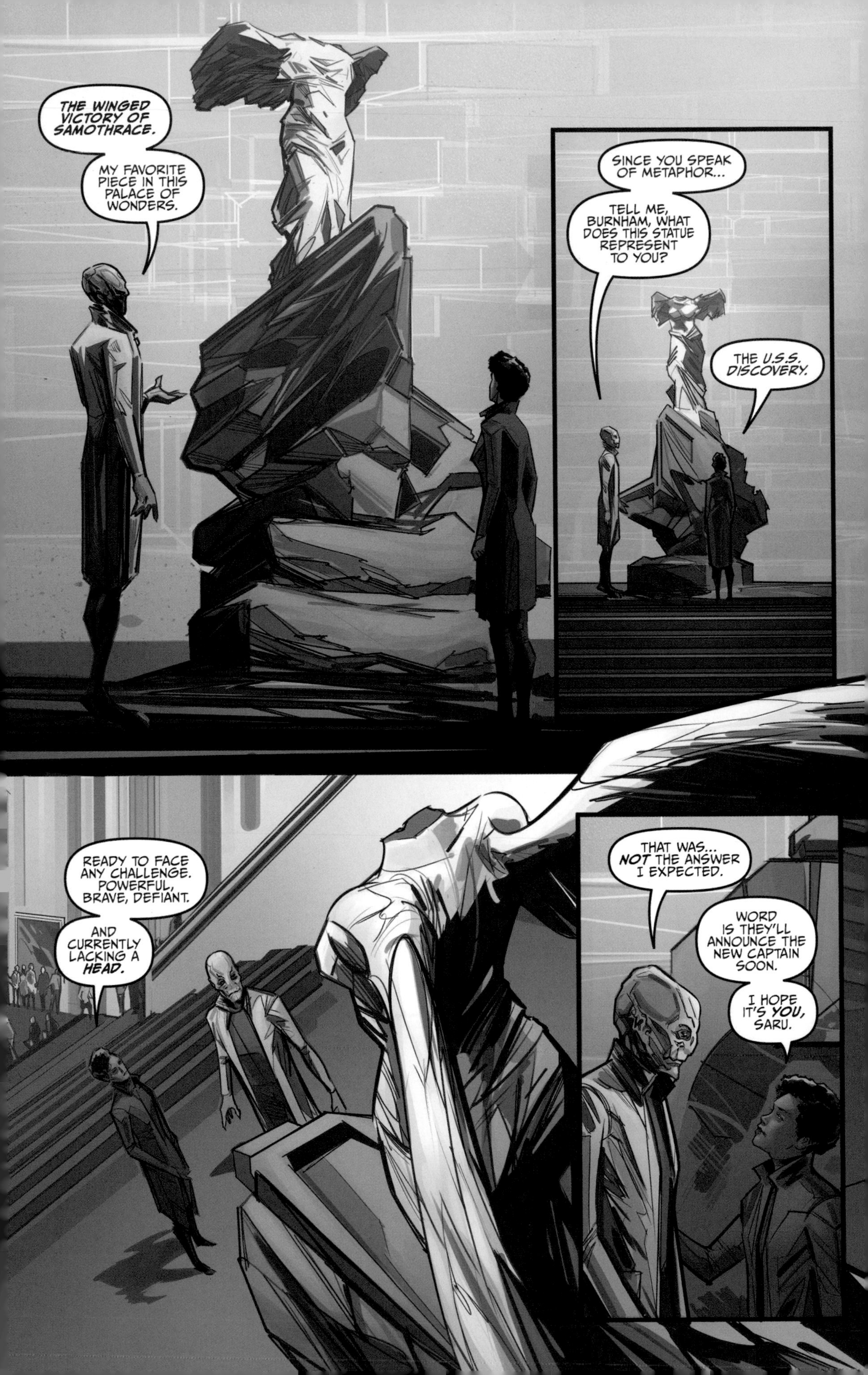
THE WINGED VICTORY OF SAMOTHRACE.
MY FAVORITE PIECE IN THIS PALACE OF WONDERS.
SINCE YOU SPEAK OF METAPHOR...
TELL ME, BURNHAM, WHAT DOES THIS STATUE REPRESENT TO YOU?
THE U.S.S. DISCOVERY.
READY TO FACE ANY CHALLENGE. POWERFUL, BRAVE, DEFIANT.
AND CURRENTLY LACKING A HEAD.
THAT WAS... NOT THE ANSWER I EXPECTED.
WORD IS THEY'LL ANNOUNCE THE NEW CAPTAIN SOON.
I HOPE IT'S YOU, SARU.

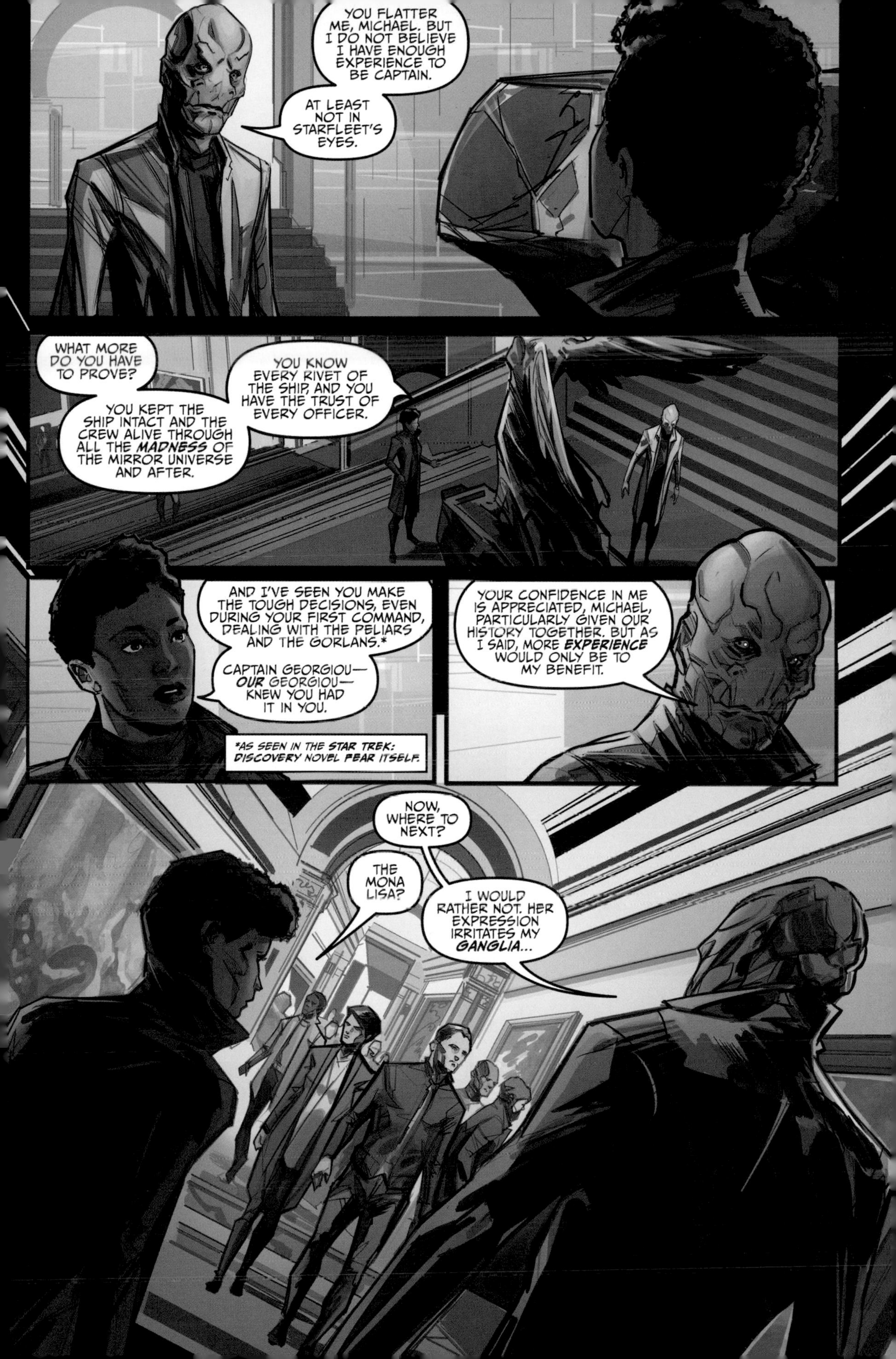
YOU FLATTER ME, MICHAEL. BUT I DO NOT BELIEVE I HAVE ENOUGH EXPERIENCE TO BE CAPTAIN.
AT LEAST NOT IN STARFLEET'S EYES.
WHAT MORE DO YOU HAVE TO PROVE?
YOU KEPT THE SHIP INTACT AND THE CREW ALIVE THROUGH ALL THE *MADNESS* OF THE MIRROR UNIVERSE AND AFTER.
YOU KNOW EVERY RIVET OF THE SHIP, AND YOU HAVE THE TRUST OF EVERY OFFICER.
AND I'VE SEEN YOU MAKE THE TOUGH DECISIONS, EVEN DURING YOUR FIRST COMMAND, DEALING WITH THE PELIARS AND THE GORLANS.*
CAPTAIN GEORGIOU— *OUR* GEORGIOU— KNEW YOU HAD IT IN YOU.
*AS SEEN IN THE **STAR TREK: DISCOVERY** NOVEL **FEAR ITSELF**.
YOUR CONFIDENCE IN ME IS APPRECIATED, MICHAEL, PARTICULARLY GIVEN OUR HISTORY TOGETHER. BUT AS I SAID, MORE ***EXPERIENCE*** WOULD ONLY BE TO MY BENEFIT.
NOW, WHERE TO NEXT?
THE MONA LISA?
I WOULD RATHER NOT. HER EXPRESSION IRRITATES MY ***GANGLIA***...

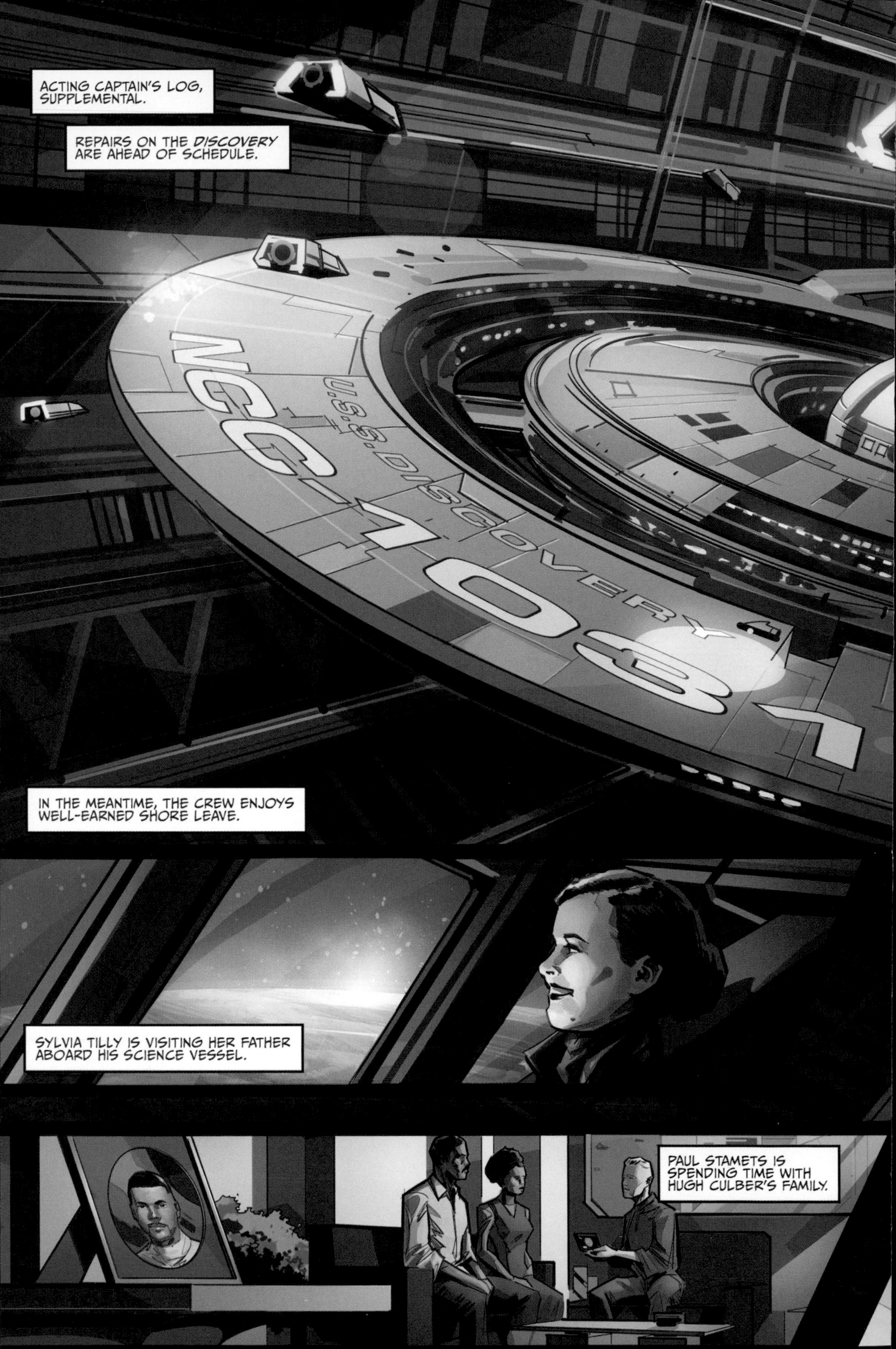
ACTING CAPTAIN'S LOG, SUPPLEMENTAL.
REPAIRS ON THE *DISCOVERY* ARE AHEAD OF SCHEDULE.
U.S.S. DISCOVERY
NCC-1031
IN THE MEANTIME, THE CREW ENJOYS WELL-EARNED SHORE LEAVE.
SYLVIA TILLY IS VISITING HER FATHER ABOARD HIS SCIENCE VESSEL.
PAUL STAMETS IS SPENDING TIME WITH HUGH CULBER'S FAMILY.

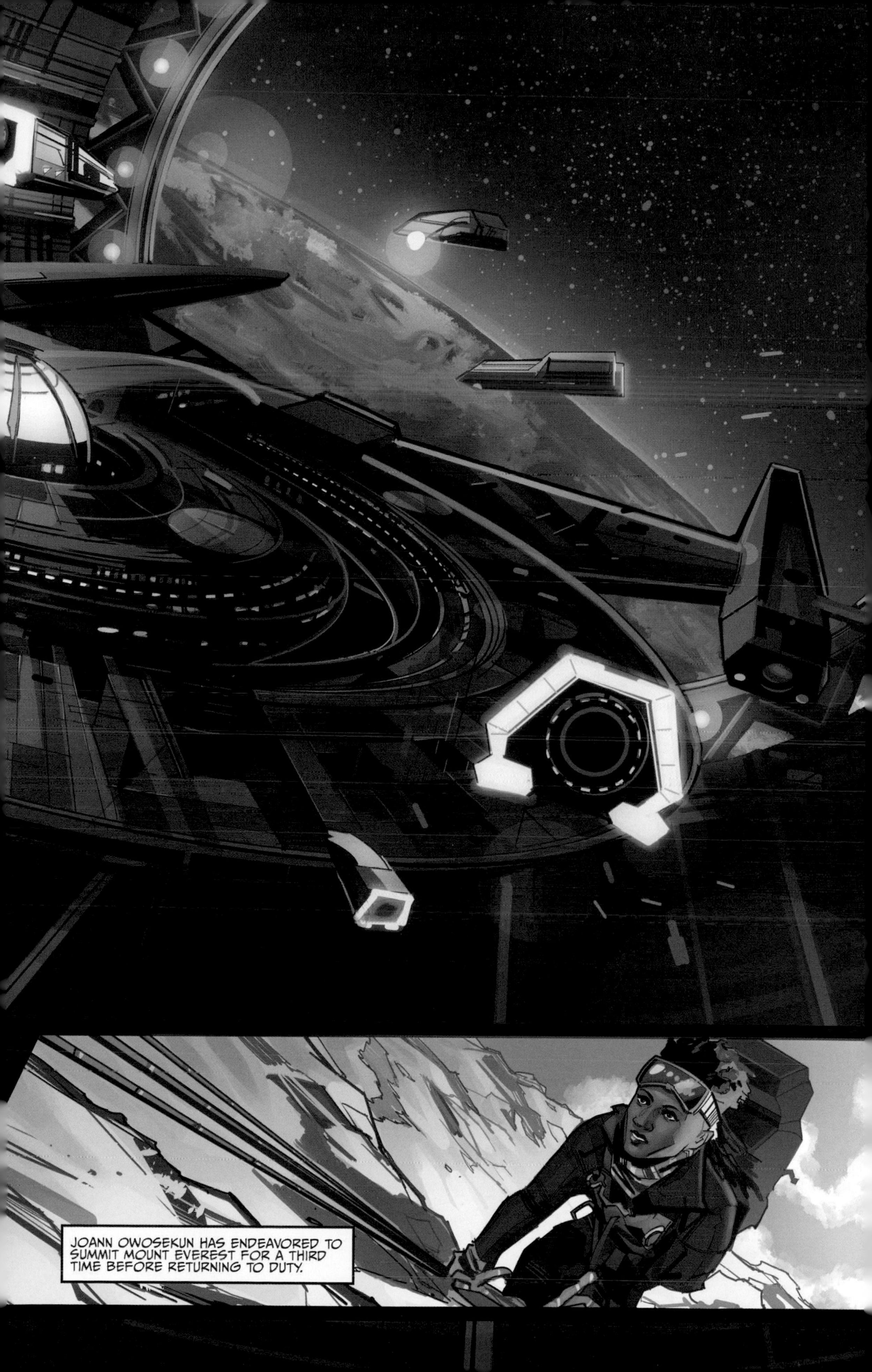
JOANN OWOSEKUN HAS ENDEAVORED TO SUMMIT MOUNT EVEREST FOR A THIRD TIME BEFORE RETURNING TO DUTY.

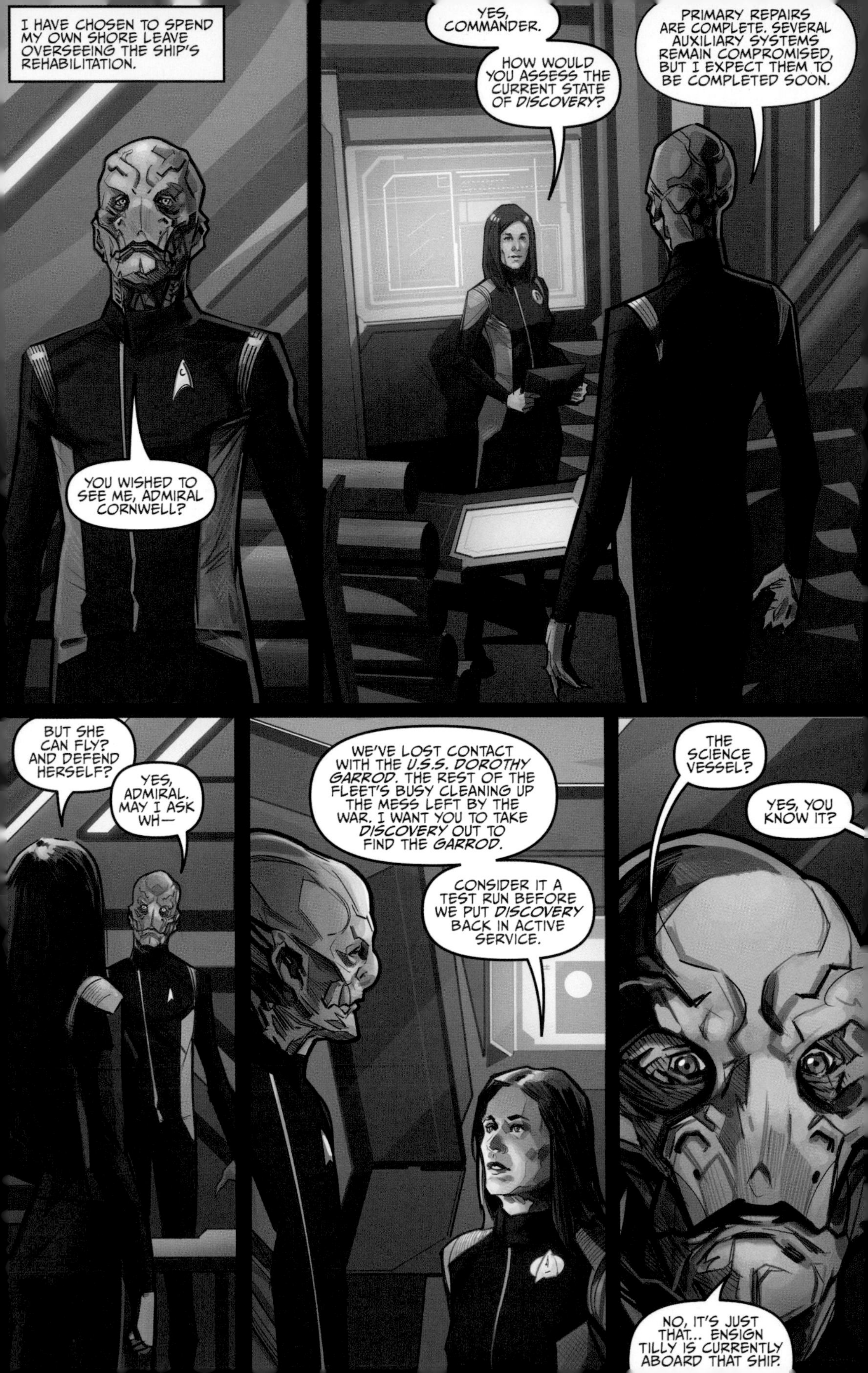
I HAVE CHOSEN TO SPEND MY OWN SHORE LEAVE OVERSEEING THE SHIP'S REHABILITATION.
YOU WISHED TO SEE ME, ADMIRAL CORNWELL?
YES, COMMANDER.
HOW WOULD YOU ASSESS THE CURRENT STATE OF *DISCOVERY*?
PRIMARY REPAIRS ARE COMPLETE. SEVERAL AUXILIARY SYSTEMS REMAIN COMPROMISED, BUT I EXPECT THEM TO BE COMPLETED SOON.
BUT SHE CAN FLY? AND DEFEND HERSELF?
YES, ADMIRAL. MAY I ASK WH—
WE'VE LOST CONTACT WITH THE *U.S.S. DOROTHY GARROD*. THE REST OF THE FLEET'S BUSY CLEANING UP THE MESS LEFT BY THE WAR. I WANT YOU TO TAKE *DISCOVERY* OUT TO FIND THE *GARROD*.
CONSIDER IT A TEST RUN BEFORE WE PUT *DISCOVERY* BACK IN ACTIVE SERVICE.
THE SCIENCE VESSEL?
YES, YOU KNOW IT?
NO, IT'S JUST THAT... ENSIGN TILLY IS CURRENTLY ABOARD THAT SHIP.

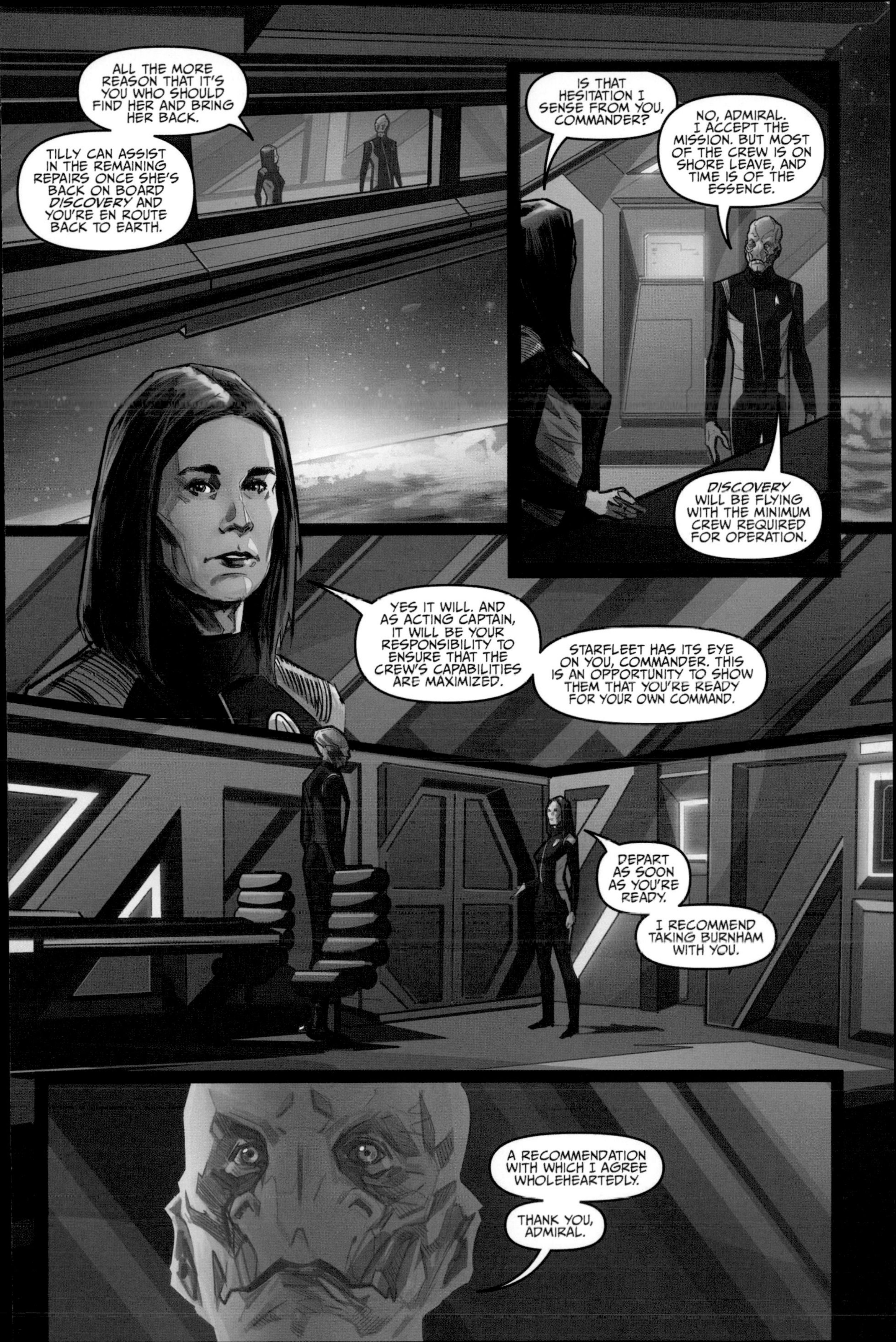
ALL THE MORE REASON THAT IT'S YOU WHO SHOULD FIND HER AND BRING HER BACK.
TILLY CAN ASSIST IN THE REMAINING REPAIRS ONCE SHE'S BACK ON BOARD *DISCOVERY* AND YOU'RE EN ROUTE BACK TO EARTH.
IS THAT HESITATION I SENSE FROM YOU, COMMANDER?
NO, ADMIRAL. I ACCEPT THE MISSION. BUT MOST OF THE CREW IS ON SHORE LEAVE, AND TIME IS OF THE ESSENCE.
DISCOVERY WILL BE FLYING WITH THE MINIMUM CREW REQUIRED FOR OPERATION.
YES IT WILL. AND AS ACTING CAPTAIN, IT WILL BE YOUR RESPONSIBILITY TO ENSURE THAT THE CREW'S CAPABILITIES ARE MAXIMIZED.
STARFLEET HAS ITS EYE ON YOU, COMMANDER. THIS IS AN OPPORTUNITY TO SHOW THEM THAT YOU'RE READY FOR YOUR OWN COMMAND.
DEPART AS SOON AS YOU'RE READY.
I RECOMMEND TAKING BURNHAM WITH YOU.
A RECOMMENDATION WITH WHICH I AGREE WHOLEHEARTEDLY.
THANK YOU, ADMIRAL.

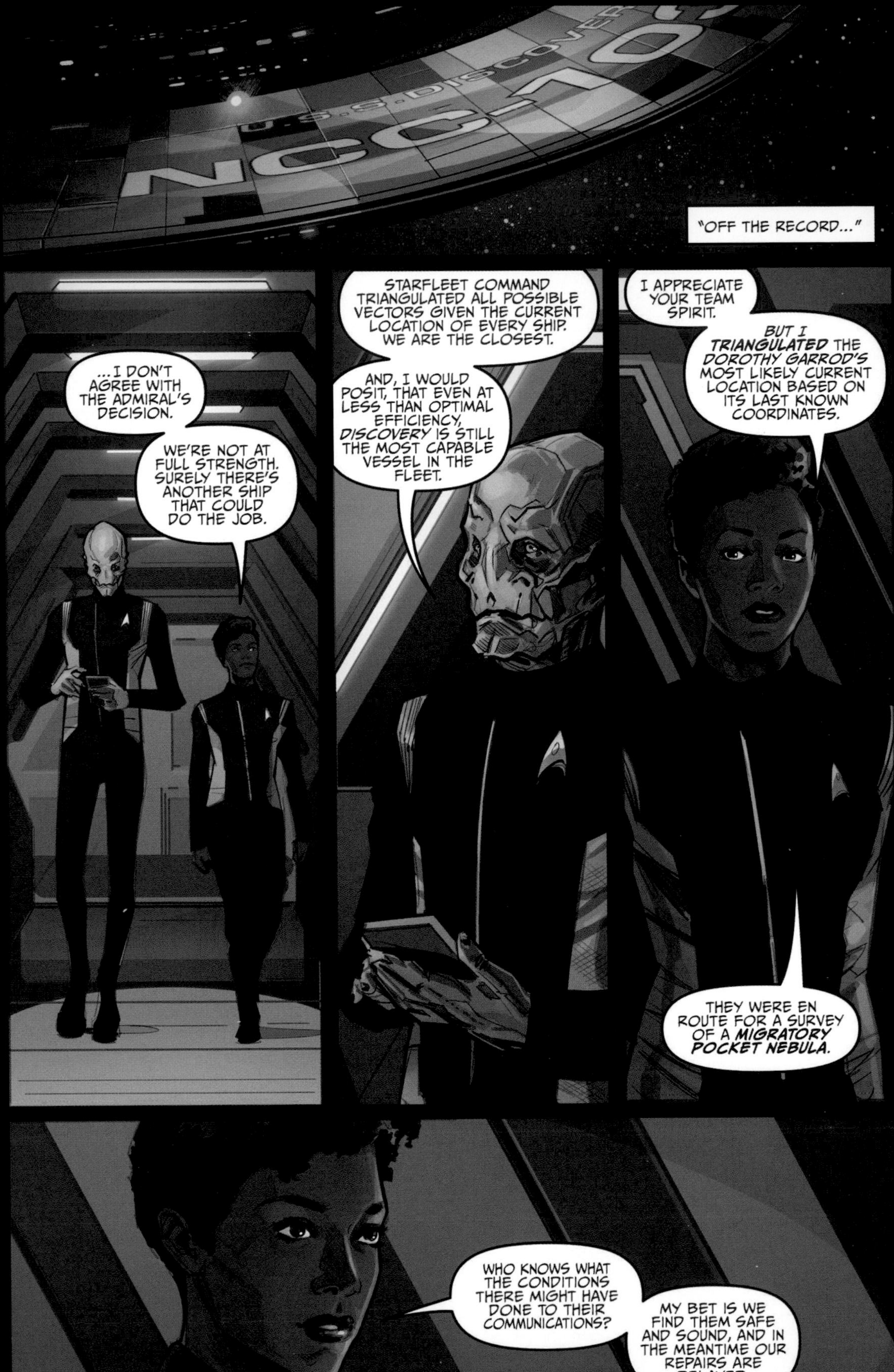
U.S.S. DISCOVERY
NCC-10
"OFF THE RECORD..."
...I DON'T AGREE WITH THE ADMIRAL'S DECISION.
WE'RE NOT AT FULL STRENGTH. SURELY THERE'S ANOTHER SHIP THAT COULD DO THE JOB.
STARFLEET COMMAND TRIANGULATED ALL POSSIBLE VECTORS GIVEN THE CURRENT LOCATION OF EVERY SHIP. WE ARE THE CLOSEST.
AND, I WOULD POSIT, THAT EVEN AT LESS THAN OPTIMAL EFFICIENCY, *DISCOVERY* IS STILL THE MOST CAPABLE VESSEL IN THE FLEET.
I APPRECIATE YOUR TEAM SPIRIT.
BUT I ***TRIANGULATED*** THE *DOROTHY GARROD'S* MOST LIKELY CURRENT LOCATION BASED ON ITS LAST KNOWN COORDINATES.
THEY WERE EN ROUTE FOR A SURVEY OF A ***MIGRATORY POCKET NEBULA.***
WHO KNOWS WHAT THE CONDITIONS THERE MIGHT HAVE DONE TO THEIR COMMUNICATIONS?
MY BET IS WE FIND THEM SAFE AND SOUND, AND IN THE MEANTIME OUR REPAIRS ARE DELAYED.

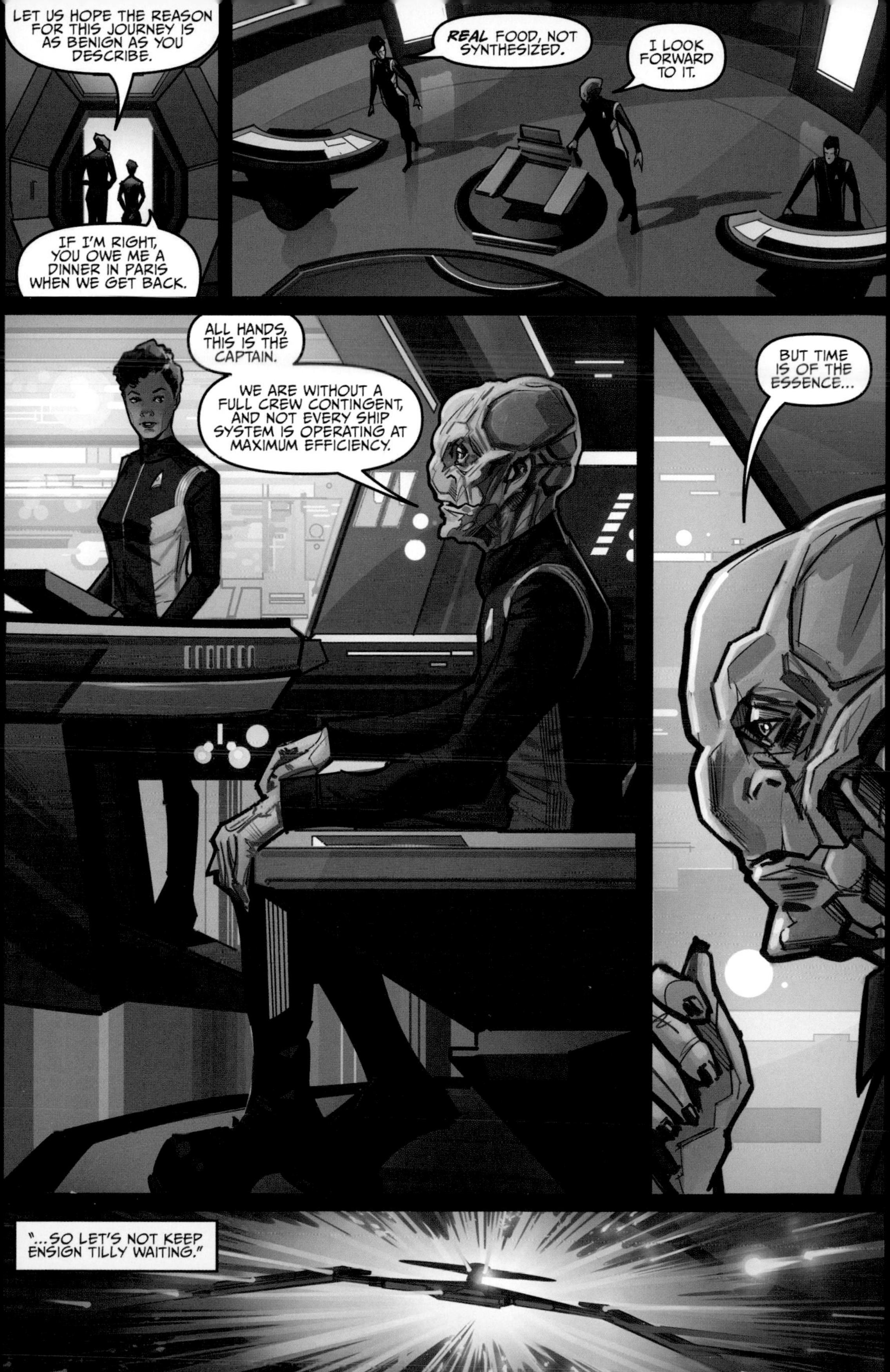
LET US HOPE THE REASON FOR THIS JOURNEY IS AS BENIGN AS YOU DESCRIBE.
IF I'M RIGHT, YOU OWE ME A DINNER IN PARIS WHEN WE GET BACK.
REAL FOOD, NOT SYNTHESIZED.
I LOOK FORWARD TO IT.
ALL HANDS, THIS IS THE CAPTAIN.
WE ARE WITHOUT A FULL CREW CONTINGENT, AND NOT EVERY SHIP SYSTEM IS OPERATING AT MAXIMUM EFFICIENCY.
BUT TIME IS OF THE ESSENCE...
"...SO LET'S NOT KEEP ENSIGN TILLY WAITING."

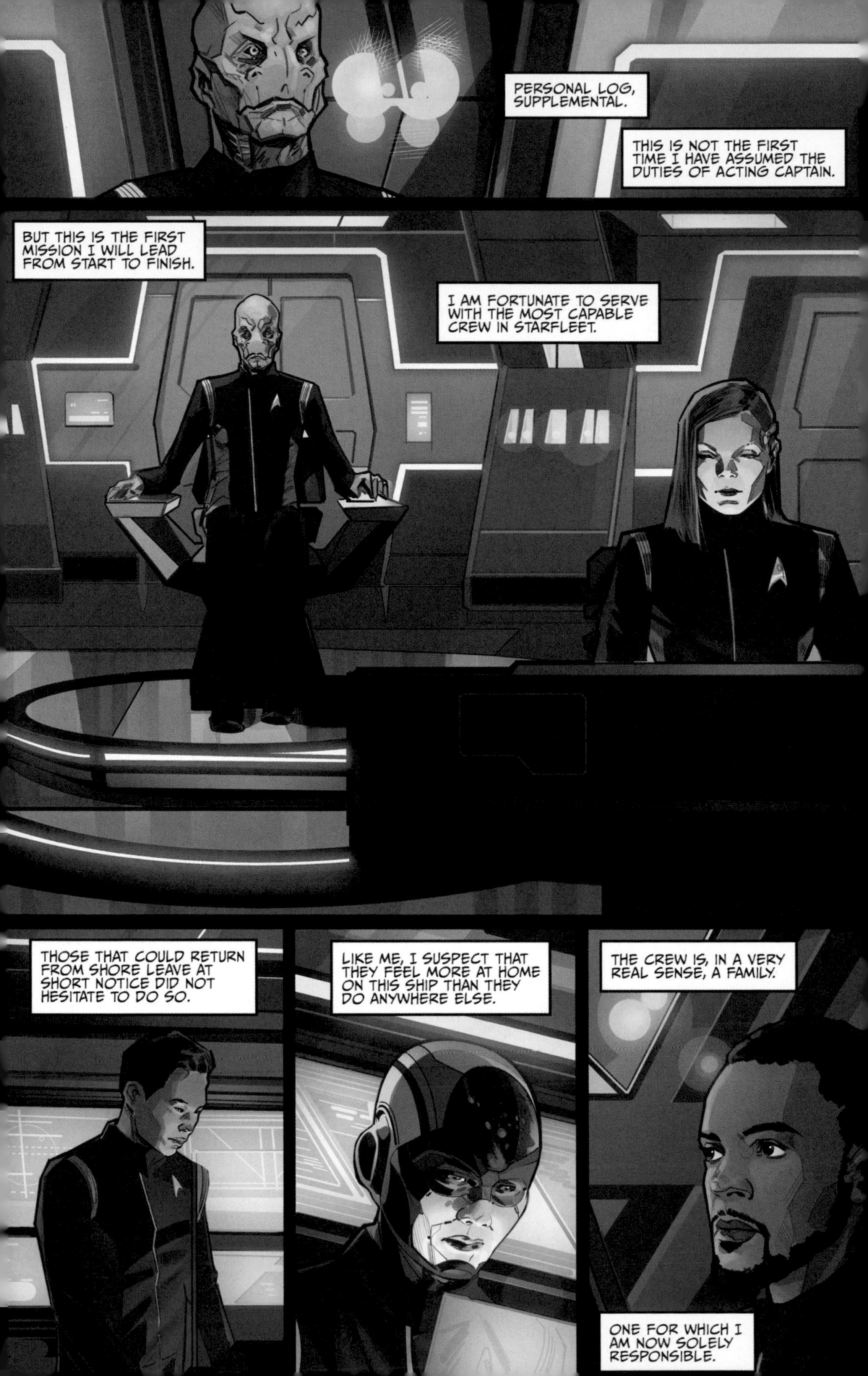
PERSONAL LOG, SUPPLEMENTAL.
THIS IS NOT THE FIRST TIME I HAVE ASSUMED THE DUTIES OF ACTING CAPTAIN.
BUT THIS IS THE FIRST MISSION I WILL LEAD FROM START TO FINISH.
I AM FORTUNATE TO SERVE WITH THE MOST CAPABLE CREW IN STARFLEET.
THOSE THAT COULD RETURN FROM SHORE LEAVE AT SHORT NOTICE DID NOT HESITATE TO DO SO.
LIKE ME, I SUSPECT THAT THEY FEEL MORE AT HOME ON THIS SHIP THAN THEY DO ANYWHERE ELSE.
THE CREW IS, IN A VERY REAL SENSE, A FAMILY.
ONE FOR WHICH I AM NOW SOLELY RESPONSIBLE.

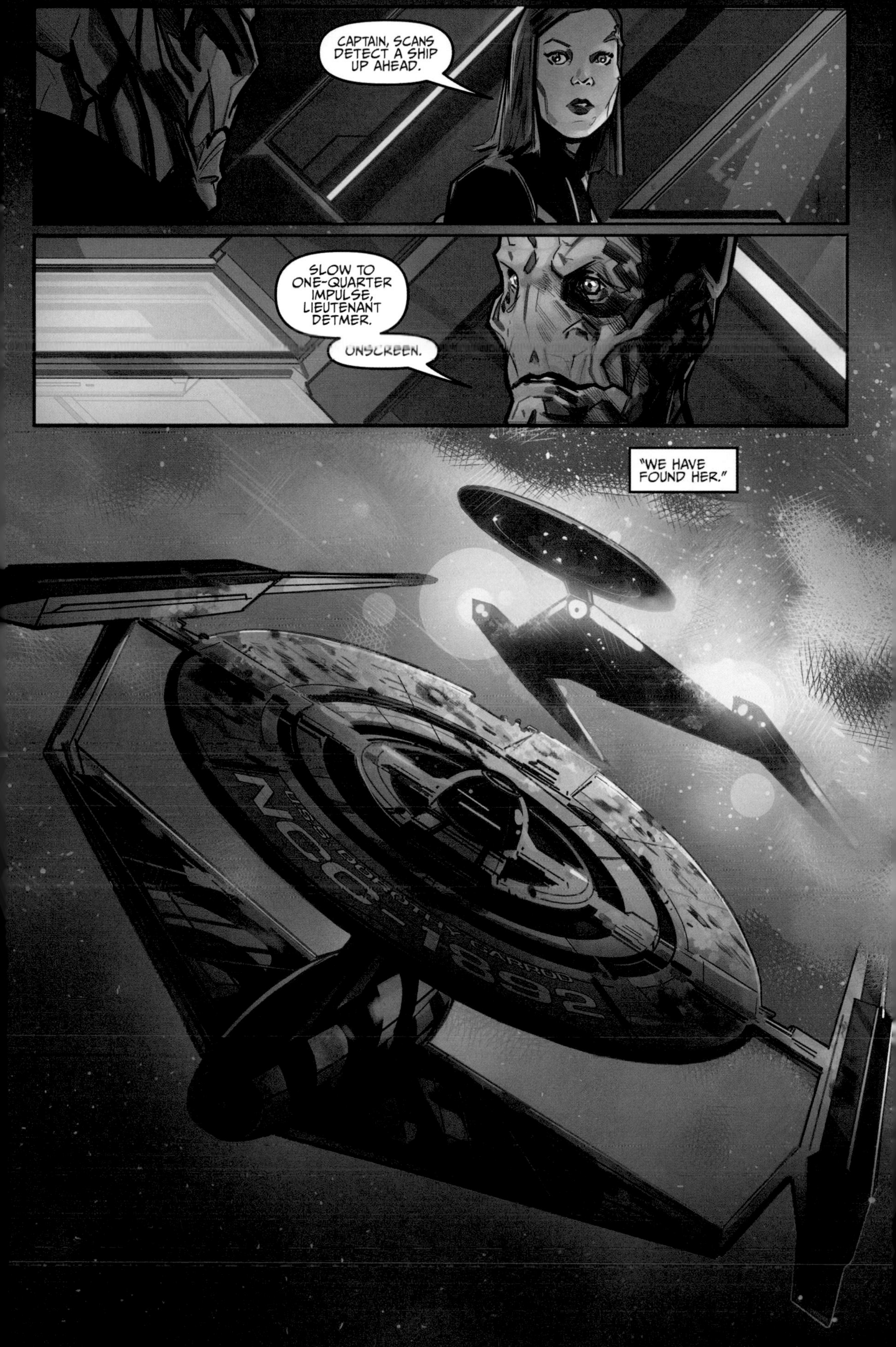
CAPTAIN, SCANS DETECT A SHIP UP AHEAD.
SLOW TO ONE-QUARTER IMPULSE, LIEUTENANT DETMER.
ONSCREEN.
"WE HAVE FOUND HER."

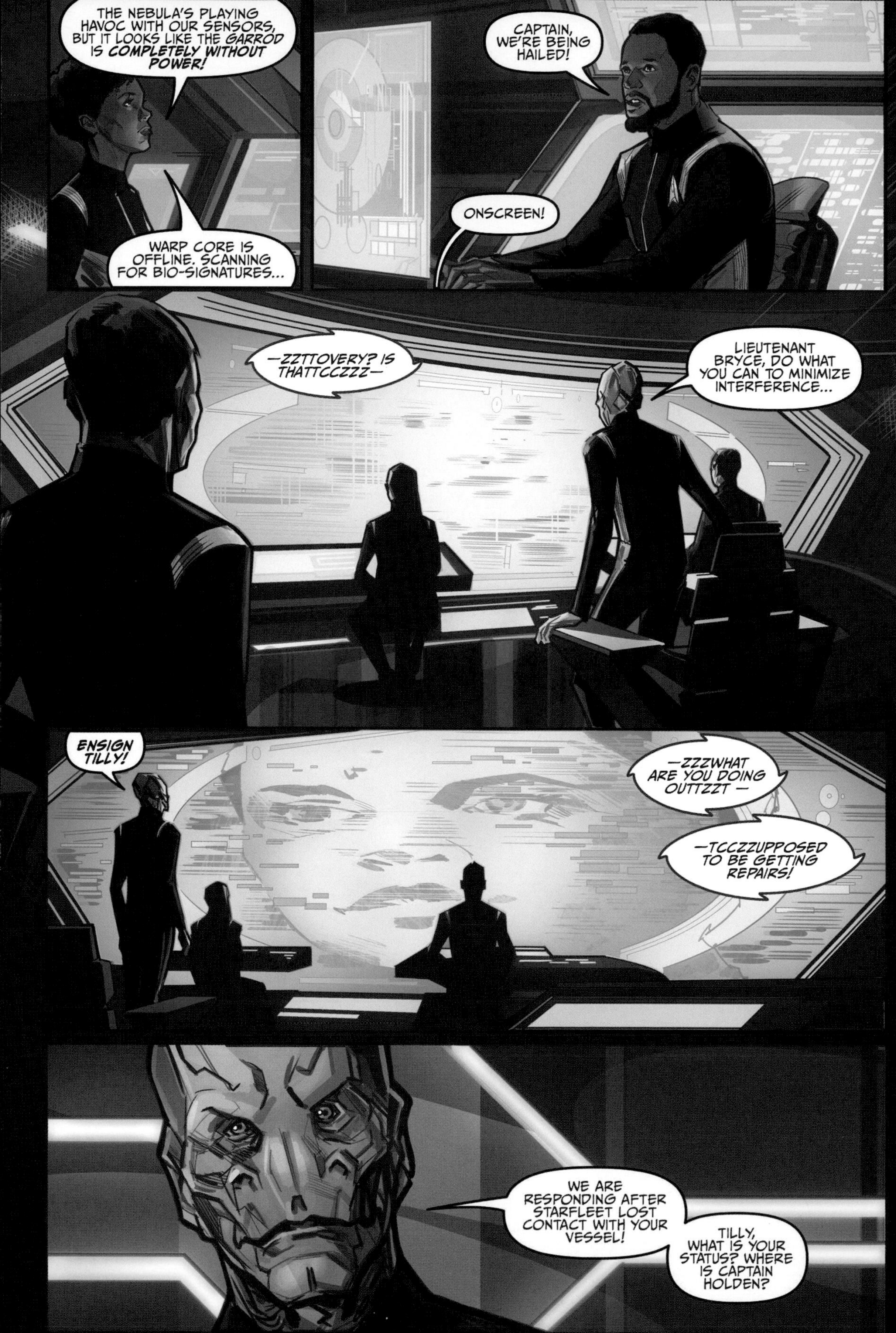
THE NEBULA'S PLAYING HAVOC WITH OUR SENSORS, BUT IT LOOKS LIKE THE GARROD IS COMPLETELY WITHOUT POWER!
WARP CORE IS OFFLINE. SCANNING FOR BIO-SIGNATURES...
CAPTAIN, WE'RE BEING HAILED!
ONSCREEN!
—ZZTTOVERY? IS THATTCCZZZ—
LIEUTENANT BRYCE, DO WHAT YOU CAN TO MINIMIZE INTERFERENCE...
ENSIGN TILLY!
—ZZZWHAT ARE YOU DOING OUTTZZT —
—TCCZZUPPOSED TO BE GETTING REPAIRS!
WE ARE RESPONDING AFTER STARFLEET LOST CONTACT WITH YOUR VESSEL!
TILLY, WHAT IS YOUR STATUS? WHERE IS CAPTAIN HOLDEN?

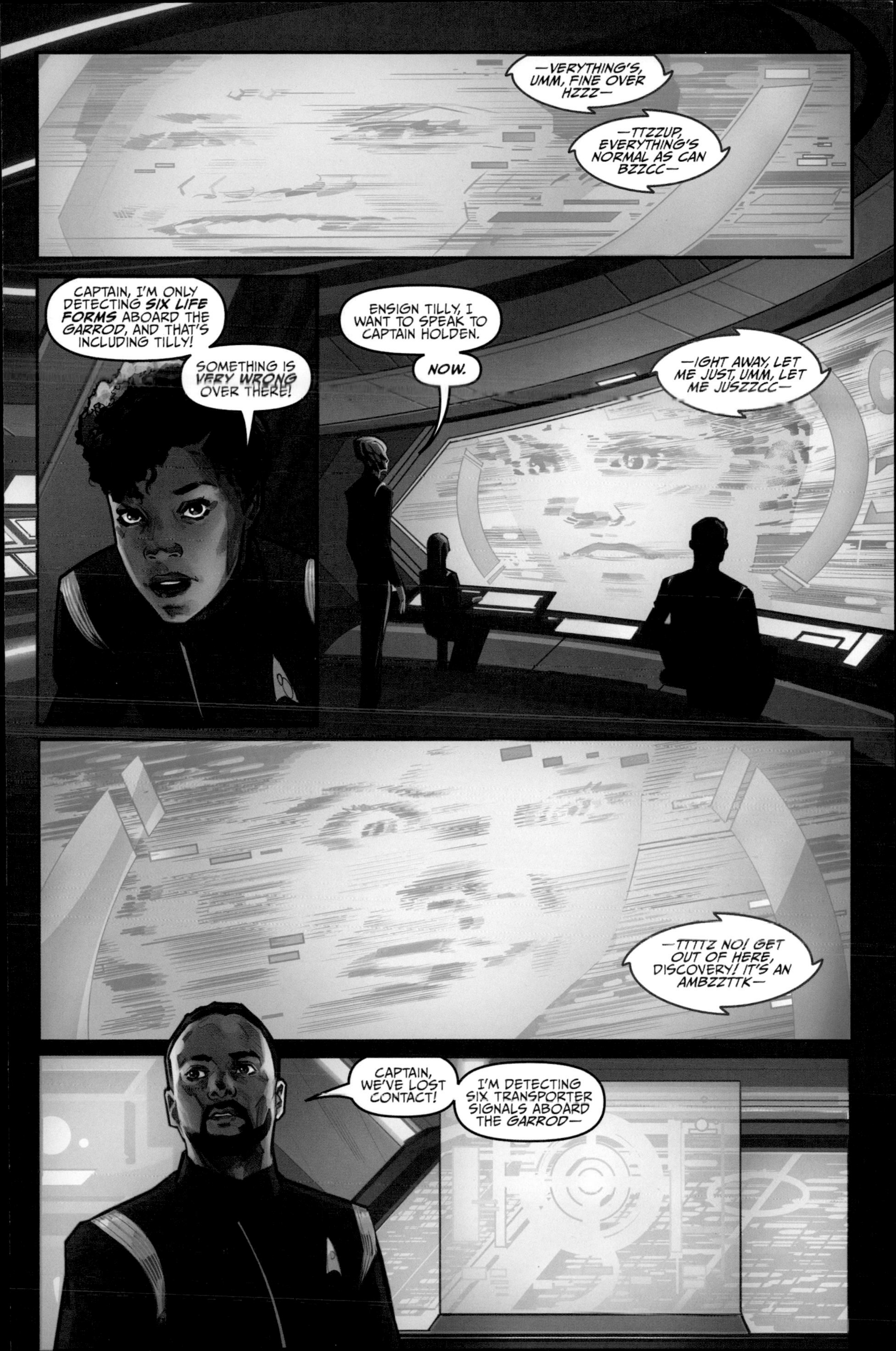
—VERYTHING'S, UMM, FINE OVER HZZZ—
—TTZZUP, EVERYTHING'S NORMAL AS CAN BZZCC—
CAPTAIN, I'M ONLY DETECTING SIX LIFE FORMS ABOARD THE GARROD, AND THAT'S INCLUDING TILLY!
SOMETHING IS VERY WRONG OVER THERE!
ENSIGN TILLY, I WANT TO SPEAK TO CAPTAIN HOLDEN.
NOW.
—IGHT AWAY, LET ME JUST, UMM, LET ME JUSZZCC—
—TTTTZ NO! GET OUT OF HERE, DISCOVERY! IT'S AN AMBZZTTK—
CAPTAIN, WE'VE LOST CONTACT!
I'M DETECTING SIX TRANSPORTER SIGNALS ABOARD THE GARROD—

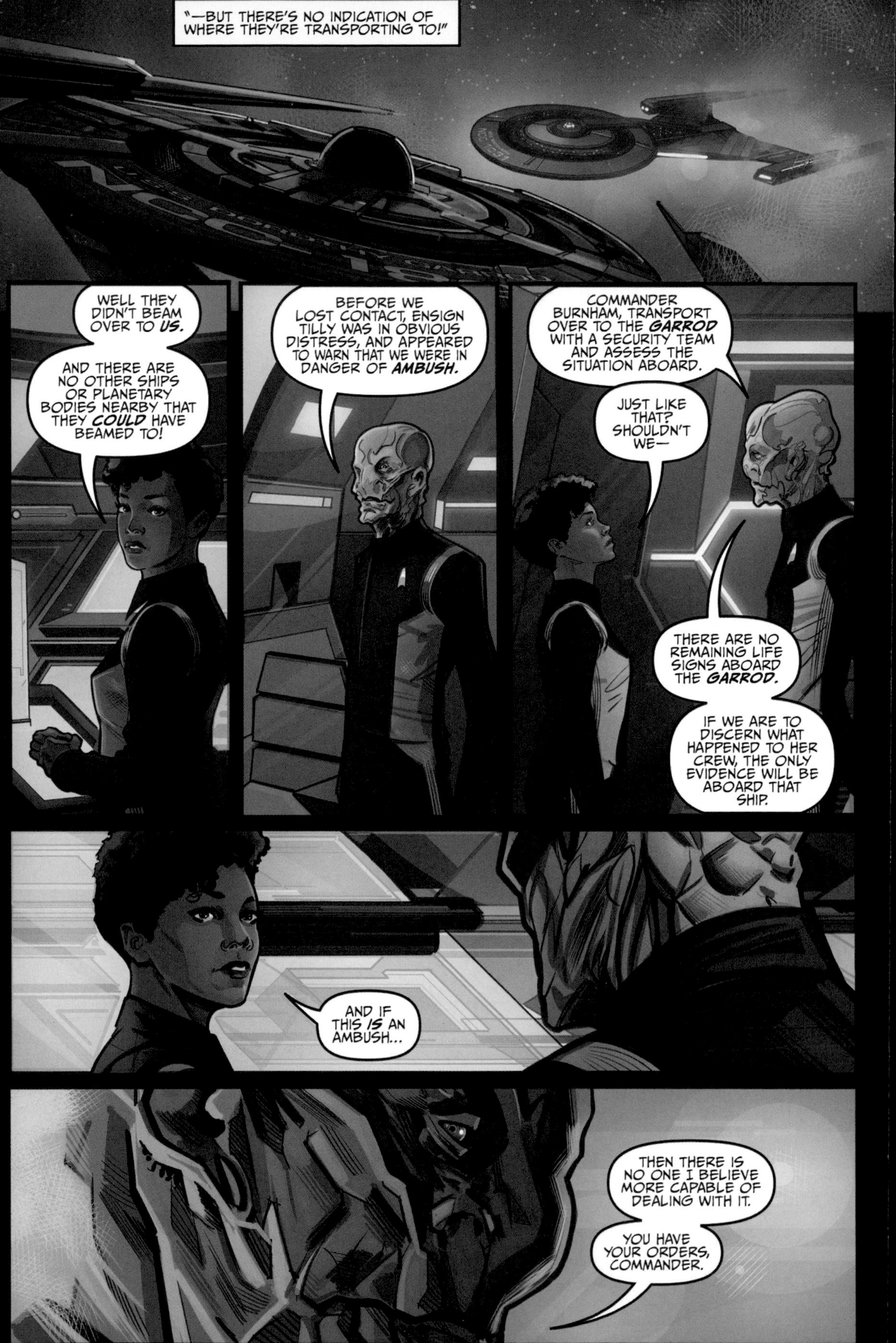
"—BUT THERE'S NO INDICATION OF WHERE THEY'RE TRANSPORTING TO!"
WELL THEY DIDN'T BEAM OVER TO *US.*
AND THERE ARE NO OTHER SHIPS OR PLANETARY BODIES NEARBY THAT THEY *COULD* HAVE BEAMED TO!
BEFORE WE LOST CONTACT, ENSIGN TILLY WAS IN OBVIOUS DISTRESS, AND APPEARED TO WARN THAT WE WERE IN DANGER OF *AMBUSH.*
COMMANDER BURNHAM, TRANSPORT OVER TO THE *GARROD* WITH A SECURITY TEAM AND ASSESS THE SITUATION ABOARD.
JUST LIKE THAT? SHOULDN'T WE—
THERE ARE NO REMAINING LIFE SIGNS ABOARD THE *GARROD.*
IF WE ARE TO DISCERN WHAT HAPPENED TO HER CREW, THE ONLY EVIDENCE WILL BE ABOARD THAT SHIP.
AND IF THIS *IS* AN AMBUSH...
THEN THERE IS NO ONE I BELIEVE MORE CAPABLE OF DEALING WITH IT.
YOU HAVE YOUR ORDERS, COMMANDER.

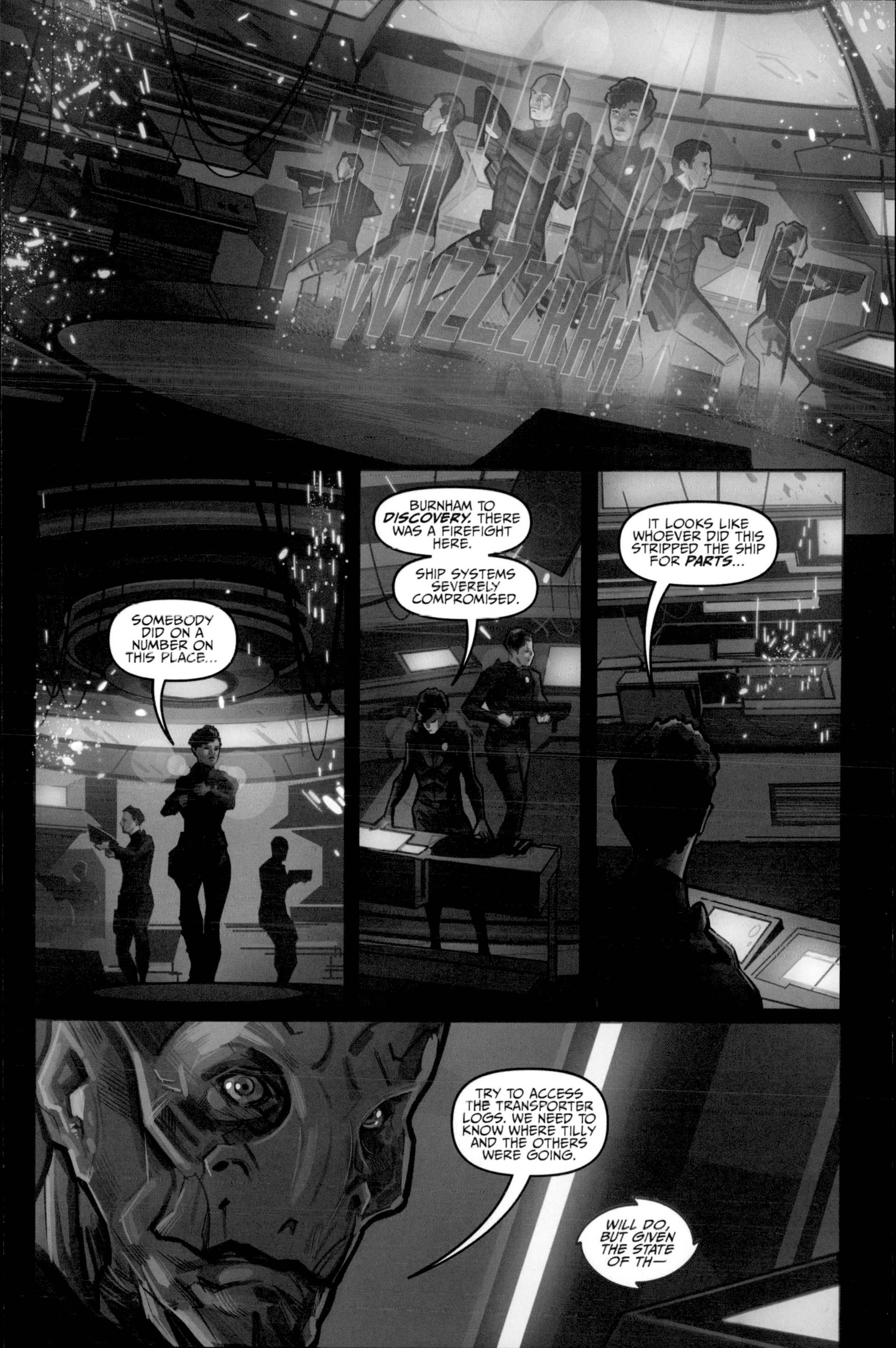
WVVZZZHHH
SOMEBODY DID ON A NUMBER ON THIS PLACE...
BURNHAM TO DISCOVERY. THERE WAS A FIREFIGHT HERE.
SHIP SYSTEMS SEVERELY COMPROMISED.
IT LOOKS LIKE WHOEVER DID THIS STRIPPED THE SHIP FOR PARTS...
TRY TO ACCESS THE TRANSPORTER LOGS. WE NEED TO KNOW WHERE TILLY AND THE OTHERS WERE GOING.
WILL DO, BUT GIVEN THE STATE OF TH—

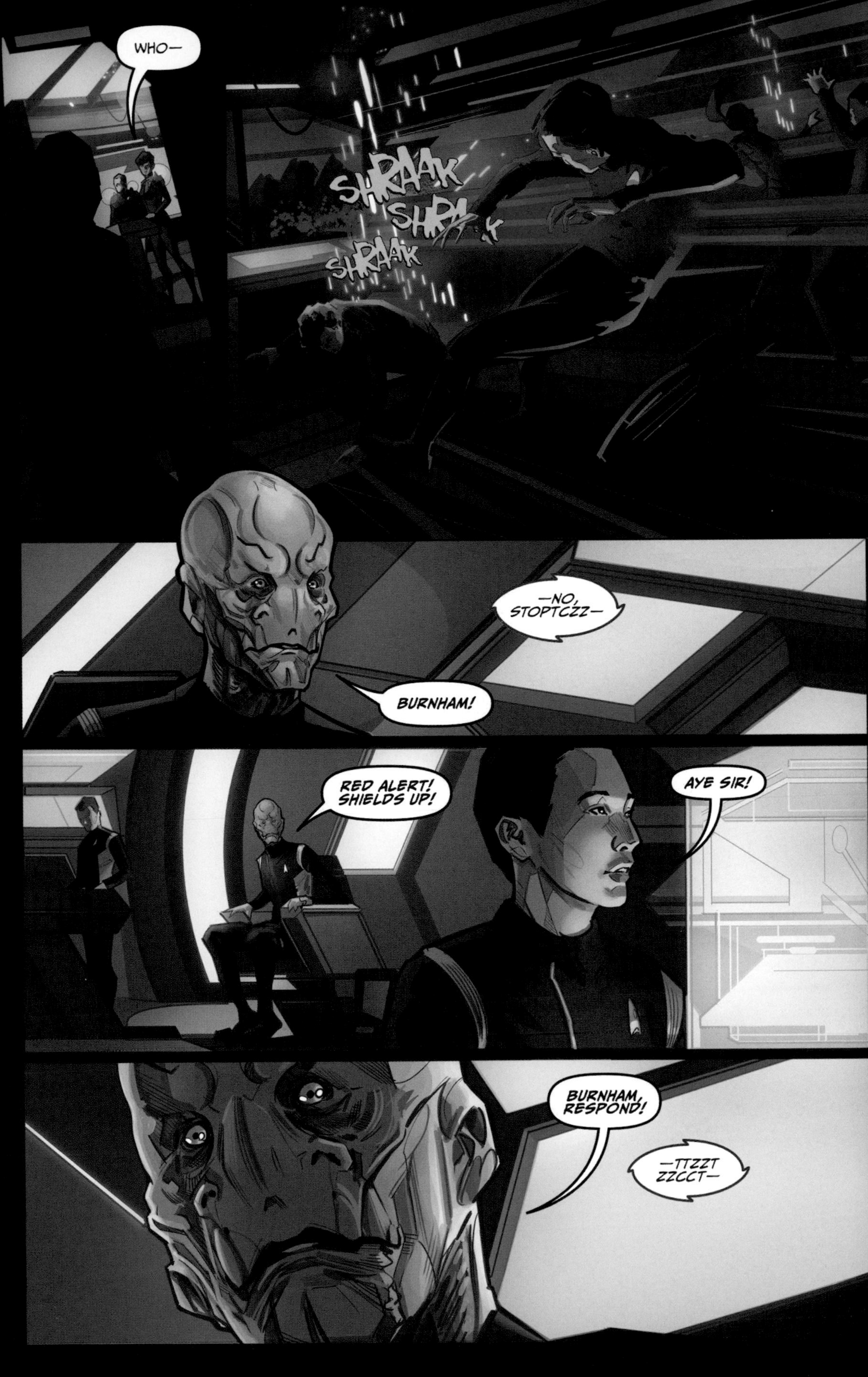
WHO—
SHRAAK
SHRAAK
SHRAAK
—NO, STOPTCZZ—
BURNHAM!
RED ALERT! SHIELDS UP!
AYE SIR!
BURNHAM, RESPOND!
—TTZZT ZZCCT—

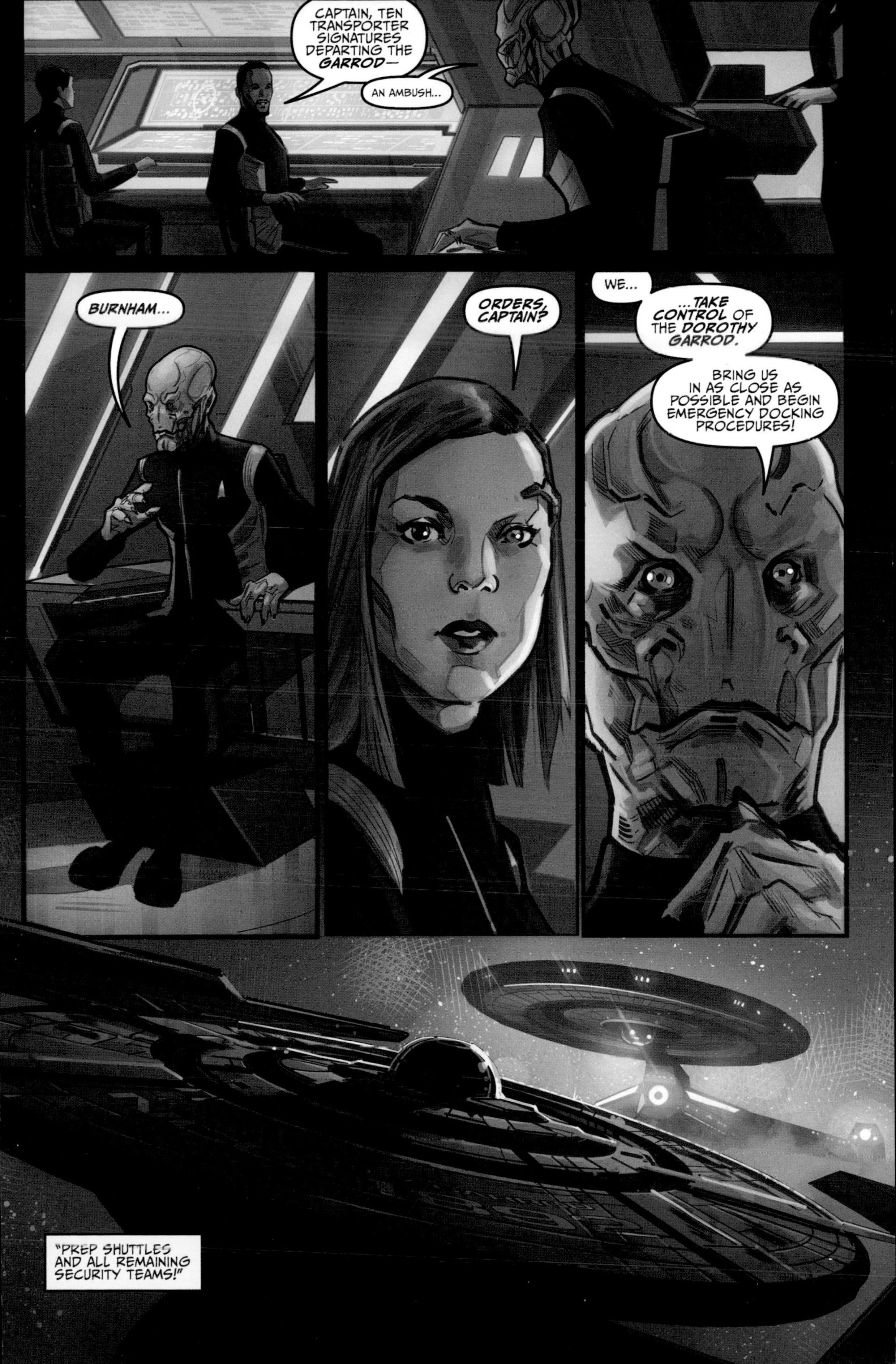
CAPTAIN, TEN TRANSPORTER SIGNATURES DEPARTING THE GARROD—
AN AMBUSH...
BURNHAM...
ORDERS, CAPTAIN?
WE...
...TAKE CONTROL OF THE DOROTHY GARROD.
BRING US IN AS CLOSE AS POSSIBLE AND BEGIN EMERGENCY DOCKING PROCEDURES!
"PREP SHUTTLES AND ALL REMAINING SECURITY TEAMS!"

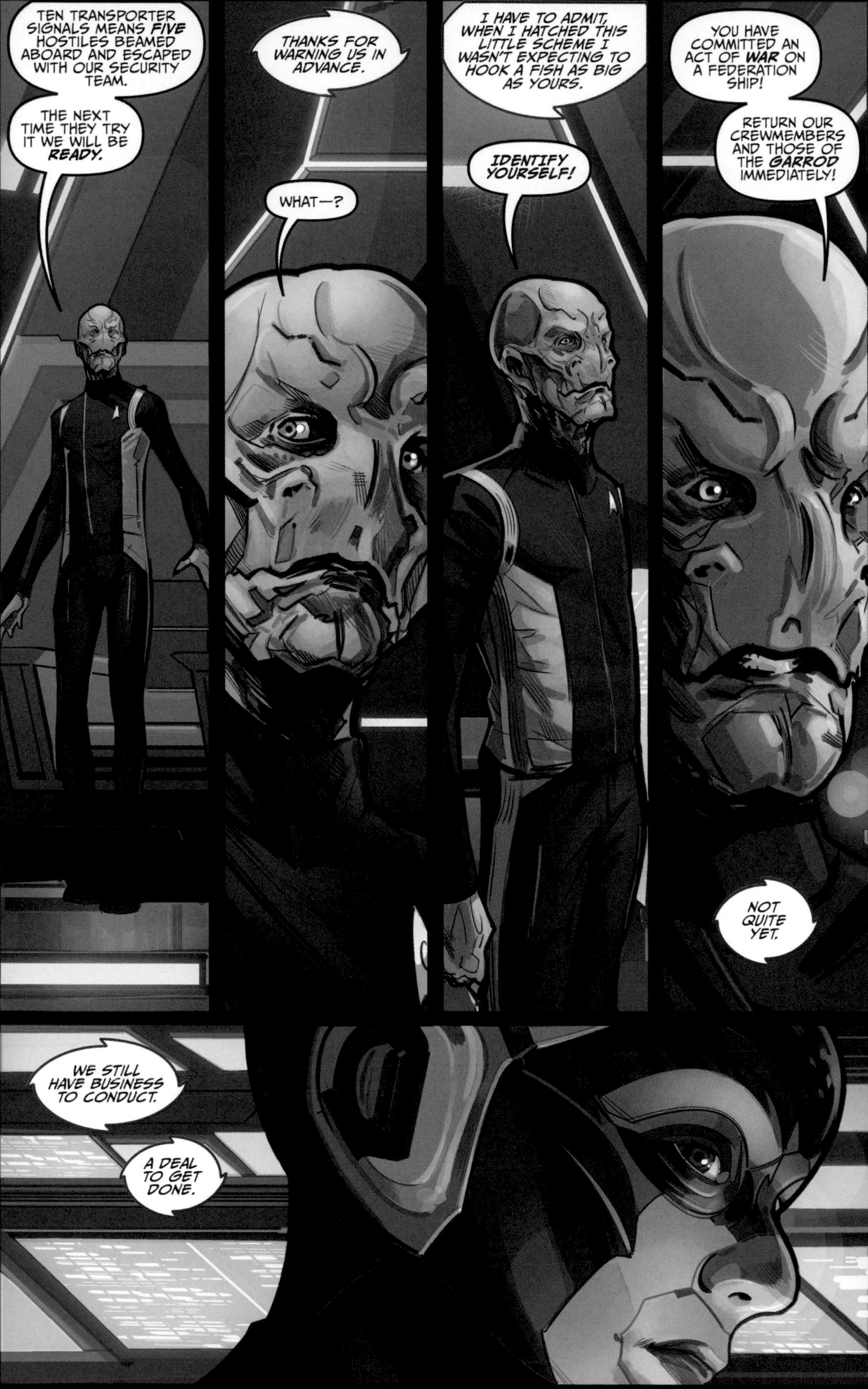

TEN TRANSPORTER SIGNALS MEANS FIVE HOSTILES BEAMED ABOARD AND ESCAPED WITH OUR SECURITY TEAM.
THE NEXT TIME THEY TRY IT WE WILL BE READY.
THANKS FOR WARNING US IN ADVANCE.
WHAT—?
I HAVE TO ADMIT, WHEN I HATCHED THIS LITTLE SCHEME I WASN'T EXPECTING TO HOOK A FISH AS BIG AS YOURS.
IDENTIFY YOURSELF!
YOU HAVE COMMITTED AN ACT OF WAR ON A FEDERATION SHIP!
RETURN OUR CREWMEMBERS AND THOSE OF THE GARROD IMMEDIATELY!
NOT QUITE YET.
WE STILL HAVE BUSINESS TO CONDUCT.
A DEAL TO GET DONE.

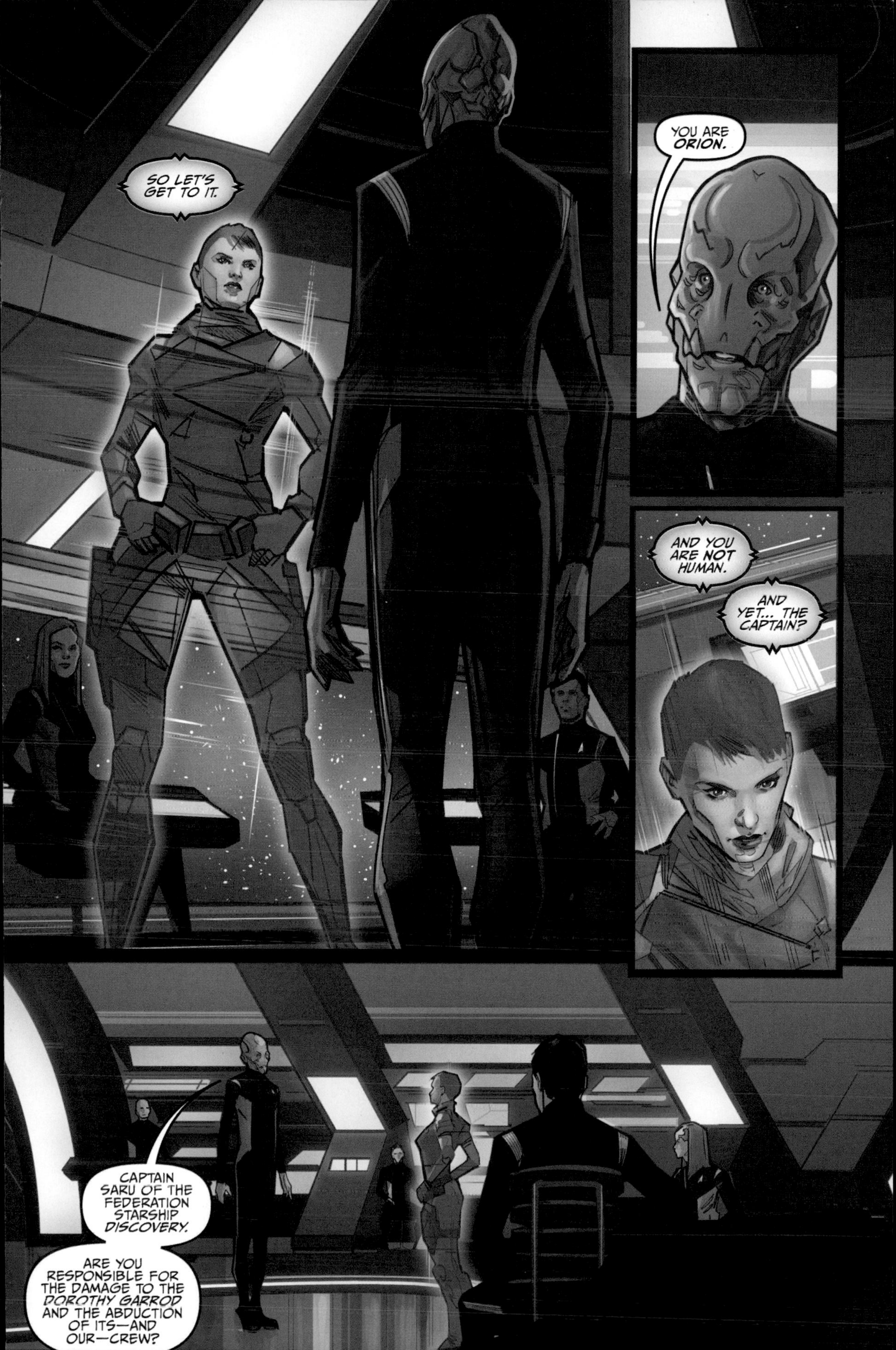

SO LET'S GET TO IT.
YOU ARE ORION.
AND YOU ARE NOT HUMAN.
AND YET... THE CAPTAIN?
CAPTAIN SARU OF THE FEDERATION STARSHIP DISCOVERY.
ARE YOU RESPONSIBLE FOR THE DAMAGE TO THE DOROTHY GARROD AND THE ABDUCTION OF ITS—AND OUR—CREW?

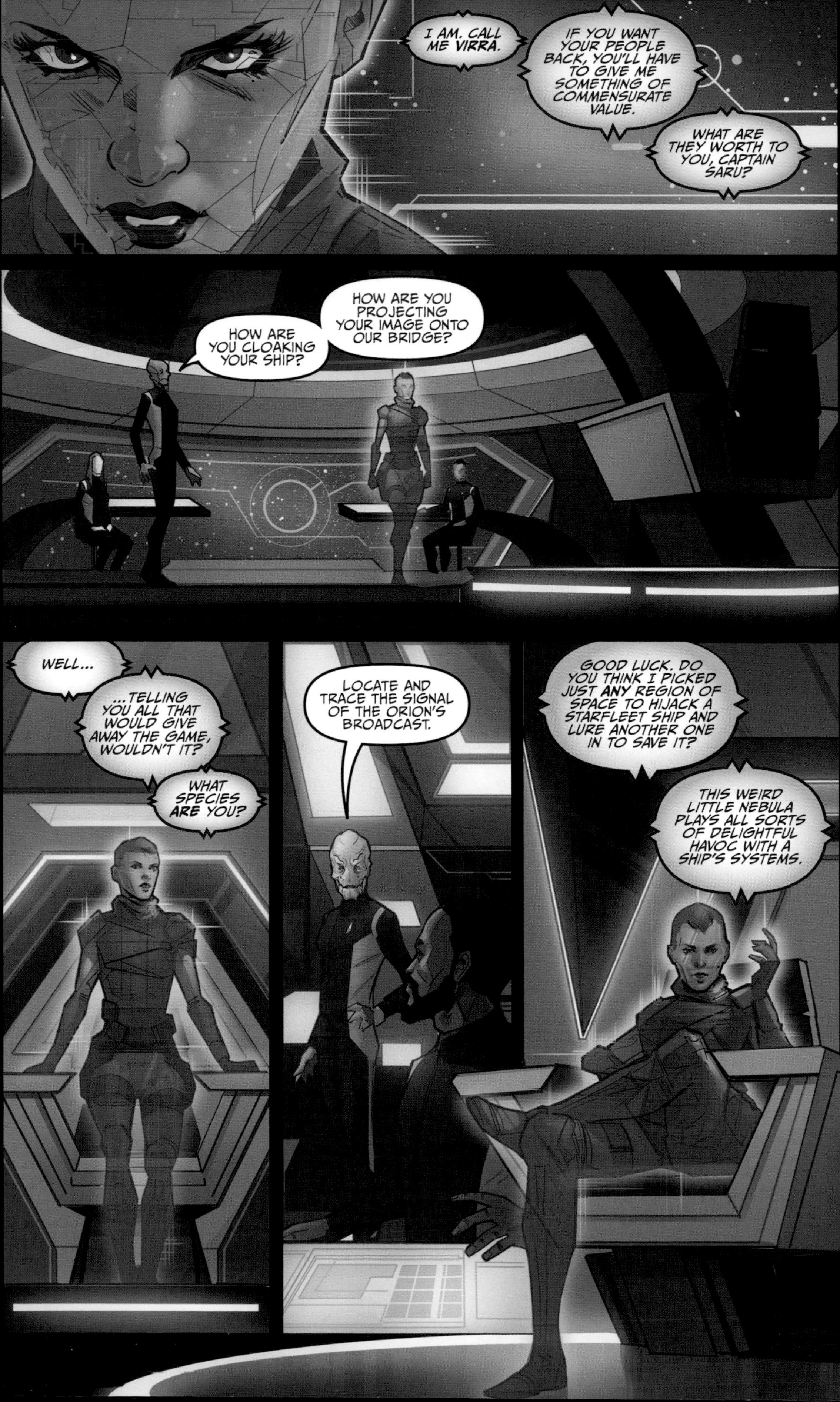
I AM. CALL ME VIRRA.
IF YOU WANT YOUR PEOPLE BACK, YOU'LL HAVE TO GIVE ME SOMETHING OF COMMENSURATE VALUE.
WHAT ARE THEY WORTH TO YOU, CAPTAIN SARU?
HOW ARE YOU CLOAKING YOUR SHIP?
HOW ARE YOU PROJECTING YOUR IMAGE ONTO OUR BRIDGE?
WELL...
...TELLING YOU ALL THAT WOULD GIVE AWAY THE GAME, WOULDN'T IT?
WHAT SPECIES ARE YOU?
LOCATE AND TRACE THE SIGNAL OF THE ORION'S BROADCAST.
GOOD LUCK. DO YOU THINK I PICKED JUST ANY REGION OF SPACE TO HIJACK A STARFLEET SHIP AND LURE ANOTHER ONE IN TO SAVE IT?
THIS WEIRD LITTLE NEBULA PLAYS ALL SORTS OF DELIGHTFUL HAVOC WITH A SHIP'S SYSTEMS.

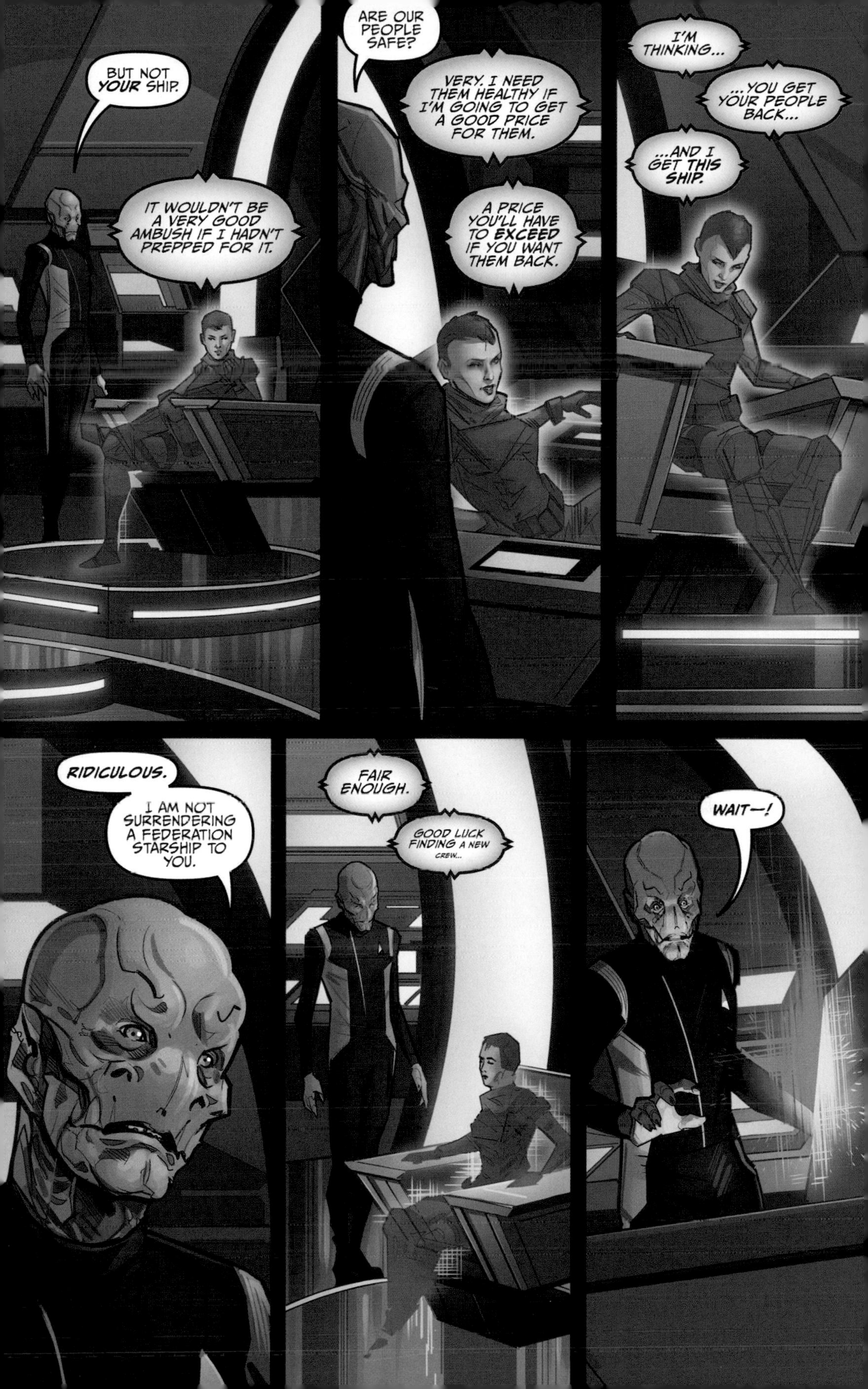
BUT NOT YOUR SHIP.
IT WOULDN'T BE A VERY GOOD AMBUSH IF I HADN'T PREPPED FOR IT.
ARE OUR PEOPLE SAFE?
VERY. I NEED THEM HEALTHY IF I'M GOING TO GET A GOOD PRICE FOR THEM.
A PRICE YOU'LL HAVE TO EXCEED IF YOU WANT THEM BACK.
I'M THINKING...
...YOU GET YOUR PEOPLE BACK...
...AND I GET THIS SHIP.
RIDICULOUS.
I AM NOT SURRENDERING A FEDERATION STARSHIP TO YOU.
FAIR ENOUGH.
GOOD LUCK FINDING A NEW CREW...
WAIT—!

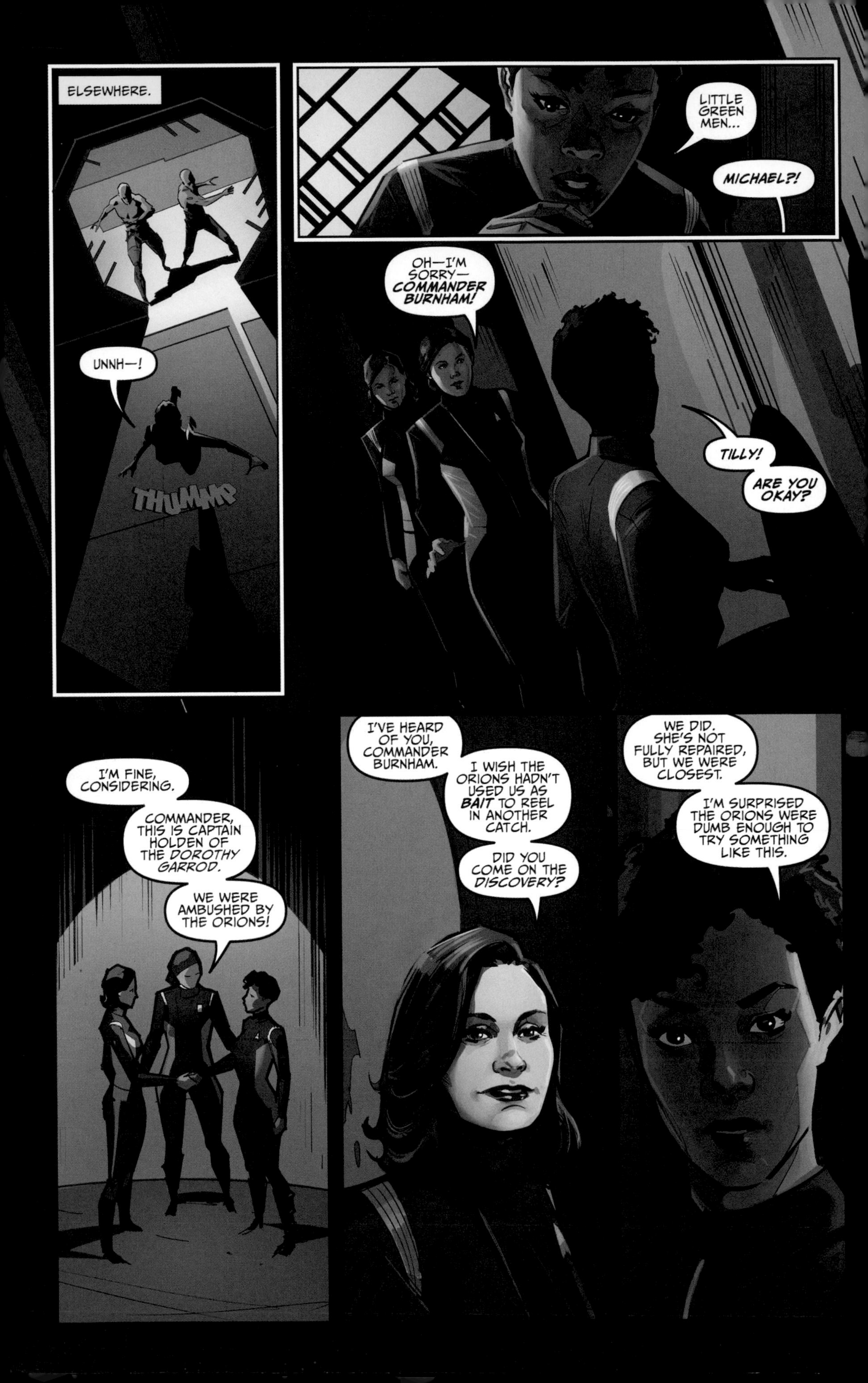
ELSEWHERE.
UNNH—!
THUMMP
LITTLE GREEN MEN...
MICHAEL?!
OH—I'M SORRY— COMMANDER BURNHAM!
TILLY!
ARE YOU OKAY?
I'M FINE, CONSIDERING.
COMMANDER, THIS IS CAPTAIN HOLDEN OF THE DOROTHY GARROD.
WE WERE AMBUSHED BY THE ORIONS!
I'VE HEARD OF YOU, COMMANDER BURNHAM.
I WISH THE ORIONS HADN'T USED US AS BAIT TO REEL IN ANOTHER CATCH.
DID YOU COME ON THE DISCOVERY?
WE DID. SHE'S NOT FULLY REPAIRED, BUT WE WERE CLOSEST.
I'M SURPRISED THE ORIONS WERE DUMB ENOUGH TO TRY SOMETHING LIKE THIS.

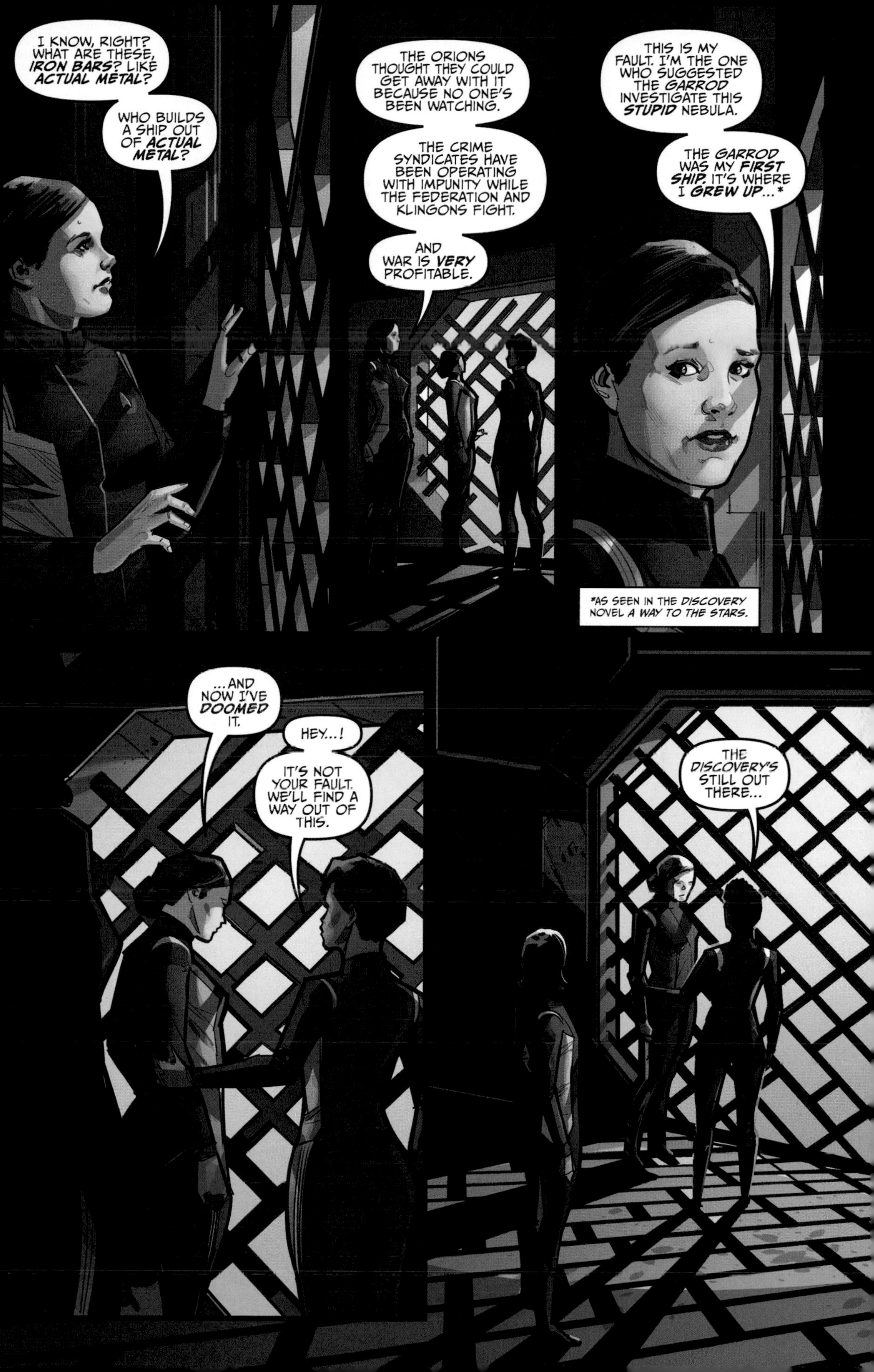
I KNOW, RIGHT? WHAT ARE THESE, *IRON BARS*? LIKE *ACTUAL METAL*?
WHO BUILDS A SHIP OUT OF *ACTUAL METAL*?
THE ORIONS THOUGHT THEY COULD GET AWAY WITH IT BECAUSE NO ONE'S BEEN WATCHING.
THE CRIME SYNDICATES HAVE BEEN OPERATING WITH IMPUNITY WHILE THE FEDERATION AND KLINGONS FIGHT.
AND WAR IS *VERY* PROFITABLE.
THIS IS MY FAULT. I'M THE ONE WHO SUGGESTED THE *GARROD* INVESTIGATE THIS *STUPID* NEBULA.
THE *GARROD* WAS MY *FIRST SHIP.* IT'S WHERE I *GREW UP*...*
*AS SEEN IN THE *DISCOVERY* NOVEL *A WAY TO THE STARS.*
...AND NOW I'VE *DOOMED* IT.
HEY...!
IT'S NOT YOUR FAULT. WE'LL FIND A WAY OUT OF THIS.
THE *DISCOVERY'S* STILL OUT THERE...

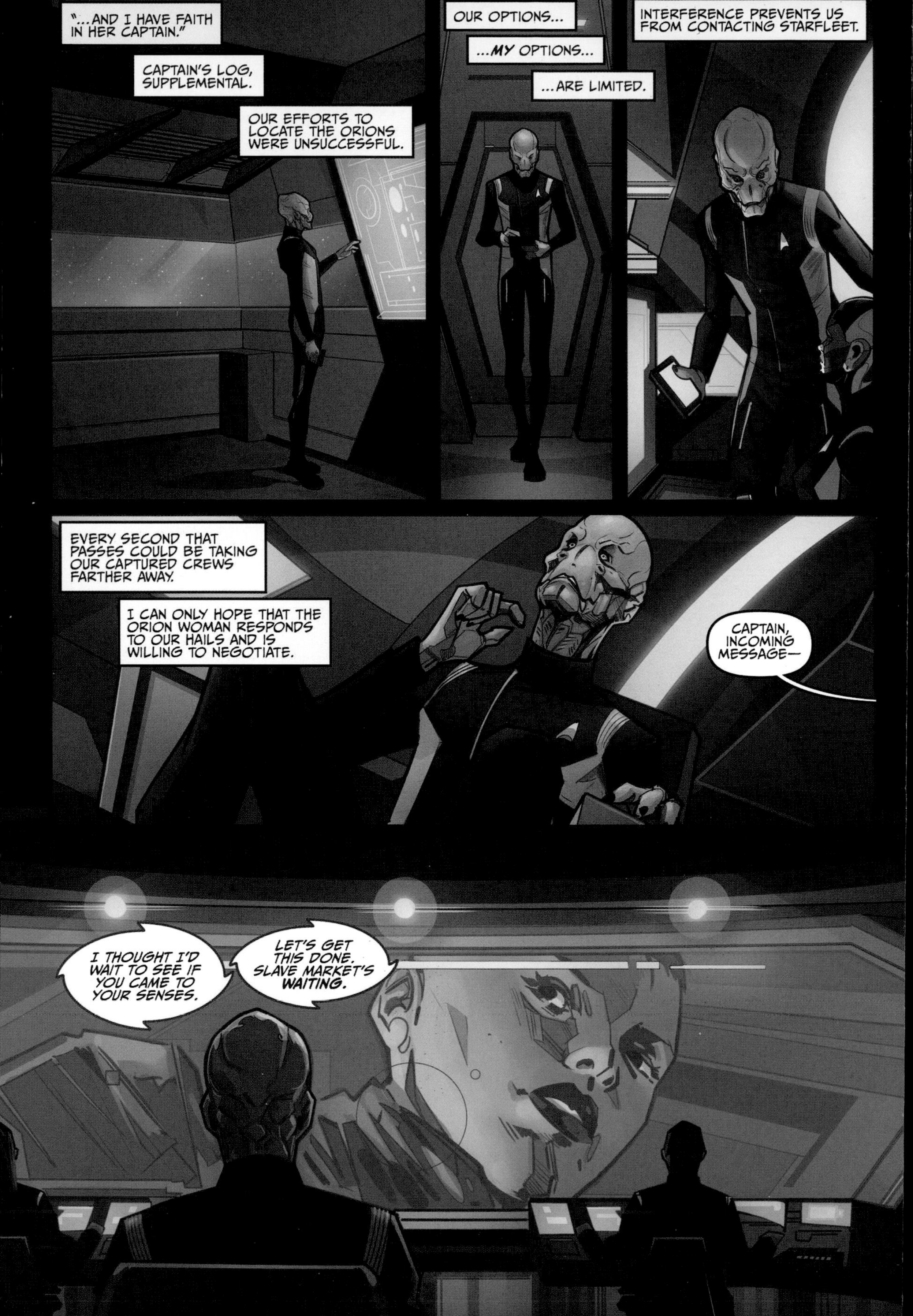
"...AND I HAVE FAITH IN HER CAPTAIN."
CAPTAIN'S LOG, SUPPLEMENTAL.
OUR EFFORTS TO LOCATE THE ORIONS WERE UNSUCCESSFUL.
OUR OPTIONS...
...*MY* OPTIONS...
...ARE LIMITED.
INTERFERENCE PREVENTS US FROM CONTACTING STARFLEET.
EVERY SECOND THAT PASSES COULD BE TAKING OUR CAPTURED CREWS FARTHER AWAY.
I CAN ONLY HOPE THAT THE ORION WOMAN RESPONDS TO OUR HAILS AND IS WILLING TO NEGOTIATE.
CAPTAIN, INCOMING MESSAGE—
I THOUGHT I'D WAIT TO SEE IF YOU CAME TO YOUR SENSES.
LET'S GET THIS DONE. SLAVE MARKET'S **WAITING.**

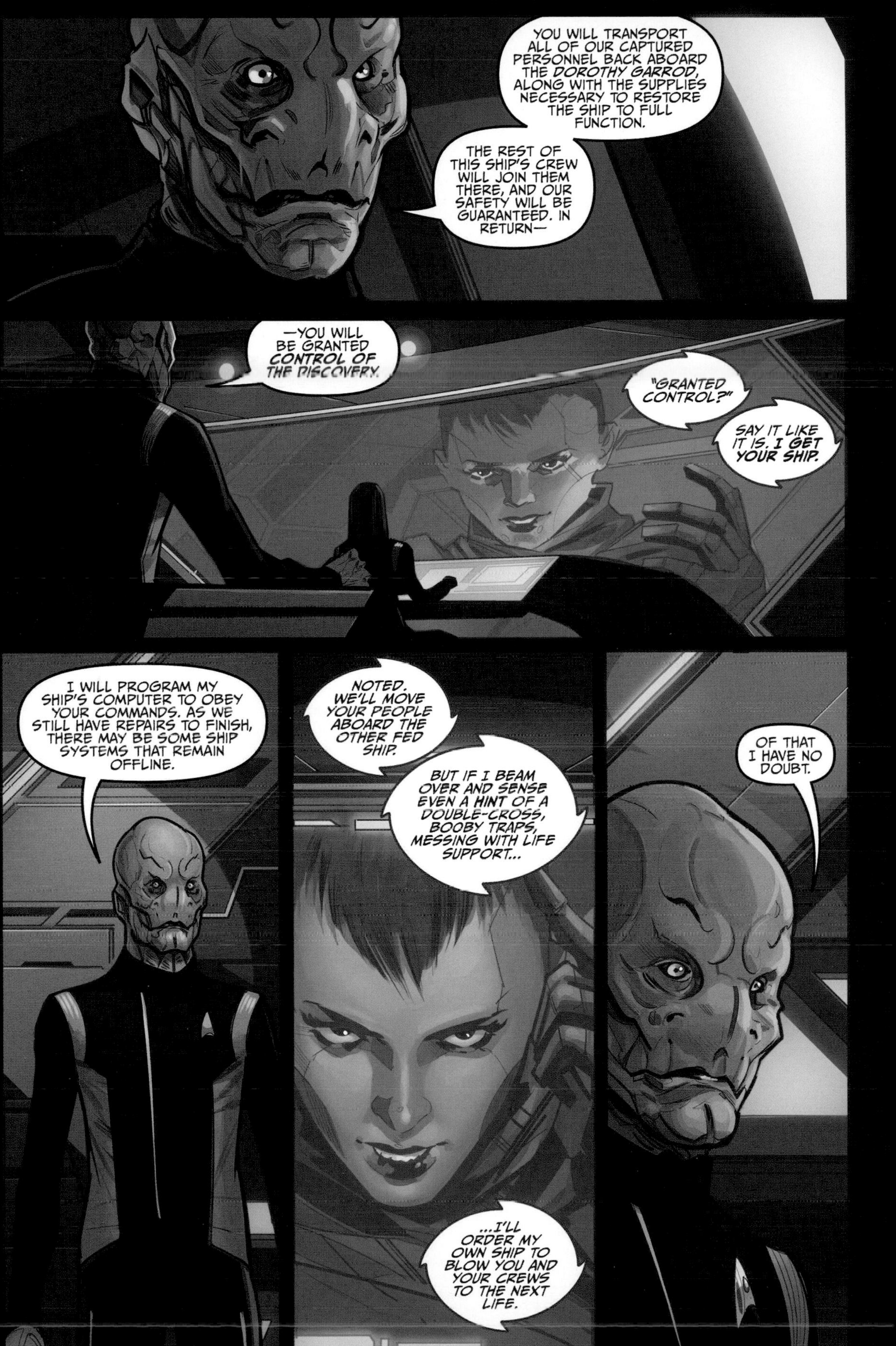
YOU WILL TRANSPORT ALL OF OUR CAPTURED PERSONNEL BACK ABOARD THE *DOROTHY GARROD*, ALONG WITH THE SUPPLIES NECESSARY TO RESTORE THE SHIP TO FULL FUNCTION.
THE REST OF THIS SHIP'S CREW WILL JOIN THEM THERE, AND OUR SAFETY WILL BE GUARANTEED. IN RETURN—
—YOU WILL BE GRANTED **CONTROL OF THE *DISCOVERY*.**
"GRANTED CONTROL?"
SAY IT LIKE IT IS. **I GET YOUR SHIP.**
I WILL PROGRAM MY SHIP'S COMPUTER TO OBEY YOUR COMMANDS. AS WE STILL HAVE REPAIRS TO FINISH, THERE MAY BE SOME SHIP SYSTEMS THAT REMAIN OFFLINE.
NOTED. WE'LL MOVE YOUR PEOPLE ABOARD THE OTHER FED SHIP.
BUT IF I BEAM OVER AND SENSE EVEN A **HINT** OF A DOUBLE-CROSS, BOOBY TRAPS, MESSING WITH LIFE SUPPORT...
...I'LL ORDER MY OWN SHIP TO BLOW YOU AND YOUR CREWS TO THE NEXT LIFE.
OF THAT I HAVE NO DOUBT.

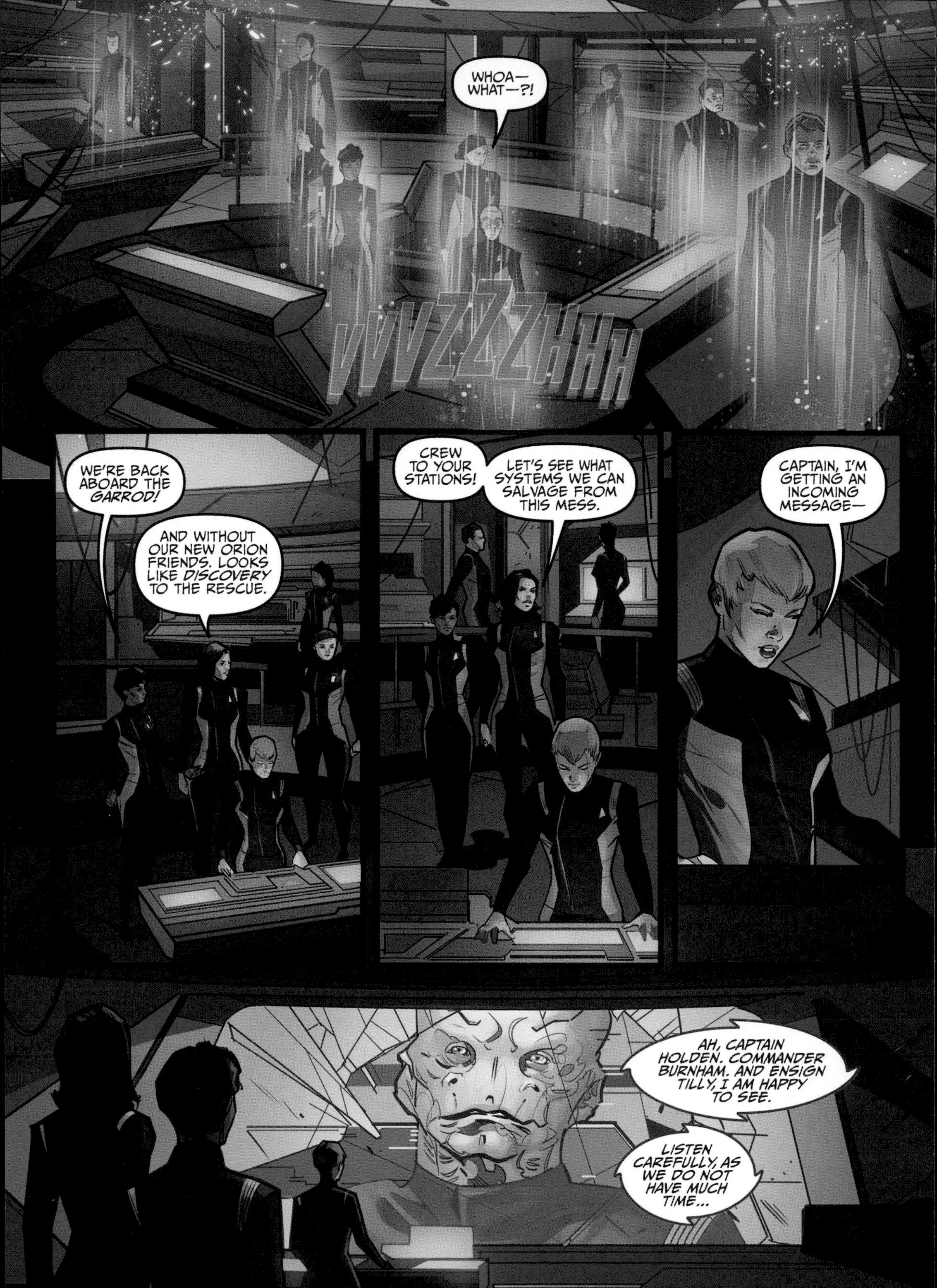
WHOA—
WHAT—?!
VVVZZZHHH
WE'RE BACK ABOARD THE *GARROD!*
AND WITHOUT OUR NEW ORION FRIENDS. LOOKS LIKE *DISCOVERY* TO THE RESCUE.
CREW TO YOUR STATIONS!
LET'S SEE WHAT SYSTEMS WE CAN SALVAGE FROM THIS MESS.
CAPTAIN, I'M GETTING AN INCOMING MESSAGE—
AH, CAPTAIN HOLDEN. COMMANDER BURNHAM. AND ENSIGN TILLY, I AM HAPPY TO SEE.
LISTEN CAREFULLY, AS WE DO NOT HAVE MUCH TIME...

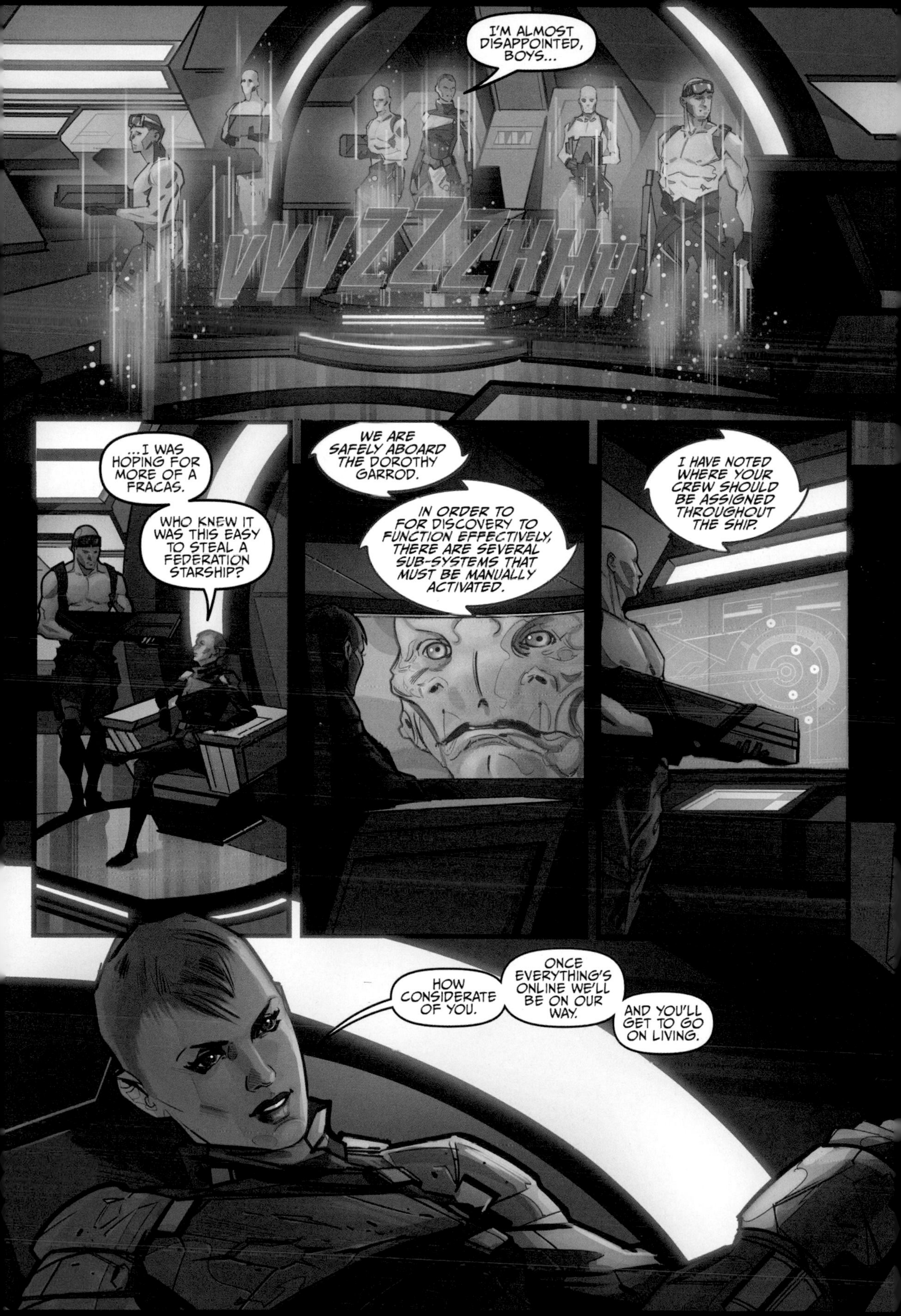
I'M ALMOST DISAPPOINTED, BOYS...
VVVZZZHHHH
...I WAS HOPING FOR MORE OF A FRACAS.
WHO KNEW IT WAS THIS EASY TO STEAL A FEDERATION STARSHIP?
WE ARE SAFELY ABOARD THE DOROTHY GARROD.
IN ORDER TO FOR DISCOVERY TO FUNCTION EFFECTIVELY, THERE ARE SEVERAL SUB-SYSTEMS THAT MUST BE MANUALLY ACTIVATED.
I HAVE NOTED WHERE YOUR CREW SHOULD BE ASSIGNED THROUGHOUT THE SHIP.
HOW CONSIDERATE OF YOU.
ONCE EVERYTHING'S ONLINE WE'LL BE ON OUR WAY.
AND YOU'LL GET TO GO ON LIVING.

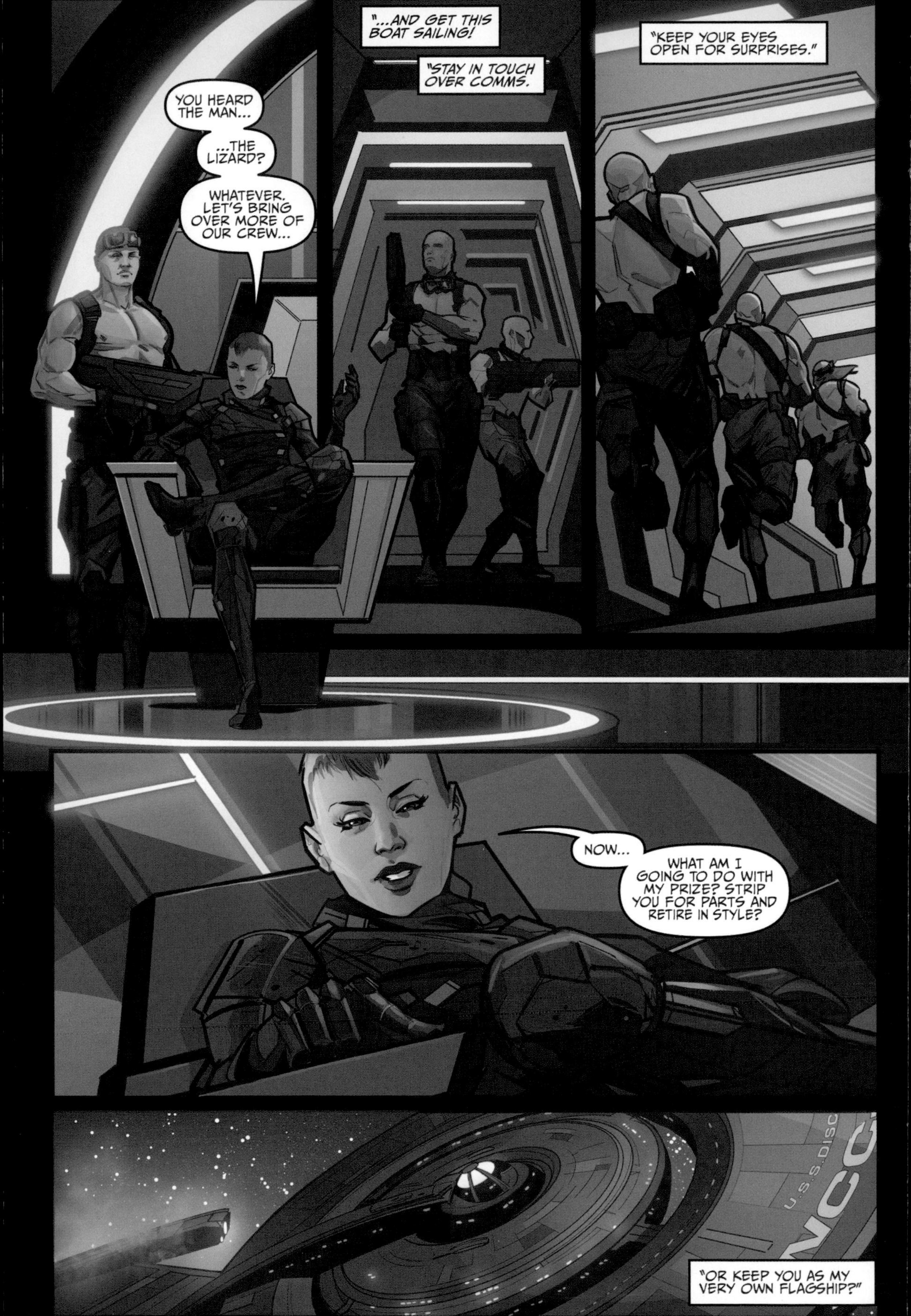
YOU HEARD THE MAN...
...THE LIZARD?
WHATEVER. LET'S BRING OVER MORE OF OUR CREW...
"...AND GET THIS BOAT SAILING!
"STAY IN TOUCH OVER COMMS.
"KEEP YOUR EYES OPEN FOR SURPRISES."
NOW...
WHAT AM I GOING TO DO WITH MY PRIZE? STRIP YOU FOR PARTS AND RETIRE IN STYLE?
U.S.S. DISC
NCC
"OR KEEP YOU AS MY VERY OWN FLAGSHIP?"

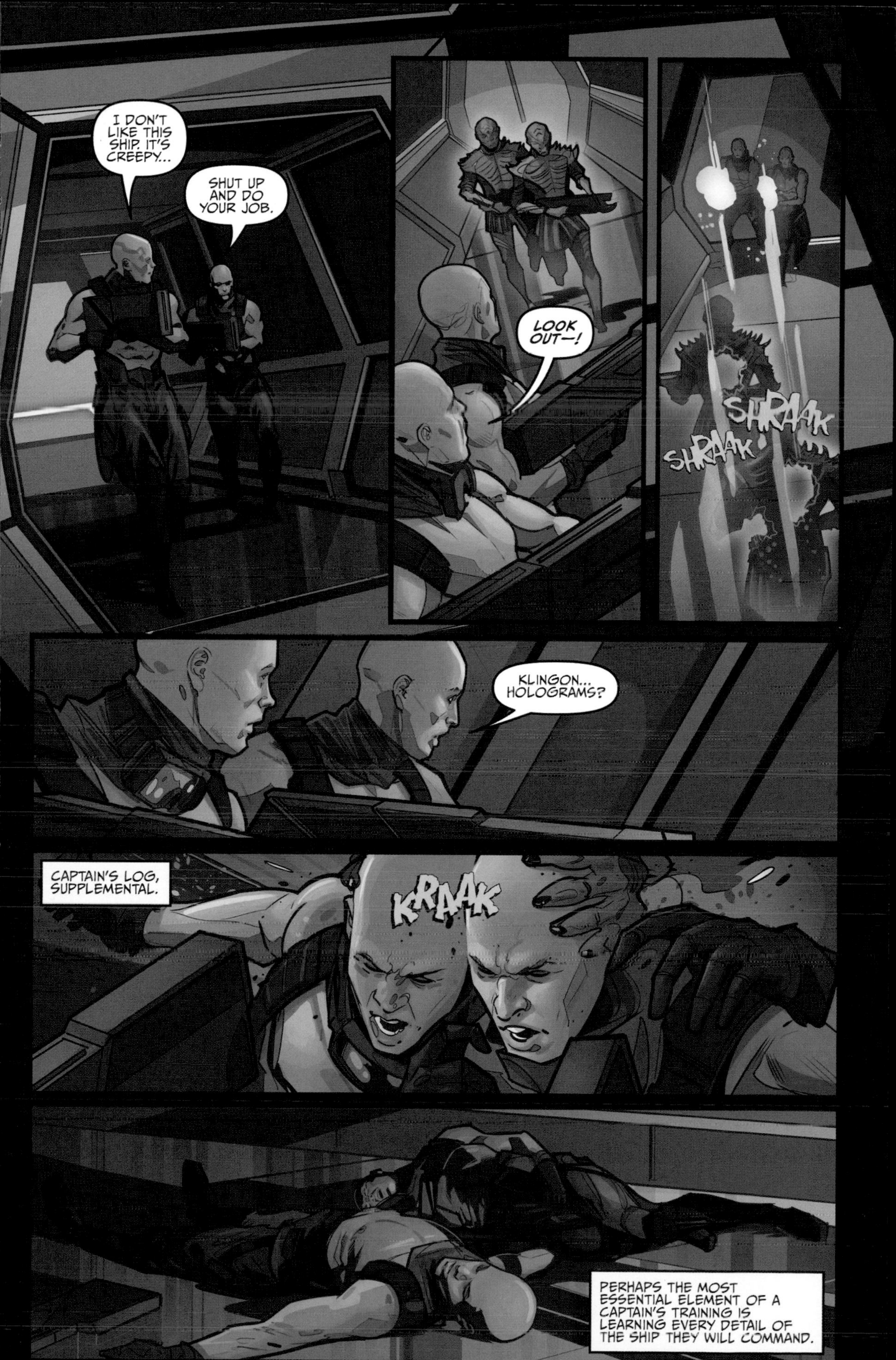
I DON'T LIKE THIS SHIP. IT'S CREEPY...
SHUT UP AND DO YOUR JOB.
LOOK OUT—!
SHRAAK
SHRAAK
KLINGON... HOLOGRAMS?
CAPTAIN'S LOG, SUPPLEMENTAL.
KRAAK
PERHAPS THE MOST ESSENTIAL ELEMENT OF A CAPTAIN'S TRAINING IS LEARNING EVERY DETAIL OF THE SHIP THEY WILL COMMAND.

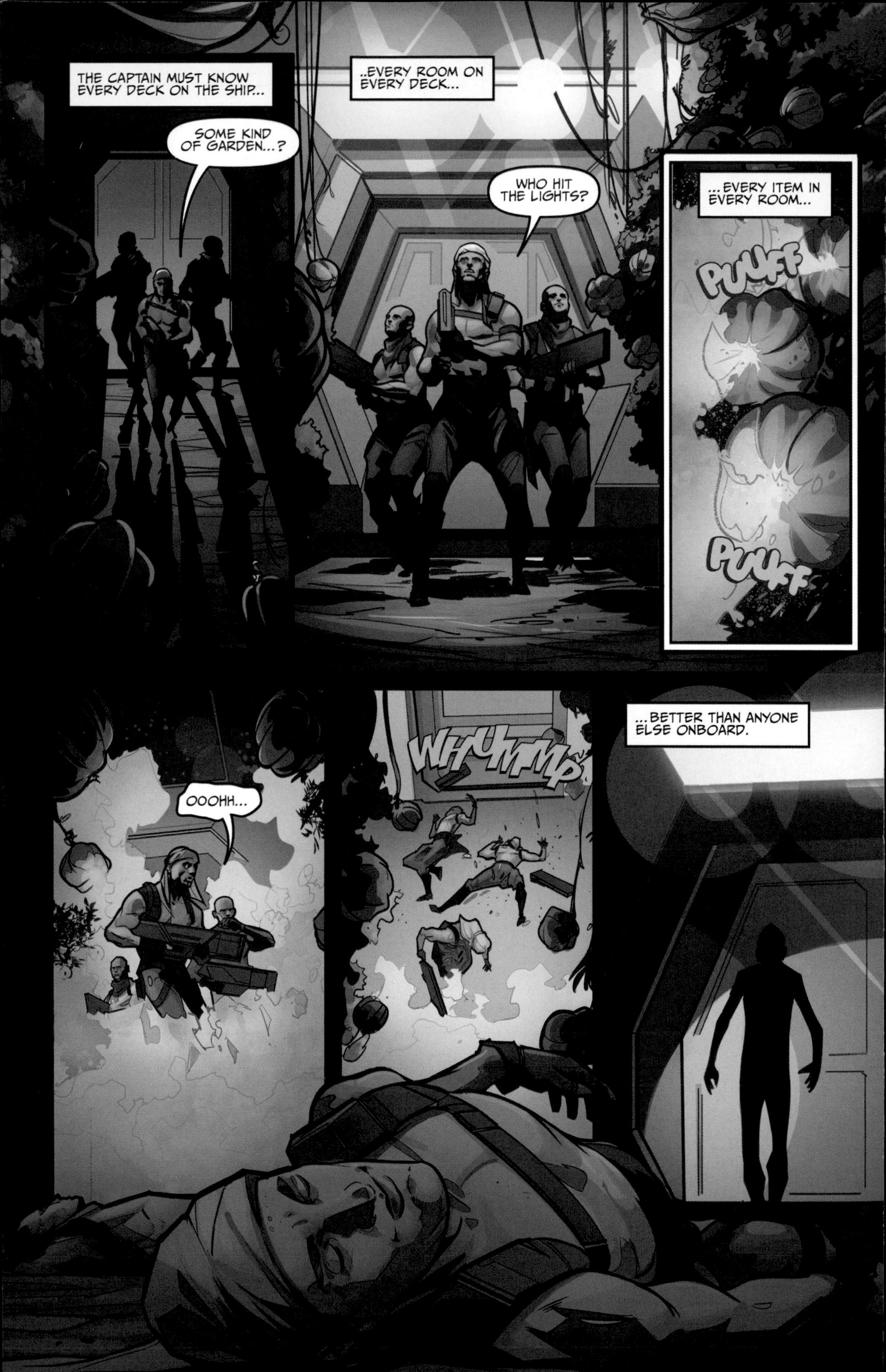
THE CAPTAIN MUST KNOW EVERY DECK ON THE SHIP...
SOME KIND OF GARDEN...?
..EVERY ROOM ON EVERY DECK...
WHO HIT THE LIGHTS?
...EVERY ITEM IN EVERY ROOM...
PUUFF
PUUFF
OOOHH...
WHUMMP
...BETTER THAN ANYONE ELSE ONBOARD.

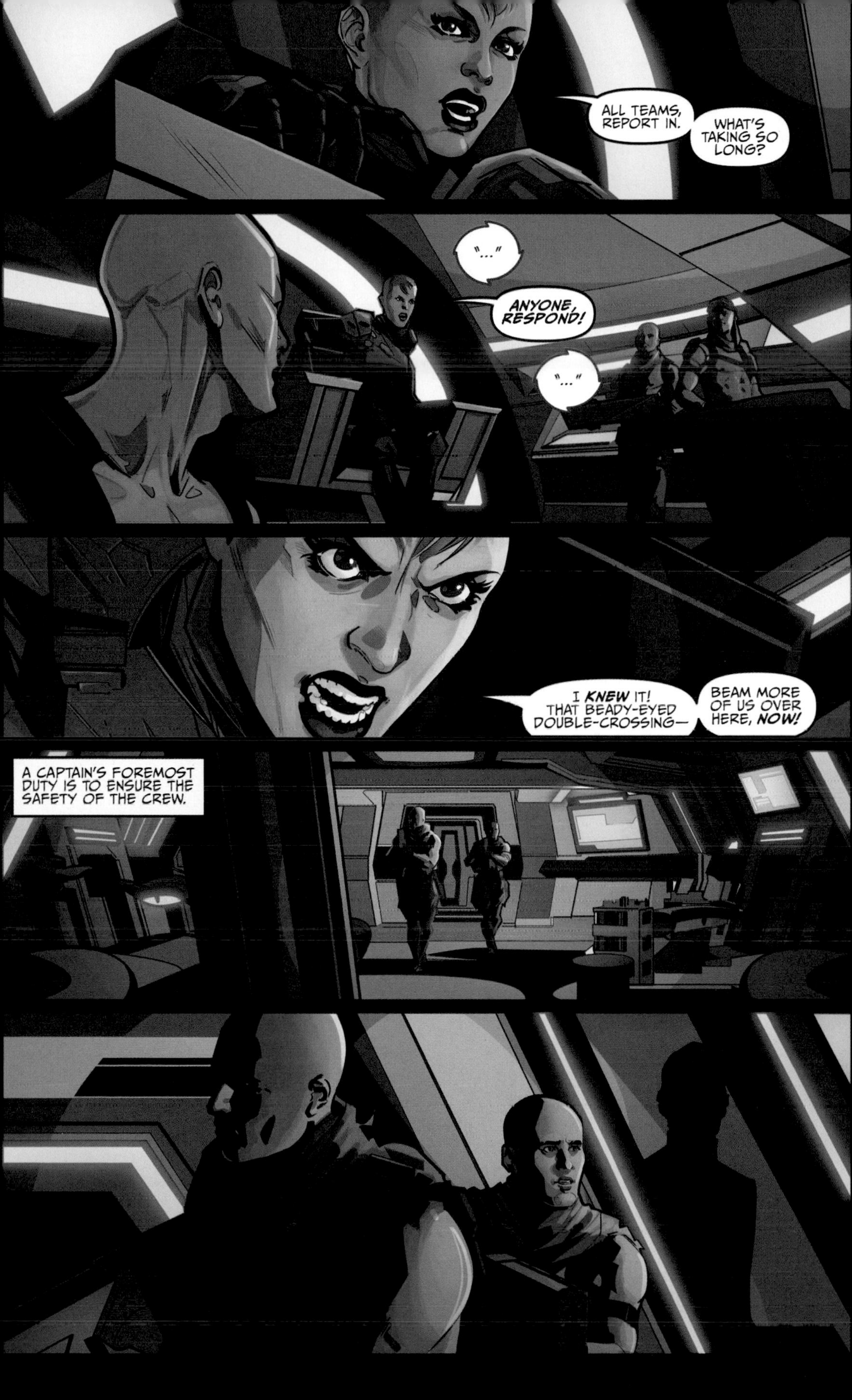
ALL TEAMS, REPORT IN.
WHAT'S TAKING SO LONG?
"..."
ANYONE, RESPOND!
"..."
I KNEW IT! THAT BEADY-EYED DOUBLE-CROSSING—
BEAM MORE OF US OVER HERE, NOW!
A CAPTAIN'S FOREMOST DUTY IS TO ENSURE THE SAFETY OF THE CREW.

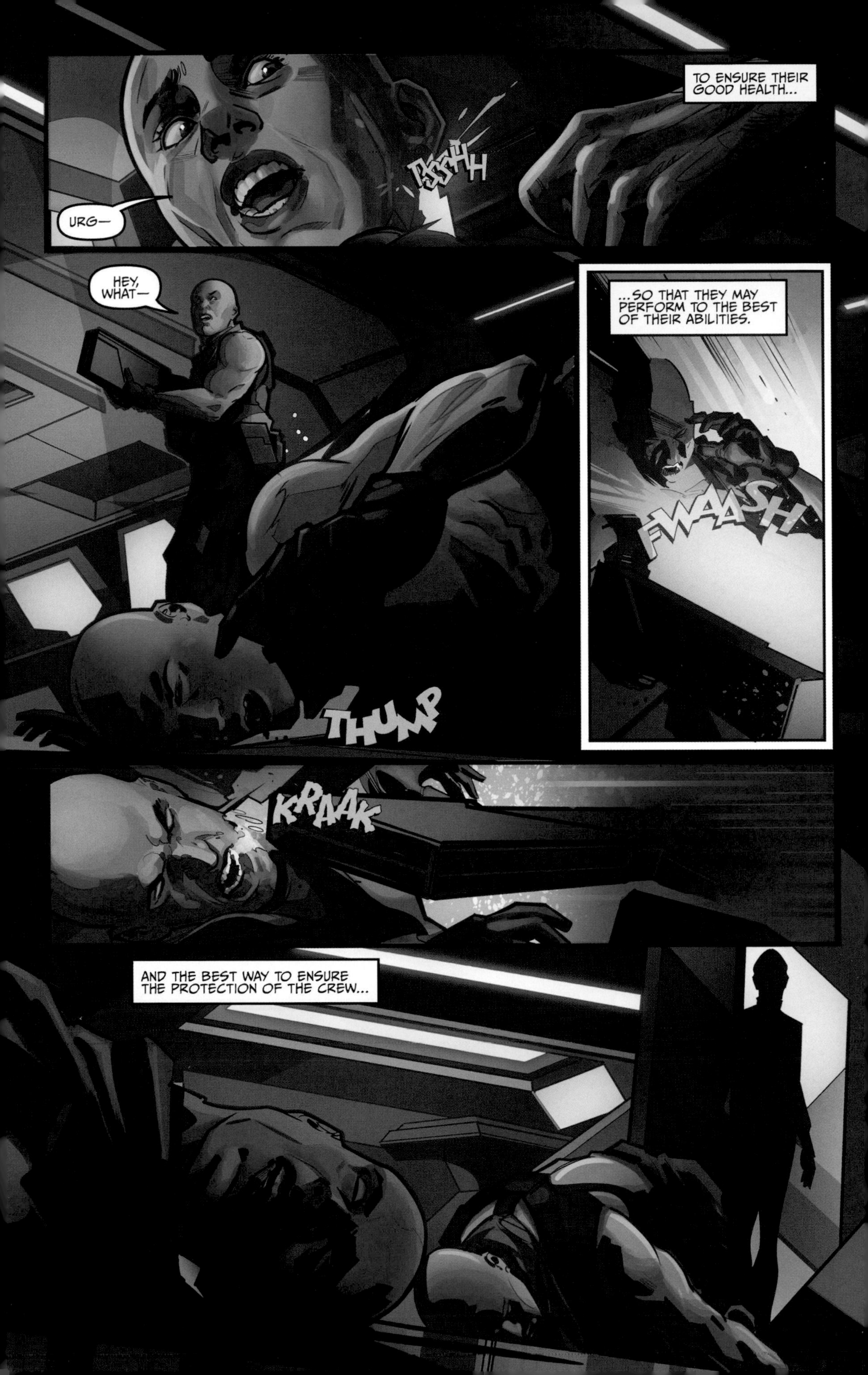
TO ENSURE THEIR GOOD HEALTH...
URG—
HEY, WHAT—
THUMP
...SO THAT THEY MAY PERFORM TO THE BEST OF THEIR ABILITIES.
FWAASH
KRAAK
AND THE BEST WAY TO ENSURE THE PROTECTION OF THE CREW...

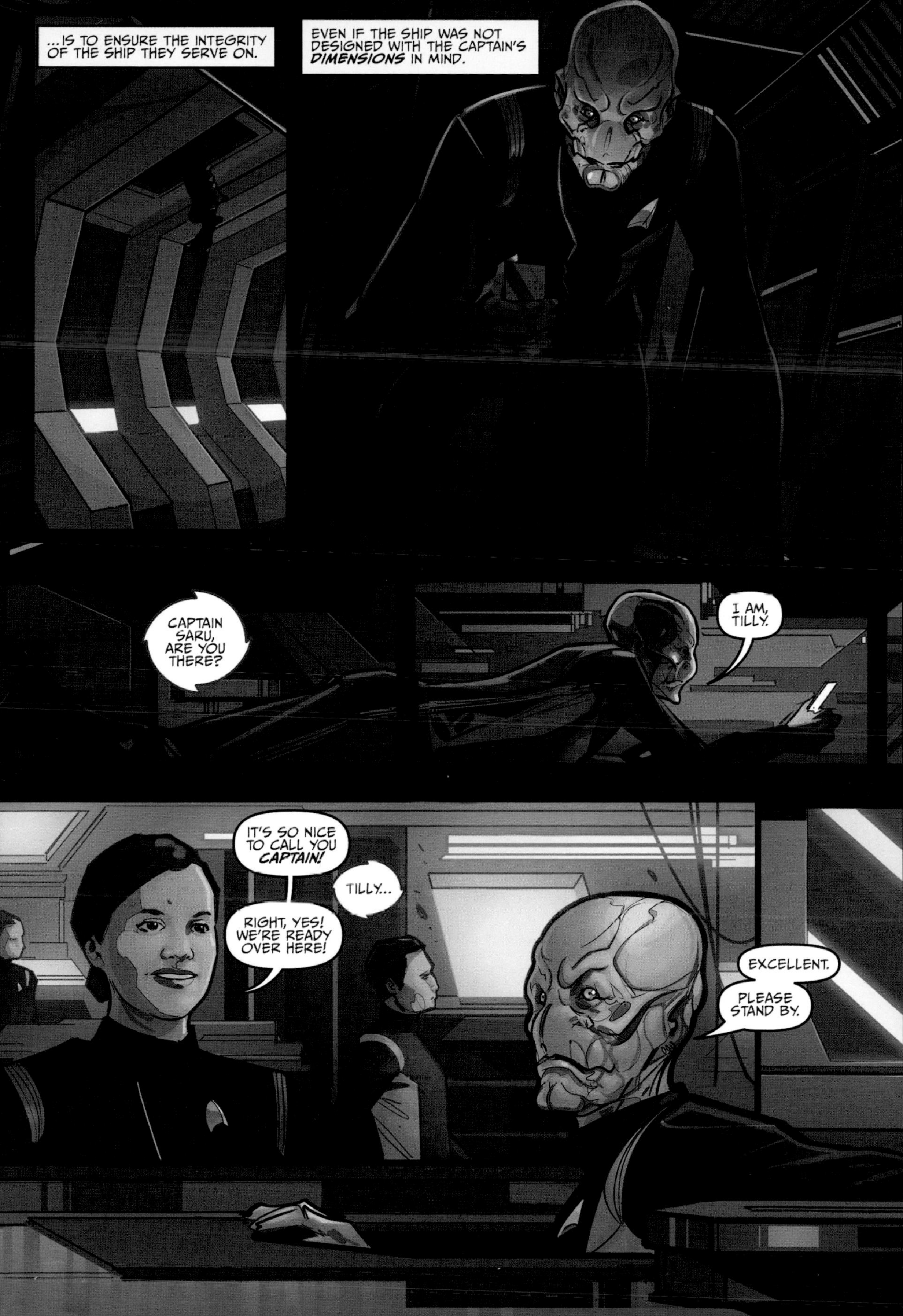
...IS TO ENSURE THE INTEGRITY OF THE SHIP THEY SERVE ON.
EVEN IF THE SHIP WAS NOT DESIGNED WITH THE CAPTAIN'S DIMENSIONS IN MIND.
CAPTAIN SARU, ARE YOU THERE?
I AM, TILLY.
IT'S SO NICE TO CALL YOU CAPTAIN!
TILLY...
RIGHT, YES! WE'RE READY OVER HERE!
EXCELLENT.
PLEASE STAND BY.

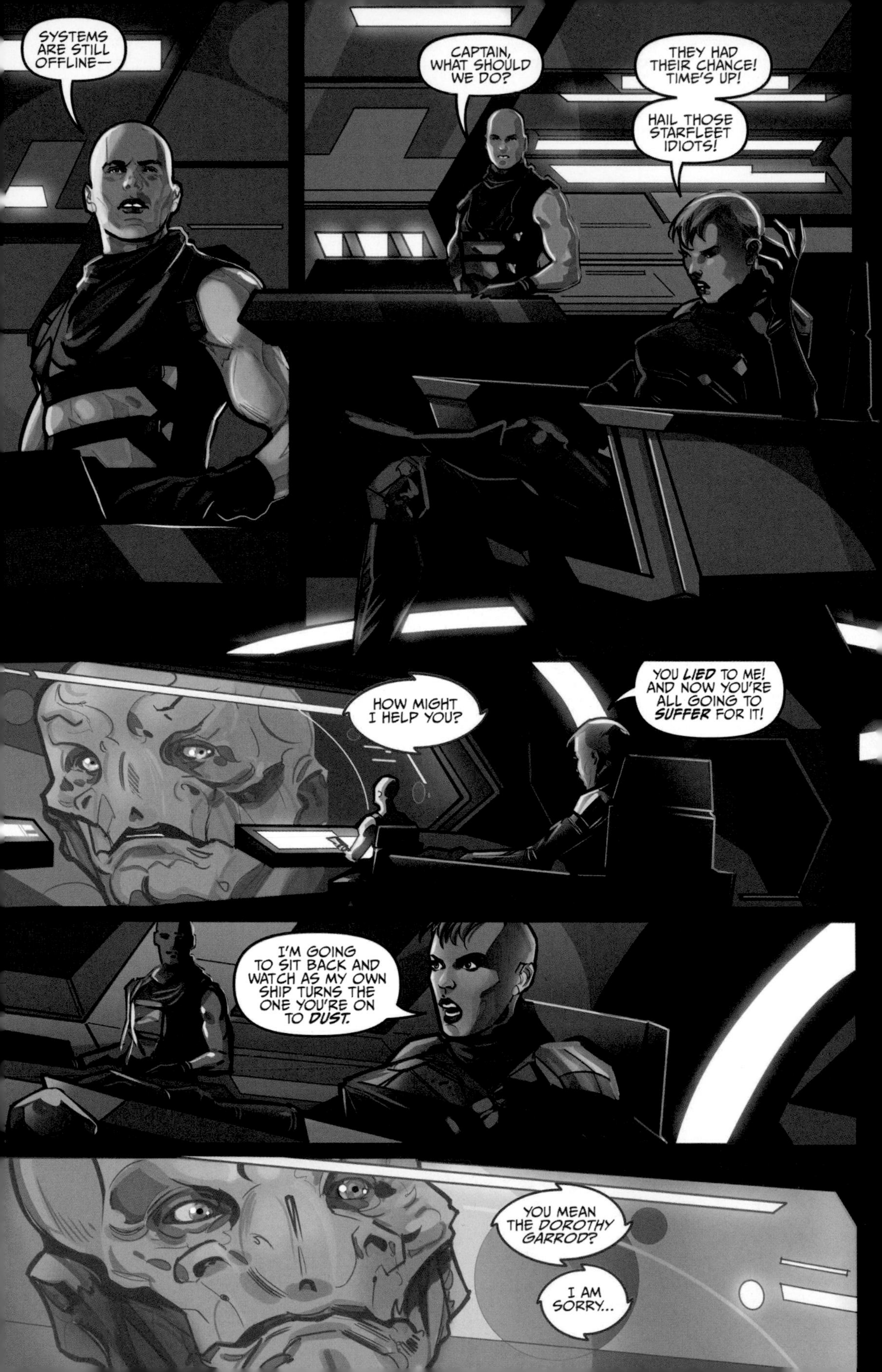
SYSTEMS ARE STILL OFFLINE—
CAPTAIN, WHAT SHOULD WE DO?
THEY HAD THEIR CHANCE! TIME'S UP!
HAIL THOSE STARFLEET IDIOTS!
HOW MIGHT I HELP YOU?
YOU *LIED* TO ME! AND NOW YOU'RE ALL GOING TO *SUFFER* FOR IT!
I'M GOING TO SIT BACK AND WATCH AS MY OWN SHIP TURNS THE ONE YOU'RE ON TO *DUST.*
YOU MEAN THE *DOROTHY GARROD*?
I AM SORRY...

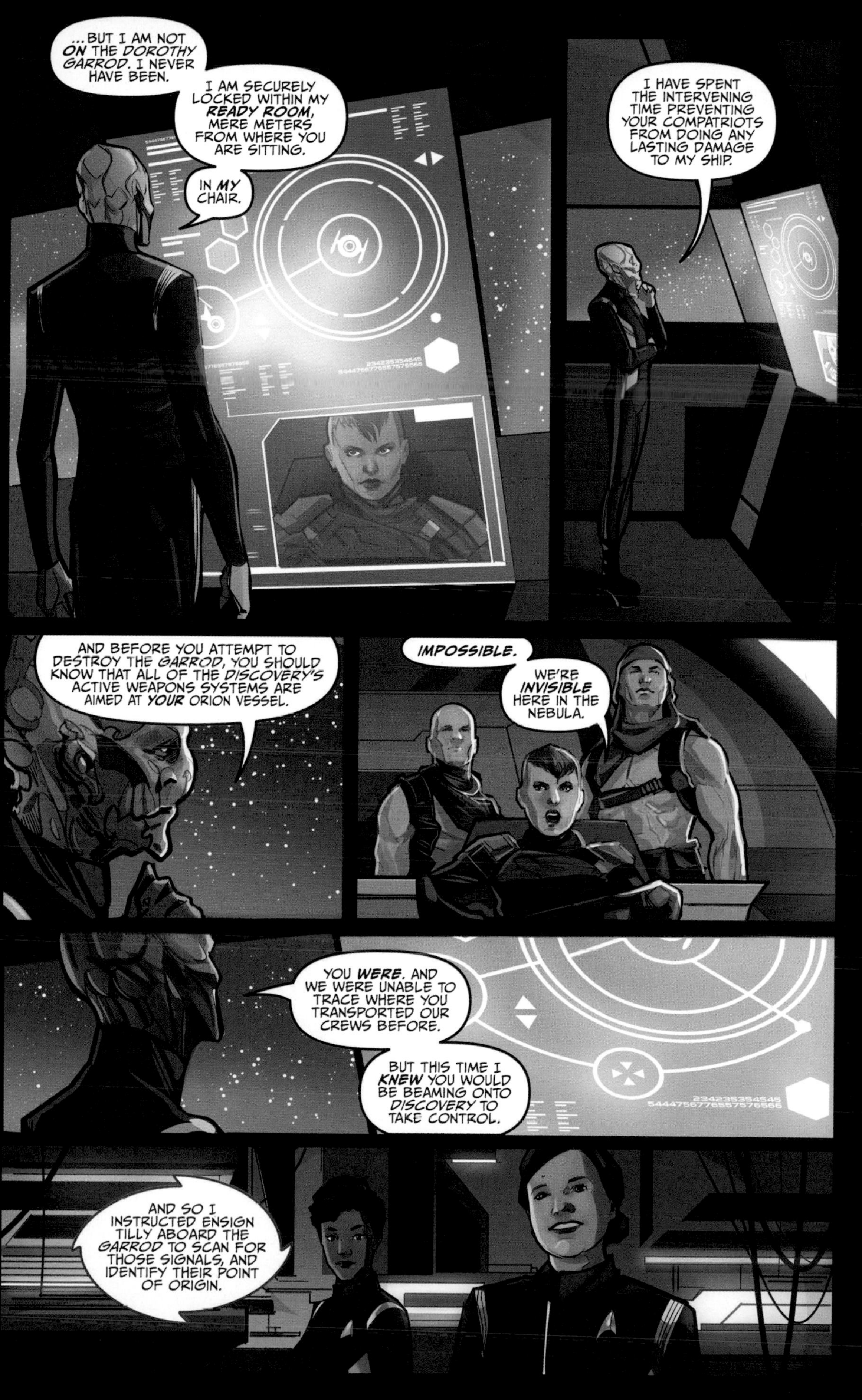
...BUT I AM NOT *ON* THE *DOROTHY GARROD*. I NEVER HAVE BEEN.
I AM SECURELY LOCKED WITHIN MY *READY ROOM*, MERE METERS FROM WHERE YOU ARE SITTING.
IN *MY* CHAIR.
I HAVE SPENT THE INTERVENING TIME PREVENTING YOUR COMPATRIOTS FROM DOING ANY LASTING DAMAGE TO MY SHIP.
AND BEFORE YOU ATTEMPT TO DESTROY THE *GARROD*, YOU SHOULD KNOW THAT ALL OF THE *DISCOVERY'S* ACTIVE WEAPONS SYSTEMS ARE AIMED AT *YOUR* ORION VESSEL.
IMPOSSIBLE.
WE'RE *INVISIBLE* HERE IN THE NEBULA.
YOU *WERE*. AND WE WERE UNABLE TO TRACE WHERE YOU TRANSPORTED OUR CREWS BEFORE.
BUT THIS TIME I *KNEW* YOU WOULD BE BEAMING ONTO *DISCOVERY* TO TAKE CONTROL.
AND SO I INSTRUCTED ENSIGN TILLY ABOARD THE *GARROD* TO SCAN FOR THOSE SIGNALS, AND IDENTIFY THEIR POINT OF ORIGIN.

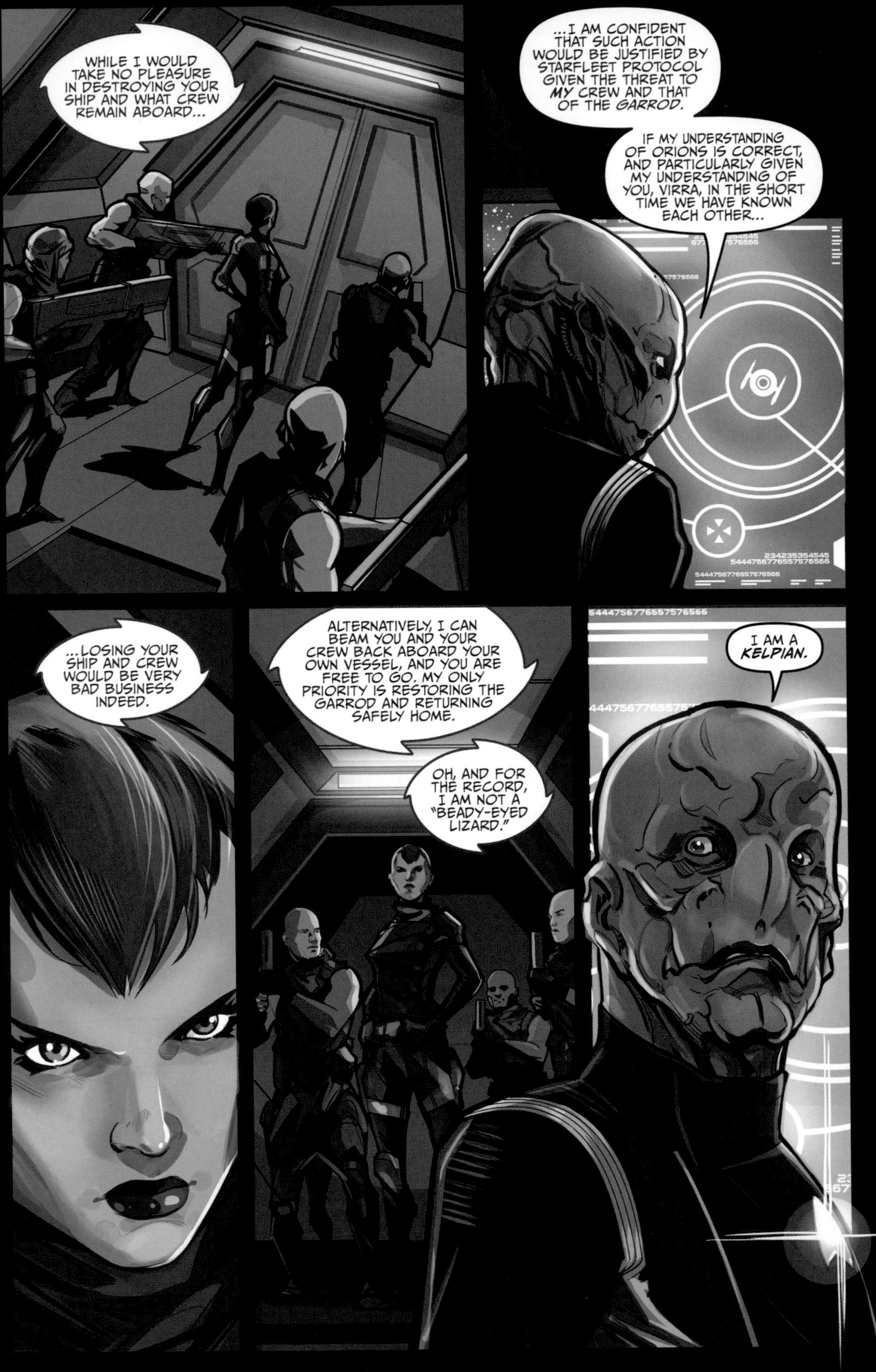
WHILE I WOULD TAKE NO PLEASURE IN DESTROYING YOUR SHIP AND WHAT CREW REMAIN ABOARD...
...I AM CONFIDENT THAT SUCH ACTION WOULD BE JUSTIFIED BY STARFLEET PROTOCOL GIVEN THE THREAT TO MY CREW AND THAT OF THE GARROD.
IF MY UNDERSTANDING OF ORIONS IS CORRECT, AND PARTICULARLY GIVEN MY UNDERSTANDING OF YOU, VIRRA, IN THE SHORT TIME WE HAVE KNOWN EACH OTHER...
...LOSING YOUR SHIP AND CREW WOULD BE VERY BAD BUSINESS INDEED.
ALTERNATIVELY, I CAN BEAM YOU AND YOUR CREW BACK ABOARD YOUR OWN VESSEL, AND YOU ARE FREE TO GO. MY ONLY PRIORITY IS RESTORING THE GARROD AND RETURNING SAFELY HOME.
OH, AND FOR THE RECORD, I AM NOT A "BEADY-EYED LIZARD."
I AM A KELPIAN.

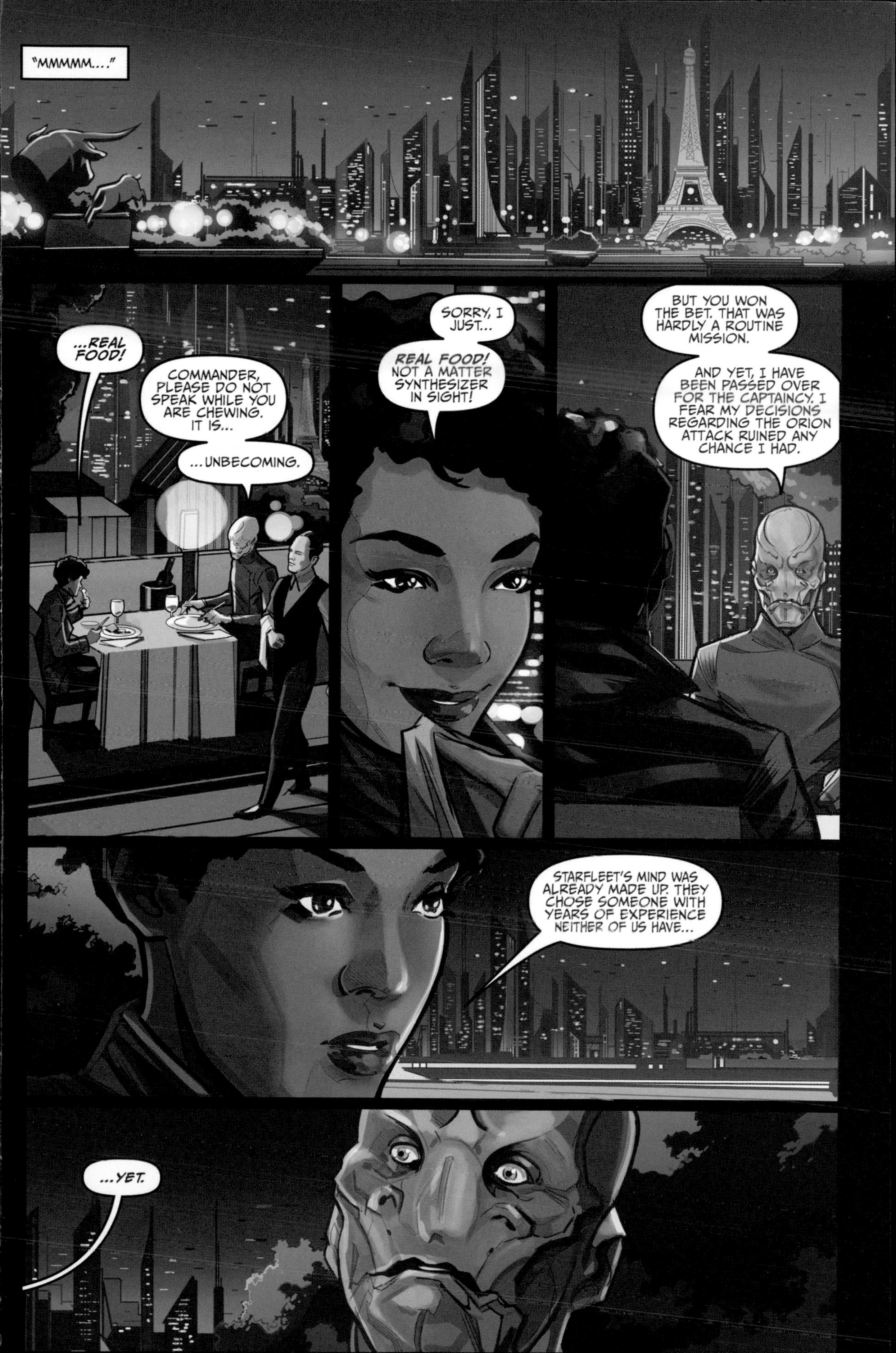
"MMMMM..."
...REAL FOOD!
COMMANDER, PLEASE DO NOT SPEAK WHILE YOU ARE CHEWING. IT IS...
...UNBECOMING.
SORRY, I JUST...
REAL FOOD! NOT A MATTER SYNTHESIZER IN SIGHT!
BUT YOU WON THE BET. THAT WAS HARDLY A ROUTINE MISSION.
AND YET, I HAVE BEEN PASSED OVER FOR THE CAPTAINCY. I FEAR MY DECISIONS REGARDING THE ORION ATTACK RUINED ANY CHANCE I HAD.
STARFLEET'S MIND WAS ALREADY MADE UP. THEY CHOSE SOMEONE WITH YEARS OF EXPERIENCE NEITHER OF US HAVE...
...YET.

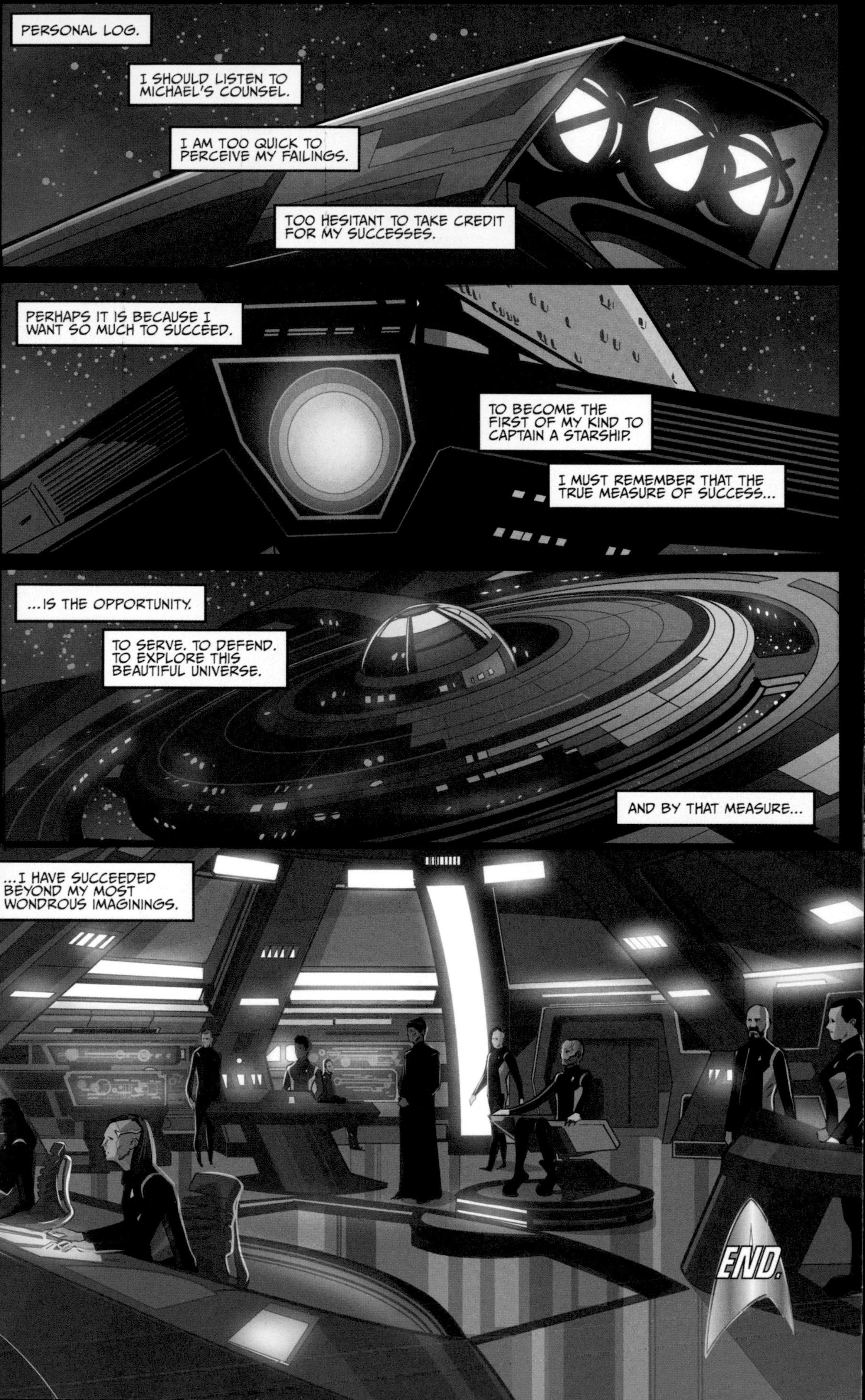
PERSONAL LOG.
I SHOULD LISTEN TO MICHAEL'S COUNSEL.
I AM TOO QUICK TO PERCEIVE MY FAILINGS.
TOO HESITANT TO TAKE CREDIT FOR MY SUCCESSES.
PERHAPS IT IS BECAUSE I WANT SO MUCH TO SUCCEED.
TO BECOME THE FIRST OF MY KIND TO CAPTAIN A STARSHIP.
I MUST REMEMBER THAT THE TRUE MEASURE OF SUCCESS...
...IS THE OPPORTUNITY.
TO SERVE. TO DEFEND. TO EXPLORE THIS BEAUTIFUL UNIVERSE.
AND BY THAT MEASURE...
...I HAVE SUCCEEDED BEYOND MY MOST WONDROUS IMAGININGS.
END.

ART BY **ANGEL HERNANDEZ** | COLORS BY **J.L. RIO**

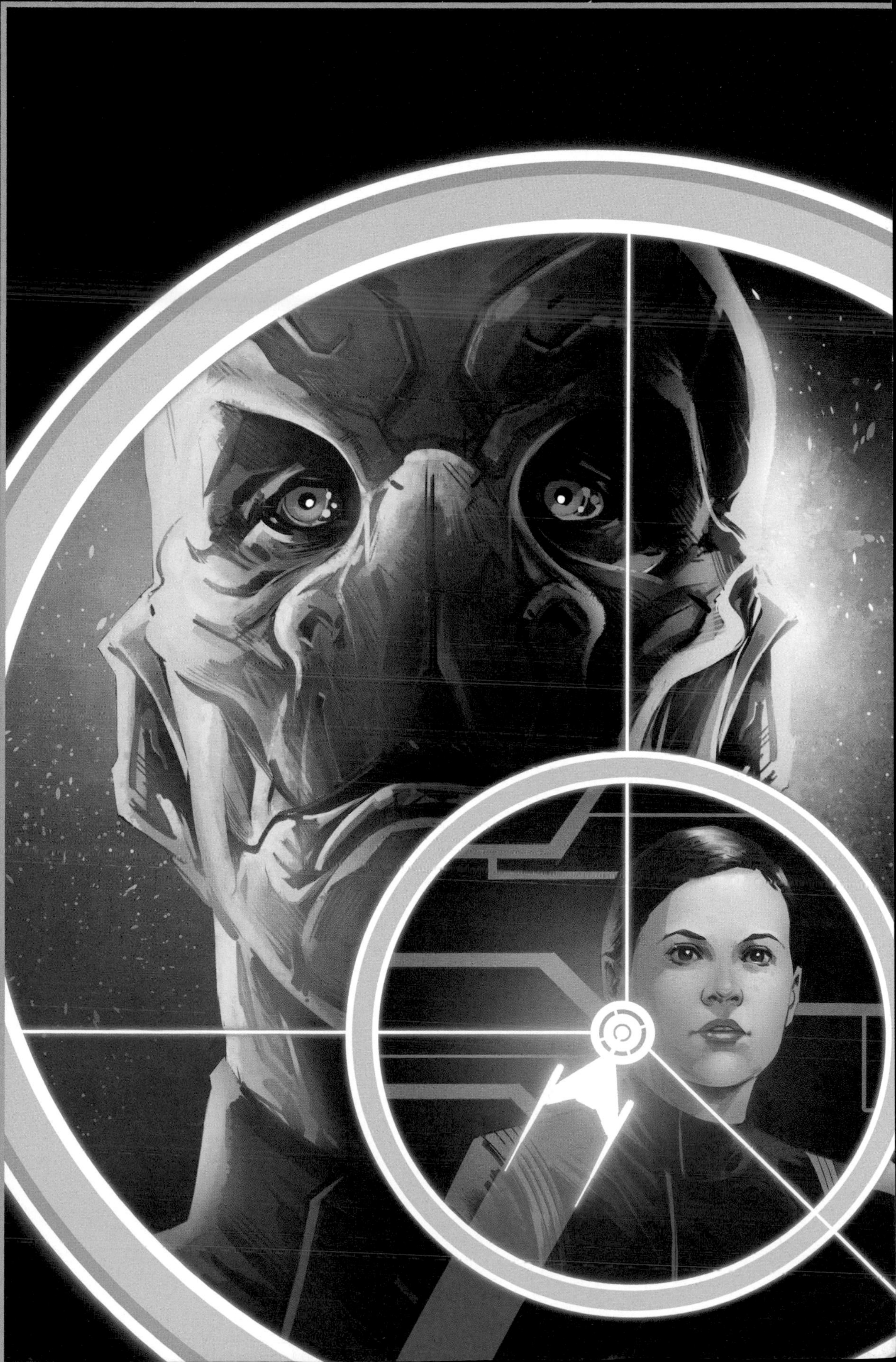

ART BY **GEORGE CALTSOUDAS**

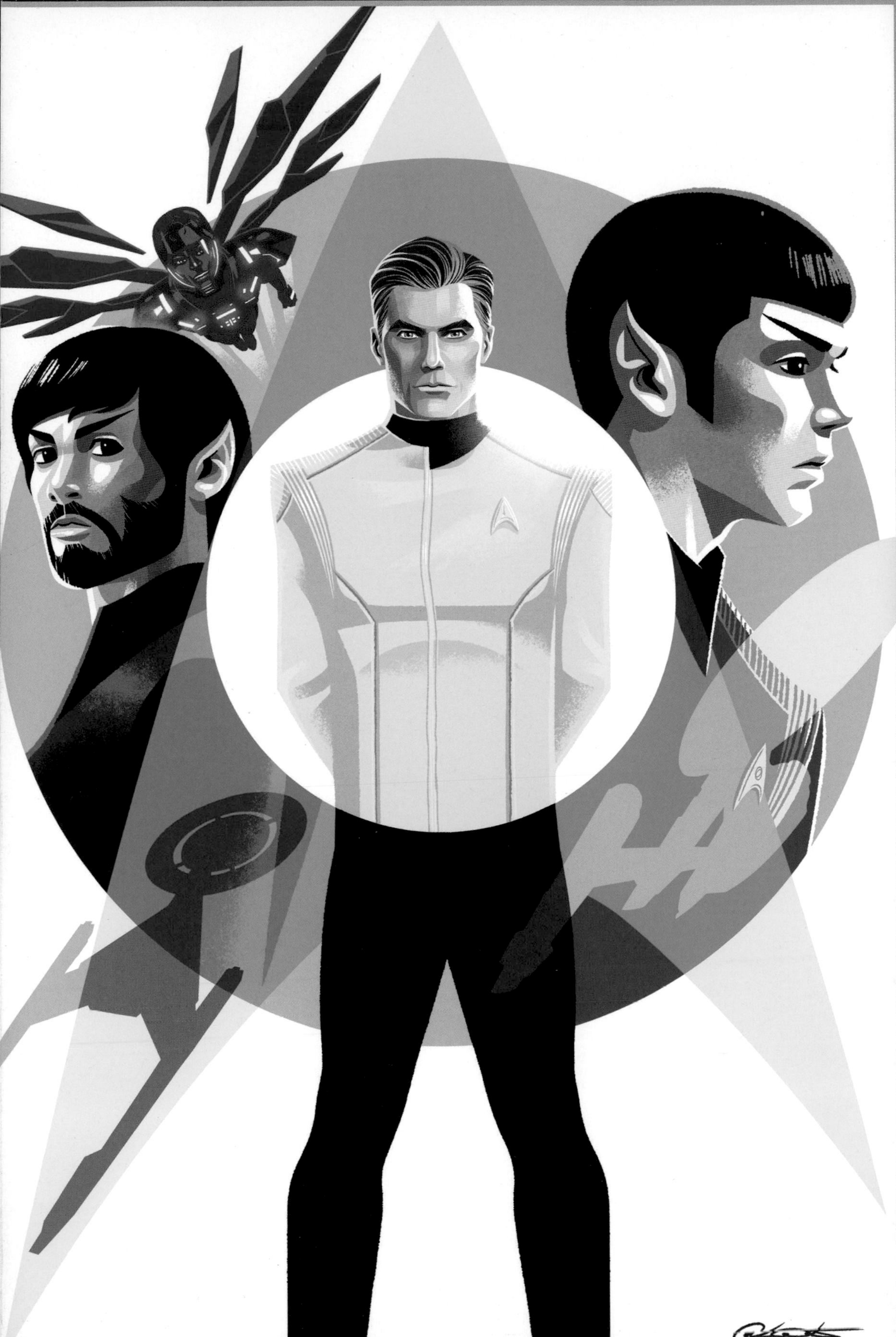